The Midnight of Eights

To Cassandra,

Enjoy. Imagine. Discover.

Justin Newton

Also by Justin Newland

The Genes of Isis
The Old Dragon's Head
The Coronation
The Abdication
The Mark of the Salamander – Book 1 of the Island of Angels

The Midnight of Eights

BOOK II OF THE ISLAND OF ANGELS

Justin Newland

The Book Guild Ltd

First published in Great Britain in 2024 by
The Book Guild Ltd
Unit E2 Airfield Business Park,
Harrison Road, Market Harborough,
Leicestershire. LE16 7UL
Tel: 0116 2792299
www.bookguild.co.uk
Email: info@bookguild.co.uk
X: @bookguild

Copyright © 2024 Justin Newland

The right of Justin Newland to be identified as the author of this work has been asserted by them in accordance with the Copyright, Design and Patents Act 1988.

All rights reserved. No part of this publication may be reproduced, transmitted, or stored in a retrieval system, in any form or by any means, without permission in writing from the publisher, nor be otherwise circulated in any form of binding or cover other than that in which it is published and without a similar condition being imposed on the subsequent purchaser.

This work is entirely fictitious and bears no resemblance to any persons living or dead.

Typeset in 10.75pt Adobe Garamond Pro

Printed and bound in the UK by TJ Books Limited, Padstow, Cornwall

ISBN 978 1835740 330

British Library Cataloguing in Publication Data.
A catalogue record for this book is available from the British Library.

To family.

Now let the story begin.
And it has been said *Ex Insula Angelorum*.
From the Island of Angels, no less.
For always was it so and always thus to be.

The Wonder Story Group, *The Tales of the Men of the Sea*

There is less danger in fearing too much than too little.

Sir Francis Walsingham

Bell, Book and Candle shall not drive me back,
When gold and silver becks me to come on.

William Shakespeare, *King John*

PART 1

THE PLOTS

1

The Plough Head

The village of Mortlake, near London, England
14th October 1580

With the shadows lengthening across the River Thames, Nelan tethered his horse to a yew tree standing guard outside the cemetery of St Mary the Virgin. Poignant memories of attending church services as a young boy with his father flooded his mind. His heart thumped against his chest. He'd waited for this moment for nearly three years, and now it was here.

Two men loitered in the cemetery. One patted the earth on a newly dug grave with his spade. The other one, with cabbage ears, pushed a wooden cross into the soil at the head of the grave.

"What's the name on the cross?" Nelan asked.

"The King a' Spain's," Cabbage Ears quipped.

"If that was so, we'd have a holy day of singing and carousing!"

"Don't I knows it. Nah, this be for Gladys Pence, a scullery maid a' Dr John Dee 'isself."

"I knew the doctor. Do you know if he is well?"

"He is, m'lord, and he's kindly paid for the services a' me and Tobias here."

"What's your name, sirrah?"

"I be Bardulf, gravedigger be me trade."

"Greetings, Bardulf."

"Who you lookin' for, shorty?"

"How do you know I'm looking for someone?" Nelan replied.

"What else does people come 'ere for?" Cabbage Ears rolled his eyes.

"Laurens Michaels," Nelan said.

"Who's he to you?" Cabbage Ears wanted to know.

"I'm Nelan. He was my father."

"Well, he be there, next to the hawthorn thicket. Buried him meself some three year ago. Wait a mo. Nelan Michaels. Me knows that name. Wasn't you arrested and sent ta' prison?"

"I was, but I'm innocent."

"Shush, that's what they all say," Bardulf hissed.

"No, it's true. I was falsely accused."

"Come, Bardulf," Tobias interrupted. "Leave the man to mourn his pa. Let's ta' tavern."

As the pair left the cemetery, Nelan made his way to the hawthorn thicket.

He wiped the pall of moss and grass from his father's tombstone. Mouthing a prayer, he read:

Laurens Michaels
Born: Sangatte, Picardy, 1543
Died: Mortlake, 5th December 1577
May his soul rest in peace

In different ways, his father and his mother had died at the hands of the Spanish. Both were terrible wrongs. Both cried out from Heaven for the scales of justice to be rebalanced. At two and twenty years, Nelan had time to achieve that.

A murder of crows roosting on the chapel roof watched as he grasped the horse's reins and walked along the riverbank. He reached the location of his old house, which had burnt down and at the same time taken his father. Fire cleansed, but it also destroyed. He stood in the midst of the scorched black outline on the ground, and howled his grief into the embers of the day. Now the land was his, he'd rebuild the house and make a home of it with Eleanor. He'd find her waiting for him at the Cross. Then he'd marry her and she'd help him achieve his dream.

Turning his back on the derelict site, he headed upriver towards a large ramshackle mansion, the house of Dr John Dee, the renowned astrologer to the court of Queen Elizabeth. Nelan desperately wanted to renew his acquaintance with the man, but he had a message from Admiral Drake to deliver, so a reunion would have to wait.

He headed east. The smells and sight of the fields and meadows were pleasantly familiar. A fox darted across the stubbled field, stared at him, and sniffed the dank air as if to ask, *Who is this who disturbs the peace of the hedgerow?* Another fox stalked the roof of his destination, Barn Elms – a black metal weathervane, a clue to the nature of its distinguished owner.

It rained and he sought shelter beneath a plane tree. As he dismounted, he nearly tripped on a piece of wood jutting out of the ground. He reached down to grab it. His gloved hands slipped off the muddy surface of the wood. He tried pulling it out of the sodden earth, but it held fast. It was a piece of rotting oak.

Something nudged him. *Take a second glance.* Lo and behold, it was the curved handle of a plough. He dug around it until his blade struck metal. Now he had to uncover all of it. With the evening shadows closing in, he knelt down, removed his gloves and felt the surface with his palms. A piece of iron was attached to the wooden handle. Ah! A plough head. He pulled it free, and it fractured in two. As he wrenched the other half from the soil, it released an odour as foul as the Devil's breath.

Ignoring the odious smell, he felt around the moist earth and found a bone. His heart missed a beat. What was this – a day of graves? If so, whose? Too small to be human. He unearthed the skeleton of a bird. It had a hooked beak, so a bird of prey. With a bell and leather thongs attached to each leg, it was a falcon, belled and jessed.

A falcon and a plough head made strange bedfellows. The jessed young bird must have got loose from its straps and died. Was he, Nelan, jessed to the straps of his past, forever strangled by his unfortunate history? Would he ever cut them loose?

It surprised him that the plough head had been left to rot, because carpenters would normally resharpen and repair the wood. When he worked as an apprentice blacksmith, he'd often reforge old plough head irons. Holding the bones in his hand, he turned it over in his mind; the straps and the share, the bird and the bell, the plough head and the falcon, belled and jessed. These were clues, but to what?

In the distance, he heard the rumble of cartwheels. Looking through the hazy light drizzle, he saw only the meadow and the manor house. Yet he could hear them trundling over cobblestones as clear as if he stood in the middle of a bustling city street. Then he heard the snort of an ox. He was hearing and seeing things that weren't there. What was happening?

Then he realised. The cart and the ox were not of this world. No, they belonged to the other world. During his voyage around the globe, Nelan had learned how to look through the veil and peer into that mysterious astral realm. Beneath the middle finger on his right hand were three wavy lines, like three letter S's – the mark of the salamander. Sometimes, when he rubbed the lines, a vision unfolded before his astonished eyes. This time, the vision pressed itself upon him of its own accord.

In it, a man dressed in white robes stood in the ox cart. He was surrounded by pikemen and pipes, louts and lutes. There was festivity, and there was terror. As the great bell tolled, the crowd chanted:

You're gonna be seen,
On the tree that's ne'er green!

Nelan's horse neighed and tossed its head, jolting him out of the vision. He felt chills down his spine.

What's a tree that's never green? As he pondered this question, he wrapped the bones of the falcon in a cloth and shoved it in his purse. He led the horse across the meadow. Moist from the drizzle, the soil smelled rich and earthy. The trees had shed most of their leaves, and a light breeze arranged them into small neat piles. The birds made softer evening squawks. He needed a place to rest for the night. Robbers and highwaymen hid in every wood, even close to the manor house of a member of the Privy Council, the most senior instrument of Queen Elizabeth's government.

Across the other side of the meadow, four watchmen emerged from the house, one of them clasping a wicker torch. A pair of hounds followed the man's every move as he lit the lanterns, spreading light around the estate.

As Nelan watched, the flames sang to him from their cradles:

You are well-come, Ne-lan.

By the Lord, the flames spoke to him. On his journey with Francis Drake, he'd witnessed fiery visions and visited the higher astral realms, but never had he heard the voices of the flames. Engraved with the mark of the salamander, he had a great affinity for the spirit of fire.

"I see you and hear you," he whispered.

Another horse and rider galloped up the track towards the manor gate house. After a brisk conversation, one of the watchmen ushered the rider into the courtyard and stabled the horse. With the coast clear, Nelan trudged across the meadow.

The hounds announced his arrival. Shoulder to shoulder, the three remaining watchmen sheltered from the rain beneath a narrow lintel at the courtyard gates. Burly folk they were, bearing pikes and swords, black capes and bonnets, with beards and looks to match. The one dressed in a fine doublet and cap and feather drew his scabbard and snarled, "Halt! Who goes there? Friend or foe?"

Nelan froze before the man's cold, empty stare, and in that silent hiatus, with the incessant drizzle, he felt helpless. Before he could answer, the man waved his scabbard beneath Nelan's chin and said, "You're speakin' ta' Roger Adden, Steward to the Secretary. So, listen to me, shorty. What with them fine and dandy Frenchies all over London and them Spaniards hidin' in them priest holes, we're checkin' every man who comes to the manor. State your name and your business."

"M-my name is Nelan Michaels. I come from the admiral."

"Got any papers?"

The other watchmen unsheathed their weapons, tapping the ground with the tips of their swords. Barking like the hounds from Hell, the two dogs pulled on the leash.

Nelan retrieved a package from his purse, saying, "See, here's Admiral Drake's seal."

"Before, the admiral sent a different messenger. Yeah, he was the whistle man. What was his name?"

"Oh, you mean John Brewer?"

"Yeah, what 'appened to 'im?"

"I'm his replacement," Nelan said, gritting his teeth. "I'm three days out of Plymouth Hoe. I smell of pigs' shit and manure, and I'm here to deliver the admiral's message to your master."

Roger Adden sheathed his sword, and to Nelan's relief, the others did the same. "Equerry'll take your 'orse. You come wit' me."

Adden led Nelan through the gates, across the cobbled yard and into the main house. Then, leaving him guarded by a watchman, Adden disappeared into an office. Nelan warmed his hands by the fire. A neatly stacked pile of logs and kindling sat by the fireside.

Nelan felt beyond exhaustion. Sleep would be his solace. Sleep. He'd rest in her sweet arms and drift off into divine bliss. Battered and bruised by the dog of a journey, he melted into the soft fabric of a chair by the fire. But then he heard a crackling whisper. It wasn't the guard. So, who? Wait. The voice. The fire spoke again:

By the warm,
I'll be sworn.

He was in Heaven. Not only was the fire talking to him but the blood coursed through him, even reaching his extremities. The office door crashed open, shaking him out of the comfort of the moment. Adden led another man into the anteroom. His long black cloak was smattered in mud and bracken. He was the rider who'd arrived a tad before Nelan. The watchman escorted the rider out of the anteroom.

"Come with me, fella," Adden said, and ushered Nelan into a wood-panelled chamber with a low ceiling. Layers of shelves, full of books, and boxes of manuscripts and scrolls lined one side. On the other side was the beating heart of the room, a warm fire burning in the hearth. Grey-black smoke billowed up the chimney.

In front of a narrow window was a man sat before a wide oak desk, covered with papers, scrolls, quills and inkwells, and a miniature portrait. The man wore a black hat and a white ruff tight around his neck. His long earlobes rested on top of the ruff. The thick worry lines on his forehead spoke of long nights and arduous days. His small mouth nestled between folds of a trimmed black beard, while his thin, pointed nose sat poised to sniff out danger. His eyes examined every detail of Nelan's appearance.

This was Sir Francis Walsingham, the Queen's spymaster. With his dark, imposing manner, Nelan understood why it was said she had nicknamed him her 'Moor'.

Adden said, "This be Ordinary Seaman Michaels with news from Plymouth, m'lord."

Walsingham pressed a paperweight down on a document he was reading, crooked his index finger several times and said, "Pass me the admiral's message."

Walsingham took the letter from him with long, spindly fingers. He broke the seal and studied the document.

"Adden, will you hear this?" Walsingham's face lit up as he read:

To Sir Francis Walsingham, Secretary to the Privy Council.

As instructed, I have shared the princely sum of fourteen thousand pounds of the Spanish treasure with the crew, who are full of gratitude at Her Majesty's beneficence.

And today, I began to transport the remaining treasure for safekeeping to Trematon Castle, on a small estuary off Plymouth's River Tamar.

Signed,
Admiral Francis Drake.
Aboard the Golden Hind on the 11th of October in the year of Our Lord, 1580.

"Good tidings, m'lord!"

"Yes, Adden. At last!" Walsingham said. "I personally invested in Drake's expedition, so I am indebted to the admiral for the bounty I'll receive."

"I'm glad you'll benefit, m'lord," Nelan said, sensing the secretary relaxing in the conversation. "Is there a reply?"

"No," Walsingham said. "But I'd like to see some of the treasure. Do you perchance have some of it on you?"

"I do," Nelan said, delving into his purse and taking out an item wrapped in a cloth.

"What have we here?" Walsingham asked, raising his eyebrows.

Opening the cloth, Nelan said, "This is a ruby salamander pendant."

The secretary's eyes lit up as he touched the rubies and the gold filigree.

"A salamander is the spirit of fire, hence the rubies," Nelan said. "Admiral Drake rescued it from the Spanish treasure ship the *Cacafuego* off the Panama coast. He gave it to me as a reward for my part in helping him find the ship."

"Exceptional workmanship," Walsingham purred. Then, staring at Nelan, he asked, "Michaels, was that your name, lad?"

"Yes, m'lord, Nelan Michaels."

"I've heard that name before. Yes, your house burned down. It was near Dr Dee's mansion in Mortlake."

"Dr Dee was my personal tutor."

"Was he now? And, before that, you attended Westminster School."

"Yes, m'lord." Nelan swallowed hard, and wondered what else Walsingham knew of his chequered past. Should he keep quiet or tell him the whole truth?

"Yes, what?" Walsingham insisted.

The rhyme played in his head:

By the warm,
I'll be sworn.

The fire told him to be honest and true.

"I swear," Nelan blurted out.

"Swear what, lad? Come on, spit it out. I don't have all evening."

"Five years ago, the school accused me of killing a boy, but I swear, I did not," Nelan said, as the emotions gripped him around the throat. "His name was Guillermo, one of the Spanish stepsons of St John of Southampton. His family once lived in Sneakenhall; a hamlet just north of Mortlake."

"I know where it is," Walsingham growled. "I remember the case well. Tell me, if you were innocent, why did you flee when the constables came to your house to arrest you?"

Of all the questions, Walsingham had to ask him that one, the most difficult one to answer truthfully. But the fires bade him try. "M'lord, the two witnesses to the incident were the school steward and the pastor, whose name was Christopher. But neither saw how the fire started, only how it ended. Their testimony would have convicted me. I ran away in order to find evidence to prove my innocence. Dr Dee himself urged me to do so."

"Is that right?"

"Yes, it is," Nelan said. "After that, I worked as a blacksmith in Queenhithe and joined a group of watchmen putting out fires around London. One day, by a quirk of fate, we were called to a fire at my father's house. On the way there, as we rowed past Sneakenhall, Guillermo's brother, Pedro de Antón, recognised me. He called the constables, who arrested me and threw me in Marshalsea prison. Soon after, I was pressed onto Admiral Drake's ship."

"That makes me very wary." Walsingham stood up and paced back and forth in front of the desk, hands clenched behind his back.

"Of what, m'lord?"

"Of you, Nelan!" Walsingham snapped. "Why would the admiral, the first Englishman to sail around the globe, entrust an important message to a fugitive from justice?"

Nelan's heart pounded. Was he to spend the rest of his life haunted by the Guillermo incident? "I am no longer a fugitive. Here, now I have this document."

Nelan delved into his purse and handed it to Walsingham, who read it aloud:

In my capacity as Admiral of the Golden Hind *and the powers endowed in me, I hereby pardon Nelan Michaels of all charges relating to the tragic death by gunpowder explosion of Guillermo, the stepson of St John of Southampton, also known as San Juan de Antón.*

Admiral Francis Drake.

Aboard the Golden Hind *on the 11th of October in the year of Our Lord, 1580.*

"You see, both Admiral Drake and Dr Dee believe my story."

"I admit, their joint voices make a convincing argument in your defence." Distracted, the secretary stared at a miniature on his desk. For fear of intruding on the man's private thoughts, Nelan shifted uncomfortably on his feet.

When Walsingham emerged from his reverie, he said, "I beg your indulgence. Your story of the incident at Westminster School evoked an unhappy memory."

Nelan heard the clear, plaintive sound of the man's grief.

Walsingham showed him the miniature, in which he stood next to a woman, while two young boys sat proudly in front of them.

"That's my wife, Ursula. We'd only been married a year. John and George were her children from her previous marriage. They should be grown up, off fighting with the Dutch against Spanish incursion."

"What happened, m'lord?"

"They both perished in a tragic accident – a gunpowder explosion, similar to the event you described."

"My condolences."

"Thank you. Alas, it was the will of the Almighty," Walsingham said. Then, snapping out of his sad demeanour, he added, "Here, have the document back. You never know when you might need it. Now, is there anything else?"

As Nelan shuffled items in his purse to make space for Drake's clemency document, a cloth fell out of it onto Walsingham's desk.

"What on earth have we here?" Walsingham said, opening the cloth.

"Oh! They are the bones of a bird of prey."

"I'm not blind. I can see that for myself. They are of a falcon. And they're wet. What are they doing in your purse?"

"As I arrived on the meadow by your estate, I found its skeleton buried beneath an old plough head. When I held it in my hand, I had a chilling premonition."

"Did you? Tell me, what did you see?"

"It was a hot, dusty summer's day. A pikeman led an ox cart through a noisy, drunken rabble. In the cart stood a man in a plain white smock and white cap. A preacher in a black pointed hat and black gown stalked alongside the cart, mouthing a pious prayer. Then, as the vision ended, a great bell tolled."

"By heavens, you're describing the procession of an execution. Did you see the visage of the man in the cart?"

"No. But the plough head and the falcon belled and jessed are important clues."

"To what?"

"I've been wondering that ever since I had the vision. I believe they point to a traitor to the Protestant cause. That's why the man in the cart is to be executed!"

"Yes, a Catholic."

"Does anyone come to mind?" Nelan asked.

"Not immediately."

"Wait... What's another name for a plough head?"

"A throck," Walsingham said.

"Exactly. The throck and a falcon belled and jessed – do they feature anywhere you can think of, m'lord, like in an insignia?"

"Now that you come to mention it, they appear on the crest of a prominent aristocrat."

"His name?"

"Throckmorton!" Walsingham said with a broad smile and a nod of his head. "Oh, yes. Francis Throckmorton is from a well-known noble Catholic family, who we've had no reason to suspect of treason. Adden, we must act! Make sure that the family are closely watched from now on."

"M'lord," Adden said, bowed and left the room.

"This is very good, Nelan. You understand, we live in times of momentous change. And that breeds uncertainty as surely as death follows the plague. You know there are Catholic plots to kill our queen, and Mary is at the heart of them. Only the Almighty knows why Elizabeth gave her refuge here in England."

"Well, they are cousins."

Walsingham ignored him, and instead waved a scroll at him, saying, "Do you know what this is? No? It's the *Regnans in Excelsis*, the first words of a papal bull, meaning Reigning on High. It excommunicated Her Majesty, released all her subjects from allegiance to her, and excommunicated anyone who obeyed her laws or commands. But we give no credence to papal bull!"

"We're safe here, though, m'lord."

"I wonder if we are," Walsingham said, as he stalked the room like an old fox sniffing out its prey. "A few years ago in Paris, I witnessed the brutal treachery of the Papists!"

"The St Bartholomew's Day massacre."

Walsingham nodded his head, and added, "And now the Spanish have invaded the Netherlands and persecute the valiant Dutch."

"I know," Nelan murmured. "The Spanish burned my mother there during the Council of Blood." The memory of it still burned in his soul.

"I'm sorry to hear that," Walsingham said with a rueful air. "And it'll get worse before it gets better."

"Why's that?"

"Just before you arrived, a rider brought news from Lisbon," Walsingham said. "A few months ago, Philip of Spain became the King of Portugal. With it, he inherited vast fortunes coming from the Portuguese spice islands in the Indies, and acquired their army and navy."

"This is awful news," Nelan said. "But we are the Island of Angels. We have Elizabeth. We have the best astrologer and the most fearsome admiral in the world."

"I like your defiance," Walsingham replied. "When our nation's existence and our way of life are in jeopardy, we can never have too many fears." He paused, and then said, "I find your premonition of the plough head timely. Understand, my business is spying. I have men and women in the Catholic houses of England, in the state offices in France and Spain, and in our embassies in Antwerp and Lisbon."

"That's an extensive network."

"That may be, but like today's message from Lisbon, the information can take months to arrive on my desk, and by then it's out of date. Yet today, you've pointed me towards a potential traitor. I can use a man with your skills. Nelan, I want you to travel into those mysterious realms, or however you perceive these things, and come back and tell me where and how the Spanish devils will next strike. Will you come and work for me?"

Nelan gazed into the open fire. The blue-violet flames whispered to him:

By the warm,
I'll be sworn.

While he'd told Walsingham the truth of his story, now he had to be honest with himself. The secretary's offer was as surprising as it was unexpected, but Nelan had set his heart on settling down with Eleanor. And he wanted to pursue the vision Dr Dee had given him; of playing a part in fulfilling England's destiny. But spying would be an impediment, like those leather thongs around the falcon's claws, to his ultimate purpose.

There he was, alone in the room with the secretary, one of the most powerful men in the country, with secret affiliations to people and embassies and nations. How could he, little Nelan, decline the man's request?

"I-I'm afraid…" Nelan stammered.

"Afraid of what? Come on, out with it, man!"

"I-I mean, I can't…" His voice was hoarse.

"What? Will you turn me down? You're an immigrant. Will you refuse the opportunity to fight for the country that gave you sanctuary?"

"I-I have to say no." Nelan had to prise the words out of his mouth, one by one.

"You need to reconsider my offer."

"Why, m'lord?"

"The admiral's clemency document…" Walsingham said, glaring at him.

"What about it?" Nelan gulped. Every moment dragged like a broken plough head.

"It's invalid."

Nelan cleared his throat. "Why?"

"Drake may command all hands on the *Golden Hind*, but on land, the admiral's legal authority is as thin as the paper the document is written on."

"I-I see," Nelan stammered. Inside, he was crestfallen. Walsingham had bound him in the chains from which for three years he'd tried to extricate himself. At sea, Nelan had built up his hopes and dreams of a bright treasure-filled future with his Eleanor, only for Walsingham to break them asunder in three minutes.

As if conceiving a new deadly plot, the secretary furrowed his brow and said, "But it is within my power to authorise the document."

So, hope did rest at the bottom of Pandora's Box. "It is?" Nelan asked.

"Yes, but before you decide, remember there's still a warrant out for your arrest for the murder of Guillermo."

Inside, Nelan felt ice bound. He had delivered the admiral's message then hoped to leave Barn Elms a free man, rich beyond measure, with his girl on his arm, chasing his dreams of saving the angels of England. But the meeting had gone from bad to worse. Now

Walsingham threatened to arrest him for a crime he hadn't committed. Unless he volunteered for a task for which he had no taste.

Begrudgingly, he asked, "What's involved, m'lord?"

"Good, that's better. I want you to go into the field," Walsingham said. "Watch out for Catholic sympathisers, uncover the priest holes. Find the messengers from Spain and Italy coming to sow discord in our land. And use your skills to uncover treachery and treason."

"And if I agree," Nelan said. Seeing he had no choice, he had to extract something from the bargain.

"If!"

"The arrest warrant…?"

"I'll issue a temporary suspension of the warrant."

"Temporary?"

"Yes, for nine months. But if you have not returned by then, I'll send my agents to find you. And find you, they will!"

"Can I have the ruby salamander back, please?"

Walsingham glowered at him. Slowly, almost imperceptibly, he shook his head and said, "I think I'll keep it."

"Why?"

"To guarantee your return."

Nelan balled his fists, bowed and strode out of the door.

2

Eleanor's Cross

15th October 1580

It was a matter of love. Because love mattered. Love was the glue, the inspiration, the grit in the oyster that had eased him through the tough times on the long voyage across the oceans of the world. He'd find his beloved Eleanor, marry her and make her his own. And he knew exactly where she'd be waiting for him.

After the exhausting interview with Walsingham, he bedded down in a large barn, a resting place for the many riders that buzzed around the manor at all times of the day and night. The Lisbon messenger lay stretched out on his bed of straw, snorting like a pig. Nelan bemoaned his own fate. He'd endured three years of mariners' snoring in the close confines of the forecastle, and the one thing he looked forward to on his return to England's shores was a quiet night's sleep.

The first sliver of dawn crept under the barn door as he emerged into the new day. He headed off to catch the Putney ferry. Even without the salamander pendant, he had sufficient funds from his share of the bounty from the voyage to buy a horse and carriage. But he relished the simple act of walking on *terra firma* as a free man, well, almost a free man. Across the river, he broke his fast at an inn on the Bath Road with some hot chestnuts washed down with cold beer. Well satisfied, he headed into London. By the time he reached the city gates, the wings of dusk were spreading over the day.

In White Hall, a trio of watchmen kept a wary eye for suspicious activity and especially for evidence of fire. One of them pulled an empty handcart, a scraggy dog keeping him company. While the second lit a lantern with a flaming torch, the third banged on the rickety door of a hovel. When no one answered, he daubed a red cross on the door. The lantern man stared at Nelan's fine cloth with a frown of envy. The trio acted as if they feared something they could neither speak of nor see.

Nelan worried about Eleanor. Only a few weeks ago, they'd met on the quay at Plymouth. The moment flashed before him. For a few blissful seconds, he'd held her in his arms. Then, Pedro had appeared out of the crowd. The Spaniard had taunted him by revealing that he'd set fire to his house in Mortlake, and so was responsible for his father's murder. The madman sought vengeance for his brother Guillermo's death. Then Pedro had knocked him out. When he'd come round, Pedro was gone, and so was Eleanor.

Now he hoped to reunite with her at the cross. Nearly three years ago, this was where he'd asked for her hand. His heart raced. Perhaps she was there, as expectant to see him as he was to see her. That would be a miracle and a blessing.

But she wasn't there. Though the other Eleanor was – her name, Eleanor of Castile, the wife of King Edward I. While on a tour of England, the Queen had died. At each place where the bier had rested for the night on the return journey to London, Edward had erected a memorial or charing cross. Of the twelve stops, this one was the last.

A simple, elegant cross crowned the top of the tall pillar. This was Queen Eleanor's Cross, also known as Charing Cross. Its intricate stonework had weathered, though the mark of it remained. Nelan recited the poem of his love for her:

I can't ask for more,
Dear Eleanor, Eleanor.
It's you I ad-ore,
Eleanor, Elean-or.

They should have been married by now, chasing after a couple of boisterous children. They'd missed three years of blithe, innocent happiness. He shunted the regret to the back of his mind.

At the base of the cross was a wreath of holly with bright red berries and shiny green leaves, interlaced with spiral threads of ivy. It was mid-October, too early for a Christ Mass offering. A sodden hand-sized canvas bag dropped out of the wreath. Inside it, he felt something small, metallic and round.

It was a ring. The ring.

With his heart thumping against his chest, he opened the pouch. Sure enough, inside it was the metal ring he'd given to her on the day of their betrothal. She'd left it as a message, which told him that she'd returned safely from Plymouth. He'd hoped to find her at the cross, but this was the next best thing. One day, man and woman, they would be the holly and the ivy, the eternal and the now, forever tied together in a dance of sympathies.

In the pouch, he found a wet, crumpled piece of paper on which the ink had run. Eleanor could neither read nor write, but from what he could make out from the smudges, it was a map. In the corner was a cross, like Eleanor's Cross. It was her mark. The map would show him where she was going.

But when he tried to open the paper, it disintegrated. His initial enthusiasm drained out of him like seawater through a leaky hull. Clutching the wreath, he fell to his knees. His heart sank into the same deep hole as his hopes and dreams. Once a shrine to their union, now the cross was a memorial to their lost love. But she had left him a sign.

Eleanor Pead, tell me, where are you?

The darkness fell from the night sky like lead pellets, and with it arose the sounds of the drunks singing and yelling. When they finally staggered out of the inns and into the alleys, cutpurses and thieves preyed on them like maggots on pieces of dead meat.

The church bells tolled slowly, languid at this late hour. The lanterns flickered with the chill of the north wind, and their flames whispered to him and spoke of the trials and tribulations they had witnessed. A dog raced down the alley, snarling and barking at him like he had the pox. The hound was followed by the trio of watchmen he'd seen earlier, their cart trundling along the cobblestones. This time, all three of them pulled it. The smell emanating from it was putrid, because it was loaded to the gills with dead bodies.

"Get thee gone from here, lad," one of them growled at him.

"Why's that?"

"Aye, you seen us daub the red cross on the door. The plague's returned!"

He turned and fled. Eleanor would have done the same, hence the haste of her message. He hoped that she, and her companion, Alexander, his old fireman friend, had escaped its fatal embrace.

He had to find her. During the three years at sea, he'd learned how to wear the shoes that never wore out and travel the mysterious realms of the astral world. Touching the ring, he brushed the holly across his palm to conjure a clue as to her whereabouts. At first, nothing came. When he tried again, there appeared in his mind's eye a tiny azure flame that grew into a clear blue light. Alongside it, he heard the tinkle of running water.

Dear Lord, the vision pointed to a place. She was near a stream or a river and nearby a flame. Fire and water linked them. With these clues to her whereabouts, he murmured a prayer of thanksgiving to the flames and the waves. But where was this place? He guessed she'd go south, so he headed for old London Bridge.

Days became weeks, and weeks became months. In early December, as he walked the snowy paths of the South Downs, he pondered his fate. He needed to find Pedro, and he needed to work out how to extricate himself from his agreement with Walsingham. He did not want to be a spy, but it seemed he had no choice. And he had frozen in the face of the secretary's imperious demands. Even though his vision had revealed Throckmorton as a danger to the realm, that man had remained unmoved. If he never returned to Barn Elms, Nelan would always be a fugitive, and he'd forego his ruby salamander pendant. Damn the man.

He felt bound by invisible leather thongs to Walsingham, and they suffocated him. Every step felt heavy. Yet he yearned to be free, to chase his dream of helping England and her angels. He resolved to fulfil his promise to Walsingham and, at the same time, find a way to escape from it.

Come early January, he settled at a coaching inn near Canterbury, Kent. No matter how many times he rubbed his salamander lines, nothing happened, forcing him to resort to more traditional methods.

Over the coming weeks, he despatched messengers to the hamlets and villages along the North Downs. He hired watchmen to question the local merchants and keep an eye on the village innkeeper. They asked after Catholic sympathisers. Making a list, he scrawled suspects' names and notes onto it. Out of the Candlemas mists, a pair of Walsingham's agents appeared and relieved him of it.

After the year's poor harvest, bread was scarce. As Easter approached, hunger gnawed at the people's lives like the rabid strumming of an out-of-tune lute. The local stocks were full of men, women and boys. Local magistrates doled out harsh punishments for vagrancy, petty theft, and wearing the wrong-coloured clothes or failing to attend Mass.

Still, there was no sign of the flame near the running waters, nor any way to escape from Walsingham's clutches.

3

Madima's Vision

23rd April 1581

He walked through a carpet of bluebells on the slopes of Shooters Hill, just west of Greenwich, with a grand view over the bends in the River Thames. The chapel bells called him to compulsory worship. After intoning the Lord's Prayer, when the service ended, he trudged across common land on the edge of a village. He grimaced as the acrid smell of death stung his nostrils. There it was, a corpse hanging from a gibbet. The dead man's flesh had shrunk to his bones. His shoeless feet dangled in the air, his head tilted to one side, and his swollen, dried-up tongue bulged out of his mouth.

To one side of the meadow, a handful of yeomen practised their archery skills. They set their arrows in their yew bows and unleashed them into the air in high, graceful crescents. They stopped shooting when they saw him.

"What brings ya here, lad?" one of them, with a scraggly beard, asked.

"Lost my beloved. She has these green eyes and curly auburn hair. A tad taller than me, she goes by the name of Eleanor and travels with a companion, Alexander."

"Not seen no folks like that," the man replied.

The one with a pock-marked face must have picked up his slight Flemish twang, because he asked, "You one a' them foreigners? You a Gyptian?"

"I was born in Picardy in Northern France. What's a Gyptian?"

"They call 'emselves Children of Ancient Egypt. We call 'em E-gyptians. That's where they hark from; E-gypt. Some call 'em Gypsies. Watch out, though, there's a bunch of 'em, three score or more, up there on Shooters Hill."

"What of it?"

"Them Gyptians be rascals 'n' thieves. They settle in a place, then shuffle on here and wander on there. Folks say they worship the Devil 'imself. An' they read ya palm 'n' tell ya fortune. It smells of witchcraft, lad. They'll slit ya throat as soon as give you a by-your-leave."

"They're that bad?"

"Yeah, listen to me," he said, pointing to the hanged man. "That fella over there on Gibbet Field, he was hung just for talkin' to 'em. It's agin' the law a' Queen Bess herself."

While the archers collected their arrows, Nelan collected his thoughts. Like Wandering Jews, these Gyptians moved from place to place, and so might have encountered his Eleanor. He loitered in the woods until the archers left then strode up to the summit of Shooters Hill, where he was greeted by a hound with wild eyes and a bark as sharp as Excalibur.

As he tousled the dog's mane, a man asked, "What you want with us?" A woman stood next to him.

"You with the Gyptians?" Nelan replied, trying to keep his nerve.

"Who's askin'?" the man said.

"I'm Nelan."

"Me is Jasper," came the reply. His voice was guttural but mellow at the same time. The man's forehead resembled a ploughed field, each furrow etched from life's profound experiences. "And this be me sis', Kazia."

"Greetings, Nelan. What brings you to our camp?" she said, in a voice as soft as a rose petal. Kazia had black hair, an olive complexion, high cheekbones and dark eyes that watched with passion. She was utterly stunning. Nelan puffed out his cheeks and glanced away so as not to offend her by staring.

He told them about Eleanor.

"We don't get many pass through our way," Kazia replied. "Ordinary folks are scared of coming close by, what with the law against us. I haven't seen your friends, but I'll spread the word."

Thinking to hide out amongst them, beyond the long reach of Walsingham's agents, he accepted the Gyptians' offer of a bed for the night. They welcomed him into their settlement of wagons and tents. The men strode off like warriors to gather kindling and firewood, hunt in the woods and fish in the streams. When they returned, they cooked, ate and drank together around a blazing campfire. As dusk set in, they danced and sang, with music and poetry, wit and humour. They told stories of the old days, the spirits of the ancestors, and the otherworld, by which the Gyptians referred to the astral realms.

Nelan slept on a bed of straw, tired out from enjoying the company of Jasper and Kazia's people and their pageantry of games and trickery, juggling and jigs. Relishing the opportunity of mixing with folks whose eyes glistened with light and fire, he stayed the next night and the next. The longer he stayed, the more he felt at home amongst these people who, like him, trod the sacred soil of the land anew.

After a week, Jasper called him to one side, a worried look on his face.

"A visitor come yesterday," the Gyptian said. "A young fella, said his name was Matthew. You know him?"

"No, I don't. What did he look like?"

"He was stocky, about your age, with curly black hair," Jasper said. "Wore a black doublet."

"Did he have an accent?"

"Not that I could say."

"What did he want?"

"He asked if we'd seen any strangers. The dogs yapped at him. They didn't like his stink. Nor did I."

"Is he still in the camp?"

"Nah, he left soon after. An' he kept fingerin' this string of beads, but like he didn't want me to see 'em."

"Ah! That's a rosary! He's a Papist. I must find this Matthew and bring him to justice. I warrant he'll be looking for the nearest priest hole."

"What's that?"

"The Pope in Rome sends priests here to celebrate Mass and ferment discord. They move under cover of night from Catholic house to Papist mansion, where they hide out in cellars, tunnels and other secret hiding places. They're the priest holes."

"An' this passes for life in England," Jasper said with a rueful smile.

The news of Matthew came as no surprise. Papist spies took messages from local manor houses to English Catholics exiled in France, Spain and Italy. Nelan had a dilemma; should he get news of this Matthew to Walsingham, or rest on his laurels and hide amongst the Gyptians? But he'd made finding Eleanor his priority. He rubbed the three wavy lines on his palm, hoping to get a vision of her whereabouts. Kazia noticed his endeavours.

"What are you doing there, little Nelan?" she asked with her infectious smile.

"See these three curvy lines below my middle finger? They're the mark of the salamander. When they itch, or sometimes when I rub them, I get visions of the otherworld, the astral realms. They revealed that I'll find Eleanor near flames and waves. I'm trying to find out exactly where that is."

Her eyes brightened, and she said, "I can help with that. D'you have something of hers?"

"Yes, a ring."

She pressed it into her hand and closed her eyes and then said, "I sense that she's well and safe enough."

"My word. What a relief! Can you see where she is?" he replied.

"The picture's hazy. I too see the flame and the water. But she's also near… a four-legged creature… with a tail and a snout."

"A dog?"

"Yes, and no."

"A dog, but not a dog? Is it a hog? Is she near a wood?"

"I can't say for sure, but I hope that helps," Kazia said, giving him back the ring.

"Thank you, I *will* find her."

"Show me these three lines on your hand," she said, cradling his palm in hers. Then she added, "Ah, they're like a little trio of flames rising out of your hand."

"I've also wondered, what do they mean?"

"That one day you might…" and she paused, before uttering the next words, as if to the spirit of fire itself "… a Fyremaster be."

"What's that?"

"A Fyremaster is a master of fire, a man who can conjure the element out of the ether. He hears the voice of the flames. A Fyremaster is a servant of the living fire that exudes the universe, and uses his mastership for the benefit of all. For does not the hearth warm all who stand by it? Does not the sun shine on everyone?"

"That's inspiring," Nelan said.

"There's one more thing." Her eyes glazed over, and she murmured:

I hear the ringing of the bells.
I hear the words of the prayers of the Almighty.
I see the light of the blazing fire.

He asked, "I don't know what that means, but tell me, who are you to know of these things?"

"She's a Chovihano," Jasper said. "That's a wise woman, a knowing priestess."

While they talked, an air of anticipation suffused the Gyptian camp. The men built two more fires, one on either side of the main bonfire. The women adorned the tents and wagons in branches, fruit and berries, and bunches of flowers. Children scampered around carrying kindling, bits of wood and coloured cloth. Before dusk, a pall of silence descended on the camp. With the juices of excitement flowing, men and women, old and young, disappeared into the wagons to dress.

"What's the preparation for?" he asked.

"Tomorrow's May Day, a special festival in our year," Kazia said. "The voices of the spirits of our ancestors are distant, and we barely hear them whisper to us. There's a veil between our world and theirs, which tonight wears thin."

"So, it's easier to hear their guidance," Nelan said. "What's this festival called?"

"Beltane. We'd like you to be our honoured guest," she said.

As the last embers of dusk merged into the night, Jasper leapt around like a banshee.

"Free the spirit!" he shouted, and poured buckets of water onto the central fire until it was dowsed. "Our fire is done for this year. Let's prepare for the new one!"

Holding an unlit torch of twigs, Kazia cried, "The Fyremaster will light the fire of this new year, the Beltane fire."

The title of the Fyremaster sat on him like a pair of oversized clothes. It seemed such an enormous task to fulfil Kazia's prophecy. Then again, when he was six years old, with all his life yet to unfold before him, he wasn't overwhelmed by the prospect of growing up. Instead, he was hungry, needful to go on. So, he resolved to learn to listen to his spirit, as it guided him towards the arts and skills he'd need to a Fyremaster be.

He pulled out his cloth, flint and a strike-a-light. The first time he tried to light the torch, the spark died before he even reached the kindling. Whispers of doubt circulated amongst the crowd when he failed on the second attempt.

On the last attempt, he struck the flint, and the spark leapt onto the canvas. The crowd cheered wildly as the Beltane torch lit the night. Kazia strode up to the bonfire and let the torch kiss the dry kindling. To the singing of the Beltane song by the crowd, the red-yellow flames spread over the new bonfire.

"Draw the flame from the Beltane fire," Kazia said. "Take it to your hearths, and let our fire be your fire. From the one comes the many, and from the many, the one."

The beacon warmth of the bonfire suffused Nelan's bones as it devoured the wood and the kindling, spitting out the air in short crackling sounds. The flames enriched his inner flame, his spirit. Behind its physical appearance sat the calling of the great spirit.

On a distant summit, Nelan saw the flames from another Beltane fire. Then another hilltop fire was set ablaze, its flames burning the night air, and then another, even further away, until a line of fires spread along the Gyptian camps of the North Downs.

The crowd gathered around the main bonfire, their faces dark in the dusk, flickering in the light. Hooting with glee, they clapped hands above their heads and danced heel-toe, heel-toe, like drunken English sailors.

"Yag, revered spirit of fire," Kazia said, "grace us with your presence, and grant the Fyremaster himself with a vision."

Walking withershins around the fire, Nelan repeated the rhyme in tune to the soft beat of the drums:

Jack be nimble, Jack be quick.
Jack jump over the candlestick.

He stared into the lithe indigo-blue flames. His mind danced with the rising smoke as it mingled with the wood, the air and the herbs. The crowd cheered. The drummers started a slow thrumming beat then got faster and louder. At the crescendo, he ran and leapt into the air. At the moment he pivoted above the fire, legs and arms akimbo, in his mind, the world juddered to a halt. Rising above the fire in the shoes that never wore out, all the worries and doubts lifted from his shoulders. Drifting above the camp, he moved through the veil into the astral world.

It was strange, because this time he noticed that he wore astral clothes. He felt quite at home in them, and wasn't surprised to see that his chosen astral form was that of a fiery salamander. He found himself standing in a meadow and staring at a young girl, shimmering with light.

"Who are you?" he asked.

"I am Madima, spirit of the earth. I come in peace, in service strong." Her voice was smooth and regular, like the waves of a lake at dawn. "I bear a message from the angels of the isle, for truly it is said… *Ex Insula Angelorum*, Out of the Island of Angels.

"The covenant between the angels and the people of the island is woven in threads of honour and respect. The angels are natural beings, and their charisma suffuses the flowers and shrubs, trees and grasses. The beauty of a flower in spring is the silent voice of an angel.

"Long ago, after the waters of the great flood receded, the land was empty of people. Lonely were the angels of the island, so they called to their people, those of kin, like a mother calls to her young. First came the Britons and the Celts, then later the Angles and the Saxons.

"The Romans and the Vikings were not called. They were cruel invaders who planted seeds here that did not belong, and that manifest as war, conflict and religious strife. After the Normans came the Plantagenets, who did just that – they planted-a-gene or a seed. They brought the three lions of England, which appear on the royal arms.

"The Island of Angels is a land of silver effervescence. The angels encourage theatrical exuberance with a love of custom, costume and ceremony. They imbue in the people of the land the spirit of adventure and urge them to discover discovery itself.

"Today, that effervescence is suffocated by a scarlet astral pall. Like a thick, heavy blanket, it sits on the moors, the valleys and the dales. It stifles the angels, forcing them to reside in underground caverns, and preventing them from fulfilling their purpose. Remove the scarlet pall and the angels will arise, and give spiritual succour to the people to realise their destiny."

"How can that be done?"

"The Gyptians know of these things. Ask them what brought them here."

When Nelan awoke, he was sitting on the ground, warmed by the Beltane fire, a crowd of faces gazing at him in wonder. He could hear the crackling of the wood and the fizzing of the branches in the bonfire. The gibbous moon shone on the clouds scudding by in the night sky above him.

"Are you well? What did you see?" Kazia asked.

"Madima's vision."

"Who's Madima?"

"An emissary of angels of the island. She entrusted me with the story of these isles," Nelan said. "She said I should ask you why you came here."

"Then, I will tell you," Kazia said. "We're an ancient folklore people who adhere to the old ways of the tor and the coombe, the ley and the stow. Gyptians respect the land and venerate its angels. We know and understand what it's like for them. They're confined beneath the valleys and suffocated by the scarlet pall. We heard their call and sailed across the seas to come here.

"We want to help the angels fulfil their purpose, which is to set free the people of this isle, the land of Arthur Pendragon, the once and future king. The angels will draw out the genius of the people and their urge to discover."

"How do we rid the land of the scarlet pall?"

"That's what we're here to find out," Kazia said.

At the end of the night, Nelan felt exhausted by the vision. On a bed of straw, he stared into the luminous night sky and fell into a deep, dreamless slumber.

The next day, with the Mayday sun on his back, he bade farewell to Jasper and Kazia, the hounds and the hill, and set forth to pursue Madima's vision.

4

Cannon Aplenty

1st July 1581

Come the warm summer winds, Nelan felt like he'd stepped into the shoes of a Jew, doomed to wander the ends of the earth. Was his sin to be born in the wrong body at the wrong time and in the wrong place?

He searched for his one and only. He knew that she was near fire and water, and a new clue – a dog that wasn't a dog! Until he found her, he couldn't restart his life. With her, he'd marry and rebuild their home. Without his Eleanor, he felt lost, alone, and miserable.

He wondered how to bring about the healing of the angels revealed by Madima's vision. It seemed like a mammoth task, but he knew he could achieve it with guidance from the astral realms.

Kazia had gifted him the vision of the Fyremaster, but what did it mean? The flames were a companion all his days. When at sea, he'd witnessed the mystery of St Elmo's fire, lithe elements of living fire in the otherworld that danced around the masts of the ships. Was he the master of the flame? He couldn't conjure fire by will alone, but maybe in the future, he could do so.

Again, he tried to detach his salamander astral persona from the back of his neck, but each time, he failed. In his astral form, he could have travelled far and wide in search of his Eleanor, and in a short time. What price, now, the shoes that never wore out?

He followed a river valley along its winding banks and came across a large stack of logs. Nearby, he found a broken axe handle. The area was covered in a sprinkling of sawdust. This was a charcoal pile. In the distance, a plume of smoke snaked into the air, blackening the skyline of low rolling hills. These were the furnaces of Lamberhurst in the midst of the county of Kent.

The town was a cluster of houses gathered in a knot around the Queen's highway. First, he smelled the charcoal-fuelled fumes. Nearer the forge, he walked into the wall of heat. The theatre of the blacksmith's yard seduced him – the clanging of metal, the cut and thrust of the constant battle with the charcoal, the wood, the flame, the heating and the cooling, the hammering, and the shaping of the moulds, the expansion and the contraction, the hottest pale blue flames in the very depths of the furnace.

As the smiths thrust their moulds into the furnaces, sweat poured from their brows. Others tended to the moulds as they cooled. The furnaces were too large to produce knives and other domestic objects. He noticed rammers and barrels, so this was no ordinary iron works. This was a foundry; they were forging cannon.

"Is that you, Ordinary Seaman Nelan Michaels?" A voice thundered behind him.

"Who's that?" he asked, peering at the man, who held the reins of a train of oxen tethered to an open-backed wagon.

"You know me well enough, as I do you," the man jested, blowing on his whistle round his neck. "Me, I'd recognise you anywhere, Little Nelan."

"Ah. The whistle and the beard. It's all turned grey, hasn't it, John Brewer?" Nelan shook the man's hand like a long-lost brother. "Well, well, well, who'd have thought it? The trumpeter of the *Golden Hind*. Tell me, how is Admiral Francis Drake?"

"*Admiral* Francis Drake?" Brewer scoffed. "You'd better call him *Sir* Francis Drake, or we might try keelhaulin' you again."

"Mmm, don't remind me of that. So, he's a knight of the realm?"

"That he is. We was all golden on the *Hind* in Deptford, and the Queen herself come on board in all 'er jewels an' finery. With all them other aristocrats, she was. She even got the ambassador of them Frenchies to knight Sir Francis."

"Sir Francis, he deserved it," Nelan said, nodding approvingly. "He drove us all to the ends of the earth and then got us home."

"Last I sees of you was in the stables of the Sailors' Return on Plymouth Hoe. You deliver that message to Walsingham?"

"I did, yes."

"Good man. What you doin' 'ere, anyways?"

Nelan wasn't sure he was going to honour his agreement with Walsingham. If he'd volunteered, that would have been different. A man was born of spirit free. He was not a slave. That he hated. Choosing his words with caution, he said, "Searching for my woman."

"What's she like, your lass?"

"She's a young, gentle soul, and big green eyes that sparkle like the sun on the waters. I imagined that she was near water, and near fire. That could be your furnace and the river and a sort of dog. They're the signs that will lead me to her. I will find her."

John Brewer dropped his eyes, as if in a moment of silent reflection. Then he said, "If she's a faithful lass, good on ya. For me, I comes home expectin' a kiss an' a cuddle from me wife, only to find meself a cuckold."

"Sorry to hear that, Master Brewer."

"Pah! I got no woman, not a farthin' in me purse. That's why I'm workin' 'ere."

"What exactly are you doing here?"

"Makin' ready for them Dons, them Spanish grandees. Our admiral reckons they'll be a comin' for us sooner or later. Look 'e 'ere," John Brewer said, gesturing to a handful of men rounding the corner, hauling the barrel of a cannon lashed on top of a cart.

"See this 'ere iron lass," he said, patting the barrel. "Got to get her onto our ships. She'll keep our England safe, mind. Her and others'll blast King Philip's ships out of the water. There's plenty more where this cannon come from. See them plumes a' smoke, each one's a furnace, turning out great guns for our British navy. There's scores of cannonballs as well, mind. Can't wait to see 'em splinter the hulls and rip through the masts 'a those Spanish galleasses. They enough ta put the fear a' God into the Devil hisself, let alone the Dons."

The men tilted a plank on the ground so the other end lay on the back of the wagon.

"Put your backs into it, lads," John Brewer said. Inch by inch, the men dragged the barrel of the cannon up the plank onto the back of the wagon. Nelan put his shoulder to the cause.

"Good work," John Brewer said. Taking off his gloves, the old bugler wiped the sweat from his brow with his forearm.

"Where are you taking her?" Nelan asked, pointing at the wagon.

"Deptford. Tell you what, come back wi' us. We'll be there in three days. Some a' the crew are still on board the *Hind*. Thomas Blacollers – Tom the bosun, remember 'im? 'Course ya does. An' the quartermaster an' the purser. Be just like old times. We're the dogs a' war. There'd be a warm welcome for ya by the galley stove, and the rush of the waters of the Thames."

There was an allure in John Brewer's words; they were attractive, summoning even. A voice inside him urged him to head for Deptford. Perhaps it would lead him to Eleanor. If not, he could join the crew, where the admiral's clemency document held sway.

"I accept your invitation."

"Well done, mate." Brewer slapped him on the back. "It'll be your second comin'."

Nelan sweated in the hot sun. He sat next to John Brewer as the ox train bumped its way across the dry trackway. There were plenty of stops at the coaching inns for water for the oxen and ale for the drivers. Each day, a swarm of mosquitoes enjoyed the rich pickings of sweaty, smelly mariners.

Nelan rode the lead wagon with the old bugler himself. "John Brewer, what happened to all your money from our escapades in the Seven Seas?" he asked. "The taking of the *Cacafuego* made us all rich beyond our wildest dreams."

"That may be true, lad. But when we docked at Plymouth, after nearly three years at sea, me was desperate to join me family. Why d'you think I offered to ride back an' forth to deliver messages to them toffs in Barn Elms an' London town?"

"Well, I suppose I thought you were helping the cause."

"Bah! Helpin' the cause! If truth be known, lad," he muttered under his breath in what sounded like a shameful confession, "I'd lost all me treasure playin' dice an' cards on the *Hind*. Me, I delivered them messages 'cos I needed the money."

"Are you still owed your bugler's wages? You're nodding your head. Oh dear. You've landed in a right old mess."

"I remembers, you got that ruby salamander as part of your treasure. Let's see it then, lad," he grunted.

"Well, now you come to mention it, I don't have it right now."

"Lost it on the dice, eh?"

"No, not at all. Secretary Walsingham's got it."

"Hah! Stole it from ya when you delivered the message, did he? Them aristocrats!"

"No, it's not like that. I'll get it back from him, you'll see."

"Bah! I never liked that man," John Brewer said. "Looked at ya askance, he did."

Nelan prayed that John Brewer was blowing hot air. The ruby salamander pendant was more precious to him than its monetary worth. Like the three wavy lines on his palm, it was a link to the mysterious astral world.

"Gee up," John Brewer cried to the oxen, and they sat in silence for the rest of the journey, both men nursing their grievances.

The gibbous moon shone down on the ox train as it finally rumbled into Deptford and Nelan joined the crew of the *Hind*.

The recently built naval dockyard was so close to Marshalsea that he could smell the fear and loathing emanating from the prison, billowing like a dark cloud over the naval ratings. By the Lord, he never wanted to return there!

On board, everything seemed as if he'd never been away. The crew moaned about a shortage of ale and ship's biscuits. Tom the boatswain returned to his best, berating the crew, the ship's cat, and even the legion of rats if they dared impede him. Nelan joined the gang hauling old cannons off the ships and replacing them with the new ones from the Lamberhurst furnaces.

John Brewer was despatched to deliver a message. Before he left, he asked about his wages, but the purser waved his complaints away, saying he was lucky to be an English mariner. The old bugler set off for the Palace of Nonsuch in a mood fouler than the bilges of the *Golden Hind*.

Every night, deep within the confines of the forecastle, the crew shared memories of the great times that had surrendered to them during the passage around the world, culminating in the taking of the Spanish treasure ship, the *Cacafuego*. On occasion, they raised the dark times. Tom reminded them of when they'd harboured off the Isle of Justice, by the coast of Patagonia in South America. The men bowed their heads and, with a sigh, Tom spoke softly of the execution of Thomas Doughty, accused and convicted of mutiny. This terrible event had cast a long shadow over the rest of their journey home. Francis Fletcher, the chaplain on the voyage, had expressed his disapproval, but only privately and certainly not to Drake himself, because everyone knew the admiral would brook no criticism of his leadership. Nelan had kept his own counsel, although he sympathised with the chaplain.

Work in the dockyard, enriched by the singing of the sea shanties, and the many small lives within it, allowed a forgetting and a healing of times past.

5

Follow the Fox!

14th July 1581

Nelan tossed and turned, half awake and half asleep. The light from the enormous moon in the sky kept him from slumber. All the while, he'd dreamed of a fox. Then, in the dream, he wasn't watching the fox; he *was* the fox, hiding in the bushes, watching… a mouse scurry into its burrow, a hog stroll through the meadow, a blackbird land on a branch. He smelled the hedgerow and the dank, earthy odours from the barley field nearby. His whiskers bristled with alarm. In the bushes behind him, there was movement.

A man shouted, "Follow the fox!"

He rubbed the sleep from his eyes. Outside, the sound of rain against the hull, splashing on the deck.

"Follow the fox!" The phrase echoed in his mind, but what did it mean? The cunning creatures were masters of deception and possessed the extraordinary ability to disappear in plain sight. He scratched his head, pulled his beard, and cast into his mind all the foxes he'd seen, and everywhere he'd encountered them.

Then he knew which fox to follow. It brought his future to a head. But it was a choice he made without hesitation. He knew it was the right one, because it lifted a weight from his shoulders.

Grabbing his doublet, he climbed the ladder up to the deck. Rain slanted into the hull. Almost slipping on the wet boards, he bade a hasty fare-thee-well to Tom, the bosun. He edged down the gangplank, onto the quay, and hailed the early morning ferry. He boarded it just as its master shoved it into the river flow.

"Don't be rockin' us, lad, or I'll be rockin' you!" the wherry master barked at him, a growl he recognised.

"Well, well, well," Nelan said. "If it isn't old Wenceslaus himself."

"Ah! 'Tis I," the man said from amidst the folds of his salt-and-pepper beard. "Now, where will I be a' takin' you, Little Master?"

"Upriver, Wenceslaus."

"Upriver's got a lot of places. Greenwich or the Bridge. Richmond or Putney. Where's it to be?"

"Just row," Nelan said. "I'll tell you when we get there."

The rain speared into them, but Wenceslaus still pulled hard on the oars. "Now, how long's it been? Last time I sees ya, that Spanish boy got hisself blown up."

"I'd no involvement in his death."

"I believe ya, an' I did so then, too."

Just beyond London Bridge, he saw his old haunt of St Michael Queenhithe, where he used to sit with Eleanor. Ah. Eleanor. He had to believe he was getting closer to finding her. As the rain clouds cleared, Wenceslaus narrowly avoided colliding with the Putney ferry.

"Dock at that mansion over there!" Nelan yelled, pointing to a nearby jetty. "The one with the weathervane."

"Is that a dog?"

"It looks like a dog, but it's not a dog. It's a fox. This is Barn Elms."

Droplets of water dripped onto the floor of the same anteroom as the day he found the plough head. Because of the chill brought by the rain, the steward had lit a fire which crackled and snapped, but it said not a word. Despite that, Nelan had a great feeling. Barn Elms was near the waters of the river. He stood by a fire in the hearth. The weathervane of the fox graced the top of the building. He'd followed the fox. Now, where was Eleanor?

The door flung open, and Roger Adden gestured for Nelan to enter the fox's den.

Since he'd last seen him, Walsingham appeared older, his face more wrinkled with the heavy concerns of keeping the realm safe from internal rebellion and foreign invasion. As he entered, the two other men in the room examined him with studied indifference.

"Please," Walsingham said to them. "Wait here while I interview Master Nelan Michaels. He may help us, you never know." The Secretary of the Privy Council ended on a sarcastic note.

"You cut your cloth very fine!" Walsingham said, staring at Nelan from the top of his eyes.

"M'lord, I fulfilled our agreement. It's nine months since last I stood here."

"Yes, to the day, Nelan."

"I'm also here for another, equally pressing, reason than to honour my promise to you."

"You are?" Walsingham looked at him with an air of feigned surprise. One of the other two men in the room chuckled quietly to himself. They were laughing at him.

"You don't know?"

"Should I?"

"Yes, you should. Please, tell me, have you seen or heard of my Eleanor?"

"Why do you ask?"

Nelan balled his fists, trying with all his might to keep his composure. He paused, and then said, "Because I believe that she is here. Is that so?"

"Well, you are right. She is." Turning to one of the men in the room, he said, "Bring the young lady to us."

The man got up and left. Moments later, he returned, saying, "She worships at St Mary's, Barnes. Adden has sent for her."

Finally, he'd found her, and in the most unlikely of places. His heart leapt with joy, and he couldn't take the smile off his face. He was going to enjoy every moment of this wonderful day. "Is she well?" he asked. "How did she come to be here?"

"She is in good spirits," Walsingham replied, "and I'm sure she'll answer all your questions. While we wait for her, I have some for you."

Detecting a tone of hostility, Nelan asked, "Why is that? Have I offended your lordship?"

"Where shall I start? I asked you to help defeat the enemies of the state, but you've shown little taste for the battle. Once again, you have run away from your responsibilities."

"As you instructed, I searched for Catholic sympathisers. I listened in the cordwainers and the coopers and stood by the smiths and the fletchers. I drank my fill in the tavern and loitered by the stable yard."

"I received information from my intelligencers to that effect. But I did not expect you to mingle with Gyptians!" Walsingham said with evident derision. "What do you take me for? I'm a queen's Privy Council. Not a queen's fool. How can you break the laws of the land with such impunity? I should clap you in irons here and now."

Nelan weighed his next words carefully. He had only returned to Barn Elms for one reason. That it now meant he had to take up Walsingham's offer of spying was, as far as he was concerned, incidental to reuniting with Eleanor. "That won't be necessary."

"Tell me why not!"

"I have something important to report."

"Good. Let's hear it."

"I have already alerted you to Sir Francis Throckmorton," Nelan said, mounting his defence against Walsingham's prosecution.

"So you have. What else, then?"

"On my travels, I heard about a young man, possibly an Englishman. He carried a rosary, so he's either a priest or an intelligencer."

Walsingham's ears pricked up. "A spy, you say?"

"His name was Matthew."

"Very good, Nelan! George, have we any intelligence on this Matthew?" Walsingham addressed the other man in the room.

"We believe he is a Catholic sympathiser."

"Nelan, this is George Eliot, one of my best intelligencers."

"May the Lord be with you, Master Eliot."

"And with you, Nelan."

The door opened, and the man said to Walsingham, "The horses are ready."

"Good. Oh, Nelan, this gentleman's name is David Jenkins," Walsingham said.

"Master Secretary," Jenkins said, "please sign the warrant, as we're keen to get going."

"Yes, of course," Walsingham said, reaching for his quill and scratching his signature. Then, he read:

> *This warrant authorises the Queen's officers to search for and apprehend the Jesuit priest, Edmund Campion, and any other like seditious persons who threaten the peace of the realm.*

"Who is this Edmund Campion?" Nelan asked.

"The most wanted man in England," Walsingham said. "Masters Jenkins and Eliot are about to set off to find the traitor."

"Good luck," Nelan said to them.

"Nelan," Walsingham said, "please hand the warrant to Eliot."

As Nelan touched the paper, his salamander mark itched, and he dallied.

"Come on, lad, pass it over. We don't have all day," Eliot snapped at him.

"Wait," Nelan said. "I've got a picture in my mind."

"What picture?" Walsingham asked.

"A house with a moat. And it's near… a horse?"

"Bah!" Eliot scoffed. "We know that already. Campion's going to be hiding in a manor house somewhere, and they all have stables, so he's bound to be near a horse!"

"Wait. Nelan has a special gift. There may be something in what he's picking up. Is there a name?" Walsingham asked.

"He's near a ford – Lin Ford, I think. Yes, Linford. Does that mean anything?"

"Nah! Linford's a village in Hampshire," Eliot said. "We believe he's in Oxfordshire. Come on, let's go. We're wasting our time here."

"No. Wait," Jenkins piped up. "Can you say anything more about the horse?"

"Yes, it's a white horse," Nelan said.

"Then I have it!" Jenkins said, jumping up and clapping his hands in triumph. "You don't mean Linford, you're talking about Lyford."

"What makes you say that?" Walsingham asked.

"Lyford is a village near the Vale of the White Horse! And Lyford Grange is a moated house!" Jenkins said.

"Of course!" Walsingham agreed.

"And Lyford used to be called Linford!" Jenkins added.

"Then Lyford Grange it is!" Walsingham chimed.

"That's where you'll find him," Nelan said.

"Jenkins, Eliot, go and get him!" Walsingham said, and the two men left. "Well done, Nelan. We must apprehend Campion. This incident again shows how useful your prescience can be in our work."

"Do you still have my pendant, the ruby salamander?"

"I do, but you can't have it back yet. It's safely tucked away in my drawer. When we unravel the truth of your vision of the plough head, I'll consider returning it."

Nelan swallowed his disappointment. Bending his ear to hear footsteps approaching, he said, "Now, where's my Eleanor? I'm so keen to see her."

"She's coming. She'll be here presently, you'll see. Well, you've returned within the nine months, as you promised, so that means you're taking up my offer of a more permanent position?"

Nelan felt awful inside. Walsingham was pressuring him to accept a longer-term position, but again he felt unable to refuse him.

"Well, what will it be?" Walsingham asked. "You know what you have to do if you want me to renew the suspension of your arrest warrant."

Nelan hissed to himself, and said, "Yes, m'lord. With my Eleanor, I'll settle here and rebuild my father's house."

"Good, I agree," Walsingham said. "From your new house, you can keep a watchful eye on the wherries and river boats. The Queen often passes by, as do other members of the Privy Council, Sir William Cecil, Sir Christopher Hatton, and High Admiral of the Fleet, Lord Howard of Effingham. We must keep them all safe."

Nelan sensed there was yet more to come.

"As the need arises," Walsingham went on, "I will ask you to visit different parts of the country to perform specific tasks. Your cover will be that you represent the Worshipful Company of Blacksmiths."

Outside the door, there was a rustle of clothing, and he knew who it was. He stood up. The door opened, and in walked a man followed by… Eleanor.

"My joy!" he cried, and kissed her hand, and they hugged. She purred inside his embrace. She whispered in his ear, "My Nelan. I always knew you'd come for me."

"And here I am," Nelan said. "Let me look at you."

"How did you know where to find me?"

"I followed the signs I saw – of running water, the hearth. I searched everywhere, then a seer helped me. She said you were near a dog that wasn't a dog. Then last night, I had a dream and realised that she was talking about a fox! So, it had to be here!"

"But I've only been here for one night."

"Then providence has brought us both to this place!"

"I've missed you so much," she murmured. "It's been nine months since I saw you on Plymouth Quay."

"I'll never leave you again… not for so long," he said.

"I know, because I will forbid it!" she said, wiping the tears of happiness and relief from her eyes.

"Let's give thanks to the Lord that we've found each other again," he murmured. As they embraced, he felt her chest heaving with emotion, her tears moist on his face.

"Why didn't you come for me? I left you a map to tell you I'd be at the Palace at Greenwich."

"Yes, I found the map, but it was soaking wet and unreadable," he hissed. "What did you do there?"

"Alexander knew a watchman in the Queen's household who got me a position assisting the midwives."

"How did you come to Barn Elms?"

"This gentleman, Master Charles, had business at the Palace where he found us. When I explained that you and I are betrothed, he said he knew of you and insisted we come here."

"Thank you for protecting my Eleanor," Nelan said.

"Charles Sledd, at your service," the man said. A tall, thin fellow, gaunt of face, he was dressed in tight breeches, a simple ruff and a woollen jerkin. "But it's Secretary Walsingham you need to thank. He's looked after her since her arrival."

"Thank you," Nelan said, pressing his hand to his heart.

"My pleasure, Nelan," Walsingham said.

Well! Of all the people to offer sanctuary to his Eleanor! The shady fox, Francis Walsingham.

"I'm glad my dreamer's found me," she said.

"The Lord has blessed you, Nelan, to have such a loyal partner," Walsingham added.

"At least someone recognises my qualities, Ordinary Seaman Michaels," she jested.

"Oh, I'm no longer an ordinary seaman," he said. "I work for the Secretary now."

She went on in a gentle, chiding tone, "Oh, is that so? Then,

Master Nelan Michaels, what I want to know is this…" She paused before answering. As pauses go, it went on long enough for Nelan to sense that he was about to encounter a serious female demand. He wasn't disappointed, for she asked, "For a man so blessed, what are you going to do now?"

"I'm going to marry you, and rebuild my father's house! Then I want to find that murderer, Pedro. He was the one who attacked me on the quay at Plymouth. Bringing him to justice will right the wrongs suffered by my father and my mother. How does that sound?"

"Mmm," she nodded, as if expecting more.

"What else…?" he murmured, then realised what she was waiting for…

"Yes, yes, I have it here," he said, delving into his purse.

She smiled with her eyes.

"May I?" he asked, taking her hand.

She nodded.

He slipped the metal ring onto her finger.

"It's back where it belongs!" she purred.

Nelan kissed the ring on her finger. "I'll replace it with a real one."

"I expect nothing less," she replied.

6

The Anniversary

15th January 1583

Nelan left his new house and walked along the short winding path to Dr Dee's sprawling mansion. The frost bit his ears and nose, and even the river flow was sluggish, with small blocks of ice floating upon it. The hoar frost crept up the trees, coating them in a sparkling dust of silver. It reminded him of the tree at Tyburn when they had hung the Jesuit priests, Edmund Campion amongst them. How Walsingham had sung Nelan's praises for securing the heretic's arrest.

About halfway across, he slipped on the frozen earth and tumbled to the ground. Getting up and brushing himself down, he glanced back at his new house with a mix of pride and nostalgia. A plume of grey smoke billowed from the chimney while a servant gathered logs and kindling in the woodshed.

His young wife, the beautiful Eleanor, said the new house was a monument to the past, and she was right. The two-storey wooden building resembled the design of the house into which he and his father had moved on arriving from the Netherlands. He and Eleanor had married in the local church at St Mary the Virgin, Mortlake. If only his mother and father had been there to witness their joyful union. He had an inkling that they watched from just beyond the gates of Heaven.

He mouthed the words to the *Turkeylony*, the song the musicians had played at the wedding reception:

If ever I marry, I'll marry a maid.
To marry a widow, I'm sorely afraid;
For maids, they are simple, and never will grutch,
But widows full oft, as they say, know too much.

Maid Eleanor had been his queen for the day, and he, her king. How they had danced and made merry!

While the new house was being built, Dr Dee had kindly offered them a place to live in a wing of his mansion. During their stay of nearly a year and a half, he and Eleanor had celebrated the wedding anniversary of Dr Dee's marriage to Jane Fromond, attended the christenings of their children, and regularly accompanied the family to Mass at St Mary the Virgin. When they finally moved into their new house on the Feast of St Nicholas in December, barely forty days ago, Dee had delighted Nelan with a gift of their own long, light rowing boat, also known as a wherry. Nelan couldn't wait to start his own family with Eleanor.

Over the months he'd stayed in Dr Dee's mansion, Nelan had learned more about the shoes that don't wear out, conjuring and astral travelling, but also about the courtiers who moved within the higher echelons of Queen Elizabeth's court.

At the house, he found Jane, Dr Dee's young wife, talking to Matilda, the local midwife, and Bridget, her pretty assistant.

"You shouldn't be up and about like this," Matilda was saying to her.

"I'm well aware of that," Jane snapped, rolling her eyes. "But I have to organise a large manor house with a horde of servants, a constant stream of visitors, from workmen to messengers, intelligencers, statesmen, navigators, occultists, scryers, mathematicians, as well as the odd spirit or two. I can tell you, some of them are very odd!"

"Yes, m'lady, that may be so," Matilda said, glancing hesitantly over her shoulder. "But with a belly that large, you'll be expecting a new arrival very soon…"

"… I know that. You know that," Jane Dee said, clearly in no mood for negotiation. "Even my husband knows that. But I still have work to do." With an exaggerated shrug of her shoulders, she waddled off down the corridor.

Nelan found the great man wearing his habitual long cape, white ruff and black hat, but his eyes shone with the light of the spirits and angels he sought to conjure. Dee's associate and scryer, Edward Kelley, pulled down his long skullcap, worn to conceal his ears, or rather the lack of them, since they'd been cropped as a punishment for forgery.

The study had a pleasant, familiar air; the smell of the books and scrolls, the towering shelves of hundreds of papers, all neatly stacked and lined up like soldiers on parade. The place suffused a pervasive sense of mystery that hovered like an angel of discovery, ready to open the doors of perception. Spread out on one table was a tranche of rare nautical charts. The Dutch geographer and cartographer, Gerardus Mercator, a friend and colleague of Dr Dee's, had signed one of them. Another table displayed navigational equipment, a spyglass, a compass and an astrolabe.

"You appear thoughtful today, Master Nelan. What's on your mind?" Dee asked.

"I was musing on the significance of this day," Nelan said. "Because it marks the twenty-fourth anniversary of our queen's coronation! Once you told me that the Queen consulted you about it. Please explain, why did you choose the 15th of January?"

"Excellent question," Dee replied, setting off around the study. "I cast up the character of this era, and the difficulties faced by the Queen, her people, and the island, and assessed the celestial influences needed to overcome them."

"And what were they?" Nelan asked, ever curious about these matters.

"The facts. In late 1559, Mary, Elizabeth's Catholic half-sister, died. Twenty-five at the time, Elizabeth ascended the throne and reinstated the Anglican religion. Like her father, Henry VIII, before her, she severed ties with the papacy in Rome. As retaliation, in 1570, Pope Pius V issued the *Regnans in Excelsis* and excommunicated Elizabeth."

"Why is that important?"

"The excommunication affected our relations with the Catholic kingdoms of France and Spain, who view us as heretics and devil-worshippers. An excommunication is a Roman Catholic rite. Vested in a stole, amice and violet cope, the pontiff is assisted by twelve priests holding lighted candles. Wearing his mitre, he pronounces the formula of the anathema in Latin, culminating with this condemnation:

> *In the name of God, the All-powerful, Father, Son, and Holy Ghost, by virtue of the power which has been given us of binding and loosening in Heaven and on earth, we declare her excommunicated and anathematised, and we judge her condemned to eternal fire with Satan and his angels.*

"The twelve priests respond, '*Fiat, fiat, fiat,*' meaning, 'So be it! So be it! So be it!' To conclude, the pontiff rings a bell, closes the Holy Book, and the priests dash the candles to the ground and stamp on them. The three parts to the rite have given rise to its common name – Bell, Book and Candle."

As Nelan soaked in the highly charged atmosphere, he recalled Kazia's prophecy:

> *I hear the ringing of the bells.*
> *I hear the words of the prayers of the Almighty.*
> *I see the light of the blazing fire.*

She may not have known it, but the Gyptian Chovihano was talking about Bell, Book and Candle.

Nelan asked, "How did this shape your thoughts about the date of the coronation?"

"The 15th of January sits within the astrological influence of Capricorn. I chose this date because it was imperative that the coronation garnered its huge celestial power. To survive these coming times, and to combat the forces of the Spanish Empire, I calculated that England would need the Capricornian qualities of perseverance and hard work, resilience and self-discipline allied with a dose of stubbornness. The planet Saturn rules Capricorn, and in mythology, Saturn sacrificed two of its moons for the greater good. I foresaw that the Queen and her people would have to make such sacrifices for the commonwealth."

"Did it please the Queen?"

"It did. Ever since then, she asks for my counsel," Dee said, puffing out his chest. "And it's a privilege to give it to her."

After his audience with Dr Dee, as Nelan returned to his new house, he had that eerie feeling that someone, or something, was watching him. Nor was it the first time, either. He stopped and looked around. The shapes of the trees and bushes were hazy in the half-light of dusk. Over by the river, he heard footsteps moving through the brush.

"Halt! Who goes there?" he yelled into the night, then ran towards the bushes. He thought he saw an animal scurry through the undergrowth. It was probably a fox or a beaver. He shrugged his shoulders and walked home. Soon, he was standing by the hearth in his new house, warming himself by the embers of his wife's love.

7

The Midwife's Oath

4th February 1583

Nelan and Eleanor arrived early at St Mary's, Barnes. The bright winter sun reflected off the craggy pieces of flint bound into the outer church wall. The warden rolled up soon after they did. With his hunchback, he stared at them with cross eyes.

"What you 'ere for then?" he said, his tone as frosty as the ground.

"To take the midwife's oath." Eleanor's voice resonated with pride.

"That so?" the warden replied. "See, we get all sorts tryin' to steal the church's silver, so I gotta be careful, else the pastor, he gives me a beatin', he does."

"We understand," Nelan said in his best sympathetic voice.

They watched the warden shuffle around the church furniture and, to their amusement, move it back to its original position.

"Well, my love, we're here now," Nelan murmured.

"I've wanted to do this since I was a youngster," Eleanor said.

Matilda, the local midwife, had suffered a bout of the ague and could not attend to her duties, albeit temporarily. The other midwife, Bridget, needed an assistant. Eleanor had helped with some births while at Greenwich Palace and readily volunteered to take the oath. Because Jane Dee was expected to give birth at any moment, they had organised it in a rush. As a reciprocal gesture, Jane Dee had kindly offered to teach Eleanor to read and write.

Nelan dabbed Eleanor's hand, and she smiled, and then adjusted her bonnet. Her palm was moist, and she said, "I hope this goes well."

"With the Lord's help, it will," he said.

The curate emerged through the vestry door waving a thurible, sending thick clouds of sweet-smelling incense into the thin, late winter air. The elderly pastor shuffled up to the altar, his footsteps echoing around the stone chapel. Nelan wondered which was older, the church or the pastor.

After conducting the ceremony, the pastor spoke the midwife's oath, and she repeated it after him in a soft, nervous voice:

I, Eleanor Michaels, née Pead, am admitted to the office and occupation of a midwife.

I will faithfully exercise the said office according to such cunning and knowledge as God hath given me. I will help both poor and rich women being in labour and travail of child.

I will not permit any woman in labour to name any other to be the father of her child, only the true father. I will not suffer any ungodly means to shorten the labour nor suffer the substitution of the infant at birth. And I will refrain from any kind of sorcery or incantation in the time of the travail of any woman. Nor will I destroy the child born of any woman, nor dismember or hurt the same.

In the ministration of the sacrament of baptism in the time of necessity, I will pour clean water upon the head of the infant, and speak the accustomed words:

I christen thee in the name of the Father, the Son, and the Holy Ghost.

Eleanor made her mark, the crucifixion cross, on the parish register, and the pastor announced her as a midwife for Mortlake, Barnes and Putney.

Outside, Nelan said to her, "I'm so proud of you."

"It's a great responsibility. Women rich and poor die in childbirth, as do many infants. I can help them."

They strolled along the Old Church Road, by the gnarled oak and the hawthorn bush, all the way to their jetty and home. That evening, the chef prepared a fish stew. The celebratory meal marked the beginning of a new life for them both.

"What is this fish?" he asked.

"It's a barbel," Eleanor said.

"Why did you choose that fish?"

"No reason, my love. Why do you ask?"

"The barbel, or the catfish, is the emblem of the St John family."

"Oh my goodness! Is that the family of the boy who died accidentally at your school?"

"The same."

"I'm sorry, my love. I didn't know."

"It's fine," Nelan said, although he had an inkling this did not bode well for her future as a midwife. "Anyway, let's drink a toast of this Spanish sack. May you exercise your craft with skill and care, safely bringing new lives into the world."

"To midwifery!" she chimed.

Three days later, Nelan accompanied Eleanor to Dr Dee's house. While his wife attended to the travail of Jane Dee, Nelan joined Dr Dee and his scryer, Edward Kelley, in the scrying room, a special place of conjuring spirits and angels. Fascinated, he absorbed every detail in the room, especially the black obsidian mirror, the scrying stone itself. What images could dance on its dark surface? Would he get to visualise an angel? When Dr Dee instructed Edward Kelley to show him the basic principles of scrying, Nelan could barely control his excitement.

Nelan sat at the scrying table. Laid out in front of him were the trappings of crystal gazing; a show stone on a copper base inscribed with symbols, including Dee's monolith and the Tetragrammaton, the four-letter Hebrew theonym.

Nelan fidgeted with his ruff and nervously touched the obsidian stone.

"Will you sit still," Kelley snapped. "The angels will not reveal the truth to us if you upset the subtle harmonies of the spirit room."

Nelan glanced at Dr Dee, who nodded in that encouraging way he had, and Nelan quietened himself. Following Kelley's instructions, Nelan placed his hands on either side of the crystal show stone. With the atmosphere in the room spinning slowly, Nelan relaxed his hands and nodded his head. He heard voices inside his soul, as if they conversed with him. The atmosphere grew fine and cool, and the muscles in his face relaxed. Even the furrows on Dee's brow smoothed.

A quiet presence descended into the room. In the middle of the show stone, there appeared a small round spark of living fire. It increased in size until it formed a bright globe of light some twenty inches in diameter.

The spirit had come.

"Please tell us your name," Nelan asked.

After a pause, he heard a distant voice say, *Agnes.*

Nelan held his breath. Agnes. There was only one Agnes who spoke in such a gentle way… someone very special to him.

"Mother!" The word burst from him with joy, surprise and amazement.

My Nelan, the voice replied.

"Oh! My!" It was her; his mother's spirit.

What do you want of me, son?

"C-can you…? W-will you…?" he stammered. His hands shook as he glimpsed the vague image of his mother's beautiful face in the shadows of the show stone.

"Are you well?"

I abide in the arms of Our Lord.

"Your visitation… is a wonderful gift."

Nelan felt waves of emotion ripple through him, like gusts of wind moving across the surface of the waters.

How can I be of service? she said.

"My mentor, Dr John Dee, is worried about his wife. She labours in the travails of childbirth."

He will have no concerns, Agnes said. *The Lord will bless them both with a healthy son.*

When scribing the conversation, Dee could barely hold the quill. "Praise the Lord our God! I shall name the boy Roland, in honour of my dear father."

What else will you ask of me, my son?

Nelan was trembling inside; he knew what he wanted to say, but he could barely bring himself to broach the subject.

"C-can I ask about…?" he stammered.

You can ask anything.

Nelan summoned every last shred of courage and asked the question that stuck in his gullet. "When we lived in Leiden in the Netherlands… the Spanish soldiers… It was the last day I saw you… alive."

I remember.

"I tried to stop them from taking you away. I grabbed the soldier's leg, and he dragged me along, scraping my knees on the ground… Then I followed you and Father to the town square, where I stood in the crowd. Father pressed a white lily into your hands. Then the soldiers tied you to the post and lit the fire."

You were but ten years old.

"Mother, why did they do that?"

What's done is done, my son. On that day, you stopped growing. You're little. But you're a good, brave boy, and I love you all the same.

Nelan wiped away the tears but couldn't wipe away the horrible feeling of being frozen inside that had afflicted him in the town square in Leiden. Ever since, the incident had followed him like a shadow, suffocating his natural response in times of danger, just as it had done when faced by Guillermo's threats at Westminster School.

"Mother, tell me please, why did the priest *bless* the flames? Did his blessing make them hotter? I watched the flames shrivel your white lily. Then I looked away."

I'm glad you did, she said. Then, after a moment's pause, she added, *Remember the words of Our Lord… Father, forgive them, for they know not what they do.*

"I can't agree to that yet."

Do not seek revenge, Nelan. Vengeance is for the Lord, not for you.

"Yours and father's deaths were wrong… wrongs I must put to right."

Do that for your father and me. Right the wrongs, but do not seek vengeance.

"I shall."

Now, as I take my leave, I absolve you of any guilt you may feel.

"Mother, don't go."

But the light in the scrying stone faded, and a normal atmosphere returned. Nelan could barely put one foot in front of the other and staggered out of the scrying room. Eleanor greeted him, and announced, "There's a new addition to the family. Mother and baby are fine. Dr Dee, you're the father of a healthy boy."

"Oh. Bless the Lord," Dee said, tears rolling down his cheeks.

When Nelan told her that his mother's spirit had visited them, she said, "This has been a most extraordinary day!"

When they approached their front door, the doorman stomped around the back of the yard.

"What's happened?" Nelan asked him.

"The chicken coop," he said, holding up a dead chicken. "An animal must have found a way in and slaughtered them. The rest escaped."

"Let me see. Bring that lantern over here," Nelan said. "No, someone took a blade to this."

"What's that mean?"

"It means we need to double the guard."

"Why?"

"This was sabotaged."

8

The Art of Being Previous

18th May 1583

The doubling of the guard had the desired effect, because whoever had sabotaged the chicken coop hadn't done so again in the three months since the incident.

As the spurges and rhododendrons bloomed in his garden, Dee invited Nelan to meet a man named Olbracht Laski. Arriving from Poland during the previous month, Laski had a reputation as a man of adventure and, as a budding alchemist, he contacted Dee to glean more knowledge of these forbidding times.

Laski strolled into Dee's study and, with grace and dignity, made his presence felt. A big man, his beard was almost as long as his black cape. After dinner, he, Nelan and Kelley retired to Dee's study.

"The four of us gather today in the presence of Our Lord," Dee said, "to conjure the future, and what it may hold for the blessed land of England. Master Kelley wants to share a vision. Let's try to interpret its meaning."

Edward Kelley smoothed down his jerkin and announced, "The Lord has granted me not one vision of the future, but three!"

"Marvellous!" Dee chimed.

"In the first one, I saw a narrow passage of water."

"Where was this?" Laski asked.

"The vision did not reveal it to me," Kelley replied. "But many vessels sailed along the small channel."

"Was it the Irish Sea?" Laski asked.

"Perhaps," Nelan said. "Tell us more about the ships."

"Huge galleons with cannon aplenty, many men, and in the stern of the ships, great towers reaching to the heavens."

"They are English warships," Dee said, fisting one hand into the palm of the other.

"I am not so sure," Nelan said.

"Why? Dr Dee is certainly correct. This vision is of the English navy patrolling your western flank," Laski added.

"Pray, Master Kelley, tell us what else you saw in this vision," Nelan said.

"Some vessels had banks of rowers," Kelley said.

"They're galleasses," Nelan said. "The Spanish and Venetians use such vessels."

"Could the English have captured them?" Laski ventured.

"No, I have an inkling whose they are," Nelan said. "Tell us, Master Kelley, what emblem did they fly?"

"Let me conjure the vision again… Yes, on the flag… I saw the unmistakable image of the Madonna," Kelley said, clapping his hands in joy.

"Then, these are Spanish ships," Nelan cried. "I suspect the narrow passage of water refers not to the Irish Sea but to the English Channel. In short, your vision signifies the provision of foreign powers against the welfare of this land, this England!"

"And," Kelley exclaimed, "it is something they shall shortly put into practice!"

"In which case, the Spanish are coming, and soon," Nelan said.

"I think you're right," Dee said. "Because the Spanish grandees hold sway across the world by the might of their arms, they'll stop at nothing to propagate their religion."

"I had a second vision," Kelley said.

"Tell us more," Nelan said.

"I envisaged the cutting of the head of a woman by a tall black man."

"A woman, you say? That is certainly a terrible thing," Dee said.

"And she wore a crown," Kelley said.

"If it is the Spanish fleet who are the invaders, then could that be your Queen Elizabeth?" Laski suggested, hesitation in his voice.

"No, don't think that," Dee said firmly.

"I meant no offence," Laski said. "Is it the other queen?"

"Mary, Queen of Scots?" Nelan asked.

"I know not which monarch it is," Kelley added. "But again, the vision suggested that the event is shortly to occur."

Laski paced the room like a lion and then stared out of the window at the River Thames. "Tell us the third vision."

"This concerns astrology," Kelley said. "You may know of last month's conjunction in the heavens involving the two great outer planets – Jupiter and Saturn."

The atmosphere in the room was charged with a fervent intensity, in which every word gripped them in the heart and the mind.

"Every twenty years," Kelley said, "the two planets appear close together in the celestial sky, but the significance depends on where in the heavens it occurs. Up to now, and for the last twenty years, the conjunction has occurred in the Watery Trigon – that's one of the three water signs of Cancer, Scorpio and Pisces. But last April, the conjunction moved into the Fiery Trigon – that's the three fire signs of Aries, Leo and Sagittarius."

"How often does this conjunction occur?" Laski asked.

"Every eight hundred years," Nelan said.

"That's a long, long time," Laski murmured.

"It marks a sea change," Nelan said, "the end of one phase of history for the Island of Angels, and the beginning of another."

"Hallelujah!" Dee chimed.

In His wisdom, God had revealed the three premonitions to Kelley: the threat of many Spanish ships, the death of a queen, and the beginning of a new stage in English history. With prior knowledge of these momentous events, the question was how best to prepare for them.

As readiness was everything, Nelan resolved to perfect the art of being previous.

9

The Dover Premonition

2nd September 1583

Several months later, Nelan approached the end of a journey. Two days previously, Walsingham had despatched him to Dover to deliver a secret message to the searcher, the man responsible for checking the port's incoming vessels and their passengers. Nelan had left the comforts of his house in Mortlake and the warm embrace of his wife, although Eleanor was busy performing midwifery duties and learning to read and write.

Nelan had wanted to stay close to Dr Dee's growing family and witness little Roland take his first steps. Although on the day he left and passed by the mansion, he heard raised voices between Jane Dee and Edward Kelley. Domestic harmony was difficult to achieve.

Along the Dover Road, he'd seen plenty of activity in the fields, farm labourers harvesting and collecting fruits from the orchards. On reaching Dover, the smell of the salt from the sea invigorated him. Once he'd spoken to the searcher, Nelan turned and headed home. But when he passed a small chapel at the top of the white cliffs, something irked him about the place, and he dismounted outside its low cemetery walls. He tethered his horse to a yew tree and gazed at the thick crenellated walls of Dover Castle in the distance.

From this vantage point, he overlooked the white-crested waves of the Narrow Seas and watched the great galleons and carracks shuffling in and out of the harbour and across the English Channel to the Netherlands. This was surely the narrow stretch of water to which Kelley had referred in one of his visions. Every day, the ships transported men and supplies to assist the war against the Spanish and returned with the dead and wounded.

Nelan stood outside the graveyard by the chapel. The wind gusted off the channel of old England, whistling through the trees, and sending a chill through the air. A holly bush and a couple of grand old yew trees yielded colour to the drab cemetery stones. The windswept trees were shedding their leaves. A crow squawked, and its cry travelled over the graveyard, and across the meadows and dales, summoning the other crows. The birds' calls, the cattle mewing and the foxes' cries in the nearby woods were muffled and indistinct.

The outlying fields smelled of hay and cow dung. Sleepy hamlets, isolated farms and derelict barns dotted the landscape. The trees resembled stubs, their growth stunted by the salt-laden winds. The place had a windswept feel, as if nothing could take root.

He slumped against the cemetery wall, jagged bits of flint protruding into his back. The bells rang out from the belfry, resounding across the empty wastes of the southern flatlands. With the pastor at its head, a harvest festival procession wound its way around the chapel. A handful of choristers sang a psalm with all their hearts, lifting the congregation.

His horse neighed, but something niggled at Nelan's soul. Unlike his mount, he wasn't ready to return home just yet. Nelan edged towards the church gate as the procession passed him by and entered the chapel, followed by the lord of the manor, his wife and children, and then peasants and landsmen. Then Nelan realised what irked him. It was the pastor. He was none other than Francis Fletcher, the ex-chaplain of the *Golden Hind*. Bumping into him again kindled memories of their extraordinary passage around the world. He remembered when the vessel crossed the Equator, or the line as it was called. And mariners, being an inveterately superstitious lot, had ceremonies for nearly everything, including crossing the line. Officiated by Fletcher himself, Nelan had undergone the ceremony which closely resembled a baptism.

Back in the church, Fletcher hadn't noticed him. A torn white ruff draped down his back, Fletcher bowed obsequiously by each of the candles, hands held in prayer while mumbling a passage from the psalms which passed for the blessing. As he lit each one, the chapel hummed with a gentle vibrancy, dispersing the oppressive sense of gloom and foreboding. The blessing over, no sooner had Fletcher heaved his old frame up the steps than he was standing by the eagle lectern and regaling his flock about the sanctity of their mission to support Queen Bess.

"Without her grace, we face the wrath of Spain," Fletcher said, thumping the lectern. "Their King Philip despatched the Duke of Parma at the head of a large army to invade the Spanish Netherlands. William the Silent leads the Dutch resistance against the Duke. Recently, the Spanish sent an assassin to murder William, but thank the Lord, he failed. Whether Puritan or Huguenot, Lutheran or Calvinist, we will defend the Protestant cause in Europe."

Nelan approached him at the end of the service.

"Well, this is a pleasant reunion. If it isn't Little Nelan!" Fletcher said, his wrinkled face breaking into a warm smile. "What brings you to my parish?"

"Some business in Dover," Nelan said. "But what are you doing here? You didn't want to stay on board ship?"

"Not after what *he* did to me during the grounding of the *Golden Hind*!" Fletcher winced as he spoke the words.

The grounding on a reef had happened in Indonesia in January 1580 on their way home, and was a watershed moment for the ship, the crew, the admiral, and particularly for Francis Fletcher. To lighten the ship and allow them to refloat, Drake jettisoned heavy cannons and even gifts intended for the Queen. But the reef held them fast, sapping the men's morale. They feared they would never see their loved ones again and die a horrible death in a strange land.

Drake turned to Fletcher to ease the men's spirits. Unbeknown to the admiral, the chaplain harboured a grievance against him for what had transpired earlier in the voyage on the Isle of Justice in Patagonia. Fletcher vented his fury and told the men that the grounding of the ship was divine justice for Drake's unjust execution of the mutineer Thomas Doughty.

Drake was apoplectic. When the ship was finally refloated, the admiral excommunicated the chaplain, chained his feet to the mast, and planted a placard around his neck. Its first words read:

FRANCIS FLETCHER, the falsest knave that liveth.

"I'm sorry Drake did that to you," Nelan said. "But I admire you for speaking your conscience. I wish I had found the courage to do the same, because I believed what you were saying was true. To toe the line, I kept my own counsel."

"I feared the wrath of my God more than Drake's, and so should you," Fletcher said, then turned and sought sanctuary in the vestry.

Well, Fletcher had put him in his place. Nelan shrunk inside. Why hadn't he spoken his mind like a man, like Fletcher had done at the time? If he had, perhaps he could have saved Fletcher from the humiliating punishment to which Drake subjected him. If he ever met Drake again, he vowed to tell him exactly what he thought of those tragic events in Patagonia and Indonesia.

Nelan slumped down with his back against one of the yew trees. The thin scaly bark dug into his skin. The incident was a poignant moment for Nelan. He too had been sympathetic to the chaplain's position, because why else, with their expert seamanship, would they have run aground if it wasn't the will of the Almighty?

Tired of walking, tired of spying, he drifted off into a fitful sleep.

A vision unfurled before him.

Filaments of mist arose out of the ground and slowly coalesced into a recognisable shape; a wall, two spires and a vaulted ceiling. An old yew tree bathed the churchyard in shadows overlooking three bonfires, each with a stake. Three carts trundled towards them over the cobblestones. Each carried a prisoner wearing a white robe and hood. Pikemen jostled them onto the bonfires and lashed them to the stakes.

The atmosphere curdled, heavy with hate, thick with tension.

An enormous crowd bayed for the blood of the three convicts.

A pikeman stepped forward, wielding the torch. The flames scorched the air.

A woman cried out from the crowd, "She's not a witch. She's innocent!"

A dog raced onto the bonfire and yapped at the feet of one of the prisoners. Then the hound tugged at the person's robe and pulled it off.

Just as the hood fell to the ground, he woke up, gasping for breath.

This was a premonition. Something terrible was going to happen to a witch.

10

A Question of Trust

21st September 1583

The Dover Road was bumpy and clogged with carriages and courtiers, merchants and messengers, and plenty of horses and carts. When he arrived home, the rays of the midday sun glinted on the waves of the river. The world was cocooned in a quiet lethargy, except for three large wherries tethered to the jetty by Dr Dee's mansion.

At home, Eleanor talked enthusiastically to him about midwifery. Now she'd taken the midwife's oath, Matilda and Bridget often asked for her to assist them with new births. He was pleased that she'd found a passion with which to fill her life. Then, he secretly wondered whether she had done so to ease the pain and continuing disappointment because the Lord had not blessed them with a child of their own. This was not the time to ask her about it, and he let her help him take off his dirty coat and muddy boots, and then told her stories about meeting Fletcher and his trip to Dover.

"While you were there, did you hear the sirens' call of the sea?" She had this way of asking questions that stretched into the very core of his being, and this was one of them.

"I'll do what England needs of me," he replied.

"I thought you'd say that," she quipped, her eyes dancing with love and kindness. Then she added, "Oh, that new man in Dr Dee's household, what's his name?"

"John Halton."

"Yes, him. What a strange fellow he is, with his deformed hand."

"And he's got this haunted look in his eye."

"Anyway, he brought a message. The doctor has a favour to ask of you. Oh, and there's been a lot of comings and goings at the mansion over the past few days."

"I'll go and see what's happening."

At Dr Dee's mansion, John Halton opened the door.

"I'm here to see the doctor," Nelan said.

"In the library," came the abrupt reply.

Caskets of scrolls and rolls of papers lined the corridors. Every room was stacked high with cases, luggage and crates.

Upstairs, he heard raised voices – Kelley arguing with Jane Dee. That was nothing new. The servants buzzed around like flies on a hot summer's day. Squeezing by all the caskets, Nelan made his way to the library. Every shelf was empty, and all the books were piled into boxes. Dee sat at a desk making notations on a paper.

"Ah! Nelan! There you are. Close the door. Now, I daresay you learned many secrets in Dover. Walsingham will flap his ears when you tell him about them."

"Both the port and its searcher were busy, m'lord," Nelan said. "But I fear you're leaving us."

"One moment," Dee said, scribbling on the scroll in his tiny handwriting. "There, I'm making the last entry to the library catalogue. Now, what did you say?"

"Where are you going? What's happening?"

"Sadly, I must depart these shores. I'm taking my family with me and Kelley. We're invited by Laski to visit the Kingdom of Poland."

Nelan hissed. "My lord, this is more than a visit. This is moving house, court and country."

"I know, Nelan."

"But you can't go now. Not when we have so much more to do. There's your inspiring work conjuring Madima and the other spirits. What will happen to all the wise guidance they have to impart to humanity?"

"Have faith," Dee said. "Our holy work with the angelic spirits will continue. Humanity needs more new knowledge with which to climb the ladder of truth to the Almighty."

"Can't you remain here to conduct that sacred work? Our nation faces the warmongers Philip of Spain and the French king. We're spiritually bludgeoned by the Pope in the Vatican. So, why now?"

"For many reasons," Dee said. "You will remember, during Queen Mary's reign, when she married King Philip of Spain, I cast the matrimonial horoscope. That's all I did. One thing led to another, and my father was ruined and I was arrested and imprisoned for calculating, conjuring and witchcraft. I can't let that happen again to me and my family."

"But that was during Mary's reign. Now there's good Queen Bess. Will she not lend you her support?"

Dee shook his head. "Once, I was her philosopher and trusted advisor. Not anymore. A while ago, she passed by the house in the royal barge. Before, it was her pleasure to stop and converse with me, but this time, she merely waved, one of those haughty regal waves. She was my last and greatest supporter. Without her, I am prey to the carrion at court, of whom there are many. No, the time is ripe to seek pastures new."

"I see," Nelan said, sensing there was more to come.

"I'm not sure that you do. Have you read a tract by Henry Howard, Earl of Surrey? You're shaking your head. It's entitled *A Defence Against the Poison of Supposed Prophecies*. In it, he attacks my methods – the scrying, the conjuring and the alchemy. It's too dangerous to tarry a moment longer."

"I have Walsingham's ear," Nelan said. "I can speak to him on your behalf."

"Hah! The Moor! I think not. The last I heard, he declared that I'm marvellously alienated from him. Where he's concerned, I am of the same humour."

"I'm sorry to hear that."

"There are other, more pressing, reasons to leave these shores. I'm in a parlous financial situation. To remedy it, I applied for a court pension, which was refused. Nelan, I have a wife and children to feed. Laski has promised some pecuniary rewards for our trip."

"What can I do to help?"

"I'm taking my tracts on astronomy, the Cabbala, astrology, navigation and alchemy. The house and its contents now belong to Jane's brother, Nicholas Fromond. You're a trusted neighbour, so please look after my remaining books. One day, I shall return, because these four walls, the garden, the river and the church hold many delightful memories."

"I shall miss you. You've been a father and a spiritual mentor to me. You welcomed me and Eleanor into your family. More than that, you gave us hope, comfort and purpose. I shall not forget your kindness. You've improved both our lives."

"Thank you for saying so. It has been a pleasure to instruct you."

"And Eleanor will miss your wife's reading and writing lessons."

"She's quite proficient now," Dee said. Scratching his beard, he added, "But listen to me, Nelan. These are changing times. A while ago, they imprisoned a man named Charles Bailly in the Tower. On his cell walls, he inscribed the following verse:

Wise men ought circumspectly to see what they do.
To examine before they speak.
To prove before they take in hand.
To beware whose company they use.
And, above all things, to consider whom they trust.

"I advise you to take these poignant words to heart, particularly the last phrase."

"I will, m'lord."

There was a scuffling noise from outside the library door. Dee put his finger to his lips and pointed to it. Nelan tiptoed towards it and opened it suddenly. There, with his ear glued to the door, was a man with a deformed hand.

"Well, Master John Halton," Dee said. "Did you hear it all, or shall we speak louder?"

The man huffed and puffed, made his excuses, and shuffled off.

"There, that's another reason I can stay no longer," Dee said.

"What an affront. What does he think he's doing?"

"He's one of Walsingham's intelligencers. Now, do you see my predicament?"

Nelan shook his head. "What has England come to when riff-raff spy upon a man of your credentials, who has given the Queen the finest advice and counsel?"

Come midnight, the Dee and Kelley families and their belongings, along with Olbracht Laski, sailed off down the river to seek passage to Europe. As Nelan watched the stern lanterns of the fleet of wherries disappear into the night, he rued the day England lost perhaps her greatest occultist.

11

The Devil Lurks

9th November 1583

It had been an early start. The first rays of dawn moved above the horizon with a languid indifference. As Wenceslaus docked the wherry, Nelan almost felt at home, since he'd spent some of the best times of his life as an apprentice just along the river by Queenhithe wharf.

Those days were long gone. Now, he was a spy, an integral part of Walsingham's secret network. Since Dee had departed, he and Eleanor were on their own. But with caution as their watchword, they could survive and prosper within the confines of their own goals. In the middle of the night, he'd awoken to a message from Roger Adden. 'Be at St Paul's Wharf. At first light.'

Nelan hauled himself up the wharf steps, where an intelligencer quickly ushered him into a room in a nearby terraced house. A murder of crows glowered at them from the rooftops.

Inside, Walsingham spoke in a hushed voice to a dozen men in black hats and long black robes. Armed with pikes, swords and pistols, they were ready for a large operation. Two of them carried an unwieldy battering ram. Amongst the hardened faces, he recognised Roger Adden and Charles Sledd.

Walsingham interrupted his briefing, saying, "Nelan, what are you doing here?"

"I asked him to attend," Adden said.

"Why on earth did you do that?" Walsingham said through gritted teeth.

"I-I thought you would want him to be present…" Adden stammered.

"Well, you thought wrong, Master Adden. I shall have words with you later. Nelan, since providence and Master Adden have brought you into my presence, you may join the fray."

"Thank you, m'lord," Nelan said, but he felt awkward having walked into the middle of a dispute between Walsingham and his steward.

"Charles Sledd will lead the raid," Walsingham went on, "which, Nelan, you might find of interest."

"Why's that?" Nelan asked.

"Oh! You'll see for yourself," came the gruff reply.

Walsingham lingered inside the house after the briefing. Outside, all was dark, except for distant dawn rays. Silent as ghosts, Charles Sledd led them in a line towards a house on Paul's Wharf Hill. The men with the ram battered the door down, releasing the hounds of Hell. Sledd, Nelan and Adden piled inside, shouting, fists pumping. The others barged in behind them. A pistol shot rang out, disturbing the crows, and all inside. Screams of despair mingled with yells of delight. Shadows moved around the inside of the house, in which two men were arrested, tied up, gagged and hooded.

Nelan cried, "All's well!"

Eyes bright with delight, Roger Adden wore a broad smile and a feather in his cap. In a voice redolent with joy and relief, Charles Sledd said, "Tell his Lordship, we've got 'em. And the evidence."

Head high, Walsingham strolled into the house. "Well?" he asked, with an air of excitement. He wasn't alone. The agents hooped and cheered, as if they had won first prize at the joust.

They crammed into a small wood-panelled office in the house. Walsingham sat behind a desk, scrutinising the evidence the agents had uncovered. Eagle-eyed, he pored over the papers, weighing every morsel of detail on the scales of justice. The two hooded men stood before him, wearing their long white gowns, surrounded by Adden, Sledd and the agents.

"Here, wear this," Adden said, with sarcasm dripping from every word, and placed a chain of office over the head of the taller of the two men.

Standing next to Walsingham, Nelan grimaced at the rank odour of the men's fear.

"This evidence is compelling. Their guilt is evident," Walsingham said with a deep note of satisfaction.

Charles Sledd motioned to lift the rim of the hood of one of them, but Walsingham wagged his finger.

"Not yet," he said. "I want these traitors to hear my words from within the confined darkness of their hoods. The Devil wears a hood, for evil is conniving and deceptive. These two are devils from the pits of Hell."

Walsingham picked up the papers on the desk and brandished them in the air, saying, "These are secret letters between Mary, Queen of Scots, and the Spanish ambassador. They reveal plans to raise a rebellion amongst English Catholics and disturb the Queen's peace. By handling them, you two have committed high treason against the person of the monarch!

"You are Catholic scum, the worst of the worst. You may believe that *Regnans in Excelsis* will save your skins, but it won't. Because here we don't recognise papal bulls. They are bull!" Walsingham spat the last word out like poison.

Adden sneered. Sledd guffawed. The hooded men remained silent.

"You," Walsingham said, pointing to the man wearing the chain of office, "were once an aristocrat from a noble family. Not anymore. Your fall from grace is shameful and alarming. The motto of your house is *Virtus Sola Nobilitas*, meaning Virtue is the only Nobility. Now you stand before me, accused of the most grievous crime, the betrayal of your queen, the betrayal of your country, and above all, the betrayal of the motto of your own house. With this heinous deed, you have abdicated from the nobility and from all virtue."

As Adden grabbed the man, the chain around the traitor's neck broke and clattered to the floor. Picking it up, Adden noticed the crest on the medallion, and jibed, "Here, this fella's got the crest of a falcon on his coat of arms."

Nelan knew the man's identity. "Wait," he said. "The falcon… It's belled and jessed, isn't it?"

"Why? Yeah, it is that," Adden said.

"This must be Francis Throckmorton," Nelan said, whipping off the man's hood. Tall, thin and gaunt, the aristocrat had a furrowed brow and an anxious look. He bowed his head and stared at the ground.

"It is, Nelan. This be none other than *Sir* Francis Throckmorton," Adden said.

Now he understood how Walsingham had connived against him. The secretary had not invited him because he did not want Nelan to share in this coup and desired all the credit for himself. Nelan could hardly accuse him of such malevolent intent, but he could still claim the success, and in a moment of vindication, he boasted, "And think, m'lord. Without my help, you'd never have caught him!"

Walsingham was ominously quiet. Roger Adden was not. "Traitor!" he said, and spat into Throckmorton's face. The spittle dribbled down his cheek and onto his gag. With his hands tied behind his back, he could not respond. He had nothing left, not even a shred of dignity.

"What about the other traitor?" Walsingham cried. "This one's driven by deceit and conspiracy. Now, reveal the face of wickedness."

Roger Adden tore off his hood.

"We believe this shadow of a man to be Matthew Gonzales, m'lord," Charles Sledd claimed.

The man was short, young and stocky, and had black hair and a swarthy, arrogant look. Nelan recognised him. Oh yes, he knew him well enough.

"Nelan, is this the man named Matthew you reported as acting suspiciously around the Gyptian camp?" Walsingham asked.

"I don't know because I never saw him myself. But I do know that this man is not Matthew Gonzales."

"No? Who is he then?" Walsingham asked.

"Pedro de Antón."

At the speaking of his name, a glimmer of recognition shone in the mystery man's eyes. He gnawed at his gag and struggled to free his hands.

"We need confirmation. Is he Pedro or Matthew?" Walsingham asked, turning to Charles Sledd.

"We may find his name in the papers we found upstairs," Sledd said.

Walsingham unrolled one of the scrolls and threaded a finger across it, word by word, line by line. "Ah yes, here it is."

"What's it say, m'lord?" Sledd asked.

"This entry is in Throckmorton's hand and concerns Pedro de Antón, alias Matthew or Mateo Gonzales. Remove his gag. He can read it for us."

Throckmorton took the scroll and read in a shaky voice:

Don Pedro de Antón is a brave young Spaniard, the younger brother of Guillermo. His father died when he was young. His mother remarried an English mariner and a Catholic, St John of Southampton, and lived with them in Sneakenhall near Mortlake on the River Thames.

Both boys attended Westminster School where, some years ago, Guillermo was killed in a gunpowder explosion. Don Pedro claims another boy murdered his brother.

St John, his stepfather, left England and joined the Spanish navy, where he took the title San Juan de Antón. Don Pedro seeks to avenge his brother's murder and works for us to unseat the heretic Queen Elizabeth.

Don Pedro speaks English without a Spanish accent, making him a marvellous asset to our Catholic cause.

Sir Francis Throckmorton.

"I told you," Nelan blurted out. "That's Pedro. He's a traitor and a murderer!"

"For what it's worth, let me hear what this Don Pedro has to say for himself," Walsingham muttered.

Roger Adden ripped the gag.

Staring at Nelan, Pedro cried, "*Asesino!* Murderer! After you killed my brother, my mother withered away, eaten by grief." He launched himself at Nelan and tried to head-butt him. Nelan darted out of the way as the agents pulled Pedro back.

"Then you robbed the treasure from my stepfather's ship. You've brought eternal shame on our family name!" Pedro ranted at Nelan. "So, yes, I set fire to your house! I killed your father. That wasn't murder. That was an eye for an eye. Now I want you dead. When you docked in Plymouth, I knocked you out but failed to kill you. I've pursued you across half of southern England. I even hunted you down in your house."

"Hah! That was you!"

"Yes. It was. I will never give up the fight for Spain and to avenge my brother's death. Vengeance is mine!"

"You were right about him, Nelan," Walsingham said. "Master Adden, escort these vermin to the Tower. They will stand trial for treason."

Charles Sledd taunted him, "The delights of the Little Ease await you!"

"What's that?" Pedro asked.

"An airless, dark cell in the Tower," Sledd went on, "in which a man can neither sit, stand nor lie. Hence, a place of little ease."

"I don't care. You will never break me!"

"Oh, but I think we will, Pedro," Nelan said.

"I am not Pedro, I am *Don Pedro de Antón*!" he shouted.

"Get them both out of my sight!" Walsingham muttered, and the agents led Pedro and Throckmorton out of the office, leaving Nelan alone with Walsingham.

"That will be all, Nelan," Walsingham said.

But that wasn't all there was. The secretary was not keeping his pledge.

"M'lord, you promised. I've contributed to today's success, and I helped you find Edmund Campion."

Walsingham twitched nervously, as if they'd caught him red-handed.

"Oh! I've so much on my mind. You'll have to remind me."

"You promised to give me a proper pardon for my supposed crimes."

"Oh? Did I? So I did."

"Then will you compose one?"

Walsingham hesitated, as if deciding how to play his cards. "No, I'll endorse Drake's clemency document."

Nelan always had it with him, and passed it to the secretary, who sat back down at Throckmorton's desk and countersigned it.

Nelan was ecstatic. Now he could realise all his hopes and dreams. This was an end and a beginning. He was truly, and legally, a free man. "And the ruby salamander?"

"I keep it in the drawer of my office at Barn Elms. Next time you are passing, come and collect it, if you will," Walsingham said.

Now that was satisfying in the extreme! His premonition had forewarned Walsingham of the Throckmorton plot, and earned him a valid clemency. Nelan felt flushed with success; he'd righted the wrong perpetrated by Pedro. Yet he still had to make the Spanish pay for murdering his mother. That would be immensely more difficult, but he knew it was his destiny to go back to sea and one day face the imperial might of King Philip's fleet.

"I will, m'lord. What now?" he asked.

"My priority as Secretary to the Privy Council is the security of Her Majesty's person and the safety of her realm. Our efforts must now be in one direction. All my intelligencers, you included, are intent on predicting, with as much accuracy as possible, when King Philip of Spain will despatch his Great Armada against us."

"What do you want from me?"

"Your gift of prescience uniquely equips you to interpret the signs of tomorrow. But I must mention one concern." Walsingham's tone was deadly serious, and he added, "Please, Nelan, close the door."

Nelan did as he was told. "What's this about, m'lord?"

"I am a devout man, and in serving my Queen, I wish to stay within the confines of the law and my religious precepts, although, for the sake of expediency, I'm prepared to extend the boundaries of what is permissible in order to defeat the Spaniards."

"What do you mean?"

"I'm referring to your astral arts," he said, rubbing his hands. "I mean those of prognostication, crystal-gazing, astrology and conjuring angels. While they can bring us success, there are senior members on the Privy Council, notably Sir William Cecil and Sir Christopher Hatton, who regard these skills as borderline heretical."

"This places me in an impossible situation. How can I continue to work for you?"

"We must proceed with extreme caution. You must tell no one else that you employ those arcane skills to defeat our enemies. Understood?"

"It is."

Nelan beat a hasty retreat from Walsingham's office. The secretary had openly warned him about employing his astral arts, yet had asked him to use them to save England from the wrath of Catholic Europe. Nelan felt an inner conflict between support for the Church and loyalty to the State. Whichever way he turned, the Devil awaited him, lurking on both shoulders.

12

The Tree That's Never Green

9th July 1584

It was early evening. With blistered feet, Nelan led his horse across the field, dried hard by the summer sun. Since leaving Tutbury Castle near Derby, he'd been in the saddle for two days. He and saddles did not mix. Lord, he had a sore arse.

Mary, Queen of Scots, was still suspected of plotting against Queen Elizabeth so, earlier in the year, Walsingham had sent him there to spy on her. His fruitful stay meant he had much to report to Walsingham. On the morrow, he'd meet the spymaster at his house in Seething Lane in the City of London. But tonight, he'd meet his beloved and couldn't wait to see her again.

He led his horse up to the summit of a hill. Looking south, the magnificent panorama of the City of London spread out before him. But the squawks and intensity of the birdsong put him on edge. If they were wary, so was he. Robbers and highwaymen could prowl in that copse or behind those bushes. He slowed to a snail's pace before entering the thicket. Moving under the canopy of the trees added shade to these shady times. Where the light was hazy, what lurked around the corner was shrouded in uncertainty.

Only nature was regular, and reliable, as spring gave way to summer, yielding autumn and winter. After the fallow, the sowing; after the sowing, the growth; after the growth, the harvest. Town markets every month. Fish every Wednesday, Friday and Saturday.

Church service every Sabbath. The inn every day. He liked that constancy.

From the hill summit, he looked for the place he'd meet Eleanor. It was near a large building that once housed the hospital of St Giles-in-the-Fields. His destination was the Bowl Inn, situated nearby.

Church bells rang out across the city, announcing evensong. Lights flickered in the evening breeze as the watchmen lit the lanterns. Nelan felt sure this was a sign that Eleanor would light his darkness, and together, they'd perform miracles. In these three long months, he'd missed her.

Avoiding the usual pack of barking dogs, mangy hounds and half-crazed canines, he stabled his horse at the Bowl Inn. Flies flitted around the piles of horse shit outside the stable. Folks sat on the grass beneath the lanterns, chewing blades of grass while enjoying beakers of ale. Some gambled with dice; others sat absorbed over a game of chess. Merchants and millers, coopers and clothiers, all conversed at table.

He found his beloved sitting alongside the old watchman, Alexander. A small whisp of auburn hair snuck out from her headscarf; the same one she'd worn on that summer's day in Queenhithe, the day he'd fallen for her. He tucked it back into her scarf.

"You're as pretty as a briar rose, and smell just as sweet," he whispered in her ear. She smiled with her eyes. He brushed her cheek with the back of his hand. Leaning over, he kissed her softly on the lips.

She swallowed her emotion and said, "It's lovely to see you, Nelan Michaels. I hear you're a man of fire, so where is it? I see no flame." She gave him one of those all-knowing smiles of hers.

"It's not outside. The fire's inside," he said. "It's the fire of my love for you."

She grasped his hand in hers. Then, feeling the roughness of his palm, she touched the three wavy lines on his right hand and murmured, "Perhaps that fire of your love for this island will one day awaken her angels."

"I pray for that," he said. "How is the fireman Alexander?"

"The poor fellow's getting old and decrepit. I brought him with me as a companion and for protection, not that he's able to provide much."

"Good, then I'll protect you."

"Now, stand back. More. I want to see how you're dressed."

He brushed himself down and pulled his doublet into place.

"You're wearing a doublet with those jags and cuts," she said with a frown.

"Yes, I like the fashion, don't you?"

"You know I don't. It looks like your tailor attacked the cloth with a scythe."

"I'll not wear it again, my love," he said. And she smiled. He was learning how to keep the peace of both the realm and the home. Neither was easy.

A trickster dressed in quartered harlequin garb spread mirth and mayhem amongst the drinkers. He approached their table, jingling the tiny bells hanging from his hat and clothes, and snorted:

You're gonna be seen,
On the tree that's ne'er green!

The phrase jolted Nelan's memory. He'd heard it before, but where and when?

"What did you say?" Nelan asked him.

The trickster sang the rhyme again.

"Pray tell, where's this strange tree?" Nelan asked.

"The same place as tomorrow's match," the trickster said, and spun around the table playing his flute.

"Where's that?" Nelan asked.

The trickster played a gleeful tune and said, "At the Tyburn Match."

That was it! The vision of the plough head. The hot summer's day. The tolling of the bells. A man in white with terror in his eyes. A man in black with fire in his eyes. The drunken crowd yelling that phrase about the tree that was never green.

Walsingham was right.

Tomorrow, Nelan would attend a hanging at Tyburn.

The next morning, the sun burst through the clouds and cast away the darkness of the night. With Eleanor by his side, the feeling of joy and wonder coursed through his veins.

Their room overlooked the Tyburn Road. They rose early. Well, they had to; the trickster banged the drum and played the flute, inciting dance, delight and derision in the courtyard. At this early hour, an excited crowd shouted and sang bawdy songs.

The innkeeper served him, Eleanor and Alexander a tidy breakfast of some leftover pie from the night before and a crust of rye bread, washed down with a jug of ale.

Nelan asked him, "We heard there's a Tyburn Match today."

"Aye, there'll be a new batch, all right. Six of 'em are gonna dance the Tyburn jig."

"That's a good 'alf dozen gonna dive into the fires of Hell," the trickster mused.

"Git on with ya," the innkeeper said to him. "Yeah, eight executions a year is good business. An' fun for the family. Even the children loves it. God bless Queen Bess, I say. Wanna hear a secret?"

"We're all ears," Nelan said.

"The Yeoman of the Halter hisself stayed here last night, he did," the innkeeper said, as he took a deep draught of ale and wiped his mouth with his sleeve. "Left for Newgate prison early this mornin' to do his duties with them that's condemned."

"What's he do then, this Yeoman?" Eleanor asked.

"He gets to tie the halter, the noose, round their necks," the innkeeper said, sticking out his chest like a peacock. "Dresses 'em up in them white robes and white hats, and gits 'em ready for their last journey into the fires 'a Hell."

"Who's dancing this time?" he asked.

"Dunno all their names. But there's a posh one, the traitor. What's he called? Oh, yeah, it's Franny Thickmitten."

"Oh, you mean Francis Throckmorton."

"Yeah, summat like that. Him, anyways."

How strange that the workings of fate had drawn him to this place to witness the end of a story. It had begun in Barn Elms three years ago when he stumbled across a plough head and a falcon belled and jessed. Nelan would get to see another wrong put to rights. His father's murderer, Pedro de Antón, would also meet his comeuppance!

Nelan had served the realm and protected the Queen. He had

helped remove traitors from her midst – first Campion and now Throckmorton and de Antón. With the country removing its poisons, it acted as an exorcism. Justice was served. Nelan felt hugely satisfied at this important achievement.

As they exited the inn, a messenger rode into the courtyard and called, "Nelan Michaels. Message for Master Nelan Michaels of Mortlake."

"That's me," Nelan shouted.

The messenger handed him a note.

"Who's it from? Must be important, that's a royal messenger," Eleanor said, peering over his shoulder.

"It's from Walsingham. It's about this afternoon's appointment. He's busy and wants a delay. We're to meet in two days."

"Then we have them to ourselves," Eleanor said.

"But first, let's see the Tyburn jig. Two traitors will burn in the fires of Hell! I helped uncover their plot. One of them you've met."

"I have?"

"Yes, Pedro de Antón, the madman who fought me at the quay at Plymouth Hoe. The man who murdered my father!"

She squeezed his hand and smiled with those big green eyes, two pools of warmth and kindness.

Carpenters and coopers, smiths and hatters, all jostled for space on either side of the road. An execution day served as a public holiday, and what better entertainment than the hanging of a couple of Catholic traitors for high treason? Plush coaches carried the rich merchants and their families to the execution site. Traders sold bread and sweetmeats, ale and posies of flowers. Not surprisingly, red roses, scarlet dahlias and blood-red poppies were popular assortments. Folk dispensed leaflets damning the Papists and broadsheets purporting to detail the last words of the condemned, which was quite a feat since they hadn't been executed yet. Others milled around the courtyard of the Bowl Inn, blowing the trumpet, playing the flute and dancing the jig alongside the trickster.

The town crier led the procession, calling out, "Hear ye! Hear ye! Make way for the condemned!" His bell clanged with the news of imminent death.

The Marshall of the City of London came next, dressed in his regalia, emblazoned with the mysterious protector, the silver griffin with the fierce red tongue, lizard scales and wings of fire. The ox carts followed behind them. Pikemen flanked the procession to prevent the escape of the convicts and keep the crowds at bay.

The first ox cart trundled down Tyburn Road. The Yeoman of the Halter had dressed the two young men in it in long white smocks and white caps. Oblivious to their fate, they waved at the crowd, laughing at their jests and exchanging banter. Friends and supporters threw posies of flowers and nosegays at them. If there hadn't been a couple of coffins in the back of the cart, Nelan might have mistaken the procession for a May Day celebration.

Two more young men wearing white robes occupied the second cart. One of them stood tall and proud, grasping the front of the ox cart.

"Oh, I know this man!" Nelan cried.

"How? Who is he?" Eleanor asked.

"It's Jasper. I met him on Shooters Hill. His sister, Kazia, helped me find you."

Jasper nodded his head and gave him the thinnest of smiles. The Gyptian stared straight ahead and ignored the noise and bustle around him. The crowd grew angry at his refusal to bow to the divine forces of the Protestant religion. His pride brought him a volley of colourful insults and rotten vegetables.

The Yeoman of the Halter announced the man's heinous crimes. "This man is a thief, a vagrant and a Gyptian!"

A man in rags and another in jags jumped out and nipped in front of the innkeeper, who carried two bowls of ale, one for Jasper and one for the other man in the ox cart.

"Let me by," the innkeeper said.

"No! This one ain't gettin' no ale," the one in rags cried, blocking his way.

"A free drink of ale for the condemned. It's tradition," the innkeeper replied.

"No ale! No ale!" the crowd yelled.

Wrapped in a presence of dignity and strength, Jasper wore this look of intense pride. Perhaps he'd settled to his lot, but the crowd hadn't. They thumped the air with their fists and chanted the Tyburn song:

Oh! Get thee down to the Tyburn tree,
The Tyburn tree, the Tyburn tree!
Oh! Hang thee high from the Tyburn tree.
The Tyburn tree, the Tyburn tree!
Oh! Get thee down to the Tyburn tree.
Down to the Tyburn tree with thee!

Nelan swallowed on a dry throat. When he'd been down in the doldrums, the Gyptians had restored to him the precious gift of hope. Kazia had recognised him as the enigmatic and mysterious Fyremaster, a title which he had yet to fully explore. Now he had an opportunity to return their kindness and goodwill. He had to help this man. But the impending execution kindled crippling memories of his mother's death. He felt numb inside. His head was spinning. He froze… again!

Then he remembered. He'd talked to his mother's spirit. She had released him from his pervasive guilt, or at least some of it. As he struggled with his inner demons, he balled his fists and gritted his teeth. He was determined to fight them with all his will. He resolved to assist his Gyptian friend in whatever way he could. What could he achieve? If he tried to free Jasper, they'd arrest him and haul him off to the gibbet. Besides, there were too many pikemen and constables. But, he could provide Jasper with a little comfort in the meantime.

Boldly, he stepped in front of the two ruffians who barred the innkeeper.

"What you doin', shorty?" The one in rags squared up to Nelan.

"Let him have a drink. He's a man, like you and I," Nelan said.

"Nah. He's a Gyptian," said the rags man.

"Doesn't he breathe the same air? Doesn't he fear death? Doesn't he warrant a last drink of ale to slake his thirst?"

"No! Let the cartman drink his ale," the jags man said.

Nelan stared fixedly at the two men, and said slowly, "He will have a last drink!"

"Who says so?" the jags man said, pushing him in the chest.

Just as fists were about to fly, the minister stepped in between them, saying, "The young man's correct. It's tradition. A drink of ale is a last kindness to the condemned. No matter what their transgression."

"Bah!" the rags man yelled, and shuffled off with the jags man, cursing and cussing.

Jasper took the bowl of ale from the innkeeper and downed it, savouring every gulp.

"Me, I enjoyed that," Jasper said, wiping his mouth with his sleeve.

"I wanted you to have your due."

"Good on ya, lad, for standing up for me."

"I wish I could do more."

"You can. Look out for my sis, for Kazia. An' make sure you fulfil her prophecy. You're the Fyremaster! You gotta believe it! I'll be lookin' down on ya from the otherworld."

"I know," Nelan said with a smile.

They shook hands, and Jasper's ox cart set off. Nelan watched him standing in the cart, unbowed, staring at the horizon. What courage!

The third ox cart trundled along to where he stood. Only one man occupied it. Palms pressed tight in prayer, it was the traitor Francis Throckmorton. Like the others, he wore a plain white smock and white cap. What of the sneaky catfish, Pedro? There was no other ox cart, so where was he?

Nelan confronted the Yeoman of the Halter. "Where's Pedro, the other traitor?"

The man frowned then spat on the ground. "Escaped from Newgate this mornin'. We're lookin' for him now."

"How could you let him get away?" Nelan spat the words out in rage.

"Dunno. It befoxed me, it did. One moment, he's there, comin' out of the gates a' the prison, guarded by the pikemen. Next minute, this fella drives up, the crowd surges, the pikemen gets pushed out of the way, an' someone cuts Pedro's rope. He hops on the cart, an' they're swallowed up in the crush."

"Who was the driver of the cart? Did you see him?"

"Nah, but just before the driver come, there's this signal… Three shrill blows."

"What was it?"

"Mmm, can't be sure. Methinks it was a flute."

"A flute, you say?"

"Yeah, but we'll get Pedro an' the flute man."

"You'd better," Nelan said. "And I want to be there when you do!"

Across the way, the minister adjusted his black robe, and called out, "All good people, pray heartily unto God for these poor sinners who are now going to their deaths, and for whom the great bell tolls."

Throckmorton drank from his bowl, and the ale dribbled down the front of his smock. He was already half-cut from all the other bowls he'd drunk along the way.

The executioner and his assistants lumbered along behind the last of the three ox carts. Amidst the hubbub, the town crier rang his bell, silencing the dogs and the crowd, and a conspiracy of ravens roosting on the branches of a nearby evergreen tree. The procession set off from the Bowl Inn for the last leg of the journey, before reaching the open fields of the Tyburn Road. Eventually, it arrived at the Tyburn Tree, which wasn't a tree anymore but a gallows, the tree that was never green. It consisted of three tall uprights arranged in a large equal-sided triangle. Three upper beams joined the tops of the uprights to make a triple gallows.

To great applause, the cartmen parked their ox carts beneath each of the three beams. The executioner's assistants clambered around the upper part of the gallows like monkeys, making the noose ready for the condemned, even if the condemned weren't ready for the noose.

The midday sun bleached the crowd, which by now had swelled to thousands. Pickpockets and cutpurses milled around, hoping to relieve them of their hard-earned farthings. Constables and pikemen tried to stop them. Simple folk hawked their wares of bread and pies. Ministers and preachers recited God's words. Separatists prayed for the condemned. Those in velvet gowns perched on rows of temporary seating. The public execution of a traitor excited every man from beggar to landsman.

Amidst the noise and bustle, the town crier's bells rang out again, calling for silence, as the Yeoman of the Halter secured each noose around the necks of the criminals.

The minister cried out above the hubbub, "You that are condemned to die, repent with lamentable tears; ask mercy of the Lord for the salvation of your souls."

The two men in the first cart showed no signs of remorse. The crowd, full of righteous indignation, hollered for them to repent.

When the minister got in their ear, they knelt before the might of the Lord.

The minister turned to Jasper. From his time with the Gyptians, Nelan knew that they regarded most Christians as hypocrites. So he wasn't surprised to see Jasper standing proud and resolute. This incensed the crowd, who chucked a volley of dead flowers, rotten vegetables and choice insults at him. But the man held his gaze steady and his self-respect firm.

Throckmorton, contrite as a monk, bowed low and held his hands up in pious sorrow, praying to the Lord for forgiveness. The crowd shouted for joy. A show of public remorse, especially from a nobleman, always impressed the masses.

The Marshall lifted a white 'kerchief, and to a great yell from the crowd, lowered his hand. The drivers whipped their oxen, and the carts pulled away, leaving five bodies twitching in the July sun, dancing the Tyburn jig. These were the final gyrations of the astral body as it shuffled off its mortal coil and escaped into the vast freedom of the otherworld. In this macabre theatre, the crowd thumped the tabor, clapped their hands and hollered like devils. Taking a last majestic bow, the conspiracy of ravens swooped over the execution site.

Nelan's spirits sagged. This wasn't justice; this was a gross injustice. A good man, Jasper's only crime was to be at odds with the prevailing spirit of the nation. If there was any concordance between the law of a land and the nature of the angels that inhabited that land, then the angels of the isle were cruel, barbaric beings. Nelan couldn't square that thought with his belief in a deity that was both fair and even-handed in all things, especially where humanity was concerned. He concluded that the law of the land often departed from, and was sometimes antithetical to, the nature of the angels of that land. Another wrong that needed to be put right.

The bell tolled on a nearby church, and as the ring subsided, so did the jerking of one of the two young men in the first cart. A woman snuck out from the crowd. With a babe at her breast, she brushed the child's cheek against the dead man's hand. This macabre act was reputed to cure all diseases and bring the child good fortune. Nelan doubted that it did either.

As the crowd surged around them, Eleanor's hand nestled in his.

The five men ended their last dance. The jig had finished. The crowd sang the Tyburn Tree song so out of tune that it sounded like a cacophony. The Yeoman of the Halter and his assistants lowered the bodies onto the ox carts. In the stifling heat, a cloud of flies swarmed around the dead.

The Marshall called out, "Throckmorton resides with the devils. The Queen is safe. Let us celebrate this pyrrhic victory for England, and for Gloriana!"

More folk sneaked out of the crowd to touch the still-warm bodies of the dead. One stole Jasper's white cap. Another snatched Throckmorton's.

Nelan noticed a man in the crowd in the temporary gallery assembled behind the Tyburn Tree. Although he wore a hood, partially covering his face, he looked eerily familiar. The man kept glancing over his shoulder, like he was afraid he was being followed.

"Oh! My word! It's Pedro!" Nelan yelled.

"*The* Pedro?" Eleanor asked.

"Yes, Don Pedro de Antón. God's teeth, not only did he escape from Newgate, he has the gall to turn up at his own execution!"

"Where is he?"

"There, opposite us. In the temporary gallery. Pikemen! Get him!"

A constable near him blew his whistle and led a thicket of pikemen into the crowd, but the crush was so great that they got nowhere near him.

"Damn," Nelan said. "He's danced away, again!"

This was an end. This was an end for Jasper, who didn't deserve it. It was an end for Throckmorton, who did. It should have been an end for Pedro, but it wasn't. The man was like a barbel fish who slid out from under the determined gaze of his captors. How could they catch him? Who was the flute man who freed him?

In two days, Nelan would ask these questions of the fox himself, Sir Francis Walsingham.

13

White Tower, Black Tidings

12th July 1584

Nelan walked northwards from the river past the oppressive White Tower of London towards Walsingham's residence. Up ahead, a drunk was shouting at a washerwoman, who took fright and ducked down an alley. A door slammed. A rat sniffed the air and then scampered down a hole. A couple of pikemen stood guard outside Walsingham's offices in Seething Lane. They were seething all right, with intrigue and duplicity. A strange brew, this spying business. Who would have thought that, in a land of high religious morals, such secretive and clandestine methods were not only commonplace but necessary for survival?

Charles Sledd opened the door and told him that Walsingham was conducting his business in the Tower. Well, only one kind of business was conducted in that hellhole. Nelan gritted his teeth and set off on the short walk to the imposing Postern Gate. He waited while the guards fetched Roger Adden, who escorted him into the precincts of the Tower. Immediately upon entry, a shiver of fear ran up and down his spine.

Adden led Nelan down some steps, unevenly worn down in the middle. The smell of piss and fear stung his nostrils. Nelan felt as sick as a dog. For a moment, he froze, believing that Walsingham could no longer protect him, and was simply going to throw him in the Tower.

"What ya waitin' for, lad? Ya comin'?" Adden's gross familiarity eased his fears, and he breathed a little easier.

Adden led him to the turnkey's office, a dark, smelly place with more ghosts than cobwebs. To his chagrin, he discovered that the office was within hearing distance of the dungeons. Adden left him on his own and went to attend to other business. Nelan paced the cobbled floor and tried desperately to shut out the terrible screams of the inmates. He struggled to breathe and to hear himself think. Even worse, the mark of the salamander was itching on his palm. For heaven's sake, not now! He did not want to see the ghosts of headless men walk past him. Nor hear their desperate cries for mercy. Nor witness their suffering on the rack. Frantically, he shook his hand until the astral visions vanished back into the bricks and mortar.

The door thudded open, and Walsingham strolled in like he'd just finished a country walk. Whatever he had been doing before stepping into the turnkey's room, the secretary had clearly eradicated from his mind. While he washed his hands in a bowl of water, he asked Nelan, "At Tutbury Castle, what did you find out about that Scottish Queen?"

Nelan heaved a sigh of relief, as he could banish the gross images of men in agony on the rack. "While I was there, I tried to peer into her inner thoughts to gauge her intentions," he said, "but she is brave and strong, like the lion rampant on her heraldic arms. Sleeping with one eye open, Mary is vigilant, a fortress unto herself. She keeps her own counsel and is reluctant to trust others. But complacency stalks the inner corridors of everyone, even a queen. In the end, she'll succumb to hubris and make a mistake."

"I wait for that. What do you suggest?"

"Get your agents onto her estate as draymen or joiners, stonemasons or messengers. That way, they can be near her servants, deal with her secretaries, and converse with her maids. Then her secrets can leak out, bit by bit."

"Excellent idea."

"What about Pedro's escape from Newgate? It made me mad to see the man in the crowd at Tyburn during the execution."

"We've not caught him yet, but we will."

"How did he escape?"

"We don't know. We suspect he had inside help from someone familiar with the schedule, the organisation of the procession... a Jesuit, a priest, a Catholic sympathiser, or..."

"… A disaffected constable," Nelan suggested. "There's famine and plague, there's the threat of insurrection and the danger of invasion. There's even talk of the end of the world."

"There's always talk of an apocalypse. Perhaps it's already happened… and we missed it," he added dryly.

Nelan frowned.

"Either way, I'll arrest Pedro and his helper," Walsingham said. "But Throckmorton's execution sends a message to the embassies and courts of Europe. It tells them we'll stop at nothing to prevent a Catholic monarch ascending the English throne."

"During these times," Nelan said, "the rules of that game change as quickly as it takes to steal a white hood from the head of a hanged man."

There were heavy footsteps in the corridor and then a loud knocking at the door. Roger Adden entered, and said, "Messenger from them Netherlands, m'lord."

"Show the man in," Walsingham said.

Hands on hips, the messenger bowed to Walsingham. He was dressed in the garb of the road – dust and dirt, sweat and horse shit.

"This is a good day, so let's hear the good news," Walsingham said cheerfully.

The man winced at this volley of optimism and said, "I bring tidings from Prinsenhof in Delft, the residence of William of Silent, the Prince of Orange."

"What news from the Dutch Provinces? Has he defeated the Duke of Parma and wreaked vengeance for the Council of Blood?"

The messenger hesitated, suggesting he carried bad news. "No, m'lord," the man said. "I'm afraid there's been another attempt on the Prince's life."

The silence in the room thickened, like blood pooling around a decapitated corpse.

"I pray that he survived," Walsingham said, pressing his hands in prayer.

"No, he's been assassinated."

"How did it happen?" Walsingham asked, shaking his head in sorrow.

"King Philip of Spain offered 25,000 crowns for anyone who killed William. This grand reward persuaded some wretch to do the evil deed."

"Another paid assassin! The Spaniards are devils," Nelan said.

The messenger added, "The prince's last words were reported to be:

Mon Dieu, ayez pitié de mon âme.
Mon Dieu, ayez pitié de ce pauvre peuple.

"It means, 'May God have mercy on my soul, and on my poor people.'"

"These are black tidings," Walsingham said. "Now William has left us, our Queen alone carries the torch of Protestant freedom in Europe. Mark my words; the Papist forces will redouble their efforts to replace her with that Scots woman."

Nelan turned to the messenger and asked, "When was this assassination?"

"Two days ago."

"The 10th of July, the same day as Throckmorton's execution," Nelan mused. "Such are the workings of fate. On the day we execute one traitor and quell another plot against our Queen, we suffer another setback, and the scales of divine justice are reset and remain in the balance. We must make sure they tilt in our favour in the future."

Walsingham had the last word. "To do that, we have to ensnare the spider at the centre of these webs of intrigue. The Privy Council is formulating an Act of Parliament called the Bond of Association. All signatories to it must pledge to uphold the honour and life of our gracious majesty, and to avenge those who plot against her. Mary, Queen of Scots, will be asked to sign it."

"We shall see how that transpires," Nelan said, as another scream echoed out of the dungeons.

14

The Bloody Letter

29th July 1586

What with the scrying, the visits around the country and the spying, the two years since Throckmorton's execution had passed quickly. Nelan had searched in the astral realms for Pedro, but the catfish with his whiskers had vanished again. The man would surface someday, and when he did, he'd stop him for good.

His love for Eleanor had deepened, and every night they prayed to be blessed with a child. His wife's interest in midwifery had blossomed too. Now Matilda had recovered from the ague, Eleanor regularly assisted her and Bridget with births in the local hamlets and villages.

During that summer, Nelan heard rumours in the corridors of Barn Elms and Seething Lane of a new conspiracy against Queen Elizabeth, again instigated by her cousin Queen Mary. In this game of plot and counterplot, Walsingham moved the pieces on the board with the skill of a master craftsman. The aim – to protect the realm, come what may.

That late July day in Mortlake was warm but blustery, heralding a change of season and fresh conflict. It started with a knock at the door when a man hailed, "Message from the Secretary!"

Nelan's instinct had been jittery for some days, so he'd anticipated the message. Opening the scroll with a mixture of excitement and trepidation, he read the typically brief note: 'Come to Seething Lane. And be quick about it.'

As Wenceslaus rowed him with the flow from Mortlake to the Tower, Nelan reflected on the hectic events of the month so far. They began when Thomas Phelippes, one of Walsingham's best intelligencers, intercepted a coded letter written by Anthony Babington, a Catholic nobleman. Its recipient: Mary, Queen of Scots. Phelippes had decoded it and sent it to Walsingham. Nelan had been present at a private reading of it:

> *Myself with ten gentlemen and a hundred followers undertake the delivery of your royal person from the hands of your enemies.*
>
> *For the despatch of the usurper, from the obedience of whom we are by the excommunication of her made free, there be six noble gentlemen, all my private friends, who, for the zeal they bear to the Catholic cause and your Majesty's service, will undertake that tragical execution.*
>
> *6th July 1586*

These dark words chilled Nelan to the bone. How could it come to this again, that another English aristocrat plotted the murder of his own queen, the so-called usurper? This letter soiled the hands of the English nobleman. The letter also incriminated the Pope, because Babington referred in it to the terms of the excommunication. The *Regnans in Excelsis* freed any Englishmen from obeying Elizabeth's statutes and instead urged them, for the sake of the Catholic polity, to execute her.

A few days later, Phelippes, still in Tutbury, intercepted and decoded Mary's reply, sealed it in an envelope, and sent it to Walsingham in London. On the outside of the envelope, Phelippes had drawn a gallows, inspiring Walsingham to name Mary's reply the 'bloody letter'.

As Nelan rushed past the White Tower, he realised that the governing astrological influence of the month was now Leo, the lion. Was it a coincidence that the heraldic arms of both the English and Scottish monarchs featured the king of the jungle? The English heraldry depicted three golden lions walking past but facing the onlooker. The Scottish arms showed a single red lion rearing up but seen in profile. Amidst the tumult and the turmoil, which of them was in harmony with the astrology of the heavens? Which possessed the mandate to proceed into tomorrow?

Arriving in Seething Lane, he wondered what Walsingham would decide to do with the bloody letter, which, although intercepted, had yet to be delivered to Babington. Would the Secretary's actions chime with or oppose the spirit of the times? That was the state of play. Only Walsingham knew the next act. Nelan was about to find out his part in it.

As Nelan entered the offices, he bumped into Arthur Gregory, a gruff, meddlesome man whose clothes, along with his breath, stank. Walsingham swore by the fellow, because he was a forger *par excellence*, copying the seals of the embassies of France and Spain, as well as supplying wax, paper, quills and ink. As Nelan passed by into Walsingham's chambers, he saw Gregory applying a wax seal to an envelope.

Walsingham had his back to him by a table full of packages and envelopes, papers, scrolls and inkpots. Thomas Phelippes, recognisable by his pock-marked face, was also present.

"Welcome, Nelan," Thomas said. A small wiry man, he had a steady gaze, nerves like steel and narrow-set eyes, a perfect combination for the Virgoan patience and love of detailed intricacy required to decipher a complex code.

"Ah, there you are, Nelan," Walsingham said, stifling a yawn as he turned to greet him. The Principal Secretary's long gaunt face wore a mix of weary fatigue and resolute determination.

"M'lord."

"Time waits for no man, Nelan."

Accustomed to these gentle barbs, he disarmed this one by saying, "I came as quick as I could."

"Then, to business," Walsingham said. "See if Gregory has finished the seal on the envelope," he said to Phelippes.

"Yes, m'lord," Phelippes said, leaving the room.

"I want you to deliver a package," Walsingham said to Nelan. "Yes, I know I could have asked John Brewer or any of the other couriers, but this is a very special delivery."

"Which one?"

"Don't bloody rush me, Nelan."

My, he was petulant today. Nelan suspected a chronic lack of sleep and the rising tension caused by the bloody letter.

"Listen, if Babington discovers we've intercepted his letters, we'll lose this precious opportunity to indict Mary," Walsingham barked.

"Apologies, I didn't mean to…" he said, trying but failing to be obsequious.

"… Then don't," Walsingham snapped. "You are to deliver the bloody letter to Anthony Babington."

"Me?"

"Yes, you."

"I see," Nelan said, swallowing hard. As the Secretary intimated, this task would brook no mistake.

"Can you do it?"

Nelan stuck out his chest and said, "Yes, m'lord."

"I trust you to do so. But not dressed like that. You're to wear a simple disguise. Here," Walsingham said, pointing to a blue coat on the back of a chair. "You must wear the livery of a household servant. See if it fits… Good, yes, it does. Babington must believe you're performing a simple menial task."

"What are your instructions?"

"Go to his residences and find a discreet place to observe who comes and goes. Use your astral skills. What is their demeanour? How fast is their gait? Do they look over their shoulder?"

"I can do that, and much more."

"When you're ready, approach the house. You must hand the bloody letter directly to Babington. Not to his servant, his wife, or anyone else. I want to know if he suspects we are intercepting his mail. When he takes the letter, is his hand shaking? Do his eyes flit from side to side? I want to know his inner thoughts. Is he about to flee to Paris or Rome? Do you understand what I'm asking you to do?"

"Yes, I do. You want me to observe the man's outward behaviour and deduce his inner state of mind."

"Exactly," Walsingham said.

Thomas Phelippes came back into the room holding a package. It looked like the one the forger, Arthur Gregory, had been sealing when Nelan arrived.

"You can give it to him now," Walsingham said to Phelippes.

On touching the package, Nelan received a powerful premonition. In his mind's eye, he saw a gibbet. Was it the one on Shooters Hill, or on Smithfield, or even Tyburn? Or did he pick up on the gallows that Phelippes had drawn on the envelope containing the bloody letter?

"What is it, Nelan?" Walsingham asked.

Nelan hesitated. He thought about telling Walsingham about the image of the gibbet, but he was unsure whose it was. Over the years, he'd learned to be cautious about first impressions to give himself time to gather confirmatory evidence. Besides, Walsingham himself had advised him to be cautious, so cautious he would be.

"It's nothing," Nelan said.

"Thomas has done his work," Walsingham crowed, "and excellent it is too. He's written and deciphered letters aplenty, but none more vital than this one for Babington."

"I sense that the fate of the entire nation rests on its safe delivery," Nelan said.

"I agree," Walsingham said. "We hold ourselves to the highest standards of integrity and trust, even while conducting these underhand activities. Because it's for God, the Queen and for England. The Almighty is not deceptive, nor must we ever be. We must conform to God's laws and the laws of the land. Although we fight traitors and heretics, we can never act as they do."

"I understand," Nelan nodded. He felt like asking why the Privy Council endorsed the rack, the thumbscrews and the Little Ease, but swallowed his objections.

"Then I bid you a safe journey," Walsingham said.

"M'lord."

Nelan made his way out of Seething Lane and walked through the sun-soaked streets and alleys of the City of London. Crowds of people hustled around the nearby market, buying bread, singing songs and playing the tabor. Passing along Fleet Street, he got a strange sense emanating from the package. Feeling it inside his doublet, his hand felt hot, like it was near burning coals. He withdrew his hand, which swelled in front of him. His eyes blurred, and he saw blotches of red on his hands. It was uncanny. Bloody letter. Bloody red blotches.

He paused by a blacksmith, and smelled the familiar odours of sulphur and charcoal, feeling the flame and the heat of the fire. As soon as he moved on, the bloating returned apace. He closed his eyes momentarily and saw a mental image of two men with their backs to him, bending over a table full of quills, paper and scrolls.

"Shall I?" one man said. "It's a risk. A terrible risk."

"We must do it," the other said. "We've no choice."

"Because it's for God, for the Queen and for England."

He recognised the phrase. He knew who the two men were. But what were they talking about?

Nelan took out the package. He turned it over in his hands, and slowly, inexplicably, the seal eased open without him even touching it. Oh, Lord. The seal had split. The wax hadn't dried properly. The envelope was open, revealing its contents. How could he deliver it now? Walsingham would think he'd opened it deliberately to read the bloody letter, but he hadn't. It had opened as if by some magical hand!

A queen, a Scottish lioness, had scribed the letter. The next dilemma was – should he read it? If he did, he'd deny the very principles of trust and integrity Walsingham espoused to him just now at Seething Lane. Besides, he had already read the letter and knew its contents. He summed up his deliberations with the saying:

I will be no traitor to myself.
Nor betray the purposes for which God put me on earth.

He turned back to the blacksmith's to ask for help, but the smith had left the furnace for a moment. So, he found a warm metal rod, carefully heated the wax and resealed the package. That would do it. It looked as good as new!

He arrived in Lincoln's Inn Fields and settled in a nook near the Temple Church from where he could sit and watch Babington's residence. The bewigged legal folk strolled back and forth, but he shut them out of his gaze. He rubbed the three wavy lines on his palm and closed his eyes. Sensing his astral body rise up, he drifted off to sleep. Then, his astral form – the fiery salamander – eased out of the back of his neck and alighted into the vast chambers of the astral world. Mentally, he despatched it to explore the Babington residence.

To his surprise, the house emanated warmth and kindness. Only one person was at home, a young man he identified as Anthony Babington. He detected that the nobleman had three distinct character features; first, a quiet, homely man who enjoyed his own company and loved solitude. The second was a young uproarious gentleman enjoying the benefits of a rich family inheritance. Yet something else moved in the young man's deeper instinct; a fear, a terrible dilemma, that weighed on his soul. Undoubtedly, the man suffered pangs of guilt and uncertainty of conscience. Babington was terrified.

His astral work done, Nelan summoned his salamander form and soon he was awake again, approaching the Babington residence.

Nelan knocked and, after a brief wait, the door opened, and there he was. Anthony Babington. As he took the package, the young nobleman must have realised what it was, and dropped it. The seal almost split again, but thankfully remained intact.

"Thank you," he said, and closed the door.

Babington had the bloody letter.

Babington had blood on his hands.

PART 2

THE REPULSE

15

The Game's Afoot

16th July 1588

Nelan sat at the window of the study and watched the river waters drift serenely past the jetty. The birds circled the woods, searching for their roost for the night. A gentle aura of evening amber settled around their house.

Eleanor came in and said, "You have wonderful abilities, but even you can't see in the dark. Here, my love, let me light a candle."

"Thank you, dear," he said, and smiled. "Join me. It's a lovely evening."

"I will," she said.

The candlelight shone on his bookshelf, where, neatly stacked, he kept his diaries. Ever since the Babington plot, Nelan had grown fascinated by the whys and wherefores of chance. Exploring the notion of 'where the rock shall fall', he'd adopted the habit of randomly picking up one of his diaries before opening it wherever it wanted to be opened. Dr Dee used the same practice with the Holy Bible to read the runes of the day.

Where would the page fall tonight? He shut his eyes and chose a diary from the shelf and opened the page. He plucked the diary for the year 1586 and the page fell open on the 14th of September. That day lived so vividly in his memory that it could have happened yesterday, and yet it was nigh on two years ago:

On this day, Walsingham secures the arrest of the traitor Anthony Babington. Across London, there's the burning of bonfires, the singing of psalms, and the ringing of bells.

He flipped a few pages to the entry for the 20th of September 1586, where he read:

> On this day at St-Giles-in-the-Fields, Anthony Babington is hung until dead, cut into small pieces, and his body parts placed in prominent sites around London. For Elizabeth and her realm, this is a hard-won victory! What now Mary, Queen of Scots, a signatory to the Bond of Association?

He took another diary. This time, it was 1587, last year. The page often fell open on the 8th of February because he had browsed the entry many times:

> Today is a momentous day.
> It's just over twenty weeks since Babington's execution.
> In twenty weeks, a pregnant woman's belly grows large with child.
> In twenty weeks, wheat can grow as high as a horse.
> In twenty weeks, a man can walk from John O'Groats to Land's End.
> But these twenty weeks changed the course of history.
> On this day, Mary ceased to be the Queen of Scots.
> On this day, at Fotheringhay Castle, an executioner wearing a black hood separated her head from her body.
> On this day, England and its Queen, Elizabeth Regina, were separated from all hope of a reconciliation with the embassies of Spain.
> If there was a threat of Spanish invasion before this day, now the danger is as palpable as the darkness enveloping the House of Tudor.

He clutched his throat, gasping for breath. The threat suffocated him, just as it suffocated the angels of the isle. He read the rest of the entry:

> Through the deciphered letters, and especially the bloody letter, Walsingham proved that Mary was the claimant to the throne in whose interest the attempt on Queen Elizabeth's life was to be made.
>   How could Mary have foreseen that, by signing the Bond of Association, she in effect signed her own death warrant? Such are the ironies of history.
>   The people call her the daughter of the Devil. To celebrate her death, they ring the church bells and light the beacons, filling the

air with the sounds of fury and the delicious woody smell of the purifying fires.

I'm reminded how Edward Kelley, Dr Dee's scryer, predicted that a queen would be executed by a tall black man. He was right. The Queen was Mary. Though the executioner wasn't black, but the hood he wore was.

Nelan read the entry for 10th July 1587:

Today, Sir Francis Drake returned in triumph from his outrageous attack on the Spanish fleet in Cadiz harbour.

This was the audacious singeing of the King of Spain's beard. Alas, that was all. It would grow back and thrive, as would the King's preparations for the enterprise of the Great Armada.

Reflecting on these momentous events, he picked up his quill and wrote:

I am minded of a famous prophecy by Johannes Müller, aka Regiomontanus:

When after Christ's birth there be expired,
Of hundreds fifteen, years eighty and eight.
Then comes the time of dangers to be feared,
And all mankind with dolours it shall fright,
For if the world in that year does not fall,
If sea and land then perish nor decay:
Yet Empires fall, and Kingdoms alter shall,
And man to ease himself shall have no way.

1588 – the year was already halfway passed in which Regiomontanus had predicted that 'Empires shall fall'. But which one? England's imperial ambition, or Spain's sprawling kingdoms? The Armada was coming. It would be a matter of weeks, if not days, before they found out.

The next day, the morning sun burst through the windows. Before heading along the Old Church Road to attend Mass at St Mary's,

Barnes, he and Eleanor made sure they dressed in the right-coloured clothing for his status. To wear the wrong colours, or miss Sunday worship, risked a hefty fine, not to say the vitriol of the local minister and censure of the congregation.

As they left the chapel, Roger Adden was waiting outside, a young, pretty damsel hanging off his arm.

"A ladies' man now, Master Adden?" Nelan said, raising his eyebrows.

"'Tis my business, lad," he said with an air of rebuke. "I'm here to tell ya the Secretary'll see ya, immediate like."

When the fox barked, Nelan ran to his den.

Hands behind his back, Nelan confronted Walsingham. Despite the heat of the day, the Secretary wore his black skullcap, his white ruff cradling his bearded face, emphasising his grim Saturnian countenance. His grey-green eyes were weary but alert. He spoke in a steady, meticulous way, inserting long pauses and profound emphases, as if reciting a passage from the Bible.

"Nelan, we face many difficulties, which range at us like a pack of wild boars. Here's another one," he murmured, waving a paper at him.

"What news?"

"It's from Rome, that hotbed of heretics. The new Pope Sixtus V is retaliating for Mary's execution. He's reinvigorated the *Regnans in Excelsis*, the terms of Elizabeth's excommunication. Then, he's endorsed his backing for the Armada by blessing its flag."

"As if they need more support!"

"Exactly. How can the Vicar of Rome bless a flag? A piece of coloured material hardly qualifies as holy or sacred."

"What about the beads of their Holy Rosary?"

"Yes, it's more superstitious Papist nonsense. Thank the Lord we've prohibited it from our Anglican religion."

"This is something to fear."

"But there's less danger in fearing too much than too little."

"What does that mean?"

"It means that fear both binds and blinds. Fear obsesses on a single thing to the exclusion of all else, when that thing is often only a symptom of a more pernicious evil. So, fear shields us from perceiving the more profound danger. We must have the courage to look beyond the smaller, and face the greater, fear."

Nelan glanced around Walsingham's office. These tidings from Rome, like the dark wood panelling, lent the atmosphere a gloomy aspect.

"There are tidings from Lisbon," Walsingham went on, his voice hoarse and guttural. "Towards the end of May, my agents informed me that the greatest fleet in the world was moored in the Tagus estuary. The quays were piled high with oat biscuits, barrels of wine, victuals, equipment, gunpowder, cannon, arms, pikes, helmets and uniforms. Tens of thousands of sailors and soldiers milled around the decks and the inns. Every ship was regularly scoured for women. Those that were found were rowed ashore. King Philip will have his men untainted by the desires of the flesh and clean from sin. That's how he hopes God will grant his fleet a glorious victory!"

"Has it sailed?"

"Yes, it has. To scout for the van, Lord Howard, Admiral of the Fleet, has sent carracks to the Lizard, the Scillies and Ushant."

Nelan sensed there was more to come before the embers burnt out.

"I commissioned Thomas Norton to explore the patterns of English history and extract the lessons to be learned. He wrote this paper," Walsingham said, tapping a scroll on his desk, his long fingers like stalks of wheat.

"What did he find?"

"That our Queen's predicament is mirrored by that of Harold Godwinson. In 1066, William the Conqueror defeated the Saxon King. Norton claimed that Harold was defeated because of his sins and those of his people."

"Meaning Harold's loss on the battlefield was God's punishment," Nelan said.

"Yes, it was. There are other similarities to our situation today. The Pope of the time supported William's conquest of England and, even though he was a foreign king, this persuaded the English clergy to accept him. The Pope sent William a banner which he blessed. Then, the Pope excommunicated Harold and absolved his subjects from their allegiance to him. It's uncanny how history repeats itself."

"It's got indigestion, more like," Nelan said. "But there are important differences between then and now. Our Queen is not sinful, nor are we, her people. Unlike when ruled by King Harold, today England is not bound by the dictates of Roman Catholic bulls. The Queen is the monarch and the Head of the Church, governing both the sacred and the secular realms, giving her a mandate to rule by divine right."

"Well said, Nelan." Walsingham heaved himself up from the chair and stalked his chambers.

"And have you thought that the Spanish are runaways?"

"How do you see that?"

"Look at the Latin name of their country."

"*Hispania?*"

"It means the land of rabbits. And don't they scare easily and run away from danger?"

"They do," Walsingham chuckled, a rare humour for the spymaster. "I have two new missions for you. I want you to attend Howard's fleet in Plymouth. I will explain that task in more detail nearer the time. Before that, you're to organise the printing and distribution of an important pamphlet. Here it is," he said, handing it over. "The Privy Council forwarded this draft to me."

Nelan read it.

"What do you think?"

"It's excellent."

"Good, I agree. Go and see Richard Jugge, the royal printer. His premises are in Paternoster Row. Then distribute copies around the country: send messengers to the boroughs and shires and finish up in London. Order the town criers to call it out on every street corner, by the village stocks and in the alleys and byways. The ministers must read it out from the pulpit and by the cross in every churchyard. Every villein in the land must know of the imminent danger and make ready to repulse it. After that, take copies with you and distribute them along the way to Plymouth. Show it to the men in command: Admiral Lord Howard; Vice Admiral, Sir Francis Drake and Rear Admiral, Sir John Hawkins."

"Yes, m'lord."

When he arrived back in Mortlake, Flint, his manservant, stood talking to another man. A shiver went up his spine. It was the constable. Surely, they hadn't come to arrest him. Besides, he hadn't done anything wrong, had he?

"Good evening, Constable," he murmured. "What can we do for you?"

"I 'ere to see your good lady."

"Then you'd better come in."

Flint showed the constable into the withdrawing room, and Nelan opened a window to let his smell drift out of the room.

"What's this all about?" Nelan asked.

"Me's 'ere 'bout Bridget," he said.

"My friend, the midwife?" Eleanor said, a note of alarm in her voice.

"Did you know 'er at all?"

"I know her very well," Eleanor said. "I've assisted her for years. Why? What's happened to her?"

"She bin arrested."

"Oh, my Lord. What did she do?" Nelan asked.

"At the last birth she attended, 'cross the river in Chiswick, the mother accused 'er a' conspirin' with the Devil. She be on trial for witchery."

"I don't believe it," Eleanor said.

"Nor do I," Nelan snapped.

"The mother's grievin' at the loss of her infant," the constable added.

"I wasn't at the birth," Eleanor said, her voice croaking with emotion.

"We know that, ma'am," the constable said. "But we may need to ask you some questions about Miss Bridget."

"I-I understand," Eleanor said. "But Bridget's a God-fearing woman and she'd never conspire with the Devil. What happened, Constable?"

"I dunno much, jus' that it were summat about darkness an' candles. Now, beggin' your pardons, I must to the magistrate. I'll say a by-your-leave," he said and left.

"This is awful, dear," Nelan said. "But... what did he mean about candles?"

"Matilda warned us to bring enough candles to light the birthing chamber. If the room is dark, the mother can suspect the midwife of wanting to steal the child or replace it with another. If Bridget was alone in the room with the mother, she'd be open to these accusations. I don't understand. Unless it was an emergency, Bridget should have asked another woman, even an unqualified one, to witness the birth."

"What about you? Can you step away from your duties?" he asked.

"No. I can't. Matilda struggles with the ague, and is getting older by the day. Without Bridget, she'll depend on me. I want to help women in the travail and their infants. I can't let her down, or them."

"But why? If you make a mistake, you'll get arrested."

"Not if I'm careful. And I always will be. Even more so now. But it's the same for you. Walsingham himself warned you to be cautious about what you say, and who you say it to. Every day, we both walk on shifting sands, hoping to find more solid ground."

"I agree, my love. But this is a strong warning. I think it's dangerous for you to continue."

"The birthing chamber is a place of marvel and mystery. Every birth is special, but it's also fraught with worry. I'm there to ease the delivery in any way I can. It's a privilege to see a new life come from the confined darkness of the womb into the light of the great church."

"I want you to stop."

"I can't. I don't want you to spy for Walsingham, but do you take any notice of what I say?"

"No, but the circumstances are different…"

"… Are they? I don't think so!"

"Well, I'm going to wait and see what happens to Bridget. After that, I'll make a final, binding decision."

"If you say so," she hissed.

The next day, Nelan waited for Wenceslaus by the jetty outside his house. Across the other side of the river, he spotted a stag. It sniffed the early morning air, saw him, and scurried off into the woods. The birdsong brought back memories of wondrous times and joy aplenty.

Grunting like an old bear, Wenceslaus rowed him downriver. Nelan alighted at Queenhithe dock and made his way via St Paul's Cathedral to Paternoster Row.

"Master Jugge, when can I collect the print?" Nelan asked.

"You can see I'm busy," Jugge mumbled through his beard while wafting a hand at the piles of prints stacked in the corner.

"This is urgent," Nelan protested.

"Listen," Jugge said, hands on hips. "This over 'ere is for Sir William Cecil 'isself. It's only on 'is say-so that I avoided a call-up to the militia. I's waitin' for a delivery of paper. Now, where is that blessed cartman?" he added, peering up the busy street.

"How long then?"

"Got a piece a' string?"

Nelan frowned and folded his arms. "Master Jugge, this is for Queen and country."

The printer shook his head and said with obvious reluctance, "Then I'll work through the night. The bells of St Paul's will keep me awake. You'll have them on the morrow!"

"Good man!"

On the wherry home, Nelan's thoughts flew to Plymouth harbour, imagining the English fleet gathering there. He couldn't wait to join the fray. Soon, he'd have to leave his Eleanor and, that evening, he broke the news to her.

"You keep leaving me and heading off on these impossible missions," she moaned. "When will you be back after you go to Plymouth?"

"It should be weeks or months rather than years," he said with a gainful smile.

"Nelan. I'm Mrs Michaels now. I'm your wife. I share this beautiful house with you. You're going to join the fleet to fight a terrible enemy, and you don't know when you'll return." She had the wind in her sails. "Sorry is not good enough. I need more than an apology and an empty reassurance."

He held her hand in his, and realised that the pain of their previously long, enforced absence ran deep in her soul, and that its scars could easily be reopened.

"I can't disappoint Walsingham. The Armada is coming. These are dire times. First the pamphlets, then I must to Plymouth."

"I know. I'm not saying don't go to Plymouth," she said, her chest heaving with pent-up emotion. "Just make provision."

"If anything happens, there's my will and testament," he said, but his words lacked conviction. A spoken promise was one thing, but the keeping of it was another.

"I don't want money or property. I just want you to come back home to me. After all we've been through, is that too much to ask?"

"I'll do my best."

"I hope so," she said, drying her eyes. "I really do, because I doubt if my heart can bear another long separation, not knowing where you are, and if you'll ever return to my arms."

"I know I'll come back safe and sound," he said, with a certainty that surprised even him. "I promise to write whenever we make landfall."

She breathed out a long slow breath and held his hand. They stared across the lawn, past the orchard, and towards the river. How many tides would ebb and flow before he returned? Would he come back in one piece? Naval warfare was barbaric. Limbs were lost. So were wits. And so were lives.

The rest of that day was filled with bliss, and of harmony between a man and a woman, in all that the word implied. It was love, and a love shared, genuine and generous, for they were of kind with one another.

All the same, he made provision for the future.

Under the heat of a flaming July sun, he returned to the printers to collect the pamphlets. That day and the next, he raced to different stables in London and arranged for riders to take them to all parts of the country. Once he'd got them a chunk of bread and cheese for the trip, and made sure they knew they handled an important document, he despatched them.

Whispers of a Spanish invasion grew into a raucous clamour. Everyone looked over their shoulder. Folk stole a wary glance at the sea.

Nelan left the most important visit until last. He headed into the City of London, protected by the legendary silver griffin. After attending midday service at St Paul's, he strode into Cheapside with its timber-covered market stalls on either side of its wide street. Housewives bartered with the stall holders, servants followed their masters, some with leather water vessels in their arms, others with casks suspended from a yoke across their shoulders.

A man with a hunched back strode into Cheapside in full regalia, the red and white livery of the City of London emblem, the silver griffin, emblazoned on his chest. This was the man he'd arranged to meet.

"John Tunnall be my name. Town crier be me callin'," the man said.

"The Privy Council wants you to read this pamphlet," Nelan replied.

Tunnall browsed through it as his assistant, a one-eyed man wielding a brass bell, placed a rickety three-legged stool on the cobblestones. Master Tunnall stepped onto it with the assumed majesty of a king of England, while his assistant rang his bell that resounded like the chimes of St Paul's.

"Hear ye! Hear ye!" John Tunnall cried. "This 'ere be the text of the Privy Council, what speak on behalf of our Queen Bess."

Folks stopped squabbling with the stall holders and came from the market. They put down their ale and emerged from the inns. Gamblers left their dice and their cards. Husbands and wives laid down their petty squabbles and came from their houses. Adjusting their codpieces, men stumbled out of the whorehouses.

All of them came to hear what, instinctively, they already knew. John Tunnall went on:

Yeomen, burgers, and merchants, we face a grave threat. King Philip of Spain ranges a fleet of warships against our gentle queen. Soon, their vessels will taint our seas, and their sails infect our skies. They'll set their armies on England's soft and gentle land. We must repulse them. Pray to God to grant us victory.

The town crier adjusted his grip on the pamphlet. His words, taut with alarm, penetrated the hearts and minds of his audience. He read on:

The Spanish may tell you they are a noble people. In truth, they are savage brutes. The Spanish may tell you they're chivalrous folk. In truth, they're devils in disguise. The Spanish may tell you they're a religious people. In truth, they're heretics.

Let us remind you of their foul deeds. In Mexico, the people there were judged as heathens and killed because they wouldn't convert to Catholicism. Over thirty years, their assassin Cortés and his army murdered four million. Four million! There are not that many souls in all the shires of England!

If the Spanish invade our shores, don't doubt that it will be the same here.

Every word cut another scythe into the flesh. Women covered the ears of their children. Men gripped their knives and stood ready to fight, to defend their family, their country, their religion, and their way of life. The rallying cry struck the fear of God in those who heard his words. When John Tunnall finished his part, he cried, "God save the Queen!"

The crowd responded with a resounding, "God save Queen Bess!"

Nelan stepped onto the stool and read the pamphlet's finale:

We will defeat the Spanish. Not one of their soldiers will set foot on our land. Pick up your pikes. Sharpen your stakes. Marshal your courage and join your local militia. Because today, men and women of the Island of Angels, the game's afoot.

16

Empires Shall Fall

21st July 1588

Playful, insouciant, Nelan and Eleanor strolled across the field, hands swinging back and forth. Hers felt soft and warm. The wheat fields bathed in the rays of the early morning sun, and the river flowed gently on its way to the North Sea. The land simmered in its glory, but he knew it wouldn't last.

They attended service in the stone chapel of St Mary the Virgin, Mortlake, and stood listening to the pastor. His sermon was as hot as the July weather.

"Deliver us from evil, sayest the prayer of Our Lord. Deliver us from evil Papists, I say!" and he smashed his fist down on the pulpit, and immediately shook his hand, grimacing in pain.

Nelan quelled the desire to smirk, but it didn't stop the pastor from raging against recusants.

"Brethren, be vigilant. Because out there, amongst the faithful, are the denizens of evil. From the Book of Proverbs, remember:

Keep thine heart with all diligence: for thereout cometh life.

"In the Papist manor houses up and down the country, they masquerade as serfs and labourers. They hide like moles in their holes. Watch for them on Sundays, saints' days and holy days, when they creep out of their hiding places. They are the scourge of humanity.

Spreading their heretical beliefs, they are itinerant Catholic priests. But we have the courage of a lion, and a lion of England too. We will expel the vermin."

The service over, Nelan and Eleanor walked back to the house, and the time came for the long goodbye.

"I have two gifts for you," Nelan said, and whistled loudly with two fingers in his mouth. At the signal, Flint emerged from the side of the house leading a dog.

"Oh! I love him. What's his name?"

"Holdfast," he said, handing her the lead.

She stroked the dog, with its fine mat of smooth hair, bright eyes and pointed upright ears. The hound yelped in appreciation of his new mistress. "Thank you. That's considerate of you, my love."

"You said you needed more than words of reassurance," Nelan replied. "Well, you'll have Alexander and Flint and Margaret to protect you. And now there's Holdfast."

"I'll keep busy. Matilda always needs my help at the birthing stool."

"Talking of midwifery, is there any news of Bridget?"

"I'll find out more when I visit her in prison on the morrow. But when are you coming back? It had better not be as long as last time."

"No, my love, it won't be."

"I wish I had your belief." Her green eyes sparkled.

"You do. You have it already."

"How do you know?"

"Because you give me every shred of my belief. I couldn't do what I do without your support, your encouragement and your love," he said. She warmed to that and smiled. He kissed her and went to meet Wenceslaus on the jetty.

Today, the 21st, marked the start of the astrological influence of Leo. The sun rose high in the sky, and the strong, implacable influence of the rampant lion simmered in the embers of his soul. He knew this time of Leo would be a turning point for England, her Queen, her people, and the angels that lent them all their power. The Queen's coat of arms pictured a pride of lions, one on the crest, and two pairs of three on the shield. The eighth, one of the two supporters of the shield, was the most fearsome of all. Crowned, with its red claws and protruding red tongue, it peered straight into his heart, examining every sinew. It roared these words at him:

Be not to your nature right and true,
Then thee I will repulse without ado.

The lion had courage and strength, but in his heart, Nelan saw the beast as the guardian of the Queen's Treasury in White Hall. As he mused on these matters, Wenceslaus moaned and groaned as he rowed him to where he was to meet Walsingham. Approaching the building, the usual coterie of watchmen greeted him with pike and frown.

"Halt. Who goes there?" one shouted, drawing his sword. The other three placed their hands on their pistols, and the four of them glared at him.

They let him into the courtyard, where a gang of pikemen milled around a covered wagon, eyes focused like it contained the crown jewels. In these uncertain times, perhaps it did. Walsingham directed them. He wore the air of a man overwrought with the problems of the country, hands clenched behind his back, stooping as if he walked into a stiff headwind. Nelan listened while he instructed two royal messengers.

"This message is for the paymaster general," he said to one of them. To the other, he murmured, "And you give this to Admiral Lord Howard." The riders mounted their steeds and set off at a gallop.

The Secretary turned and, on seeing Nelan, said, "Ah, about time you showed your face." Well, he had to have a grumble about his timing.

"M'lord. What will you have me do?"

Walsingham stared at him and said, "This wagon contains a casket of silver coins. You and Adden are to deliver it to Admiral Howard in Plymouth. He'll see it gets to the paymaster general of the fleet."

"I will, m'lord."

"The men need paying," Walsingham said, his voice a low whisper. "The fleet needs more food, ale, equipment, sail, cannon and, above all, gunpowder. Howard has requested the funds to pay for this."

"Yes, m'lord."

"With all that money, this is a dangerous mission, so I've assigned you these guards. Meet their leader," Walsingham said, pointing to a mountain of a man.

"That be me, m'lord. Bartholomew be me name. Guardin' be me business," the man said with a loud guffaw. "Folks call me Big Bart."

"Greetings, Big Bart," Nelan said.

"And you'll have the cartman for company," Walsingham added.

"Well, well, well, if it isn't John Brewer holding the tiller," Nelan said, recognising his friend from the crew of the *Golden Hind*.

"'Tis me, Nelan," John Brewer replied. "Needs must, lad. And I got needs. Now, can we get goin' or are we waitin' 'til them Dons come tickling the beard a' Old Father Thames?"

Walsingham narrowed his eyes and said, "Adden, where the devil are you? How I detest tardiness."

From one corner of the courtyard, the errant steward strolled towards them while hastily adjusting his codpiece. A young damsel Nelan had seen at the chapel a few days before ran up behind Adden, pulled him by the arm, and pressed him to her breast. Not that the steward resisted. She planted a hefty kiss on his lips, wrapped her arms around him, and almost had him there and then for breakfast, lunch and dinner. Fortunately for Adden, the Secretary had his back to him. Should Walsingham have seen the two of them, the steward would have faced the wrath of God.

John Brewer jumped down from the wagon and sidled over to Adden, saying, "Put Mistress Ready down, will ya? An' git you a'lumbering over here! We's all waitin' for ya."

Adden prised himself away, smoothed his jerkin, and joined the entourage.

"Ah! Adden. There you are," Walsingham said. "Can you get going now?"

"Aye, m'lord," Adden said, mounting his steed, and blowing a parting kiss to the damsel, who, at least according to Nelan, did not appear to be in any kind of distress. Far from it, Mistress Ready seemed united with the joys of summer, her face quite flushed and radiant.

"God's speed!" Walsingham said, and the wagon party of Nelan, Adden, Big Bart and a five-horse guard set off. With a parting glance, Nelan could have sworn that he saw the damsel mounting a mare and heading out of the side gate. Sure enough, as their party hugged the river and broached London Bridge, there she was, the pink tails of her pretty bonnet flying in the breeze, calling out, "Wait for me! I'm coming!"

Adden brought the party to a halt, greeted Mistress Ready with yet more hugs and kisses, and then helped her up onto the wagon next to John Brewer.

"She's...?" Brewer said with a heavy sigh and a disparaging shake of the head.

"Yes, Master Brewer. She's comin' with. Any questions?"

"Me, I ain't too keen to share me seat with one so ready," Master Brewer muttered.

On the first night on the Plymouth Road, they rested at the Fox and Hounds, a coaching inn in Street Cobham. As they bore a warrant to prove they pursued the Queen's business, the innkeeper afforded them special dispensation. After ejecting several disgruntled merchants from their rooms, they grabbed a good night's sleep. Big Bart and his watchmen bedded down in the stable, where they took turns guarding the wagon.

To avoid the morning traffic of horses, carts and carriages, they intended to set off early, but first light came and went, and the sun's rays failed to shine upon good Master Adden. When Nelan thumped on the steward's door, it wasn't the man's snoring he could hear but the creaking of the bed coupled with cries of ecstasy. He rapped on the door several times but to no avail. So, he returned to the wagon and watched the guards play dice. After Adden and Ready showed up, the party set off into the mid-morning sunshine.

"Wenchin' 'til mid-morn', you'll bring us misfortune, Master Adden," Brewer rounded on the steward.

They slept at coaching inns along the way until they reached the broad sea at Southampton. Wherever they stopped, Nelan handed out the pamphlets to town criers.

As the days passed, the west-bound coast road grew more crowded with coaches and wagons heading to Plymouth. Donkey carts hauled foodstuffs, barrels of ale and loads of hay. The wagons carried ship's biscuits, crates of cheese, loaves of bread, as well as marine equipment and tools. Men and boys bore yoke poles packed with goods. Messengers rode back and forth delivering royal decrees, encrypted letters and military despatches. Merchants in their plush coaches travelled the roads and byways, following their noses for a business opportunity.

During the journey, Nelan bore witness to the general health of the country. Many a village green had a man in the pillory or a woman in the stocks. Often, when passing through woodland and forest, they saw lumberjacks chopping down trees and loading them onto wagons.

"Wood for ships' timbers?" Nelan suggested.

"Or undertakers preparing for a bumper crop!" John Brewer chortled.

Here and there, a rotting corpse hung from a gibbet or a tree. Archers practising their craft crowded onto every village green, ready to repulse the invader. In market towns, men and women were whipped and chastised through alleys and streets.

What he witnessed shook him to the quick. Because nestling in the nooks and crannies were those clouds of dirty scarlet ambiance from Madima's vision. Now he remembered where he'd seen it before – in the Andes Mountains when sailing up the Pacific coast of South America. Engendered by the Vatican, the scarlet pall was Spanish. The Dons had sent it. That meant that the Armada was coming, and, because of the presence of the scarlet blanket, the Spanish were in effect already in occupation.

The Dons had their universities, like Toledo and Grenada. The English had Oxford and Cambridge. The Dons had their occult ways. They boasted the exquisite beauty of Alhambra and their esoteric Moorish heritage. England had John Dee and Edward Kelley. The Spanish sought to win the battle before it was fought. Wasn't that how every battle was won? That was why he saw the murky scarlet pall nestling in the valleys and dales. Spain laid claim to the land before they had invaded it. Thence the wisdom – obtain the surrender before the surrender.

The Spanish occultists had despatched their scarlet force ahead of them so that when they set foot on England's sacred land, their soldiers would feel at home, and receive the power of that. When they subdued the people, the scarlet pall would give them the authority, a mandate to govern. Nelan shook his head. They faced not only the greatest fleet on earth but the greatest occultists too.

Crossing the bridge over the River Exe brought them ever closer to old Plymouth. But the delays increased. Shepherds herded pigs, sheep and cattle towards the Hoe, the highest point of the city. The approaches were packed solid like a barrel full of ship's biscuits. Carrying themselves with pride aplenty, clumps of marching militia chewed on their straws and sang songs of yore to the angels of the land.

"We'll ne'er be defeated with this army!" crowed Master Adden.

Nelan grimaced; to call it an army seemed a tad generous. While some carried swords and pistols, many sported bows and arrows, but a lot of the rabble comprised farm labourers, old men and young boys with nothing more than pitchforks, rakes and spades to defeat the crack Spanish troops of the Duke of Parma.

The journey took seven days. On the last night, they rested at the George Inn in the village of Plymton a few miles outside of Plymouth. John Brewer, Big Bart and the guards tended to the wagon and horses. Roger Adden and Mistress Ready snared the last available room for themselves.

During the night, foxes made merry in the nearby woods. Their eerie cries of love disturbed the horses, who brayed and stomped their hooves. Like them, Nelan endured a troubled night. Not from the discomfort of the straw on the hard wooden floor. Nor from a tinker and a cooper on the floor next to him, who snored like a couple of wild boars. No, it was his dream of blazing fires, explosions, smoke and burning wood lighting the moon-filled night sky, evoking the vision of an empire falling into a flaming pit.

Empires shall fall, the prophecy said. But which one?

17

The Whistle Man

Fore Noon on 29th July 1588

The first sliver of dawn crept through the cracks and splashed into his room. The cock crowed thrice, its noisy, petulant shrieks heralding a portentous event; one that he had an inkling would enter the scrolls of the history of the Island of Angels. On fish Friday, the wagon, the horses and the guards stood to attention. Adden and his mistress were missing. More surprisingly, so was the cartman.

"Where is he?" Nelan asked. "It's unlike him to be tardy."

Big Bart had something to say. "Master Brewer was 'ere earlier in the mornin', and then, well, he weren't 'ere no more."

"But why would he just leave like that?" Nelan said.

"He may be gone on ahead," Big Bart grumbled.

The sun had risen, the dogs barked, and the inn had emptied. Except for Adden, who entertained his strumpet, Miss Ready, with his latest morning glory. Horses and carts trundled along the Plymouth Road towards the city's East Gate. Steaming lumps of animal excrement sat like small hillocks along the road. There was a fractious note in the air and yet inside that tension was peace and calm. It reminded him of the ocean when on the surface it raged, but in the depths, it was serene. He climbed into the back of the wagon and lifted the tarpaulin. The lock on the casket remained intact. What a relief. Despite that, he had an uneasy feeling, and it wasn't going away.

The guards shuffled on their feet, scratched their codpieces, and spat on the ground.

"Let's go, Adden and Brewer can catch us up," Nelan said. "It's vital we get this wagon to the Lord High Admiral."

"As you wish, sirrah," Big Bart said, and for a man so large, leapt onto the wagon, grasped the reins, and off they went, bumping along the dried track. The path narrowed when entering a wood. The party halted behind an overturned cart that blocked the way ahead. It had spilled its load of turnips onto the grass verge. The cartman argued with a lad with a yoke.

"You! It's your fault! Pick up my turnips," the cartman said.

"Nah!" said the yoke man. "You pick 'em up."

A whistle blew, high and shrill, splitting the relative peace of the morning. Five horsemen surged out onto the track from behind a clump of trees. Nelan recognised both the whistle and the lead horseman's scraggy grey beard.

"John Brewer!" he cried. "What are you doing?"

The cartman and the yoke man drew their sabres, turned and rushed towards the guards. Surprised by the ambush, the guards frantically drew their swords.

The sound of steel on steel. Grunts and shouts of fury filled the air. Hooves aloft, horses neighed in fear. Nelan fought the robbers with thrust, parry and slash.

John Brewer drew a pistol and fired it at Big Bart. The sheer force of the impact threw the man mountain off the wagon and onto the grassy knoll. He didn't get up.

"You bloody traitor!" Nelan yelled, and lurched at John Brewer. With his height advantage, the bugler whipped Nelan on the forehead with the butt of his pistol. Nelan fell to the ground, his head pounding, his vision blurred. Nearby, he smelled the rank odour of death.

As his head cleared, he saw the other guards lying spread-eagled and motionless on the bare earth. Brewer's gang dragged the guards' bodies across the road, leaving a trail of blood behind each one, then concealed them in a clump of trees. The cartman and the yoke man unhitched the horses from the wagon and mounted them. That left the wagon without horses.

John Brewer emerged from the back of the wagon carrying the casket of coins and wearing a smile as wide as Plymouth Sound.

Nelan saw images of trees, an upturned cart, a load of white turnips and the red trails of blood smeared across the green verge. God, his head hurt. At least he lived. For the moment. Not so the guards.

"You won't get away with this!" A last defiant burst of anger shot from his mouth.

"You don't know nuttin', Little Nelan." John Brewer spat the words out like poison. "I told ya, I got no treasure money."

"You gambled it all away!"

"Don't get all 'igh an' mighty wit' me, Master bloody Nelan. I ain't bin paid me pieces of silver. Not a farthin'. An' me wife, when I gets 'ome, what do I finds? She's ran orf wit' another man. Took me kids, me 'eart, an' me soul. Me's a cuckold. A cuckold!"

"That's no reason to steal the Queen's silver. They are the difference between victory and defeat!"

"Bah. What does I care?" Brewer said, making three shrill blows on his whistle. His men gathered around him.

"That whistle... Three shrill blows on the... No, wait. It wasn't a flute the constable heard at Newgate. It was your whistle!"

"Yeah, I freed Pedro. So what if I did? Damn it. He still owes me for that service I done 'im."

"You're a thief *and* a traitor!"

Brewer lifted the casket and crowed, "By the Lord, with these coins, I'll be a rich man. Like you!"

He pointed his pistol at Nelan.

"You going to kill me as well?" Nelan blurted out. "Go on then!"

Brewer cocked the trigger and shot but... the pistol failed to fire! Nelan missed several heartbeats, then caught his breath. From further down the path came the rumble of a horse and cart.

"There's folk comin'!" one of the gang yelled.

"Let's be gone!" Brewer cried and blew his whistle. Cradling the casket to his chest, the bugler rode off with his outlaw gang.

Nelan's world spun away, and he lapsed into unconsciousness.

His astral body eased out of the back of his neck as he detached from his carnal aspect. Nelan peered down at his injured body, blood smeared on his head. By a stream, a line of willow trees swayed in the summer breeze. Long strands of wispy clouds were pure white against an azure blue sky. He rose higher still and peered down on the Sound, the Hoe and the river as it divided into the Tamar and the Plym.

In his salamander astral form, he drifted with the currents, the astral ones he followed when wearing the shoes that never wore out. This was release. In this realm, the mind and the spirit roamed free from the confinement of the physical body.

A rhyme played in his mind:

The fresh wind blows.
The white foam flows.
The furrow follows free.

Then he knew; it mooted not just the wind, the sea and the foam; it spoke of the astral currents, where all was silent, with no sense of the passage of time. Drifting above the Cornish coast, he passed the stacks above the tin mines and watched the blue waves beat against the sandy beaches, dressed in white foam. He glided from cove to cove, the same way as the mariners who sailed along the coast.

He sensed his astral body was being pulled towards a destination. Moving through this strange astral realm, he encountered serpents and panthers, elephants and eagles. He met pillars of wisdom. At one point, he passed through a field of eggs of the ethereal variety, all different sizes and shapes, from Emerald Green and Yellow to Pink and Turquoise. Strange, these were the colours of E.G.Y.P.T. Then he encountered a clutch of dead souls, of men slaughtered in a recent battle somewhere on earth, wraiths vainly seeking their way home.

He passed along streets with mysterious buildings made of smoke, with not a brick in sight. He saw a man climbing down a mountain carrying two stone tablets, another man with the head of an ibis, and elsewhere, a naked woman plucking an apple from a tree and eating it. In the astral realm, these moments were alive, if alive was the right word, for they emanated, they had soul and presence. Then he knew that the trace of events from history and incidents in people's lives never died. Instead, they were preserved in this realm in a minute form. These episodes from history could be, and often were, re-enlivened or re-membered by any living person.

In the astral world, there was no sense of substance either. After a while, he grew accustomed to occupying a body of no weight. If there was one body – the astral body – of no substance inside him, were there others? He wondered if he really knew who and what he was. How many were these inner lives? Did they talk or sing to him? Did they try to guide him, but because of his preoccupations, he never heard them?

He recalled a rhyme he'd learned at Westminster School:

I had a little nut tree,
Nothing would it bear,
But a silver nutmeg,
And a golden pear.
I skipped over water,
I danced over sea,
And all the birds in the air,
Couldn't catch me.

How could someone skip over water, or dance over the sea… unless they were lighter than a feather and wore the shoes that never wore out?

As he travelled on, he realised he was being drawn somewhere, but where? Another ambush? Near Penzance, he saw two huge lines of astral force, ley lines; one from north-west to south-east, and the other from south-west to north-east. They crossed over at St Michael's Mount, off the Cornish coast. A port was a place of exchange where goods were imported and exported. Perhaps St Michael's Mount was an astral port, a place of ingress and egress of those energies out of and into the Island of Angels.

The Lizard came next. What a strange name. Was it a coiled one? Was it benign or malign? Beyond that came the Atlantic Ocean. Edging west, he encountered a group of small islands, spread like pearls on the face of the waters. Huge rolling waves smashed into the rocks of Bryher Island, flecks of white foam breaking onto its crags.

On the horizon, he glimpsed another island. Yet, according to his memory of the area, no island existed there. So, what was it? There were specks of white and gold dotted against the backdrop of the azure blue sea. Getting closer, he understood what had instinctively drawn him to this place.

Frozen in mid-air, he hovered. Below him, ships were spread a broad expanse. Flying back and forth over them, he counted se score and ten. So many vessels. No doubt all loaded to the gunwale with cannon and powder, sword and sabre, pistol and flintlock. A floating killing machine that brought rack and ruin, death and destruction, to the Island of Angels. With their high castles and sails like wings, the galleons were the biggest and the most fearsome.

Having embarked from Lisbon, the Armada must have tacked up the French coast as far as Ushant and sailed the thirty-five leagues from there to the Scilly Isles.

He drifted higher and noticed that the fleet was oddly arranged – a thin, curved shape, thicker in the middle than the two ends. Oh! A crescent. No, not quite. The formation resembled a giant bird, with its two wings spanning from its body. And it wasn't any bird; it was the royal bird of Spain, the eagle. The Dons had brought their imperial eagle with them to destroy the Protestant devils of England.

He found the flagship; its admiral, the Duke of Medina Sidonia, stood on the high castle deck at the stern. Sails fluttered in the breeze while hundreds of troops guarded its portals. The vessel boasted cannon aplenty top and broadside. All around the Duke, the Spanish mariners and soldiers had gathered on deck. A priest blessed the Armada emblem. To the blare of trumpets, an officer hoisted it high up the mainsail until it fluttered over the entire fleet. On one side, it was emblazoned with a crucifix. On the other was the Madonna, the Virgin Mary herself.

Prior to the invasion, the Spanish had already mentally deposited the scarlet astral clouds in England's valleys. Now their ships had this eagle formation and flew the religious emblem, drawing power from the occult influence of Spain. This convinced Nelan once and for all that the fight against the Armada would first take place in the realms of the hidden and the subtle, the implied and the suggested – this was an occult war.

The flagship let off cannon fire; once, twice, thrice. Dressed in scarlet robes and a red hat, the priest raised his hands in prayer, no doubt to thank their God for bringing them so far and to prepare them for what was to come. All the peace negotiations Elizabeth's ambassadors had conducted with the Duke of Parma in the Spanish Netherlands, all the anxious years and raised hopes and false alarms – had come to nothing.

the Armada had breached English waters.

He had to inform Howard, Drake and Hawkins.

Preparing to leave, he spotted a shimmering serpent, its scales glistening in bright astral colours of reds and greens. The astral creature crawled along the yard arm, gazing intently at the proceedings on the Spanish flagship. With four legs, scaly skin and a long, winding tail, it was a fiery dragon! Someone had adopted the astral form of a dragon. As soon as it spotted Nelan, it alighted into the astral plane.

Dr Dee had once told him that astral travellers typically clothed themselves with a cloak or shield. They'd adopt the form of an insect, animal or bird in which to traverse the astral realms. Ancient Egyptian pharaohs, when flying in the astral realms, often wore the cloak of a jackal or a black panther.

But who clothed themselves in the scales of a fiery dragon? He followed it through the astral realms and in a flash found himself hovering above the centre of the Spanish web of intrigue, the cathedral monastery of El Escorial. Although unschooled in astral etiquette, he knew that the boundaries of churches, temples and palaces were protected by the outside use of black railings with gold tips and sigils like gargoyles, and the inside use of alternate black and white square floor tiles. That day, the abbot must have forgotten to guard the entrance with occult devices, because Nelan flew into the monastery unhindered.

Having few astral skills, he plunged through the roof into the main cathedral. The abbot was in the throes of a service to bless the Armada and seek a holy mandate for its success. Fortunately for Nelan, the monks were so enthralled in singing a rhapsody to their Lord that they failed to notice an errant astral form appear amongst them.

All the congregation wore the Hieronymites' religious habit of brown hooded scapular, white tunic and brown mantle, except one. That had to be King Philip himself. The man was kneeling on the stone cathedral floor without a cushion and, from his grim, taut expression, seemed to revel in the obvious discomfort of his penance.

Out of the corner of his eye, Nelan glimpsed the fiery dragon scudding away into the otherworld, so he followed. On the way back, the dragon figure led him around the twists and turns of the astral pathways, and Nelan lost him.

18

Kiss the Mistress

After Noon on 29th July 1588

Nelan woke up on a bed of straw. A man stood over him.

"Get away," Nelan cried and jagged back, moving awkwardly with his feet and hands on the ground, and his knees sticking in the air.

"He's awake now, he is," the man said to someone else in the room.

Wiping her hands on her apron, a young woman appeared in his line of vision. She smelled of onions.

"What shall we call you?" she asked.

"Nelan. Nelan of Queenhithe. Who are you?"

"Me's Jonas, Jonas Mythorpe. This be me daughter, Cordelia."

"What happened to me?"

"Hit on the 'ead. Dreaming wit' the angels, you was."

"Phew!" he hissed. "Now I remember... El Escorial... The Scillies... The Armada... it's here. I gotta..." He tried standing up, but the room spun round like a top. Jonas grabbed him and stopped him from toppling over.

"No, you ain't goin' nowhere, Master Nelan," Cordelia said. "That's a brute of a bruise on ya 'ead. You better stay 'ere."

"Where's here?" he asked, his head pounding.

"I be a tin miner at local stannary," Jonas said, with an air of pride.

"Local? You mean...?"

"Aye, we's at Plympton St Maurice."

Damn. He was still in Plympton. The church bell chimed one of the clock. He'd been knocked out all morning.

"I must to the Hoe," he said, gritting his teeth. "I have to get a message to the Admiral of the Fleet."

"Oh, them's the big wigs. You fit for to see 'em, little fella?" Cordelia asked.

"I must tell them what's happening," he said, and stood up with her help.

"Well, if you insist," Jonas murmured. "I'm takin' me brodder Robert ta' the harbour. Look, 'e's just rolled up. There, outside."

"The angels are shining on ya today," Cordelia chimed.

"Not sure about that," Nelan murmured, as he staggered out into the day. He climbed into the back of Jonas's cart and nestled down amongst the nets and fishing gear. There he was, like Little Jack Horner, sitting in the corner, except there was no plum pie. He could have eaten a whole one, just like his mother used to make them.

"What did you see where you found me?" he asked, as he devoured a tranche of bread and cheese that Jonas shared with him.

"We finds ya in the middle a' the rubble of the robbery," Jonas said. "All them poor guards. Dead as crows, they was. An' my Cordelia, she saw you movin' an' twitchin', so she says to bring you 'ome, so I brung you 'ome."

"Thank you for taking care of me," Nelan said.

"Oh, an' the constables was bringin' 'orses to move the wagon."

"Do you know where they took it?"

"They says there was food and other supplies on it, so they was takin' it to the quay at Plymouth."

"Well, at least that will help the effort to smash the Spanish."

"Amen to that, sirrah!"

The cart trundled along the road. His wounds and bruises bumped along with it. They crossed the rickety old wooden bridge over the River Plym and then got stuck in a queue.

"It be the East Gate. 'Tis always busier than the path to Hell," Jonas said.

The gate was closed. The gateman was nowhere to be seen. After a while, he appeared from around a corner, suckling on a tankard of ale and wiping a few stray droplets from his salt-and-pepper beard.

"Ah, Jonas, how be the Lord with you today?" the gateman said, in a voice as gruff as his temperament.

"Lookin' for the admiral. Know where he be?"

"At his game on the Hoe. He'll be wit' the two giants," he said.

On the promontory, Nelan spotted the famous fortress sitting atop the limestone and granite crags of the Hoe. The mid-afternoon sun glinted on the azure blue waters, more shallow than deep because of the ebbing tide. Upwards of fifty ships from men o' war to merchantmen, from carracks to galleons, were moored across the waters in Sutton Pool. The sight lifted his flagging spirits.

There was a last desperate race to supply the ships. The quay was crowded with barrels, armaments, cannon, weapons, flags, sails, rigging, equipment, even an anchor or two. Row boats and wherries, piled high with goods, waited for the tide so they could victual the ships. Marauding gulls dived down and snatched stray bits of food.

The cart weaved its way along the quay, where Robert left them to join up with his crew on the fishing boat. Jonas guided the cart up the hill, passed the fortified Barbican, before halting it on the edge of the Hoe.

"Tell me about the legend of the giants," Nelan said.

"Over there, see, lad." Jonas pointed towards two large etchings on the ground. The turf had been cleared, revealing the white limestone beneath. "There be two giants, Goemagot an' Corineus, as this 'ere West Country of ours bein' the Land a' Giants. Goemagot was our man, the giant of Albion. Corineus was the invader from 'cross the seas. The two fought 'ere, on the Hoe. That's what these 'ere rock figures is about."

"Who won?"

"Corineus threw our Goemagot into the Sound, he did, right 'ere. Then he claimed the land a' Cornwall as 'is own."

"Jonas, so long as Corineus is on our side to fight today's invader."

"Amen to that," Jonas said and went on his way.

Near to the low cliff edge of the Hoe, a group of six men played bowls. Nelan breathed in the view of the green and the game, and the sea and the Sound. Sir Francis Drake and Drake's brother Thomas he knew. He assumed that the two men in the admiral's garb were Lord Howard and Sir John Hawkins. The fifth man, wearing a captain's uniform, Nelan didn't recognise. Nor the lieutenant standing next to him.

Francis Drake rolled a small white ball – the jack, also known as a mistress – onto the smooth carpet of grass. Then Drake grabbed his black wooden bowl, took aim, and rolled it onto the green. The bowl started out to the right of the jack and, taking the borrow and with Drake stalking it, crying, "Rub on! Rub on," it curled around before nudging the mistress. Each of the wooden bowls had a built-in bias, so they traced a crescent shape across the grass.

The game was not about straight lines. Nelan thought it resembled archery, where, to allow for the play of wind and moisture, an archer never aimed directly at the target. The winner of the game read the elements and used them to their advantage. This was a game for seafarers.

When his bowl came to rest close to the mistress, Drake howled with joy.

Next, Lord Howard, Francis Drake's opponent, took his turn. An older, distinguished man, Howard bent down, took three practice swings, and released the bowl. Taking the borrow, it curled in towards the jack, and stopped just inside Drake's bowl.

"There! That's how it's done!" Howard crowed. "Even at my age, I can still kiss the mistress! One point to me."

"Twenty more to go, Howard. I'll be having you by the end of it all," countered Drake.

Thomas Drake spotted Nelan's approach and went to greet him.

"Ordinary Seaman Nelan Michaels," he said. "It's been a long time! The Admiral of the Fleet's expecting you."

"I'm glad I've finally made it!" Nelan replied.

"Nelan. Meet Jacob Whiddon, captain of the *Roebuck*," Thomas Drake said. "And his first lieutenant, Simons."

"Welcome, Nelan," Whiddon said, and bowed. Simons grunted a cursory greeting.

Before Nelan could deliver his news, two horses galloped across the Hoe towards them. Another naval captain rode one, his equerry the other. Wearing this wild look in his eye, the captain dismounted in haste.

"Captain Fleming, what dread tidings do you bring us?" Drake asked. "You look like you've met the Devil himself."

"Not the Devil, but the next closest thing – the Spanish," he panted. "They're here."

"Oh, I know," Drake said, casual as you like. "Moored off Bryher Isle, near the Scillies."

Fleming's mouth dropped open. Once he recovered his wits, he said, "M'lord, I thought I was the only scouting ship in that area."

"You were."

"Then how did you find out?"

Nelan knew exactly what Drake was going to say.

"The Spaniards don't call me *El Draque*, the Dragon, for nothing. But, if truth be told, it should be a fiery dragon."

Fleming probably didn't know that Drake was referring to his astral cloak, but Nelan certainly did.

Lord Howard was making ready to leave, when Drake called him back. "Lord High Admiral, where are you going?"

"To fight the Spaniards, of course," Howard replied.

"Why? We've plenty of time to finish the game and then smash the Dons."

"If you say so," Howard said.

Drake introduced Nelan to the Lord Howard, who said, "Well, young fella, I received a message from the secretary that you would be here a few days ago. Time, lad, is of the essence. But I see you're here now, but where's the casket? You hiding it in your doublet? Come on. Out with it. The paymaster general has to pay the suppliers. No good setting sail without gunpowder, ale or ship's biscuits, eh? And how did you get that bloody wound on your head? It looks recent."

Nelan took a deep breath, and said, "Early this morning, m'lord, highwaymen attacked our convoy and stole the casket. Their leader was John Brewer."

"Damn!" Howard slammed the bowl down on the grass. "This could cost us the war! What am I going to do? I can't pay the merchants and the shipwrights in briny."

"I-I know," Nelan said.

"Who else was with you?" Howard asked.

"The escort of five guards, and Walsingham's steward, Roger Adden."

"Where's he now?"

"I don't know. I've not seen him since last evening."

"A robbery." Howard threw up his hands in despair. "I need

those silver coins. The fleet needs them. The country needs them. We must retrieve them at any cost. I'll find them myself if I have to. I'll interrogate the guards."

"You can't, Admiral," Nelan said. "Brewer and his gang slaughtered them."

"You're the lone survivor?"

"Yes, Admiral. They ambushed us. But I tried with all my might to prevent it. That's how I got this," Nelan said, tapping the wound on his head.

The old sailor gritted his teeth and said, "Where did it happen?"

"Just outside Plympton, first thing this morning."

"Why did it take you this long to get here?"

"Admiral," Nelan snapped. He was losing his temper. He bit his tongue. He couldn't afford to do that with admirals. "I told you, they knocked me out and I've just come round. I got here as soon as I could."

Drake stepped into the breach. "You claim that John Brewer was their leader. Yet, I knew him as an honest God-fearing man."

"Not anymore, he's not. John Brewer's a traitor and a thief. They convicted Pedro de Antón as a traitor, but he escaped on the way to dance the Tyburn jig. And Brewer bloody well helped him!"

"These are grave accusations. Do you have any evidence?" Drake asked.

"You have my word. Why do you keep asking me these questions? Send out constables to find Brewer, why don't you?"

"We will, Nelan," Drake said. "But first we need to get all the facts."

What with his head wound, the strangeness of the astral travelling and the critical importance of the casket, Nelan felt the ghosts of the past rise up in him. He suspected the admirals didn't believe his story. He lost his temper and said, "My Lords. I'm innocent. I'm not a murderer or a thief. If you want to know what I really think, this is divine justice, Admiral. Yes, that's exactly what it is!"

"What did you say?" Drake hissed.

"I said this is divine justice… against you, Admiral."

"Oh! Is that what it is? What would that be for?" Drake's face resembled a vortex of contortion.

"For the murder of Thomas Doughty on the Isle of Justice. There, I've said it now. That's why the *Hind* grounded in Indonesia. Yet the next day, a divine wind blew and released us from the clutches of the reef. What saved us was Fletcher speaking the truth, for which you humiliated him. You wronged him, and you wronged Our Lord. Now that I've spoken in true conscience, I feel better."

The wound on his head stopped throbbing, and he breathed easier. Not for long, though.

"By all the angels! Enough!" Drake yelled, scorn in every word. "How dare you question my authority! My decision then was final and absolute. My acts against Doughty and Fletcher were those of divine retribution. Then I acted for and on behalf of the Almighty. And I shall do so again, now. Thomas, arrest this man."

"What for? Telling the truth?"

"I'm convinced you collaborated with Brewer and stole the Queen's shillings."

"I'm innocent, I tell you!" Nelan hissed.

"Come on, Nelan," Thomas Drake said, tying Nelan's hands and whispering, "You should know better than to goad the bear, lad."

Nelan cursed his angry impatience as Thomas Drake led him across the Hoe towards the fortress. From there, Nelan could see the frenzied activity of stevedores coming and going on the quay. He spotted men unloading goods from a wagon. He recognised it as the one from the robbery. The constables had already brought it to the harbourside.

Sailors moved around on the vessels in the harbour, pacing the decks, waiting for the tide. He thought he recognised the vessel nearest to the shore.

"What ship is that? It looks familiar," he said.

"It should do," Thomas Drake said. "She's had a refit since you last saw her, and Captain Fleming's her master now. She's the *Golden Hind*."

On the ship, he spied a man with a shock of black curly hair, olive skin, and a familiar height and build. The man saw him and seemed to glare back at him.

When Nelan had got up that morning, he knew the omens pointed towards a portentous day, but it was turning into a nightmare. Because the man was none other than Pedro de Antón. The barbel with the whiskers must have used his excellent command of English to wangle his way onto the *Hind*. At last, Nelan had found his father's killer, but in the unlikeliest of places! But he was about to go to prison and was powerless to prevent him from running amok amongst the English fleet.

19

Beacons and Bells

Evening of 29th July 1588

Nelan slumped against the prison wall. First, it was London's Marshalsea and now Plymouth.

The prison building was a large wooden structure with small cells, each one as dark as the path to Hell, and stinking as much. A dozen inmates squeezed into each one. Most wore barely a glaze of fluff on their chins. The oldest prisoner had probably crawled out of his mother's womb some forty years ago. This old fellow had a straggly white beard, long earlobes and the eyes of a dullard, as if a demon had sucked the life out of him.

In the next cell, two drunks sang so badly out of tune that even the dead turned in their graves. A couple of inmates played cards in the evening light that drifted seamlessly through a west-facing window. Another small vent looked north, yielding a distant view of the hills beyond the city walls.

The evening wore a subtle, ethereal cloak. To the west, the low-lying hills beyond the River Tamar shone with an enticing luminescence. Nelan realised what it was. Dusk descended like a pall on the land of England, and the yellow orb of the sun dropped below the horizon. It happened so slowly, so quietly, like a leaf falling in an ancient forest, with no one to witness its evanescent glory. That night of all nights, a green flash of light shot through the air like a celestial arrow piercing the gloom, like the time Diego,

Drake's manservant, on the *Golden Hind*, had revealed one of the great mysteries.

On this night, something stirred deep in the astral that heralded matters of huge import. Change was in the air. It was as if the world shifted on its axis, and would never return to its old alignment.

The news that the Armada had reached the Scillies spread from the Hoe into the byways of Plymouth. Despite the clarion call of Walsingham's pamphlet, a tremulous fear disgorged itself onto the streets, smearing people's faces. It drew its frozen talons across their lives. It left scars that would never heal again in their lifetimes and would haunt their sons and daughters. Their souls emitted a silent, raucous cry that rose to the heavens. It was a cry for help, for pity and, above all, for absolution.

Children cowered behind their mothers' aprons. As the tidings crept like an invisible serpent around the alleys, the shout arose:

Hark! Hark! The dogs do bark.
The beggars are coming to town.

But it wasn't the beggars. It was the Spanish.

In his mind's eye, Nelan saw that the old town of Plymouth remained in flux. Rumours circulated like vultures. The Spanish would invade the town, use it as a base, and threaten the rest of the Island of Angels! Folk were terrified, but they did not run away. They may feel the threat of desperation, but English blood coursed through them. Practical and stubborn, they reached for the cloth, flint and iron. They sharpened their kitchen knives, whittled wooden poles into pointed sticks, and retrieved more arrows from the fletchers. He felt waves of their anxiety. Playing on the chords of his soul, it made harsh, dissonant music.

Peering through the small barred window, a bright luminescence on the distant hills lit up the night skies. One by one, starting on the far western hills, the yeomen climbed the winding path to reach the beacon. Gently, they caressed the flames from a wicker torch onto the beacon. On the next hill, the yeomen saw the light across the valley and took the torch to their beacon. Orange and red flames leapt high into the darkening night, signalling to the next summit. And so, from beacon to beacon, did a pulse of light spread across the hilltops, sending a message of the greatest threat to the island and its incumbent angels. Now the island of England had become the land of fire.

To Plymouth folk, that meant they did not stand alone. The rest of old England shared their plight. Along the rugged Cornish coast, the beacons flared, then across Rame Head near Plymouth, and on to Devon, Dorset and Hampshire. On and on, the flame leapt from bonfire to bonfire, to the North Downs, to Surrey, and northwards to Ely, York and Durham. That night, the beacon light even crossed the cold, dark waters of the Narrow Seas, and informed the English troops battling to lift the Spanish yoke from the Netherlands. And, to London, and the royal palaces, where, Nelan predicted, the Queen and her Privy Council would receive the dire tidings. They would know. They would know what all of Europe would know.

The Armada had come.

As the flames lit the night skies, the bells tolled in the little chapels deep in the moors of Cornwall, in town churches with their belfries, in the great cathedral cities of Salisbury, Winchester and London. Nelan heard them from his cell and listened to the tone of their call. For call they did to the heart of every English man and woman. The flames and the bells spoke to the island and to the people of the island. And the island and her angels listened to the people's response, to see if they would take up arms against the tyrannical foe, and shout, boldly, fearlessly, with challenge aplenty:

Honi Soit Qui Mal Y Pense.
Evil be to he who thinks evil of me.

Nelan saw flickering images of animal forms scudding about the astral realms, from great bears, fearsome in their intent, to imperial eagles full of majesty, to snarling jackals guarding the boundaries of graveyards. At one time, a herd of bulls pursued him. From his time with the Miwok tribe in America, he saw they were bison. Other astral entities were equally fascinating: a giant bee hovered above him before he shooed it away, and a huge black scarab beetle scuttled past him. Swarms of black and yellow hornets, and ants of the black, red and white variety, flew nearby with uncanny freedom.

The bell and beacon were the same as the bell and candle, two of the three elements in the excommunication rite of Bell, Book and Candle. An excommunication removed something unwanted or poisonous from the astral realms to a safe place. It was an exorcism. This revelation renewed his belief that the combined action of this night's bell and flame had dispersed the clumps of scarlet force nestling in the island's valleys.

As he glanced towards the hills, his heart sank. Because in the first vale upon which he set eyes was a dense scarlet cloud, more menacing than those he'd witnessed before. In the dawn light, clumps of scarlet force crept out of the ground, snaked up the tree trunks, and climbed the church spires like eerie fingers of mist.

Beacons had fired. Bells had chimed. Yet the land remained blanketed by the scarlet pall. The occult threat hadn't dispersed. Nor had it diminished. It had grown stronger.

Nelan refused to feel sorry for himself. He'd done that once too often. All the same, he felt a tinge of regret that he had vented the stresses and strains of the robbery out on Admiral Drake. On second thoughts, he wished he had shown him a tad more respect and bided his tongue rather than let it loose like the dogs of war.

Either way, he'd informed both Drake and Howard so they could retrieve the casket and bring the perpetrators to justice.

Ah! What was done was done, and couldn't be undone. He was desperate to join the fleet, because in the battle against the dire threat posed by the Armada lay his destiny. For now, he prayed that Drake had lost his temper with him, and sent him to prison, not because he had committed a crime but because he had undermined Drake's authority in front of the high admiral. He prayed that the passage of time would heal the wound and that Drake would forgive him. Perhaps one day they'd meet, and Nelan would offer him a profuse and abject apology.

Until then, he had to escape this confinement.

20

The Shining Ones

30th July 1588

As the rays of the rising sun slunk into the prison cell, Nelan waited. A man of action, waiting was never his strong point, and waiting in prison less so. Besides, waiting for what? Redemption? Pity? A pardon? None of these was remotely possible. His future seemed more like trial and judgement than humiliation and hanging.

He sighed, as if that would help him settle to his new lot, which comprised the stench of piss, sweat and fear, all enjoyed in the confines of a small cell shared with drunks and debtors, rats and rascals.

These terrible accusations were more than a troublesome interruption to the smooth passage of his life's journey, and this one – high treason for challenging the admiral's authority and theft of the casket – was potentially worse than the first. Strange that today's predicament always appeared more severe than yesterday's.

The drunks packed away their playing cards because one inmate had emptied the other's purse, as well as taken his shoes, his bodkin and the doublet off his back. The prison warden didn't care.

The day dragged like no other. Not only because in prison, everything in his life had ground to a shuddering halt, but also because it was a momentous day, a day he so desperately wanted to be part of. Faced by the greatest navy in the world, England, her people, and her angels, needed all the help they could get. And he had the skills in his esoteric armoury to assist. In frustration, he kicked out at the rats of both the two- and four-legged variety.

His mind turned to Pedro. What diabolical ploy was the man plotting? He possessed this devilish knack of turning up in the very place, and at the very time, where he could wreak the most havoc. With what connivance did he get aboard the *Golden Hind*, a vessel whose name was engraved on the scrolls of the greatest achievements of the Island of Angels? Stuck in his cell, Nelan was helpless to warn Captain Fleming of the imminent danger.

The atmosphere in the prison swirled with tension. Later that afternoon, he heard a hubbub outside the prison gates – drunks carousing, singing and hollering. Moments later, the prison warden, intoxicated as a lord, came bursting into the cell, crying, "They're 'ere. Been sighted, they 'ave. 'Undreds of 'em. Sails fillin' the blue sea all as far as the 'orizon."

"What? Where?" Nelan wanted to know.

"The Dons. They're 'ere! They're 'orf the Eddystone!"

The Eddystone Rocks protruded out of the sea about ten miles south-west of Rame Head, which itself overlooked the Plym estuary. That was close; that was just around the corner. But would they sail into Plymouth Sound and storm the city, a bold move if ever there was one? Bold – was that part of the Spanish make-up? Or was it tempered by the inveterate caution of King Philip?

At dusk, the birds roosted in their flocks and made their shrill evening calls. The light of the setting sun reflected on the low-lying clouds, giving them a purple, almost violet, hue, stark against the deepening azure blue sky. As the sun set, Nelan's head throbbed from John Brewer's pistol blow. He slumped down, his back against the only vacant corner in the cell.

Once again, he rubbed the three wavy lines beneath his middle finger and soon drifted off into the vast realms of the otherworld. He directed his astral body to detach from his physical body, and it did! He was so surprised that it had obeyed his instruction. Immediately, he felt the utter relief of feeling no pain, smelling no odours, and, above all, sensing no confinement.

In his salamander astral form, he hovered above the prison and peered down on its occupants. As the dusk thickened, so did the astral around the prison. Slowly, like early morning mist gathering above the moors, a thick, bright clump became visible. It sat above the building, but his instinct told him there was a connection between the two. It was a cloud of brilliant light. A shining beacon, it was in stark contrast to the dull, dark astral emanations of the prison.

As he willed himself towards the cloud of light, his astral body glowed; a brightness both rich and energising. Once he'd merged with its brilliant lucidity, he knew what it was. He trilled with awe and wonder. Because he had entered a cloud of souls, and not just any souls; they were human souls, and they belonged to those same poor sods in the prison.

What on earth were they doing there, hanging together in a cloud? Didn't a soul reside *inside* a body? Could it still perform its many duties if it resided *outside* the body of its host? But through the prison walls, he could see that the inmates breathed, walked and talked. That meant one thing; though separated from their carnal host, their soul still served them faithfully, allowing the men to function normally.

Why had these souls congregated in a cloud at distance from their respective hosts? The reason struck him like a thunderbolt. Why hadn't he thought of it before? The souls could not abide residing in the carcasses of the prisoners. The men were full of revenge, violence and cruelty. Their souls couldn't abide it, and so departed their hosts to clump together with those of kind.

Oh. My. God. The bright cloud was a shining entity, a silent gathering of the souls of the inmates. He'd discovered another layer of the mystery of the soul's aversion to bitterness. Years before, Dr Dee had given him a clue about it from the Geneva Bible, the Book of Job, Chapter 10, Verse 1:

My soul is cut off though I live.
I will… speak in the bitterness of my soul.

Now he gleaned its inner meaning. The human soul liked sweetness, not sweet physical things like honey, but human sentiments such as kindness and generosity. Conversely, the soul disliked bitterness caused by cruelty and wounds in the mind. Then, while maintaining its subtle connection to its host, the soul moved away from that bitterness. While the soul was cut off from its host, it still performed its many functions.

These itinerant souls, ejected from their home, searched for a new one, and so sought to join with other souls likewise removed from their carnal hosts. There they hovered, witness to their hosts' bitterness, bound by the closeness of separation. When the person, by the warmth of his or her sentiment, banished the bitterness and allowed the sweetness of soft humanity, the soul re-entered its host.

With it came a supreme well-being, courtesy of the Shining Ones.

21

The Incendiary

31st July 1588

The church bells rang out across the roofs of old Plymouth, disturbing the pigeons' and the swallows' early morning roost. That alerted the foxes, scavenging in the back alleys, sending them scurrying back to their dens. The rats sniffed the air and, afraid of nothing, blithely searched through the piles of organic detritus dumped in the middle of the streets. Undeterred by these dawn goings-on, the people of Plymouth opened their doors and followed the well-trodden path to the church, escorted each step of the way by the rhythmical chimes of the church bells.

It was the first Sunday service since the sighting of the Armada. The bells woke Nelan from a restless slumber, full of dreams of angels bound under the valleys of the earth by invisible golden cords, perpetually broken and retied. It reminded him of the Ancient Greek myth of Sisyphus, whose crime was to murder guests who stayed in his palace. For his hubris, the gods of yore condemned Sisyphus to push a heavy boulder up a hill. Whenever he reached the summit, the rock rolled back down, forcing him to walk down the hill and start again the dance of eternal repetition.

Nelan's mouth tasted like the bottom of a sewer pit. He felt as rough as the old prisoner opposite him looked; haggard and drawn. The others roared and snored. That morning, the stench was as near to the sulphurous smell of Hell itself as he could imagine.

Nelan's mind resembled that flight of errant souls. Next on his list of anxieties was the retrieval of the casket. Only with those funds could they victual the fleet. Sir Francis Drake knew this; his motto, *Sic Parvis Magna*, meant From Small Beginnings Do Great Things Grow. The outcome of the battle to come would hinge on a tiny detail. England's future was weighed in the balance so finely that a feather could tip it either way.

How could he escape? He delved into his purse and ran his finger over the ruby salamander pendant, which Walsingham had finally returned to him. Nelan also felt his cloth, flint and strike-a-light, the source of a spark of flame. In a wooden building, that would be a risk, and he didn't want to jeopardise the lives of others, just for his own salvation. Although he had gleaned that the prison building and walled enclosure had once belonged to a prominent local Catholic family. When the family had been arrested for treason, the Crown had acquired the building and converted it into a prison.

The warden rattled the bars and woke the prisoners. His breath stinking of ale, he hollered, "Git up, wills ya?" and unlocked the cells. Roused from their collective stupor, the inmates followed the wardens out of the darkness of their cells into the blinding light of dawn, across the yard to the tiny chapel. This was the Sunday service.

Nelan stood at the back while the chaplain harangued them to be good prisoners. Losing interest, he cast his mind back to the extraordinary events of the previous night when he'd entered the shining astral cloud above the prison, that strange congregation of prisoners' souls. While ensconced in it, he'd been connected to the prisoners' souls, and had become aware of their histories. He wasn't interested in their previous thieving and skulduggery, but he was in their knowledge of the prison's layout.

With all the inmates and wardens gathered in the chapel, he had an idea. After all, he was the Fyremaster. If he could create a diversion, he might contrive an escape. He delved into his cloth purse and rubbed his fingers over the ruby salamander pendant. Drifting off into an astral slumber, he conjured a pale blue flame above the church. It didn't stay long and promptly disappeared. But he persisted, and after repeated efforts, the azure blue flame sustained. Directly above the chapel, it grew brighter and more illumined, until a tiny ember, a spark of living fire, dripped from it, fell through the air and landed on the warm, dry timbers of the church roof.

Nelan waited for the flames to spread. He smelled the smoke above him wafting around the rafters. It wouldn't take long before the other inmates smelled it too. A short while later, the warden spotted it. From quiet, ordered prayer, the congregation quickly degenerated into a rabid collection of scared rabbits. In moments, as the flames crept down the pillars and circulated around the balcony, the inmates yelled and rushed back out into the yard, shepherded by the wardens.

Nelan put his escape plan into action. When everyone was safe outside, and with the smoke and flames pulsing down the pillars and across the choir, he headed past the altar into the sacristy. At the base of the steps into the crypt, he searched for a door. Where was it? He'd learned in the astral from the inmates that a door was there. Ah, look behind the vestry wardrobe. Yes. He'd found it.

He retrieved his flint and strike-a-light, and lit a candle. After some serious negotiations with a crowbar, Nelan eventually prised the door open and stared into a dark cobwebbed tunnel. With the smoke billowing out of the church and through the sacristy door, there was no way back. He slammed the tunnel door and inched his way along the cold, damp passageway.

As Nelan edged along the tunnel lit by the light of a single flickering candle, he gave thanks to the Catholics. He'd found one end of the tunnel, but what he didn't know was where it ended. Perhaps it didn't have an end. Or went nowhere, like his life. Here he was, with the candle burning down to the wick, pale shadows on the wall, lost in a tunnel beneath a church in a prison. Even a small man like him struggled within its narrow confines. What was this place… a birthing canal?

He stopped. He had to. There was no way forward and he couldn't go back. He'd reached an impasse. To add to his dilemma, the candle was flickering. Oh. Wait. There was a light breeze. He reached up. There, he could feel it coming down a shaft. A way out… He almost fainted with relief.

He pushed the board that held the roof in place, and it gave way. He hauled himself up the vertical shaft, moving like a stick insect, legs and back against opposite sides of the shaft. It couldn't be much further.

Sweat pouring from his forehead, he reached the trapdoor, steadied himself, and then pushed it open. He crooked an ear, but there were no sounds from the other side. Where had he ended up? Was he still inside the prison? An escapee who escaped to inside the prison! The inmates would ridicule him.

He pushed open the trapdoor, hauled himself up and sat on the lip. As his eyes adjusted to the light, he took in his surroundings. A bench full of hammers and chisels, punches and pincers. Piles of logs. A leather hat and apron, gloves and boots. A floor sprinkled with metal fragments, shards of wood and charcoal dust. Oh! And in every crevice, the lingering smell of embers. Where else would a Fyremaster end up than in a forge?

For once, that strumpet fortune smiled on him. Because it was a Sunday, the forge was closed for business. As a disguise, he borrowed the smith's hat and covered his bandaged forehead, then strolled out of the side gate. The streets of Plymouth were not what he had expected on a typical Sunday morn. Rushing past him were men and women, shouting and pointing towards the summit.

"Fire!" they shouted.

"Where?"

"In the prison, lad!"

He grimaced. What else could he do or say? The enclosed yard surrounding the church would act as a firewall, so their houses would be safe, but he couldn't tell them that.

As he headed towards the harbourside, he enjoyed the brisk, uplifting smell of the salt air. He'd requite the wrongs perpetrated against his life, his family and his adopted country. He remembered an odd phrase that Walsingham had said to him before they left the Queen's Treasury building. At the time, he thought nothing of it. Now, after all that had happened, it held a different meaning. For the moment, he was too busy to think any more about it, and rushed towards the stables on the quay.

Carracks, boats and small vessels of every description sailed into the harbour, loaded up with shot, cannon, powder, ship's biscuits, barrels of ale, more barrels of ale, anything they could lay their hands on. There they stayed, moored to the quay, presumably waiting for the paymaster general to settle their bill before heading out on the tide.

Although the main body of the fleet had sailed, many support and supply vessels remained. The quay burst with mayhem. Stevedores unloaded barrels, marine equipment and foodstuff onto the quay. From outside the stables, he heard the shouts of alarm from within. He burst through the doors. Two men wrestled with a third; a tall, burly man with a whistle around his neck. Oh. My. Lord. John Brewer. The other two men were Roger Adden and Big Bart.

Nelan piled into the melee, grabbed Brewer by the ankles, and cut him down. Like a Titan felled by the gods of yore, the casket thief tumbled to the ground. Adden and Big Bart turned him on his face and tied his hands behind his back.

"Got 'im at last. Brewer's brewed for good!" Big Bart crowed.

"There, we have him, Adden!" Nelan cried, brushing himself down.

"With your help, Little Nelan!" Adden chimed. "Last I heard a' you, you was in the clink."

"You knew where I was and didn't think to come and rescue me, Master Adden?"

"Bah! I would have, wouldn't I? But me wanted to nab the casket thief first before I come to get you. That way, Drake would see you was innocent of the theft."

"That the best you can do?" Nelan muttered.

"Yeah, it's true. That Mistress Ready, she diverted me, don't you know it? That mornin', I was dippin' me spoon in her gravy. By the Lord, she girded me nether regions. Dunno whether it was 'er delicious smell or what, but they stood to attention for 'er at every opportunity."

"God's teeth, Roger Adden!" Nelan snarled. "You risked the future of the Island of Angels because you couldn't keep your codpiece in place!"

Adden gave a guilty shrug.

"Tell me, what happened on the morning of the robbery? Did you see the wagon and the dead guards?"

"I did, lad, an' terrible it was. When I gets there, I'm findin' a constable an' a watchman tryin' to find out who killed the soldiers, and where the casket had got to. You weren't there, and neither was John Brewer. Where'd you go?"

"Some kind folk helped me," Nelan said. "Talking of kind people, I see, Big Bart, that you remain in the land of the living. I feared you'd taken one of John Brewer's bullets."

"Yeah, I took a bullet, sirrah," Big Bart growled. "But it takes more than a flesh wound to fell Big Bart."

"What are you doing 'ere anyways?" Adden asked.

"I might ask you two the same question," Nelan replied.

"For nearly two days, me an' Big Bart scoured Plymouth for Brewer an' his gang," Adden said. "This mornin', we come to the stables 'ere on the wharf for some fresh 'orses, and who do we see, but the man hisself. We follows him into the stable, and there was the wagon, ready an' waitin' like a good'un. How about you?"

"Ah! Do you know that Walsingham only told us half the story?"

"What d'you mean?"

"I mean, John Brewer took a big risk to come to the quay stables, so why did he do it?"

"Nah, I ain't asked him that yet."

"I'll tell you. It's because the casket he stole was worthless. Isn't that right?" Nelan asked him.

"You bet, lad. It was full of iron weights," Brewer hissed. "I's furious."

"Ha! That God's truth! Damn you, Brewer. All those dead pikemen for nothin'," Adden scoffed.

"Yes!" Nelan said. "John Brewer, you worked out that the other casket, the real one with the silver shillings in it, must be hidden somewhere on the wagon."

Brewer frowned and nodded.

"By the Lord," Adden crowed. "You're sayin' there was no theft? An' the Queen's shillings are still in our possession?"

Nelan smiled.

"Then where?" Adden asked.

"I'll show you," Nelan replied.

"An' how did you know?"

"Before we departed from the Treasury, Secretary Walsingham said something odd."

"What was that?"

"He said, 'I want you to guard *this wagon* with your life.' You would have thought he would have said, 'guard *the casket*', but no, he said 'guard *the wagon*'. He hadn't told me there were two caskets."

"He hadn't told me neither, lad. This is all new to me," Adden said.

"Then let's find the real casket," Nelan said.

"Where is it?"

"I have an inkling," Nelan said, and, using his diminutive stature, crept beneath the wagon, and in the darkness, felt the wooden boarding until… "Yes, here it is," he murmured, and crawled out from underneath, pushing the casket.

"Let's see," Adden said.

Nelan opened the casket. There they were, sunlight glinting on a hoard of newly minted silver shillings.

Adden shook his hand. Big Bart slapped him on the back. Brewer looked disconsolate.

"Now what?" Adden said.

"We deliver it ourselves," Nelan said.

"Thing is, lad, we was to give it to Admiral Howard," Adden said, "but he's off chasin' the Dons."

"Then we'll take it directly to the paymaster general. When we do that, he'll give us a clemency document, confirming the delivery of the casket and all its contents, with not a shilling missing. Now, do you know where he is?"

"I 'eard he's in Torbay, down the coast a while from 'ere."

"We can go, but what about John Brewer?"

"Big Bart can look after him," Adden said. "Take 'im to the constables, will you?"

"It'll be my pleasure," Big Bart said with a big smile.

"So Gawd 'elp me, let's find a sail to Torbay. Comin'?" Adden asked.

"You bet!"

They searched up and down the wharf, but boat after boat was fully occupied victualling the fleet. Then, out of the corner of his eye, Nelan caught sight of a man he recognised strolling up the quayside, shoulders rolling with the waves. It was Robert, who'd given him a ride into Plymouth.

"Nipper Nelan! By the Lord, fancy runnin' into you. What you doin' 'ere?" Robert asked, shaking his hand. Nelan had to pull it away before the man wrenched his arm out of its socket.

"Know where we can get a sail to Torbay?"

"Well, the Lord's a shinin' on ya today," Robert said, his eyes bright with a simple joy, and his giant hands lifting the air around him. "'T'other day, we got taken by those Papist devils. Our nets got torn 'n' ripped, so we sent 'em to Torbay for stitchin' an' repair. Going there to pick 'em up right now, as it 'appens. The admiral wants fish for them sailors, y'know. We're fishin' for the fleet," he muttered. They followed him down the steps to a dinghy moored at the wharf, and rowed out to a small coastal fishing vessel.

As they tacked out on the flowing tide, Nelan asked, "Tell us about the Spaniards. How were you taken by them?"

Robert spat on the deck and ground his heel into the spittle. "That's what I thinks a' the Dons."

"When did they take you?"

"Couple a' days ago. Fish Friday, it was," Robert said. "We's fishin' for mackerel, pollack an' a bit a' plaice, off Bryher Isle near the Scillies. Then this pinnacle races over to us fast as a sou'wester. Thought she were one of ours. But when she closes on us, we sees she's one a' the Dons. We fought 'em orf with our knives an' our fists, but they done us with their swords an' their muskets."

"What happened next?"

"Their commander, he comes aboard. Clever fella spoke our lingo. 'Is name was Gil, like in the fish."

"Juan Gil," the captain piped up.

"Yeah, by the Lord, that was 'is name. They bound us tight as a sailor's knot," he added, rubbing his wrists. "Took us to their flagship. Me, I reckons the boat was bigger than the bloomin' Ark, a wooden fortress with masts 'n' sails aplenty. Huge castled tower at one end. Oh, an' more soldiers than trees in Plymbridge Woods."

"I warrant they wanted to know about our fleet."

"You got it! And we told 'em. Our fleet be moored in Plymouth Sound, an' be waitin' on the tide. Then I warned 'em, once the tide turned, *El Draque* would be a' coming for 'em. That struck the fear a' th'Almighty in 'em, it did that."

"Then what?"

"You can see that for yourself, can't ya? They give us back our fishin' boat," Robert said, spiky as ever.

Then a cry came from the barrel man. "Fish ho!"

A school of dolphins cavorted in the distance, so smooth and lithe in their movements, so at home in their element, so marvellous in their shared joy.

"Don't see 'em that often," Robert said. "Them dolphins be a good omen."

Nelan watched them swim in and out of their wake. The most adventurous darted in front of their bow and almost collided with them. The dolphin swam backwards then let out a shrill cry, as if celebrating the daring near-miss. The school followed their boat, delighting them and each other with their exuberance, then departed to play amongst the currents and cats' paws along the coast.

Later in the afternoon, a huge plume of black smoke appeared on the seaward horizon to the east.

"It be the Dons," Robert insisted. "They takin' a whuppin', I can feel it in me bones."

"Or could be one of our ships?" Adden suggested.

"Nah," Robert said. "That be a traitor's talk. You wanna see 'em win us?"

That shut Adden up, and they sat in silence, listening to the sails flapping in the wind. High above them, the seagulls squawked, witnesses on high to their voyage along the coast.

Torbay harbour was choked with vessels of all shapes and sizes ready and waiting to supply the English fleet. The merchants wanted their money, and as soon as he and Adden found the paymaster general, they'd get it. Suspended around them like a gentle pall, a crescent moon rose in the evening sky. Amidst the mayhem, they failed to find a spare room at the Fisherman's Inn or the Crown and Anchor.

As they bedded down on a bed of straw in a large barn, Nelan asked, "And the paymaster general?"

"We'll find 'im on the morrow," Adden said.

"Can't wait too long. Those supply ships need to victual the fleet before it's too late. Then, once we've handed over the silver and got the reprieve, I'm heading there myself. This battle is the culmination of a war between two great powers; one young, mobile and fledgling; the other huge, powerful and established. We may be the underdog, but we are brave, and God is on our side!"

"Amen to that," Adden said, pressing his hands together in prayer.

While asleep, Nelan had a disturbing dream of a man; tall, slim and gaunt of face. It was the ghost of his father, Laurens Michaels. In the dream, the tolling of the church bells called the congregation to prayer. Laurens walked up the church steps, through the large wooden door, and knelt in the lady chapel. His father prayed before a statue of Madonna in her pale blue and white robes.

A woman entered the church and knelt next to Laurens. She wore a black lace mourning headscarf. Although it hid her face, Nelan recognised her smell. He knew it as a child. It embraced him. It was sumptuous. She was Agnes, his mother. Memories of his early childhood flooded back, when they lived in the hamlet of Sangatte, just south of Calais, in the Picardy region of France. After that, they had moved to Leiden in the Netherlands, where the occupying Spanish forces had arrested and burnt her at the stake. His father had promptly fled with him to England. That was twenty years ago.

Now he faced the demons that had haunted him ever since that awful incident, when, as a child, he watched his mother burn at the stake. How could he forget it or deal with it? He couldn't. It would always be with him, as she would be. But, from this day, he resolved to leave the horror, and only take forward the good memories.

Agnes's veil concealed the disfigurement she'd endured at the hands of the Spanish when they burned her during the Council of Blood. It was bloody, and it seared the memory of that horrific event into his mind.

In the dream, his mother delved into her pocket. Something dropped out of it and onto the floor.

Laurens asked, "Have you got them?"

Agnes bent down and moved her hand around on the floor as if she was blind and only had the sense of touch.

"No, I can't find them," Agnes said.

"Are they lost?"

"Nelan will help us."

"Nelan, find the rosary," Laurens said.

Agnes picked up what she'd dropped on the floor and handed it to Laurens. It was a string of beads. A Holy rosary. That struck him as extremely odd. Because the Protestant faith forbade the rosary. Which meant the church was Catholic. Yet his parents were Protestant. The dream confused him.

Tears in his eyes, his father took the rosary and fingered the beads, each one a prompt to say a prayer. He mouthed an Our Father, then the first set of ten Hail Marys.

He awoke mouthing his father's words: "Nelan, find the rosary."

Flames of guilt scorched his heart. He felt like he had betrayed his parents' memory. What was he doing dreaming of a Catholic church, and what were his parents doing in one? He hadn't thought about his mother since she had appeared to him in a vision. He had no grave on which to lay a wreath for her. Her astral remains were dispersed across the spirit worlds.

Find the rosary… how could he do that?

22

Our Lady of the Rosary

1st August 1588

They found the paymaster general in the Queen's Arms.

"We're here to deliver the monies from the Secretary Walsingham," Nelan said to him.

"About bloody time!" he muttered, with more than a touch of aristocratic arrogance. "Just when the merchants were going to cancel the contracts and sail off with their supply ships, here you are! Good, then show me to the wagon. Where is it?"

"Housed in the stables in Plymouth," Nelan said.

"Oh. My Lord! That's where the monies are."

"What do you mean?" Nelan asked.

"A rider delivered a note from Walsingham," the paymaster said, "telling me where to find the real casket."

"I know," Nelan said. "We found it in a secret compartment in the bottom of the wagon."

"You weren't supposed to know where it was," the paymaster said.

"The lad's got special gifts," Adden said, slapping Nelan on the back.

"Either way, these monies will replenish the fleet."

The old soak signed their reprieves with a flourish. Released from all repercussions, Nelan tucked his in his purse and heaved a sigh of relief.

"I must find a carrack to take me to the fleet," he said. "You coming?"

Adden shook his head. "Nah, not me. I'm headin' back ta Plymouth

Sound. We snared John Brewer, but we got to get the rest of his gang, especially a certain lady who led me astray. She was part of it, too. This was my mess, so I got to clean it up, ain't I?"

"The Lord be with you," Nelan said.

"And with you," Adden said, shook his hand and sidled off along the wharf.

Nelan raced along the quay. By late afternoon, with the tide on the flood, he still hadn't found one.

"Ship ho!" the harbour watch shouted, and pointed out to sea at a vessel on the horizon.

"Ours or theirs?" Nelan shouted up to him.

"Can't see no flag," came the response.

The usual hubbub on the quay softened to an anxious expectant hush. Even the stevedores stopped and gawped. Men scrambled to crew the seaward defences. They prepared the cannon guarding the harbour entrance for firing. Barrels were rolled into place to make crude barricades. They drew sword and dagger. They grabbed a pitchfork or spade. The wind blew lightly, and the ship took an age to arrive on the tide. Whichever side it was on, it headed towards Torbay harbour. The unusual heat of the afternoon fanned worries of a Spanish invasion.

The Mayor of Torbay paced the wharf. Nelan marched alongside him, sword in his sheath and revenge in his heart. The harbour watch peered over the sapphire blue seas.

"Can you see her flags?" Nelan asked.

"Yup! It be hoisted high on the foresail… it's… the royal arms… of Elizabeth," he cried.

Everyone heaved a sigh of relief. Even the seagulls stood down from screeching over the harbour wall.

"But wait," the harbour watch said. "There be something odd about it. The mainsail's too large for one of ours."

As the ship approached the harbour entrance, he saw it had another behind it. The towed vessel was a galleon, a towering Spanish warship. The populace raised a cry of relief mixed with excitement.

"First blood to Her Majesty!" Nelan cried.

The two vessels were piloted into calm waters and dropped anchor in the harbour.

"Ours is the *Roebuck*," the harbour watch announced.

"And the other?"

"Dunno, name's in Spanish."

A dinghy launched from the *Roebuck*. Roars of patriotic fervour greeted every pull of the oars. She moored by the harbour steps and up strode two officers from the English vessel. The mayor stepped forward to greet them.

"Captain Whiddon at your service," one said. "And this is my first lieutenant, Simons."

"Welcome to you both," the mayor said. "Captain, can you tell me how the battle fares? Are we in danger of invasion?"

"No, not at present," Whiddon said, taking the mayor to one side and lowering his voice. "The fleets are equally matched. The Spanish keep to their defensive eagle-winged formation. Our ships are smaller, faster and equipped with better cannon. If the Spanish maintain that tight line, we can't engage them. Our orders are to shadow them and pick off their stragglers."

"What happened to the Spanish galleon you have in tow?" the mayor asked.

"It's the flagship of the squadron commanded by Don Pedro de Valdes. Last night, it exploded and collided with the *San Salvador*. The admiral of the Armada, the Duke of Medina Sidonia, abandoned both ships to their fate. Early this morning, Drake found the wrecks floundering in the Channel. He instructed me to leave the *San Salvador* and tow the other ship here to Torbay."

"Thank you, Captain," the mayor said. "How can the good people of Torbay be of service?"

"My orders," Whiddon said, "are to load any cargo of value from the Spanish vessel onto the *Roebuck*, and return to the fleet on the next tide. While in port, I have a job for someone who can speak Spanish."

"I can do that, Captain," Nelan said, stepping forward.

"And you are?"

"Nelan Michaels."

"I recognise you from the Hoe," Whiddon said. "Admiral Drake ordered your arrest. What happened? How did you come to be here? Did you escape?"

"The arrest was a terrible misunderstanding. To prove it, I've a written reprieve from the paymaster general."

Whiddon read it through, and said, "Yes, it's in order. And you speak Spanish?"

"I do, Captain."

"Good. I need you to interrogate the skeleton crew the Spanish left aboard their vessel."

"I'd be glad to help. And, Captain, I'm desperate to join the fight. I'm an experienced ordinary seaman. When the *Roebuck* returns to the fleet, can I join your crew?"

"We need every man jack," Whiddon replied.

"Thank you, Captain."

"Good," Whiddon replied. "Let's get to it."

The Mayor of Torbay took Captain Whiddon to one side, leaving Nelan stood beside First Lieutenant Simons.

"When you sailed with the fleet, did you see the *Golden Hind*?" Nelan asked.

"I did that," Simons replied.

"There's a dangerous man aboard, a Spanish spy. His name is Pedro de Antón. If I can't do it, can you inform Captain Fleming?"

"I'll see to it, lad," Simons said. "Don't ya worry no more 'bout it."

As the mayor addressed the crowd, Captain Whiddon joined Nelan and Simons.

"I'm curious, Captain," Nelan said. "What's the name of the captured Spanish galleon?"

"*Nuestra Señora del Rosario*. But you know what that means."

"I do. It means *Our Lady of the Rosary*."

Ah! He'd found the meaning of the rosary in his dream; his mother and father pointed him to the *del Rosario*. Over years of travelling the astral realms, and of wearing the shoes that never wore out, he'd learned that dreams resembled an onion, full of layers, their meaning hidden at first but unravelling later. What other secrets could he discover aboard the *del Rosario*?

Nelan had goosebumps as he trod the main deck of the Spanish vessel. This was enemy territory. The stench hit him first; it was a sweet, thick odour of burnt gunpowder, grape juice, blood and rotting corpses. The deck was a contusion of broken equipment, scores of discarded muskets and harquebuses. The main mast had split in two, its sails tangled and flapped like a pall laid across a corpse. Spanish ships also served as troop carriers, and dead soldiers and horses lay strewn across the deck. This was less a ship, more a floating cemetery.

"Show us around your vessel," Whiddon asked the Spanish officer. Bartolome Gomez had blackened teeth, a torn uniform and an angry look in his eye.

Gomez growled and folded his arms.

"You'll do as the capt'n asks," Simons replied, digging a sword into his ribs.

Nelan, Whiddon and Simons followed a reluctant Gomez and his adjutant as they picked their way over scarred planks of wood, and stepped over cadavers, as well as shrouds, sails and rigging. Disturbed from their scavenging, a flock of gulls flew off in a huff, circled the boat and found another section higher on the castle with more carrion on which to feast. Whiddon ordered the remaining crew of the *del Rosario*, some of them wounded, to be rowed ashore and placed under armed guard in a barn. Other than the creaking joists and the squawking of the birds, a ghostly silence cloaked the imposing vessel.

Near the high castle at the stern, Nelan stepped around a dead sailor, who in his hand grasped a piece of crumpled fabric. It was stained black with powder and speckled red with blood. He wrenched it from the man's hand.

"What's that you've got there, Nelan?" Whiddon wanted to know.

"A flag, Captain."

"It's much more than that." Gomez snatched it from him and unfurled the bloodstained flag. "It's the emblem of the Great Armada. Here's the figure of Christ on the cross, and on the other side, Our Holy Mother Mary."

"We can see that," Whiddon said with an air of tired impatience.

"Then you can see this too," Gomez added, and read the motto at the base of the flag:

Exurge Domina et Vindica Causam Tuam.

"Arise, O Lord, and vindicate thy cause." Nelan added the translation.

"This is our *casus belli*," Gomez went on. "We sail in these waters to do God's work. The English wander the hills like lost sheep. We come as good shepherds to return them to the Catholic fold. Our cause is holy, our flags are blessed. The Armada will be victorious. As it is written in Heaven, so it will come to pass on earth."

"Bah! Papist nonsense," Whiddon said. "We will wrestle back the true faith from the appalling state into which the Pope has taken it."

Whiddon snatched the emblem from Gomez, rolled it into a ball, and threw it with disdain over the side.

"You will regret this," Gomez hissed. Encouraged by Simons's liberal use of the sword, Gomez took them towards the ship's stern.

"*Capitán* Gomez, where are you taking us?" Nelan asked him.

"You will see," he scowled. Nelan had encountered this arrogance in their officers before. The Dons believed they occupied a higher moral plane than lesser mortals, entitling them to special dispensation.

"You will show us all of this ship," Whiddon insisted.

"*Sí, Capitán*," came the bland reply.

Gomez adjusted his ruff, smoothed his silken doublet, stuck his chin in the air, and followed his adjutant, who held the lantern and led the small party down the steps of the ladder.

"Here are the commander's quarters," Gomez announced, as he ushered them into what was once a sumptuously decorated cabin. The mahogany table was tipped on its side and had spilled the silverware, maps, scrolls, quills, inkwells, goblets and plates all over the carpeted floor. Rich wall tapestries hung off the walls and were torn and scarred with smoke.

Gomez and his adjutant showed them the gun decks, the magazine, the officers' mess, and the cargo holds. Despite the damage caused by the collision and the subsequent blast, Nelan spotted some intact cannon, cannonballs, a variety of weapons including a stock of arquebuses and muskets, soldiers' body armour, as well as barrels of ship's biscuits, sails, marine tools and carpentry equipment. Several holds contained barrels of red wine.

"The deckhands'll love it," Simons chimed. "It'll make a change from drinkin' ale for breaking the fast, lunch, an' supper."

A chicken ran past them, squawking and clucking.

"What! A live chicken! They've enough supplies to sail around the world without docking in port," Nelan said. Whiddon nodded, his expression a mix of admiration and disappointment.

"And the bilges, please, *Capitán* Gomez," Whiddon said.

"*Sí*, if you insist," Gomez replied, and duly showed them to him, even though they could smell them well before they got there.

"Well, that's it. No more to show you," Gomez said. "I'm sure the power and grandeur of the *del Rosario* has impressed you."

From the dream about the rosary, Nelan had a nagging feeling that they had yet something to discover. But he didn't know what.

"We have, *Capitán*, thank you," Whiddon said.

They snaked their way back past the cargo hold and walked along a long corridor. As they neared the end, another brown rat scurried past them. They'd seen and heard so many of them scuttling around in the dark places that they'd grown accustomed to the furry intruders. Heading towards the ladder to the quarterdeck, Nelan strolled past a gap in the wall, and then, as if something tapped him on the shoulder just like it had done with the plough head, he stopped and doubled back. The corridor was swathed in shadows. Gomez' adjutant, the lantern holder, had walked on, the light flickering towards the far end of the corridor. Standing next to the gap, Nelan felt a draught of soft air on his face.

"Wait," he called. "Come back."

Simons turned to come to him, but Gomez laid his palm on his chest, saying; "No! No more to see. We must go. I wish to visit my crew."

"Captain Whiddon," Nelan said. "Please, there's something here."

"Give me the lantern," Whiddon said, snatching it from the adjutant. "Nelan, what is it?"

"Put the lantern here, that's it," Nelan said. "Now, look at that. There's a draught. See how the flame is flickering? There's something behind this facade."

"So there is," Whiddon said.

Nelan ran his finger along the gap as Whiddon moved the lantern up and down the false wall, trying to establish the extent of the door. It was not so much a door, more a flap in the lower part of the wall, and barely visible to the naked eye.

"What's behind this opening?" Nelan asked.

Gomez declined to reply.

"I warrant it's part of the King of Spain's treasure," Whiddon quipped, rubbing his hands with glee.

The flap was so small that only Nelan could fit through it. He pushed his shoulder against it until it gave way and he tumbled into the darkness. The hold had no light or sound. Just stillness and a pervasive smell of damp. Whiddon handed him the lantern through the open flap.

Nelan lifted the lantern.

He'd witnessed his mother's burning at the stake in Leiden. He'd seen terrible things in Marshalsea prison. Sailing around the world, he'd witnessed the beheading of a traitor. But what confronted him in that compartment made him gasp. He stood in the corner of a vast hold, with bulkheads on either side. It was full of hundreds of bundles of sticks tied together and laid one on top of the other in long, high, neat rows. The wood, a mix of red and white oak, was of different lengths, shapes and sizes. He guessed they were offcuts from the construction of the Armada. He edged down the rows before coming to the next load. Every hold was the same: stacks of bundles of sticks, tens of thousands of them.

A premonition informed him of their purpose.

How could any normal person believe that this was acceptable? This was a betrayal of humanity. A betrayal of everything decent and godly. His parents had pressed him in the dream to find the rosary. He thanked his parents, grabbed a bundle, and crawled back through the flap.

"What's in the hold?" Whiddon asked, his voice shot with impatience.

Nelan brandished it, and said, "There are half a dozen holds, each one packed with thousands of these."

Whiddon puffed out his cheeks and shook his head in despair.

"There's also kindling, twigs and branches, irons and flints, as well as other fire-lighting equipment," Nelan added, waving the twigs in front of the Spaniard's face. "The intent is as clear as day; to bring Hell to Protestants and to send them to Hell."

"*Capitán*," Whiddon asked, "how on God's earth do you explain these bundles?"

Gomez' face was a mix of fury and righteous indignation. It was as if someone had desecrated the grave of the man's father. "These are all blessed by the holy powers of the Inquisition! So, ours is a just cause."

"In what world is it a just cause to burn our sons and daughters, and for our mothers and fathers to endure a painful and horrific death?" Nelan was apoplectic.

"You are wrong," Gomez replied. "We come to save your souls. The burning of the heretics cleanses the land of pollution and purifies the church so that we true Catholics can hear the voice of God in our hearts."

"Yes," Nelan said, spitting out the word. "You Roman Catholics want to destroy anyone whose faith is even tinged with Protestantism."

"What are you talking about?"

"When we die of natural causes, our spirit gathers all its parts unto itself, so that it is whole again, because only then can it rise up and return from whence it came – to the source of its arising in Heaven. But if we die under torture or extreme agony, like being burnt at the stake, it prevents the spirit from gathering itself unto itself, and stops it returning."

"This, I don't know."

"Oh, yes you do." Nelan was angry. "You know exactly what death by burning achieves. Your Inquisition has honed this method of execution to a fine art. These bundles of sticks are a grisly means to a horrific end. You are not only people murderers; you are spirit murderers. The Armada is not just an enterprise to invade England. It's a barbaric attempt to rid the world of the Protestant scourge."

"You are heretics. How can you say this?"

"We all want to hear the voice of God, but this is evil," Nelan shouted in the man's face. "You're evil for acting in this heinous way and defending this intended atrocity."

Gomez made no conciliatory remark or gesture. He stood there, defiant, determined and shrouded in delusion.

While Nelan pitied the Spaniard, at the same time he realised something about himself. Gomez believed that the fires of the Inquisition could purify the soul of the Church. The fires could only achieve the exact opposite and taint the very thing Gomez wanted to cleanse.

King Philip's motto of *Non Sufficit Orbis*, meaning The World is Not Enough, was apposite in the extreme. The Spanish had sacrificed at the altar of that motto once too often. They suffered the unfortunate consequences of an empire that had expanded too quickly and harvested the fruits of other nations, but had paid insufficient attention to their own natural progression. As a result, the nation had lost its moral compass when dealing with other peoples, races and religions. After all, in the eyes of God, all were of equal merit. Even Walsingham had warned in his pamphlet that 'The Spanish will burn you'.

They escorted Gomez and his adjutant to the barn in Torbay harbour, where the skeleton crew of the *del Rosario* were held. As the warden locked the barn door, Gomez mouthed a prayer, his fingers clutching a rosary.

23

The Coupling

2nd August 1588

To speed the cargo transfer, they lashed the two ships together. The *del Rosario* and the *Roebuck* made for a pair of unlikely lovers; Spain and England, the eagle and the lion, the established empire and the upstart rogue with imperial ambitions. Like the vessels, Nelan realised that the two countries were so different, yet so alike.

King Philip of Spain was a tough, hardy and down-to-earth Taurean. Elizabeth herself was the Virgin Queen, and a double Virgo to boot, meaning she had Virgo as a rising sign and her main astrological sign, doubling the power of the Virgoan influence in her life. How ironic that the King of Spain was known as Philip the Prudent, a quality cherished by Virgoans. The Queen of England was also as frugal as the lowliest peasant. The other irony was that Philip had emblazoned the figure of the Virgin, in his case, the Madonna, on the Armada flag.

Whiddon invited Nelan into his cabin to break the fast. "I wanted you to enjoy this moment with me," he said. "Here's a goblet of fine wine, straight from the hold of the *del Rosario*."

"My, and it's tasty too," Nelan purred. "The Spanish wine is a balm to the irritation that comes from dealing with their hubris."

"It is that," Whiddon said, before tucking into his eggs with his knife and spoon.

The crew transferred the cannon, powder, equipment and

foodstuffs from the *del Rosario* to the *Roebuck*. Whiddon recruited aid from the rough and ready Torbay locals. With every half hour rung on the church bells, more men and boys drifted into town from the surrounding farms and markets. Arriving aboard the *del Rosario*, the volunteers gaped in awe at the vastness of the castle, masts and decks of one of the enemy's flagships. They joined in the shanties and put their backs into the work like patriotic Englishmen.

Later that morning, Whiddon summoned the first lieutenant to his cabin. Simons seemed a dedicated navy man, whose distinguishing mark was the absence of a little finger on his right hand, lost in a bet.

"When can we raise anchor?" Whiddon asked.

"Not for a goodly while, Capt'n," Simons replied. "Transfer's takin' long. Them cannon makes for heavy liftin', an' we gotta be right careful with the gunpowder. An' there's a lot a' them wood bundles."

"Simons, leave the damn sticks. We don't have time to move them."

"Then, wit' God's will, we'll be raisin' anchor on the late afternoon tide."

"Good, get to it then."

"Aye, aye, Capt'n," Simons said, and left.

Nelan finished his wine and asked, "Do you know Sir Walter Raleigh?"

"I do. He's a fine man, a learned gentleman and an influential supporter of the stannaries and the West Country. He's at his home near here in Budleigh East. He sponsored the building of the *Ark Royal*, the Lord High Admiral Howard's flagship. And I hear you know Dr John Dee."

"Yes, Captain," Nelan said. "Some years ago, Dee was my tutor on a range of subjects, including astrology."

"Did he say anything about these times?"

"Dee predicted that a naval war between England and Spain would begin when Mars moved in conjunction with the moon. This has just come true."

"How does that work?"

"It's simple, Captain. Mars is warlike, while the moon is watery. Combine the two and you get the idea of warfare on water. Their conjunction occurred on the 22nd of July."

"On that day, the Armada raised anchor in Corunna harbour and set sail for these waters."

"So, that day marked the beginning of the campaign."

"Fascinating! Did he also predict the outcome of the war?"

"That's what we all want to know," Nelan said. "Although now he's somewhere in the Carpathian Mountains, I suspect he yet exerts an unseen influence on our affairs."

"I believe it to be true."

Early that afternoon, the watch yelled, "Ship ho! Ship ho!"

They raced on deck to see a ketch tacking towards them.

"It's one of ours," Whiddon said.

After it dropped anchor in the harbour, its captain rowed over to the *Roebuck*. He was an old sea dog by the name of Jeremiah Horsfield. With legs as bowed as the curvature of an apple, he waddled over to them and said, "Gonna need some 'elp 'ere, Capt'n. Got dead and wounded men aboard from the battle."

Without a moment's hesitation, Whiddon said, "Simons, stop the men moving the cargo. Get them to bring the dead and injured ashore."

Dinghy after dinghy, wherry after wherry, rowed out from the quay, and returned with brave men and boys. Some hung to life by a slender thread, while others had already joined the Almighty. Nelan watched this sad procession of vessels back and forth across the harbour. It stirred mixed emotions; pride in the fight the men had shown, but sadness that it had cost them a limb or even their life.

Captain Whiddon hung over the gunwale and asked, "How did this come to pass?"

Horsfield cleared his throat, spat on the deck, scrunched the spittle with the toe of his boot, and said in a croaky voice, "The Armada stood off Portland Bill. Drake led our boys in an' we attacked 'em, hard an' fast, like Admiral Howard ordered us. Me, I'm loath to admit it, but them Dons ain't made of smoke an' dough. Oh, no. Their big galleons fought us good 'n' proper. Then came their galleasses – that's them big boats with sail 'n' oars. A real fight, it was. Our lads took some 'eavy punishment, so we withdrew for fear of comin' too close to 'em. That's their strength. When they get near, they throw grappling hooks, an' send in their soldiers to board us. We stopped 'em doin' that."

Nelan nodded, smoothed the ruffles in his jerkin, and begged his leave.

"Where are you going?" Captain Whiddon asked.

"I have to see to those brave lads. A man who's prepared to give up his life for his country and his religion deserves my full respect."

"I like the sentiment, Nelan. I'll send my barber surgeon to help as well. It'll delay us a little, but it's worth it. We'll catch tomorrow's late morning tide," Captain Whiddon said.

"Thank you, Captain," Nelan said.

Nelan rowed over to the wharf. He grabbed one end of a stretcher and moved the wounded into the barn, now a makeshift hospital. Some of them were as young as seven or eight. The poor little sods were caught up in the maelstrom of a religious war they knew little about and understood even less. Nelan's heart broke to see their faces taut with pain, tears rolling down their ruddy cheeks.

The ship's barber surgeon attended them. His assistant was a boy not much older than a kid, who froze at the smell and sight of the blood and gore. So Nelan stepped into his shoes and assisted the barber surgeon by removing soiled and bloody clothing, cutting bandages and cleaning festering wounds.

Nelan offered solace to a powder monkey, a mariner who supplied the cannon crew on the gun deck with powder. Powder burns were an occupational hazard, but this boy's face had been blown off. His body was a torment of burns. All the barber surgeon could do was give him a sup of ale. But the lad could barely swallow his own spittle, let alone any ale.

The little fellow's screams resounded across Torbay. Thankfully, the end was nigh. As the sun set, his Maker called to him and he heeded the call. He gave out this pitiful cry for his mother, but she wasn't there. Nelan held his hand and watched the life drain from the boy's fearful eyes as his soul winged its way out of this world into the next.

As dusk fell, Nelan slumped into a corner. The day had sucked every emotion from him. A bundle of sticks sat in a cradle, spreading a meagre light across the barn. Shadows flitted across in front of it, moving from one patient to another, like wraiths between the seen world and the astral world and back again. Something had died in him after his gruelling experience with the powder monkey. Was it his compassion? Or his willingness to forgive? Or had his conscience wilted in the face of such cruel injustice?

He climbed onto a bed of hay and slumped onto his back, staring at the roof joists of the barn. He blinked, trying to get rid of the horror of those memories of the faces of those brave little boys. The solitary lantern with its orange-yellow flames sat across the other end of the barn. He scrunched up his eyes and saw the scene through blurred vision. The lantern glistened and seemed to send imaginary sparks around the barn. Exhausted from the ordeal, his breathing slowed. He'd witnessed enough suffering and death for one day.

He puffed out his cheeks and opened his eyes. The lantern had burnt out and a new one was needed. A watchman noticed it and crossed the barn carrying a wood bundle. The man removed the lantern and replaced it with the new bundle, one that Nelan thought looked familiar. It had the same fleshy white oak wood he'd seen in the hold of the *del Rosario*. Fascinated, he watched it catch light and burn, sending a gentle pall of silver-white light into the barn.

As he drifted off to sleep, he heard a voice emanating from the flames:

Don't leave me.
Keep me.

24

The Voice of the Flames

3rd August 1588

The next morning, Nelan got up with the phrase 'Don't leave me. Keep me' spinning in his head, because the voice that spoke it was the same one that had told him:

By the warm,
I'll be sworn.

It was the crackling voice of the salamander, the mysterious spirit of fire. It was a sign, and he knew what it meant. Now, he simply had to follow its guidance.

Difficult though it might be, he had to convince Whiddon at all costs. Before he could speak to the captain, another pinnace arrived carrying more wounded men and boys, some ambivalent news, as well as fresh demands for gunpowder. The destiny of a nation, and the empire Dr Dee predicted it would give birth to, hung on a mixture of burnt wood, sulphur and dung – the ingredients of gunpowder! Such were the vicissitudes of fate.

A dinghy from the pinnace drew up next to the dock. Nelan recognised Jonas's brother, Robert.

"I thought you went fishing," Nelan said.

"'Tis true, our Queen Bess needs fish, but today, m'lad, she needs Robert to put 'is shoulder to the sail on this 'ere pinnace."

"You're the salt of the earth and the sea!" Nelan chuckled at his own joke.

"If you says so, master," Robert said, his voice as hoarse as chains dragging on a dry road.

"Tell us, what of the Spanish ships?" Nelan asked.

"Our fleet blew 'em apart," Robert said, his hands as animated as his voice. "Gave them Dons a good beatin', we did. There was fumes an' the noise a' the cannon fire. There was cries a' pain an' death. Me was in the midst of the fierce heat a' battle!"

"Go on," Captain Whiddon said, as he joined them on the wharf.

"Soon after that, the gunfire stops," Robert said. "At first, we don't know why. Then a wiseacre says, 'Oh, powder's low.' Then the wind, the strumpet, she shifts, changes from sou-wester to nor-easter. That prevents us fightin' anymore, so we licks our wounds. But them Dons is sufferin' more than us. The Lord, He be on our side, the admiral says. That's what I believes too. The Lord'll see us through."

"We've powder for the fleet," Whiddon said. "And we're leaving on the next tide."

Nelan cleared his throat and said, "Captain, I'm afraid to say that we can't leave yet."

"What? No. We've got to raise anchor. Simons, get me a dinghy."

"Please, hear me out."

"No. We've waited for the tides. We've loaded the cargo of the *del Rosario* and yesterday we delayed to help the sick and wounded. I can't justify staying any longer. I've orders to follow."

Nelan bit his tongue in frustration. He had to persuade him to stay longer. In his guts, he had a strong inkling that the fate of the nation depended on it. It was that important.

Whiddon strode off towards the wharf.

Nelan called after him. "Yes, Captain, I know you must follow orders. When you anchored in Torbay, you told me the order of the day: prevent Spanish troops from landing on our soil. What I have to say can achieve that."

Whiddon reached the steps leading down to the dinghy. He turned to Nelan and said, "Why should I delay again?"

Nelan heaved a sigh of relief. By getting Whiddon to stop and listen, he'd won half the battle. He said, "Last night, the flames spoke to me again."

"What flames? When was that?"

"The first time I heard them, their words helped Walsingham identify and arrest a traitor of the realm, Sir Francis Throckmorton."

"That was you?"

"And this time, the voice of the flames had the same distinctive tone."

"What did they say?"

"Don't leave me. Keep me."

"What do you think they're telling you to do?"

"I heard the voice as I watched the flames light a bundle of sticks in the barn."

"You think... Wait... This is about those wood bundles?"

"Yes, we need to move them from the *del Rosario* to the *Roebuck*."

"I'm not loading those damned bundles onto my ship!" Whiddon threw his arms up in despair.

"That's exactly what we have to do."

"It's madness. They'll turn the *Roebuck* into a floating powder keg. What with the gunpowder an' all, it's too dangerous to load them. Besides, every cargo deck is full."

"It doesn't matter. I don't know why, but we'll need them to defeat the Spanish."

"Hah! They shipped them over here to burn us!"

"Captain, sometimes history happens in twisted, ironic ways. In the end, this will be stark justice. It's because we are a nation protected by a strong, enduring principle."

"What's that?" Whiddon said with a smirk.

"*Honi Soit Qui Mal Y Pense.*"

"What's the motto on the royal arms of England got to do with this?"

"Everything. You said it yourself. They planned to use those wood bundles to destroy our religion and our way of life. We must turn it back on them and use it to destroy them. That's the repulse. The motto – Evil be to he who thinks evil of me – describes the reflective action of a mirror. It says... Any evil you throw at me will rebound back to you. It returns in equal measure what was given. It requites, which is exactly what a lady should do."

"What lends it this power?"

"To succeed, we must be in harmony with the times, and with

the nature of the Island of Angels. We need the help of higher powers. *Honi Soit Qui Mal Y Pense* is not just the royal motto, it's the song of the angels of the island. It's their guarantee of protection. Trust that the higher entities will give us the knowledge, power and wisdom to conquer the Spanish."

Whiddon furrowed his brow and said, "How do you know you're right?"

"I had a dream that there was something to discover aboard the *del Rosario*. You trusted me then. I beg you, trust me now."

Whiddon shook his head. With a wry smile, he said, "I don't know why, but I agree. I'm disobeying orders. I could end up in Marshalsea."

"You won't. You'll be a hero, a saviour of England. Besides, if the voice of the flames is wrong, we'll both be for the fires of the Inquisition."

"Simons, load the bundles!"

"Aye aye, Capt'n!" Simons replied.

25

Bittersweet

4th August 1588

They had worked through the night to transport the wood bundles from the *del Rosario* and were greeted by a glorious morning. The sun had risen and shone brightly on the *Roebuck* as she finally headed out to join the English fleet. Nelan enjoyed the sight of the cats' paws and the glint of the sunlight on the heaving swell. The spray refreshed his face and tempered his fractious soul.

After the chaplain had delivered the morning service, they passed another ketch heading west, transporting the wounded to hospital and seeking supplies. From them, they learned that the two fleets shadowed one another off the coast of the Isle of Wight, a couple of days' sail to the east.

These good tidings calmed Nelan's anxiety about Pedro. He was sure Simons had got word to Fleming on the *Golden Hind*, who had dealt with the Spaniard accordingly. But Pedro was a catfish, an artful, wily opponent, so Nelan was taking nothing for granted.

Hugging the coast, the *Roebuck* ploughed through the familiar waters of the south coast of England. The crew hung over the port gunwale and waved at the throngs of people gathered on the clifftops, who shouted back at them, cheering wildly.

These folk were a little people with a large heart. Many had only a Christian name, a Thomas or a Bethany. If they had a surname, it marked a skill or a craft, such as carpenter or cooper. Mostly, during their brief lives, they never left the locale of their farmstead or village. They were as familiar with its dales and woods as they were with the lines on their palms. They knew the badgers' setts and the rabbits' warrens. They could trace the foxes' dens and where the sounders of wild hogs gathered in search of food. It was their pleasure to watch the glory of a murmuration of starlings and witness the herds of red deer graze in the meadows.

Once a week, these landsmen would hoof off to the local market for essential supplies, to catch up on the latest gossip and hear titbits about the Queen. Then in the town square, they'd mock some poor sod consigned to the stocks or enjoy the high-spirited antics of the visiting gleemen and troubadours.

Come evening tide, these folk would wander home on the old beaten track, serenaded by the song of the nightingale, the bells of evensong and the twinkling stars on a summer's night. On the way, they'd dance and sing to the rhythms of the land. They knew where to witness the sylphs dancing on the bluebell slopes, the special places the gnomes made prodigious leaps across the rocks, and the undines swam in the gurgling stream. These local nature spirits would hear their songs, and, in return, give them well-being, renew their love of the land and rekindle their instinctive belief in a higher purpose.

The Armada's arrival was a rude, unprecedented shock. A powerful enemy fleet drifting along the coast was unheard-of in their short lifetimes. The threat of invasion hung over them like the Sword of Damocles. None had forgotten the stinging words of Walsingham's pamphlet.

As dusk fell on that momentous day, the evening softened, and the noise quietened. The seagulls stopped squawking. A flock of swallows sought their roost for the night, as did the folks on the beaches and the hilltops.

Nelan glanced across to the valleys and the hills and saw, to his horror, fingers of scarlet rising inexorably from the land. Slowly, they gathered into clumps, and the clumps into clouds, until they coated the entire valley, like drops of moisture from a dense fog on long grass.

This was the real invader, the occult invader. It eschewed the sword and the dagger, the warship and the cannon. Instead, it used subtle persuasion to touch the deep, inner fabric of the mind. But the horror of it was that most folk were unaware of it! That was more than coaxing. This was inveiglement.

The swathes of murky scarlet force swirling around the valleys and dales of England were just that horror. The scarlet oppressed the silver in the same way that overbearing parents smothered a child's natural freedom of expression with excessive discipline. He'd hoped that the cleansing fires of the beacons and the thunderous clamour of the bells would disperse the scarlet pall, but they hadn't.

Dee had warned him, as had the Gyptians. He needed to understand the origins of the scarlet force. What made it settle here? It was anchored here, like a ship was anchored in a port. While a ship had a metal anchor, what tethered this scarlet force?

His mind recoiled. What if, even if they defeated the Spanish, the scarlet pall remained, bound to the hills and dales of England, dulling the people's love of discovery, adventure and pageantry? That would leave a poisonous legacy in and on the island, preventing the release of its angels, and smothering its future unfolding. On the one hand, there was such a supreme possibility to flower, but on the other, there was the danger the nation would never blossom into the greatness its potential warranted. Like a child striving to become an adult, these times were both exciting and bittersweet.

Under the soft glare of the waxing moon, Nelan passed the captain's cabin and noticed Whiddon tuck a sachet beneath his pillow. Sensing it was a private matter, Nelan said, "I'm sorry, Captain. I don't mean to pry."

"Please, I'll tell you what it is," Whiddon replied, and waved him inside the cabin.

Whiddon pulled out the sachet and said, "This contains dried leaves and berries. Once, I went to see a Gyptian Chovihano to find a cure for my melancholia. He said to put it under my pillow, and it would heal my sadness and protect me from the evil eye. And it helped."

"I've encountered the Gyptians too. They're a good folklore people but maltreated by the English."

Whiddon nodded. "That may be, Nelan, but not by me."

Nelan hesitated to ask what had caused the sadness in his friend's life. Was it the death of a loved one or an infant? Feeling awkward, he got up to leave, when Whiddon blurted out, "Beatrice, my beloved, left me at the altar."

"That's terrible."

"The worst of it was that she ran off with my brother."

"I'm so sorry," Nelan said.

Whiddon choked on his emotion. "It's painful for me even to think of it. I loved her, she was mine, and… I knew nothing of what they were doing behind my back! Listen, Nelan, you're the scholar. What does the name Beatrice mean?"

"It means 'bringer of happiness'."

"If ever there was an irony in a name."

The heavy silence was punctuated by the waves crashing against the bow sprint, the sails beating against the wind, and the call of the hours from the watch.

"What's the herb in the sachet?" Nelan asked.

"Woody nightingale; it's also called bittersweet."

"A herb for these times," Nelan murmured.

26

The Joy of Homecoming

5th August 1588

Rung as four pairs, the ringing of the eight bells signalled the end of the middle night watch. It was four of the clock. Drifting in and out of sleep, Nelan dreamed that he stood astride the quarterdeck. The wind and the cleansing spray of the surf brushed his face. He heard the joyous cries of a school of dolphins. The scene changed as a dark cloud appeared on the horizon. A shadow came towards him, drifting along as if pulled by an ebbing tide.

As the grey-white cloud approached, he realised it was a ghost. A branch grew out of the top of the spectre and protruded into the ether. It shifted shape and coalesced into a man's index finger. Then attached to it came a hand, a forearm, an elbow… a man's arm, with the hand and index finger pointing up towards the heavenly realm.

Like a distant echo, a voice spoke to him, saying, "*Ayudame, por favor.*"

"How do you want me to help you?" Nelan asked.

The voice sounded clearer, and said, "*Es este mi barco?*"

"No, this isn't your ship. This is the *Roebuck*."

"*Dónde está mi casa?*"

My Lord, the mariner wanted to know how to get home. Before Nelan could answer, the ghost drifted past the boat, following the prevailing currents in the astral.

Shivering with fear, Nelan awoke. The dream stuck in his gullet and he gasped for breath and dry retched. Nothing came up, leaving him with a ghastly taste. In the dream, he'd seen the lost soul of a dead Spanish mariner, vainly seeking his way home. But where was 'home' in the astral realm? He staggered up the ladder to the deck to greet the first stirrings of dawn, then paced the boards until he'd shaken off the deathly vision.

Busy like a bee, Whiddon stalked the wheelhouse, first seeing to the watch, calling to the barrel man, consulting the purser, berating the bosun, talking to the navigator, and then examining the soundings with an eagle eye. The *Roebuck* was coving, sailing from one cove to the next, standard practice when hugging the coast.

"Is that Beachy Head?" Nelan asked, pointing to the line of white cliffs.

"It's the first of the Seven Sisters," Whiddon said, "so named as there are seven great cliffs, each separated by a valley."

"Many years ago, I sailed past them and I remember they gave me goosebumps," Nelan said. "I love their enduring vitality, the stark whiteness of the chalk. They seem to hold the nature of Albion, the White Isle."

"They're like old friends, stalwarts, always there, never changing. You talk about the flames having a voice. Well, these cliffs sing to me."

"I know that feeling," Nelan mused.

Whiddon said, "One day, I will return to the island. For now, we've a battle to fight and a war to win."

"The island calls to you, beckoning you to come home."

"Long ago," Whiddon said, "an ancient folk lived on this isle. They loved and cherished it and understood its nature. The people lived on the land, and in their loving of it, they heard the songs of the angels, and they sang them to each other, and the angels of the island heard their songs, and grew and were fulfilled. These folk named it the Island of the Mighty. That's who and what we are; a mighty people living on a mighty isle."

"In those days of yore," Nelan said, "the Druids held sway and dressed in colours denoting their function. The Sacrificers were the soldiers and wore red. The Bards, the poets, the minstrels and the mummers wore blue. While the High Priests dressed in long, flowing white robes."

"There's more," Whiddon said. "Come, I want you to see something."

They went to the captain's cabin, where Whiddon showed him a book.

"This is one of Dr Dee's, and it's entitled, *General and Rare Memorials Pertaining to the Perfect Art of Navigation*. The figure on the frontispiece is the Ancient Roman goddess Britannia. With spear and shield, she's the warrior queen who rules these isles. Because when we are far away and fighting for our country, what gives us the courage to persevere is the sure knowledge that Britannia keeps the home fires burning."

As the evening drew in, Nelan sat by his hammock, and his thoughts turned to his home in Mortlake. In the soft light of a candle, he scribed a letter to his beloved:

My dearest Eleanor, my one and only.

I live for you, to see you, to be with you.

When I am by your side, you make me feel whole. The thought of you near me inspires me to do what I can to lift this country up to where it truly belongs in the world. I don't know exactly where that is, but I sense it has a long way to go.

I'm aboard the Roebuck under Captain Jacob Whiddon, sailing to join the fleet. Tomorrow, we'll dock at Dover to pick up supplies. Most of all, we need ale. By the Lord, mariners love the stuff so much, sometimes I wonder if they'd suffer the indignity of a Spanish invasion rather than endure a day without it.

When moored in the lee of the white cliffs, I'll come ashore and find a willing hand to whom I can entrust this letter, and get it delivered to you. After that, we head across the Channel to confront the Spanish fleet. The battle to come is more important than we can ever imagine. The world will hold its breath to see which side prevails. It will be us. Howard and Drake, the Queen and the mighty Island of Angels, must prevail.

Whatever happens in the impending battle, pray to God that I shall see you again.

I hope to stand on our threshold, open our door, look into your soft green eyes, lift you in my arms, and hold you tight. Your love has given me a purpose to live for.

I look forward to the joy of homecoming.

Your ever-faithful husband,

Nelan.

27

The Once and Future Times

6th August 1588

They passed more white cliffs along the coast, but soon sailed into a dirty brown film on the surface of the water. The nearer they got to Dover, the more it smelled of filth. At first, Nelan noticed planks of wood, broken oars and staves from the barrels of a ship.

"Have the Dons thrown all this overboard?" he asked.

"No, nothing's wasted. We're the same." Whiddon was emphatic. "They'd keep every bit of spare wood for the furnaces – or bind them in bundles. Let's see what else there is."

Nelan had grown accustomed to the pungent odours from the ship's bilges, but this was of a different order.

"The Armada numbers over one hundred and fifty vessels," Whiddon said. "Each of the turreted warships has a crew of mariners and officers, commanded by gentlemen aristocrats who are themselves waited upon by servants. Their slaves row the galleasses. The Armada is transporting thousands of infantry as well as the cattle to feed them. They also have cavalry and horses. Then there's our navy and the men on our ships. They all create effluent. You can imagine what happens when all these ships empty their bilges."

"Oh, Lord! I get the picture. I can smell it," Nelan said, holding his nose.

The *Roebuck* drifted through the middle of the tan-coloured slick. It was like sailing through a floating cesspool. Every man waved their hands in front of their noses to get rid of the stench.

"Look! Over there!" Whiddon pointed at more debris bobbing up and down amidst the brown coating on the surface.

"I can see planks of wood," Nelan said. "No, they're oars. And that's a broken rudder. And there's half a mizzen mast with the sail hanging off it."

Whiddon ordered a change of course to avoid a large section of a ship's hull. Then, with an air of triumph, he cried, "Our mariners have hit the target. This is the wreck of a Spanish galleass. Wait, look over there. See it?"

"I do. It looks like an arm," Nelan said. He'd seen this man before… it was the corpse of the ghost in his dream. The Spanish sailor had died and his ghost had escaped from his body into the great caverns of the astral. His corpse floated on his back, his arm sticking up in the air.

"His finger's pointing to Heaven," Whiddon said.

"Is that where he's gone?" Simons asked.

"Nah, he's a Papist," Whiddon said. "He's going to the other place."

"'Tis the first Don we've seen in the water," Simons said.

"Yes, the Spanish are more superstitious than we are," Whiddon added. "They'd never throw a corpse overboard."

"How did this seaman get there?" Nelan asked.

"Could be the gunpowder store on his vessel took a direct hit from our cannon fire," Whiddon said.

"Then we have to lend him our respect and give him his last rites, or the Commendation for the Dying, as we call it," Nelan said.

"Bah! He be Catholic," Simons said. "We got no business giving him a blessin'."

"They'd do it for one of ours," Nelan said.

"Would they? You anglin' for another delay, eh?" Simons asked.

"What are you implying?" Nelan said, rising to the challenge in Simons's voice.

"I'm sayin' you'd rather be sailin' than fightin'. What is it? You afraid of the Dons?"

Nelan grabbed Simons by the collar, and the two grappled like a couple of feral beasts.

"Break this up," Whiddon said, stepping between them. "We're here to vanquish the Spanish, not each other."

"So, we're sailing' on, Capt'n?" Simons growled.

"No, Simons, we're not," Whiddon said. "I know we need to get these supplies to the fleet, but this is a man's afterlife we're talking about here. It's sacred. It'll cost us an hour or two. Nelan's right, we must pay him all due respects. Simons, take a wherry and retrieve the mariner. Then fetch the chaplain and assemble the crew."

Simons slouched off to do the captain's bidding.

Despite the odious smell of the slick, and the dead sailor's Catholic heritage, the men hauled the corpse aboard. With all due solemnity, they wrapped it in a spare hammock and loaded it down with a cannonball at his head and two more at his feet. The chaplain recited the Commendation for the Dying, albeit Anglican, not Catholic. No one thought he'd mind.

As they dropped the corpse into the sea, the chaplain raised his hands above his head in supplication and said, "May his soul rest in peace. Into the arms of Our Lord, I commend the spirit of this unknown mariner."

"Amen," said the crew in unison, as the corpse sank into its watery grave.

With a prevailing wind, they made Dover harbour by nightfall where they were hailed and then boarded by a pair of English warships controlling ingress and egress. Howard, Drake and Hawkins were taking no chances. Scores of ships, from carracks to pinnaces, crammed into the harbour. They were all taking victuals on board, ready to supply the English fleet.

After the *Roebuck* had anchored, Whiddon addressed the men. "We need ale and fresh water. Get to it, and be back here to catch the early morning tide."

Nelan went ashore and strolled through the alleys, avoiding the dogs howling at the ripening moon. At the White Greyhound Inn, just off Union Street, he sat down to enjoy bread, eggs and potatoes, washed down with a tankard of ale. Amidst the comings and goings in the inn, two men exchanged blows until the burly innkeeper separated the assailants.

In another corner, men were talking.

"I saw every last one a' them," one fellow said.

"Where was ya, Charlie?"

"On the Castle, on Dover cliff, I was. Could see scores and scores a' them. Took them most a' the day to sail by. As many as sheaves of wheat in a field, they were. Seven mile across, they reckon. Strike me down if it wasn't like a giant eagle. Tooks ya breath away, it does, just lookin' at them, tackin' down our own English Channel. So close ya can reach out an' touch them. Gives me the jitters, it do."

"One good thing," another said, "they didn't stop over in Dover harbour."

"Good for them, ya means? We'd av' given 'em a good wuppin', we would," he added, downing his tankard in one, and wiping his long pointed beard with his sleeve.

"Where've they gone now?"

"Towards the French coast. Climb up to the top of the cliff, and up to the turrets a' the Castle, an' you'll see the glimmer a' the lights from their stern lanterns."

Sailors and victuallers, ne'er-do-wells and watchmen, cutpurses and mistresses, crowded into the inn drinking their ale, and talking of the final battle, and how its outcome hung in the balance. In this turning moment, they knew that life in England, as English men and women, would never be the same again.

Every man wore a steely look in the eye. They stood by Britannia, as she stood by them, making them strong in the one, and one in the strong. Together, they would defeat the Armada. What on earth made the Spanish believe they could sail along the southern coast of England, in sight of her gleaming white cliffs, unhindered? That they could suffocate the angels of the island? What impudence!

At first glance, these English folk were a noisy, drunken rabble. But looking closer, he noticed they'd stare right back at him with withering indifference. They regarded you with an unwavering eye, waiting to see if you glanced away or kept the gaze. Should you waver, they pounced. These were the lions of England, a pride of them in the royal coat of arms, eight in all. The lions of England roared, and they did so in Leo, the astrological time of the lion. The Island of Angels was in harmony with the celestial forces in the heavens.

A familiar voice thundered across the inn, jolting him out of his contemplation.

"Well I never, if it ain't Master Nelan Michaels."

"My, my, Master Roger Adden," he replied. "What brings you to Dover?"

"I might ask you the same thing," Adden said, squeezing through the crowd and plopping down on a stool next to him.

"I'm aboard the *Roebuck*. We've called in for supplies. Tell me, did you get the rest of Brewer's gang?"

"Yeah, they's all locked up in Plymouth jail," Adden said.

"Glad to hear it. And the young lady? You know which one."

Adden flushed with embarrassment and said, "Yeah. Took old Adden for a pretty ride, she did. She was neck 'n' crop wit' Brewer. But she's in the clink, too."

"Good. What are you doing here?"

"Came to talk to the searcher before ridin' back to Barn Elms tomorrow."

"When you get there, could you deliver this letter to my wife?"

"Of course, I be glad ta'. Gotta go now," Adden said, taking the letter and sliding it into his doublet. "I'll see she gets it."

With a twinkle in his eye, Adden shook his hand so hard it hurt and said, "Good luck tomorra', lad. Give them Dons a whuppin'. See you when you get back."

Nelan did not want to swap this moment for all the spices in the Orient. These were the times to live and die for.

Tomorrow, he would set right the wrongs of his past.

Tomorrow, he would confront his own demons and banish them forever.

And tomorrow, he would head into a battle for the Island of Angels and for the once and future times.

28

A Participant, not a Spectator

Midnight to 8pm on 7th August 1588

A ship is a ship is a ship; well, that was true enough. But a ship was so much more. It was a marketplace, an inn, a gambling den, a bilge and a floating hamlet. It was a farmyard for its chickens and goats; a storage barn for the cargo in its holds; a place to make friends and enemies; a keep for its treasures, spices and silks won on the Spanish Main; a place of execution for traitors and mutineers; a chapel of worship for the ship's chaplain to celebrate Mass; a haven to share memories and moments; a place to sound the eight bells and mark the end of a life; a galley for food preparation and the eating of meals; a place where the time was measured, like in a monastery, every half an hour; but it was also a school where the young learned about life and the sea, and, as they did, grew up into men; a place of refuge from the vicissitudes of life on land; a place of solace for those escaping an unrequited love; a dungeon for those pressed into reluctant service; a freedom for others to try on the shoes that never wore out, and explore the esoteric side of life at sea.

The *Roebuck* waited along with all the other ships tacking out of Dover harbour. The Island of Angels waited, too. That day, a Sunday, was a momentous day, when all good Englishmen girded their loins, fierce in the defence of the realm, and of its new Britannia, Queen Elizabeth.

One after another, the vessels sailed out of the harbour, witnessed by the noisy seagulls diving for their breakfast, and by the great silent white cliffs looming above and behind them, and the thousands of invisible villeins and yeomen of England. The vessels joined what looked like a never-ending column of supply ships, taking wood, ship's biscuits, rope and uniforms, as well as much-needed gunpowder, ale and fresh water.

So many boats were coming and going across the Channel's choppy waters that they merged into one gigantic vessel. Black and white gulls swooped down and perched on the hatches and on the *Roebuck's* main mast, only to be shooed away by the bosun's mates and the bugler. The barrel man in the crow's nest called out in alarm, pointing frantically to the treacherous Varne sandbank. Whiddon's pilot called the knots and navigated the waters with a master's ease. Simons looked on, arms folded, a deep frown on his gaunt face, and still only three fingers and a thumb on his right hand.

Halfway across the Channel, the waters grew murky and grey. The bugler trumpeted the alarm, calling for all hands on deck. It wasn't needed, because every hand was already leaning over the gunwale. Some hummed and whistled to themselves. Others stared across the waters. A few glanced up to see the distant French coast. But they all wanted to see the two fleets. And, more than that, to participate, and not spectate, in the most exciting moment of the age, to surf upon the crest of the wave of the spirit of the times.

There they were. With the *Roebuck* several miles offshore, Nelan had a perfect view: the Armada sat directly ahead, the English to the south-west of them.

The Duke of Medina Sidonia moored his grand fleet of warships, troop carriers and cargo transports off the low-lying coast, yet far enough out to sea to steer clear of the sandbanks. Anxious about the speed and mobility of the English, the Duke strung his vessels out like a long pearl necklace in the defensive eagle-winged formation. Flying the flag of the Virgin Madonna, the warships were built like towers, castles that floated in the air, they were so high, and whose masts pointed upwards like so many fingers jabbing into the heavens. If the world was not enough, perhaps the heavens would do.

What a sight! Nelan had gazed at the Armada off the Scillies, but that was in the astral. This was real. This was *magnifico*. Scores of ships and sail, masts and marines, guns and gunwales. It loomed ahead, sails furled, banners fluttering in the stiff breeze. To see it was a rare privilege, a moment he'd never forget.

Yet, he felt strangely at home in these waters and the distant sandy coast.

To avoid the Spanish scouting ships, Whiddon changed course and tacked towards the English fleet. With the wind gusting from the south-west, that anchorage yielded Howard and Drake the advantage of the wind, the vital weather gauge.

A carrack pulled up alongside the *Roebuck,* and an excited messenger brought news from the lord high admiral. He'd divided the fleet into squadrons; Admiral Howard led one in his flagship, the *Ark Royal.* Drake led another in the *Revenge,* Frobisher another in the *Triumph,* while Hawkins commanded a fourth in the *Victory.* Seymour and the Dutch, together in a fifth squadron, prevented the Armada from heading north up the Dutch coast to seek refuge in a large inland harbour such as Antwerp. The English had sprung a trap on the Great Armada.

The *Roebuck* squeezed through the lines of the English fleet; carracks and pinnaces at the back, warships and galleons facing the Spanish in the van. Slipping between the crowded lines of boats towards the *Ark Royal,* the crews shouted greetings and yelled banter at one another.

"Ahoy the *Roebuck!*" was a popular cry.

"Praise the Lord Howard!" was another.

"God save Queen Bess!" was a third.

This stirred the blood. But why *were* they fighting? Was it for religious freedom, for Queen Bess, or for yet another reason?

In days of yore, the Ancient Greeks went to war for an ideal and for beauty, for the honour of Helen of Troy and the injustice of her abduction. Today, it was different. Today's era sought freedom, and religious freedom in particular. The apex of all pursuits, religion was the highest, most superlative endeavour in the world, and therefore the most important freedom, not only for the individual but for the Creator, who planted the passion for truth in every living person.

Nelan fought for religious freedom not just for himself and his companions but for the freedom of the angels of the island of England to exercise themselves in the people freely, and without boundaries imposed by an outside influence or orthodoxy. He would have no shackles, no Papist fences, and nor would they.

They edged forward in the *Roebuck*. Through the myriad white sails and oaken bows of the English squadrons, he glimpsed gentle slopes of a coastline he knew so well.

Whiddon sent a wherry to request orders from Howard on the *Ark Royal*. While they waited for a reply, Nelan took in the sight. The *Roebuck* straddled the van of the fleet. The rest of the English ships spanned the area to the south-west of them as far as the white cliffs of the Cap Blanc-Nez – the White Nose Cape. Directly east of the *Roebuck* ran a long strand of sand that ran all the way to the port of Calais to the north-east where the Spanish had moored. The soft light shimmered on the chalk and the sand, which yielded its name, the Cote d'Opal – the Opal Coast. For him, this was a sight of wonder, a special place. Because nestling in the gap in the sand dunes was the hamlet of Sangatte.

After all these years of false accusations, prison cells, graves, a voyage around the world, a return to grace and favour and a marriage to his sweetheart, he'd returned to where it had all begun. What invisible forces had brought him back? The chains of fate or the chimes of destiny? He had come into the world in a small house set back from the beach. This was his second coming.

This wasn't the first time in his life that the unseen hand of fate had conjured an extraordinary coincidence. When traversing the globe, the *Golden Hind* sailed along the Pacific coast of Panama where they intercepted a Spanish treasure ship, the *Cacafuego*, only to discover that her captain was none other than St John of Southampton. Years before, this man had been Nelan's neighbour and stepfather to Guillermo and Pedro.

Pedro, now where was he? Nelan kept an eagle eye out for Fleming's *Golden Hind*. The crazy Spaniard trod its boards and wanted to wreak havoc with England's plans. It and he were nowhere to be seen. Nor was there any news from Simons about Pedro's activities.

Nelan wondered what purpose these bizarre second returns served. Were they echoes in the fabric of life that induced a person to go back to where they'd once been, to discover something anew at the scene of an important moment in their life, and rewrite that part of their history?

After that extraordinary encounter in the Pacific Ocean, Admiral Drake sailed to the Isthmus of Panama. Years before, Drake had landed on the Atlantic side of the Isthmus and hiked across the hills to the Pacific side. From the vantage point of the summit, he'd gazed at a vast ocean he'd never seen before. It was the Pacific. There and then, he vowed to return and sail in it for his Queen, and for the angels of the island of England, who thrived on exploration and discovery. And he did. That was Drake's second coming.

Drake's defiant pursuit of his dream impressed Nelan. Drake had remembered the promise he'd made to himself, and its fulfilment must have given him immense satisfaction. Nelan never forgot the importance of making and keeping promises to himself.

What winds and tides of fate had guided him back to the village of Sangatte? And in these tremulous circumstances? Returning to his place of entry into this world offered him a superb opportunity to reconnect to the originating power of his life and its deeper spiritual meaning.

Perhaps it was a law that meant that everything that lived bore the mark of its birth and so knew its origin, its home. Like the call of the wild, it was perpetually trying to return to the source of his arising. Perhaps this constituted the ultimate enticement of life, the perfect spiritual destiny, to go back from whence one came.

At death, did the human spirit, that spoonful of God, return to the source of its arising when released, along with whatever spiritual experiences the person had gathered during their lives? Perhaps the greatest religious feeling was that sense of belonging. Born away from home, was the human spirit a universal errand carrier, a scout for God, and a warrior for the angels?

As the afternoon wore on, the seagulls squawked and the smaller birds darted amongst the long grasses in the sand dunes. He played there as a child, building a formidable sandcastle and then watching the tide come in, sending fingers of water towards his castle, as it gradually dissolved and then crumbled in a heap back to become one again with the beach.

All Nelan could hear were the sounds of the waves breaking on the shore, the wind whistling through the rigging of the ships, in chorus with the anxious and excited shouts of the men. The English van closed to within hailing distance of the Armada. With the wind at their backs, the English could make themselves heard, which they did by sending regular and colourful profanities towards the Spanish like stones skidding on the surface of the waves.

Howard ordered the *Roebuck* to distribute any spare munitions to the rest of the fleet. And in the middle of the first dog watch, at five of the clock, his orders were to attend an evening service followed by an officers' meeting on Drake's ship.

The men set about unloading the cargo on the *Roebuck*. The work proceeded briskly until a barrel toppled over and crushed Whiddon's leg. With the man in agony, Nelan and Simons helped him to his cabin, where he slumped into his hammock. Confined to his quarters by the surgeon, Whiddon ordered First Lieutenant Simons to accompany Nelan for the officers' meeting on the *Revenge*.

On the wherry, Simons had words to say to him. "Me, I don't get why the captain's asked you to come to this meetin', I don't. When all you done is keep the *Roebuck* outta the action."

"What! How did I do that?"

"First, you delayed us in Torbay, and for what, a few bundles of sticks? Then you tended to the injured. Then a dead Spaniard. By the Lord Almighty, if t'were me, I wouldn't have tarried for any of 'em. Not bloomin' likely. I'd have raised anchor, and hurried to catch up with the admirals, I would. Oh, but not precious bloody Nelan."

"No! That's wrong, Simons. We salvaged the wood bundles for good reason. We helped our wounded, and we respected the dead mariner," Nelan protested. Not that it made any difference. Simons had made up his mind. It was a thankless task to prise a man away from his treasured opinions.

As they were piped aboard Drake's command, the *Revenge*, Nelan felt decidedly uncomfortable about the first lieutenant. He mingled amongst the officers and men gathered below the quarterdeck. Using his diminutive stature, Nelan sneaked to the front of the crowd and climbed up on top of a barrel. Scanning the sea of faces, he saw in the men's eyes a mix of stubborn defiance, the richness of comradeship and a hint of fear. Pedro was nowhere to be seen.

At the ringing of the two bells marking the middle of the first dog watch, at five of the clock, the fleet chaplain stepped forward. In purple vestments and scarlet scapula, he raised his hands, and the assembly quietened. He recited an evensong service and concluded by blessing all the ships in the English fleet, their captains, commanders and crew, as well as their cannon, shot and powder. *Not much different to blessing the Armada flag*, Nelan thought ruefully to himself.

"Let us go forth," the chaplain said, his voice raised higher than the main mast, "and repulse these arrogant Spaniards. We'll exorcise the Narrow Seas of the vermin, and God will grant us victory."

To a resounding roar of approval from the ratings, Howard led Drake, Frobisher and Hawkins onto the quarterdeck.

The High Admiral of the Narrow Seas, Charles Howard, planted his hands on his lapels and strode forward to address them. "As good Protestants, we fight for our religion and our freedom. We defy the Spanish to set foot on our green pastures. Men, beat your fists on the anvil of purpose, for we shall never surrender! We are the lions of England. We rule the waves and ever shall it be so!"

The admiral's fiery manner and never-say-die spirit stirred young Nelan to the quick. He felt as tall and as strong as a shire horse, which said something for a shorty like him. The men's cheers resounded in the caverns of Heaven and stilled the hearts of the Spanish sailors listening across the waters.

The high admiral went on. "This month of August 1588 is profoundly significant for all of us. Our gracious Queen was crowned at Westminster Abbey twenty-nine and a half years ago, a cycle that corresponds exactly with that of the planet Saturn. That means Saturn has returned to the same position in the celestial sky as it occupied on the day of the coronation. Today, we are in harmony with the astrological destiny of the nation. So, men, we can expect another crowning, which bodes well for our victory."

Drake stepped towards the gunwale, glanced at the men, and noticed Nelan. The admiral grabbed his brother and pointed at him.

Thomas Drake arrived at his side, saying, "Michaels, come with me. The admiral wants to see you."

Nelan had expected a summons to attend the admiral. Climbing the steps to the quarterdeck, he felt queasy in his stomach. It was a familiar feeling in his life and one that ran his mouth dry with trepidation. This time, he resolved to stand up to his demons. Drake would harangue him, but he knew how he would answer him.

Drake dispensed with the formalities. "The last time I set eyes on you, I sent you to prison, from where you've obviously escaped. Now, you've the gall to show up on my ship! Thomas, arrest him. Again! Throw him in the bilges!"

"Admiral, you have me all wrong," Nelan said, digging in his heels so Thomas Drake couldn't drag him. "Please, m'lord, let me speak about that morning on the Hoe. Earlier that day, John Brewer had nearly killed me. My head was spinning like a top. In a mire of confusion, I said words to you that I deeply regret, and I apologise."

"Nelan, words are like barbs. They hurt, and your words on the Hoe were painful to my soul. I accept your apology, but never, ever speak to me like that again!"

"I won't, m'lord."

"There's still the very serious matter of the theft of the Queen's shillings."

"I had nothing to do with the attempted robbery."

"*Attempted* robbery? What are you talking about?" Drake asked.

"Oh, you don't know? It was only attempted because John Brewer stole a decoy, a casket full of metal shards. And yes, I escaped from prison. With Roger Adden, we apprehended John Brewer. We also found the real casket and returned it to the paymaster general."

Admiral Howard stepped into the fray, saying, "I know nothing about that. The paymaster general is an old acquaintance of mine. If he had received the monies from you, he would certainly have sent me a despatch to that effect."

"It must still be on its way to you, m'lord. Besides, I have a document from him, a signed reprieve," Nelan said, reaching into his purse.

"Show it to me," Howard said, tapping his foot on the deck.

"It's... not here," Nelan hissed in frustration. "Ah! I remember. I showed it to Captain Whiddon, who must have forgotten to give it back to me."

"Well, he's on the *Roebuck*, isn't he?" Howard snarled.

"Wait. Simons was there when I showed it to Captain Whiddon. He'll be my witness," Nelan said.

"Thomas, fetch him to me," Howard said, heaving a weary sigh.

As Thomas went to find Simons, Drake had a quiet word with the bosun, whom he despatched on a separate mission.

Nelan gasped for air. This was awful. If only he had got the reprieve document back from Whiddon, all would be well. He felt angry with himself for mislaying it. Now, he had to turn for help to Simons, an unreliable character at the best of times. As Simons arrived, the watch stander rang the four bells, marking the end of the first dog watch. It was six of the clock.

"First Lieutenant," Howard said, "Nelan Michaels claims that he showed a document to Captain Whiddon, a reprieve from the paymaster general. He says that you were present at the time. Can you confirm that?"

"Nay, m'lord," Simons replied with a grunt. "I was not there."

"What! He's lying. He was with us. Simons, you can't deny it!" Nelan said.

"Simons, this is very important. Are you sure about your testimony?" Howard asked.

"I swear on the Bible," Simons added. "An' since this man come aboard the *Roebuck*, he done tried every which way to delay us gettin' back to the fleet. Days 'n' days we was moored in Torbay!"

"Thank you, Simons," Howard said. "Vice Admiral, a word in private."

Howard and Drake spoke behind him, but Nelan overheard their conversation.

"What shall we do with the little thief?" Howard asked.

"Admiral," Drake said. "If you want me to be candid, I doubt that Nelan was complicit in this theft."

"Why do you say that?"

"Because he has twice shown his face to us, once on the Hoe, and again here. A guilty man would have run away. Besides, I gave him a rich reward for helping take the *Cacafuego*."

"But the reprieve document? And there's no word from the paymaster general."

"Then restrain him until the truth reveals itself," Drake said.

"I agree," Howard thundered. "Strap him to the main mast."

So, there was hope at the end of this dark tunnel. Until then, he was a captive, a helpless witness. Thomas Drake and the bosun's mate lashed him to the main mast, bound and gagged him. If they dangled a few bells on him, he'd be well and truly belled and jessed! The bile rose in his throat.

All I want to do is serve my adopted country, and this is how they repay me. Damn them!

Thomas Drake called the assembly to order and Admiral Howard addressed them again. "Captains and masters, hear our plans for the coming battle. Remember, I spoke of the planet Saturn. In mythology, Saturn sacrificed two of his children for the greater good. To harmonise with the forces of providence, we'll mould our tactics with this example. Because this night, our navy is going to sacrifice our children, namely, our own ships. The vice admiral will tell you the details."

"Thank you, Lord Howard," Francis Drake said. "The high admiral is referring to fireships. We will turn some of our vessels into floating furnaces. Then, under full sail, we'll light them up and set them adrift towards the Spanish lines. That'll prise them out of their safe mooring and then we'll pick them off, one by one."

The men threw their caps in the air and raised a raucous cheer. Drake went on. "During the recent Siege of Antwerp, the Dutch sent fireships against the Spanish van, so they'll be expecting the same. With this big round moon – tomorrow, it's full – the Spanish will see us preparing the ships. So, we'll play on their expectancy like a master musician strums the lute."

Drake paused, and then said, "Now I want to introduce you to Master John Young."

John Young wore a ragged beard and torn, jagged doublet. But his features – his nose and chin, eyes and ears – all wore this sharp look of intense, searing interest and heightened awareness.

"Tell us the plan," Drake said.

"First, prepare the fireships. Their crews'll retrieve their gear, then we'll remove the water barrels, valuables, foodstuffs and any cargo. Next, we'll prepare the pitch, the wood and tar. We'll pack the decks with old sail, spars and rigging, and other flammable material. The fireships will sail into the massed ranks of the Armada. They'll create a massive explosion and scatter fear amongst the Spanish crews. We're going to wreak terror and destruction on the enemy."

Applause and excited cries greeted the plan.

"Let me introduce my assistant," John Young said. "Master Peter."

A young man emerged from behind the mast and bowed to the assembled company. The bow struck Nelan as strange because it had a hint of mockery and derision. His black beard hid his features, but Nelan recognised the young man's arrogant brown eyes, piercing the world with disdain. He sighed in despair because he knew him. He knew him very well. It was Pedro de Antón.

"He'll help prepare the fireships," Young said.

Oh, I'm sure he will, Nelan thought.

While Howard and Drake asked the captains and masters which of their vessels they would sacrifice, Pedro sidled over to Nelan.

"You watch, I'll be preparing the fireships," Pedro whispered in his ear. The wicked grin on his face revealed his true intentions.

At the mercy of his Spanish foe, Nelan bit down hard on the gag and grunted.

"Think, English. I've done away with your father, and now I'm going to finish off the rest of the family!"

Nelan glared at him.

"No good scolding me with your eyes, they can't hurt me," Pedro went on. "You are all milk-livered cowards and runaways. Look! Even now, your vaunted English navy is afraid to grapple with my nation's great vessels."

Pedro pulled out a rosary from his cloth purse, kissed it lovingly and said:

Vengeance is mine.
I will repay saith the Lord.

As John Young approached them, Pedro shoved the rosary back in his purse.

"Peter, we're to prepare three fireships," Young said. "We're goin' ta' send them into the Spanish fleet and let them all burn in Hell!"

"Yes, master," Pedro said.

As Young left, Pedro got in Nelan's ear. "After you murdered Guillermo, I vowed to seek vengeance on my brother's behalf. He died a slow, agonising death; the heat, the scalding, and the terrible burns. I shall do the same to you. The fireships aren't all that will burn in Hell!"

The masters, captains and their crews returned to their ships.

Nelan bit on the gag and chewed on the dry threads of the rope. Tied to the main mast, he could only watch on, helpless to do anything except rue his lot. Was he now an Elizabethan Odysseus waiting to hear the terrifyingly beautiful call of the Sirens? Injustice had again bound him by hand and mouth, rendering him mute before his dire fate. There were no Sirens on the *Victory*, no alluring songs sung by mysterious bird-women, enticing men to their deaths, and no release from this awful confinement. He desperately wanted to tell anyone who would listen the truth about Pedro the Papist saboteur. But no one appeared remotely interested.

At the time of gloaming, normally a gentle quiet descended on the fleet. Not tonight. From Nelan's position on the deck of the *Revenge*, he could see the vessels of the rest of the fleet teemed with frenetic activity. Scores of small boats criss-crossed to and from the three fireships, carrying old planks, torn sail and broken barrels to stuff in between the decks. Firing the furnaces, they hauled the boiling pitch on deck, then daubed it on the masts. Then they rammed gunpowder into the cannon, ready to explode when the heat reached ignition temperature. They transformed the three ships into floating furnaces. After the Siege of Antwerp, some wiseacre named them Hellburners, because that was where they despatched anyone unfortunate enough to stray too close to them when they exploded.

Nelan loved fire. The rancid smell of the pitch and the powder, and the excitement of the men, stirred his blood, and his wrists fought against the binding of the rope. Again and again, he bit on his gag.

Glancing around the deck, his eyes fell on the barrel on which he'd listened to the chaplain's evening prayers. Something about his sermon nagged him. Yes, that was it! The missing piece of the puzzle – how to permanently dispel the scarlet pall from the valleys, release the angels, and inspire English men and women to greatness. This would fulfil Madima's vision. He needed to amend the ceremony of the Bell, Book and Candle. But why did it reveal itself to him when he could do nothing about it? He hissed air through his teeth.

Tied and bound, he couldn't even go for a piss. He felt haunted by the ghost of what might have been. All he'd ever wanted to do was be a participant, yet now he was forced to be a spectator.

29

The Crowning of the Fire

8pm to Midnight on 7th August 1588

Exhausted and depressed, Nelan's head drooped, and he drifted off into a restless slumber and another vision. It started with a pair of eyes, which was odd. Nor were they attached to anything like eyebrows, a face or a head. They hovered above the top mast, watching him watching them. They unnerved him because, in all his astral travelling, he'd never seen eyes. Not until now. They wore a hint of mischief and a touch of menace. After a while, he got used to them glaring at him. Whose eyes were they anyway? And why were they looking straight at him?

They grew eyebrows, lashes, a nose and nostrils. A mouth appeared with thick lips, a pair of gaunt cheeks, a salt-and-pepper beard, hair tucked into a sailor's scarf, eventually revealing all the face. A brilliant light shone behind its tanned skin.

The face looked familiar, but before he could take another look, a second face appeared. Then another, and another, until there were as many shining faces as stars in the night sky, staring at him, on the boat on the Narrow Seas, amid two huge opposing fleets. The eyes regarded him with a gentle gaze, like those of an old friend seeing him after a long absence.

What strange calling had drawn these faces to this place at this hour, on this day?

Clang. Clang. The ship's bell sounded; four pairs of rings in all. It wound him out of his reverie. Eight bells. Eight of the clock in high summer meant the light remained good. Eight bells signalled the end of the second dog watch. What else did it signal the end of – the Spanish Empire? English defiance? Dutch resistance?

How he would have valued Dr Dee's advice. The good doctor had departed England's shores nearly five years previously and currently occupied the position of alchemist in the court of the kingdom of Bohemia. Was Eastern Europe too far away for him to affect the outcome of the battle? Perhaps not, if he had a pair of those magical shoes, the ones that never wore out. Such a pair of shoes must be made of an insubstantial material, such as the great qualities of life, love and care, kindness and forbearance, honour and loyalty. These lasted forever. They spanned time and crossed the bridge of generations and epochs. If Dee had these qualities and wore the shoes, had he astral travelled to the Opal Coast to influence the unfolding of these crucial events? In which case, did one of these pairs of eyes belong to him?

If he cried out loud, would Dee hear him? But Nelan could barely raise a whimper with this gag stuffed in his mouth. As a young child, he remembered when he missed his mother, her smell, and the warmth and comfort of her embrace. He had cried for her. His father had tried to comfort him by saying that she couldn't hear him because she'd gone to Heaven, a place where people dwelled in the spirit of the Lord.

Nelan saw the glory of Heaven on earth, but he also saw how people preferred to go to battle over a principle. Everyone recognised that the colour of the sky was blue. Everyone slept at night in the absolute trust that they'd awake in the morning. Everyone delighted in the aroma of the rose in spring. These simple truths formed a foundation for peaceful coexistence amongst mankind.

As the orb of the sun rested on the horizon, it sent eerie shadows onto the waters, a kind of luminescent glow casting the sails of the hundreds of vessels in flamboyant scarlets and flaming oranges.

The English fleet had the advantage of the elements; a spring tide, a strong following wind, and the Channel currents all working in harmony. The lion of England roared, and the timing was perfect to send the fireships into the heart of the Spanish fleet. John Young gave the signal to launch the three ships, one after the other. The wind filled their sails, and flames raced across their decks, hungrily seeking more flammable material. Lithe tongues of flame rose up to the heavens. The raucous cheers of the English mariners sped the fireships towards their foe.

The masts on the ships were alight, the flames wrapped around them like lovers in a ghostly embrace of self-destruction. The searing heat and fierce flames danced to the tune of the wind, sucking in the air. Thick black smoke billowed into the glowering night sky. As expected, the enemy despatched screening vessels to repulse the fireships.

The Spanish closed on the first fireship, and, in the glowing heat, attached ropes to the flaming hull. They manoeuvred the vessel towards the shore, but as the fire quickened, the heat burned through the ropes, which snapped, so they returned to try again. With the fleets so close to one another, the gusting wind and the flowing spring tide, their seamanship had to be supreme. Men standing on their bows threw grappling hooks, which clasped the fireship and successfully towed it away from the Spanish van. The English mariners groaned in disappointment. The Spanish cut the ropes to the grappling hooks, and the vessel drifted harmlessly away to burn itself out on the Calais shoals.

As the second fireship drifted towards the Spanish lines, its anchor chain mysteriously plunged into the sea. The flaming beast came to a juddering halt between the two fleets. Plumes of black smoke issued from the beast, but floated harmlessly above the Spanish ships. Their mariners sang the praises of their king, to the intense annoyance of the English, who retaliated with their own songs of yore. The fireship burnt itself out and sank into the mire.

That left one Hellburner, one more chance to send the Spanish to their personal Hell. As it headed towards their lines, fires snaked up the mast then kissed the sky with yellow-red flames, sending clouds of pitch into the cooling night air. But the fire never peaked nor reached the ferocity to explode the cannons. Despite that, it headed dangerously close to a turreted warship, with its castles and high careened hull. With all their marine ingenuity, the Dons used long wooden poles to prod and shove the smoking wreck away to safety. To cheers from their mariners, the floating furnace drifted past their fleet and got snagged in the Calais sandbanks, where it toppled over on its side. Like a beached whale, it sunk into the cold, dark waters of oblivion.

As the third bell of the first watch rang across the fleet, Drake railed against all and sundry. It was half past nine of the clock. Turning to the bosun's mate, he said, "Get me John Young. Now!"

Soon enough, the bosun's mate was rowing back to the *Revenge* in a wherry with Young and his assistant.

"What's happening!" Drake demanded. "We're a laughing stock in front of our own men and, even worse, before the damned Spanish."

If Drake had removed Nelan's gag, he would gladly have told him the simple truth.

Drake gave John Young a piece of his mind, saying, "I want you to turn these ships into the ultimate Hellburners. Can you do that?"

"I can that, m'lord," Young replied.

"I hope so, or I'll have you chained to the mast of the next fireship. Then you'll know what it's like to burn in Hell."

While Drake thumped the gunwale in frustration, Pedro directed a torrent of abuse at Nelan.

"The Pope excommunicated your precious Queen and anyone who supports her," Pedro whispered in his ear. "As far as the Catholic Church is concerned, which is all that matters, you're a nothing, a peabody, a shrimp."

Pedro ensured no one saw what he was doing then kneed Nelan in the guts, winding him. "Bah!" Pedro went on. "You're pathetic. Look where your heretical religion has brought you to, eh? Stuck to a mast like a limpet when all around you is mayhem. My people follow the true faith. We believe in the one God who supports us in this war. Soon, we'll wear the garland of victory."

As John Young approached, Pedro stopped taunting Nelan.

"Master Peter," Young said, puffing out his cheeks in frustration. "Why are you waiting? Prepare two more fireships. Jump to it, lad."

The two men scuttled off to work. Soon after, they sailed the two ships up to the stern of the *Revenge*, but too close for Nelan's comfort. To create a gigantic explosion, Young lashed the two fireships together. The fireship crews worked with frenetic energy to fill the Gemini pair with offcuts, logs, matting, old sail and anything flammable gathered from the fleet. Young and Pedro reported to Drake that the ships were ready.

The admiral gave the signal for the unwieldy pair to be set alight and launched, and the Gemini pair drifted by the *Revenge*. In the dry, still moonlit night, fires broke out on the top deck of the fireship and quickly spread across the poop deck. A finger of flame shot up the mizzen mast and licked the starboard hull of the fireship nearest the *Revenge*. A tremendous explosion rocked the paired ship. Fragments of boiling tar, flaming pieces of wood and hot embers rained down on the *Revenge*. If it hadn't been so fearsome, the firestorm would've been beautiful. The decks resembled the fires of Hell. Nelan knew that this was not an accident.

That damned Pedro must be laughing inwardly.

Amidst the chaos, the bugler called for all hands on deck. To douse the fires, the coxswain ordered them to empty barrels of precious fresh water onto the deck. The barber surgeon scuttled around the crew and officers, tending to cuts, burns and scalds. A piece of burning wood hit Nelan in the shoulder, making his clothes smoulder. By this time, the flaming Gemini ship had drifted by the *Revenge*.

Drake plunged to his knees.

"M'lord, do you pray for victory?" Pedro asked in a mocking tone.

Drake clutched his forehead and let out a deep moan. "I'm hit," he said. "Shrapnel. Fetch the barber surgeon."

"I'll do that, m'lord," Pedro said. "But it's bleeding. Let me see what I can do."

Pedro ingratiated himself with the admiral. Nelan bit his gag in frustration.

Pedro pulled out a 'kerchief from his purse and dabbed it against Drake's forehead. As he did, something fell out of it onto the deck. Drake didn't notice it. Nelan did. It was his salvation. Nelan grunted and stamped his foot, trying to draw Drake's attention to it. Nelan chewed on the gag. He had to get rid of the damned thing.

In the evening light, shadows flitted back and forth. Men rushed to put out the legion of small fires and tend to the wounded. But Nelan was alert and watched Pedro grab the object. As Pedro's fingers closed around it, a hefty boot landed on top of them. It was John Young's. "What you got there, lad?" he asked.

"Nothing," Pedro snapped, trying but failing to pull his hand away.

"Don't look like nothing to me, Master Peter. Let's take a look-see."

"D'you mind? It's precious to me," Pedro said.

"Let it go," John Young said.

"Take your boot off my hand!" Pedro snarled.

Drake butted in, saying, "Come now, Peter. What have you got there, the jewels of the Orient? We're God-fearing people with nothing to hide."

"No!" Pedro's face creased into a tight ball of indignation.

"Must be something mighty precious," Young said, scrunching his boot hard on Pedro's fist until he let go, and the object spilled onto the deck.

Young stooped to pick it up and unfurled it in front of Drake.

"Oh, so now we knows why he's hidin' it," Young said.

"It's a small crucifix on the end of a chain of beads," Drake said. "I've seen them on Spanish trading vessels in the Caribbean and the Pacific. This is a fine specimen of a Dominican rosary."

"M'lord, I can explain," Pedro said.

"Oh, you're going to have to, lad," Drake said. "Because a rosary is Catholic and anathema to our Protestant faith."

"I found it. It's not mine." Pedro's eyes twitched uncontrollably.

"Who's is it then?"

"His," Pedro said, pointing at Nelan.

"No, no, no. I don't know if this man is a thief. But I do know he sailed around the world with me, and that he's definitely not a Catholic. That's one lie too many. Then what else have you lied about?"

"I gotta say, m'lord, I prepared those Hellburners good 'n' proper," Young piped up.

"What are you saying?" Drake raised an eyebrow.

"They got sabotaged by this one 'ere," Young said, pointing at Pedro.

"N-no, that's a bare-faced lie. The fires were an accident," Pedro stammered.

Another cannon exploded on the Gemini ship, sending shards of fire and brimstone into the twilight rays. In the ensuing commotion, Pedro pulled a dagger and stabbed Young in the heart. Racing across the deck, the Spaniard dived over the gunwale. But the coxswain and his mate grabbed him. One foot each, they dragged him kicking and screaming along the deck to face Drake.

"Young's right. You're a traitor and a heretic," Drake said.

The barber surgeon hurried to tend to the wound on the admiral's forehead.

"No, please attend to Young," Drake ordered. "His need is greater than mine."

Blood spilled from Young's wound and expanded onto the deck into a large scarlet pool. The barber surgeon examined him and said, "Too late, m'lord. He's gone to meet his Maker."

"Now we can add murderer to the list," Drake said, rounding on the man. "And I warrant Peter is a false name. That makes you a liar, and I hate a man who bears false witness. If you're not Peter, who the hell are you?"

Nelan chewed the last stitching in the gag, and it fell away, freeing his mouth.

"I can answer that, m'lord," Nelan yelled.

"Oh, Nelan, who is he then?" Drake snapped.

"At one time, he masqueraded as Matthew, but his real name is Pedro de Antón. He plotted with Throckmorton to free the Devil's daughter, Mary, Queen of Scots."

"The rosary marks him as a Catholic, and that's enough to damn the man," Drake said. "But have you any proof of this mighty accusation?"

"I do. I warrant you'll find it on his person."

Thomas Drake delved into Pedro's purse and pulled out a canvas, a flint and a strike-alight-iron.

"Please, look at the mark of provenance on the strike-alight-iron," Nelan said.

Thomas Drake turned the iron in his hands. "I can see a fish with these long feelers on either side of its mouth. They look like cats' whiskers."

"Exactly, they're barbels," Nelan said. "It's a catfish."

"Yes, and it's the emblem of St John of Southampton," Drake said. "Then, Nelan, what you say about him is true. This is indeed Pedro de Antón."

"He's the stepson of San Juan de Antón, the captain of the *Cacafuego*, the Spanish treasure ship."

"Well, Pedro," Drake said, raising his eyebrows. "It's a shame you've none of your stepfather's sense of duty and honour!"

Pedro struggled to free himself, but the coxswain and his mate held him fast.

"M'lord, untie me, please," Nelan asked.

"Not so fast," Drake said. "Peter may well be Pedro, but you're still a suspect in the theft of the casket."

The bosun returned from his mission and joined the gathering.

Drake said, "Bosun, you have excellent timing. Did you do what I asked you to do?"

The bosun nodded and handed Drake a paper.

Drake read it and said to Nelan, "Let me explain. After Howard had you arrested, I asked the bosun to take a wherry to the *Roebuck* to ask Captain Whiddon about your story. He furnished this document."

"I know what that is," Nelan said.

"It's the reprieve written by the paymaster general." Drake winced as he touched his head wound, and went on. "I doubted that you were a liar and a thief, and I said as much to Admiral Howard. This document proves you are neither. Bosun, untie this man."

"Thank you, m'lord," Nelan said, rubbing the rope burns on his wrists. "I bear no grudges; I only want to serve."

"You're fully exonerated, and here's the document."

"Thank you. That's a huge relief," Nelan said.

"Just don't let Walsingham catch you for burning down the prison church!"

"How... did you know about that?"

"*El Draque* knows about many things!"

The five bells rang, marking half past ten of the clock. Across the way, the stern lights of the fleet beaconed into the night, lit by the Harvest Moon blazing down on them like a lantern in the sky.

"These are special times," Drake said. "Like fertile ground, they nurture those whose lives have a purpose greater than themselves. I am one. Now that my folly has fallen away, I see that you are another. We both face a national crisis. I've lost the master of my fireships. Nelan, I need a master of fire. I need a Fyremaster."

Nelan remembered his meeting with Kazia, the Gyptian soothsayer. Seeing the three wavy lines on his palm, she had prophesied that, one day, he would a Fyremaster be. This was the day.

With his voice quivering with emotion, he said, "Yes, of course, I will a Fyremaster be."

"Good," Drake said. "But we face a huge impediment before we can taste victory. We need more fireships, but we're short of kindling. Without it, we'll never move the Armada from its anchorage."

"I know where there's a lot more," Nelan said.

"You do? I should have known *you* would. Where's that then?" Drake asked.

"On the *Roebuck*," Nelan said, and explained how they had come by the wood bundles.

"Magnificent!" Drake was ecstatic. "And they were cut from Spanish oaks! Instead of the Dons burning us in an *auto-da-fé*, we'll use the wood bundles to spread terror in *their* ranks. What a delicious irony. It tastes sweeter than Spanish sac. Remind me to thank Don Pedro de Valdes of the *del Rosario* for providing them."

"We'll send the wood bundles back from whence they came," Nelan said. "We'll do the same thing to the Armada. We'll not annihilate it. Instead, we'll repulse it. That's the secret meaning of the royal motto, *Honi Soit Qui Mal Y Pense*. The Spanish will get back what they tried to give us, but they'll get it back inverted. They'll swallow their own antithesis. It's the most lethal weapon in the world."

"I agree," Drake said.

"There are enough wood bundles to furnish three fireships."

"We've two ships whose masts and decks are already tarred. Prepare those immediately," Drake said. "As a last resort, use my ship, the *Thomas* of Plymouth. Thomas, head to the *Roebuck* and start transferring the wood bundles."

"Yes, m'lord," Thomas Drake said.

"I have a request for you, Nelan. Do you have it on your person?"

Nelan instinctively knew to what the admiral referred and said, "Yes, of course." He pulled out a small canvas cloth from his purse. "Here it is," he said, handing it to Drake.

"The salamander pendant!" Drake said, touching the gold filigree and fingering the rubies. "Now I know we'll defeat them. Do your job, Fyremaster."

"M'lord," Nelan said, and scampered off to oversee the preparation of the fireships.

At the crescendo of his life, he was at the full of his full, riding the crest of the wave of his destiny. Everything up to this moment was imbued with a relevance which only now took on a profound significance. He'd filled his quiver with many skills, the mark of the salamander, the astral arts, the dexterity with the fire and the flame, and the wearing of the shoes that never wore out. The separate notes and skills of his life combined to sound a unified chord. Now, he could assist a purpose far greater than himself.

The mariners worked with frantic speed to transfer the bundles and prepare the fireships. In the blink of an eye, they were ready.

Nelan rejoined Drake on the *Revenge* and pointed to lights flickering on the shore.

"Can you see those cottages?" he asked. "That's Sangatte, the hamlet where I was born. I know these waters and the channels that flow through them better than the fish. Please, look there," he said, pointing to another thread of water, "send the fireships down that channel and they'll race along. The Spanish won't have time to tow them away. We're in harmony with the wind and tide. Even the moon's ripe and bright. On tonight's Harvest Moon, we'll harvest the Armada!"

"Well said, that man!" Drake said.

Nelan gave the order. It was nearly eight bells on the watch, so just before midnight, but none of the English snored in their hammocks. All hands were lined up along the gunwales, cheering and waving, stoking the fires of vengeance in the Hellburners.

With the coast to starboard, the first of the three fireships set off. As it drifted towards the massed Spanish ranks, the flames beat against the deck, burning the gunwale, the barrels of pitch and the wooden sticks. The Dons despatched a screening ship to intercept and ram it. The two ships got entangled and floated towards the sandy beach, while the blaze spread to the mizzen mast and sails of the Dons' vessel, forcing the crew to abandon ship.

"That was a hard-won victory," Nelan said.

"One burning Spanish carrack is not the victory we need," Drake said. "I despair we'll ever break their damned eagle-wing formation."

"Send in the next one, and it'll work," Nelan protested.

"If we keep doing the same thing," Drake said, "we'll get the same result. We need to change tack. Now's the time to use your hidden arts!"

Drake was right. Nelan had to conjure the uncanny. His right hand itched. That wasn't unusual, because after years of work with flax, rope and barrel, his palms were rough-hewn, like leather. He expected to see a bruise, a cut or a fresh burn. What he saw surprised him. His connection to the salamanders, the three wavy lines beneath his middle finger, throbbed red raw. Yes, this confirmed his role as Fyremaster.

Mentally, Nelan sent a summons to the fiery salamanders and waited. Would they respond? Then, above the mizzen mast of the second of the three fireships, he noticed a flicker of light, a lithe spark of St Elmo's fire, but then it disappeared. All that remained was the stars and the night, the crash of the waves against the wooden hulls, the creaking of the anchors mooring the ships, the expectant cries of the sailors, the shadows of midnight, and the moonbeams lighting a sorry, sordid battle between two nations over how they should worship the same God.

With no sign of the salamanders, Nelan wondered if he'd lost his silvery touch. He rubbed the mark of the salamander again, with a cry from the now to the past, and from the past to the now, and from the now to the now. In the same place, above the mizzen mast of the fireship, he watched in wonder as a lapis blue flame coalesced out of the astral. Another appeared above the main mast and a third above the foremast. Then a serpentine thread of flame spread from each of them down their respective masts, but without heat, barely visible, yet there, present, like something quick, seen in a flash out of the corner of the eye.

The flames licked the masts. Within a moment, they crossed the mysterious veil 'twixt the astral and the corporeal. They kissed the top of the masts and fired the pitch, the timber kindling and the old sail shreds. The fire snaked along the gun decks and ripped through the ship. A cannon exploded, and then another, sending shards of hot metal and ripples of fear into the cool August night air. It rained fire and brimstone, like the thunderstorm of hail and fire that Moses conjured against the Ancient Egyptians. Scalded pieces of wood, bits of molten metal and flaming fabric showered the nearest Spanish vessel, a huge galleass with scores of rowers.

Drake howled in satisfaction. As the fires spread over the deck of the galleass, some of its crew dived overboard. A few tried to smother the raging inferno. Their courage inspired the rest of the Spanish fleet. A convoy of wherries and dinghies sped to its rescue and soon the men had dowsed the fires.

Nelan bit his lip. He'd tried to invoke supernatural help, but the fireship had failed again to split the Spanish line. They needed something else. Behind them, Nelan heard a taunting laugh. Pedro.

"Do you really think a bit of fire will scare our brave mariners?" the Spaniard crowed. "You stupid English are weak. You'll never win. Remember what happened at San Juan de Ulua."

"What did you say?" Drake snarled.

Pedro didn't know when to be quiet. "Years ago, in Vera Cruz, Mexico, the viceroy killed many English sailors. What did *El Draque* do? He abandoned them and ran away back to England."

Clenching his fists, Drake strode up to Pedro and stopped right in front of the man's face. His gaze unwavering, Pedro stared at him. Drake glared back until Pedro looked away.

Drake hissed and said to Nelan, "Prepare the *Thomas*. Stuff her with every bit of sail and plank of timber, and don't forget those Spanish wood bundles!"

As Drake turned away, Pedro spat at him, the spittle running down the admiral's cheek. Drake wiped it away. With a stare as cold as ice and a voice to match, he said, "This man does not belong amongst us. Let him return to his own people."

"Will you free him?" Nelan asked.

"In a manner of speaking, yes," Drake said, staring at Pedro. "Lash him to the mast of the *Thomas*. Let him feel the heat of the flames of the English Inquisition!"

"There!" Nelan said to Pedro. "You promised me vengeance. You promised I'd die on a Hellburner. Well, now you'll get your own back!"

Pedro groaned as the seven bells rang, marking the half-hour before midnight.

Despite the onslaught of seven fireships, the Spanish had resisted all attempts to break their formation. So far, the eagle had repulsed the lion. The *Thomas* was their final attempt. Nelan set it alight and despatched it towards the Spanish anchorage. Again, he conjured the salamanders. Lithe blue astral flames snapped into life above its three masts. They were there in the astral, but then they went out. He called them and they appeared, flickering on the edge of the veil, and again they disappeared.

For a third time, he summoned them, appearing in the astral as pale blue flames above the masts. Then, with every fibre of his being, he willed them to cross the veil, the invisible boundary between the two worlds. Their flames sparked into life, bringing a gasp of awe from the mariners of both fleets. The three masts were drenched in lithe azure blue flames. The fire spread like quicksilver and the wood bundles caught fire. The cannon exploded, sending hot shards of burning metal and flaming nuggets of wood onto the decks of the Armada.

Pedro's screams pierced the night air, prompting memories of Nelan's mother's death. Back at Westminster School, Guillermo's shrieks had paralysed Nelan, and he'd failed to help the boy. This time, not only was he equal to the fear, he conquered it. This was his requital.

The Spanish held their mooring. The *Thomas* buttressed a large Spanish vessel sent to divert it. Locked in a fatal embrace, the two ships floated harmlessly away from the massed Spanish ranks towards the Calais shoals.

30

The Midnight of Eights

Midnight on 8th August 1588

Nelan needed to conjure a miracle.

As the sands of time of the Sabbath ran out, the future of the battle, and of the Island of Angels, hung in the balance. Despite them sending eight fireships, the Armada held their anchorage. There was a tide in the affairs of men, which, when taken at the flood, led on to fortune. This was one of those times. Something deep in his soul knew how to achieve that fortune. He just had to surrender to it.

He plunged into his quiver of astral arts and skills and pulled out one last ruse to change the course of the *Thomas*, and, with it, that of the battle. Guided to his cloth purse, he pulled out the salamander pendant. With feeling, one by one, he touched the rubies and, each time, a powerful presence gathered.

He was being watched... the crowd of eyes attended in silent witness, their faces shining with a brilliant silver hue. In that moment of power, and in the power of that moment, with the potency lent by the eyes and the silver faces, a new astral presence manifested above the *Thomas*.

The watch bell rang twice on the *Revenge*, one ring quickly followed by another.

In the pause before the next double ring of the bell, everything slowed down. In that suspended moment, a solitary ruby flame appeared in the astral above the eighth fireship. Each time Nelan touched one of the rubies on the pendant, another flame appeared out of the ether, and then another, until the three coalesced into a flickering red tongue, pointed at the end, like a lizard's. Then the nose, deep-set jaw and mouth appeared, alongside a set of sharp teeth, all with a shiny silvery hue.

The astral creature wore pointed ears and a tail. Tucked close to its body was a pair of lizard-like wings. He'd seen it emblazoned on the coat of the arms of the City of London.

Silver griffin.

Silver faces.

This happened as quickly as a cloud scudding across the face of the full moon, yet it seemed slower than an old carthorse trundling up a steep hill.

The astral beast spread its wings and hovered above the *Thomas*, still entangled with the Spanish vessel and drifting away from the Armada. The sporadic flames shot here and there on the fireship, which billowed clouds of blackened smoke into the night air. Once again, the Spanish mariners had prevented the fire from spreading.

The second pair of bells rang.

As the griffin flapped its astral wings, a downdraft of air fanned the flames, sending a panoply of scarlet, gold then azure flames from the deck of the fireship across the gunwale and into the heart of the stricken Spanish vessel. The flames had transformed the *Thomas* from a ship into Pedro's burning coffin. With hungry alacrity, the fire spread from port to starboard, creating more gusts of wind, further fuelling the fire. The Spanish vessel and the fireship merged into a drifting furnace of intense heat.

The third pair of bells rang.

They sent further echoes into the astral. The astral responded, requiting the signal.

Unrecognisable as seafaring vessels, the two ships were a single huge inferno of ruby heat and blue flame, making it impossible to tell them apart. A huge plume of red and yellow flames rose up from them, sending light, smoke and fumes into the air, showering the ships from both fleets with hot violet embers of molten metal, wood and material.

The ships formed a dual destiny, a Gemini. Inextricably entwined with the Spanish vessel, the *Thomas* changed course and, catching the flow, drifted straight towards the heart of the Armada's eagle formation.

Even at a distance, the fierce heat scorched face and hands. He turned away and covered his eyes. It reminded him of the days he worked the furnace in Queenhithe.

The voice of the fire roared like thunder. The colour of the flames changed from pinkish red to a furious white and stark yellow. A plume of black smoke snaked up in front of the full moon. The ship splintered into a thousand pieces and lit the night sky with a blazing trail of smoke and heat. The fury of the fire smashed into the van of the Armada.

Nelan gazed in wonder at the smoke billowing out of the *Thomas*. The plume had an oval shape with a fin at one end, and feelers hanging from the mouth, like a catfish. Evoking the emblem of the St John of Southampton family, it signified both an end and a beginning. Pedro's death ended Nelan's feud with the Antóns, one that had claimed both brothers, Nelan's father and his house. The barbel was gone; it was over. He offered a prayer of thanks.

The ship exploded again. The fire grew into a furnace, with heat scalding the very air they breathed. Perhaps it singed the King of Spain's beard. Philip would have felt its repercussions in the astral, as would his court astrologers in Granada and his occultists and alchemists in Toledo.

Did the furnace-like heat of the fire attract the silver griffin? Or did the silver griffin itself summon the great heats and blistering gusts of winds? If summoned, was the silver griffin called by someone far away with the curious surname of Du? In the Welsh tongue, the name meant black, suggestive of the unseen astral realms. When all seemed lost, was it Du, or Dee as his name was in English, who had plunged the Spanish Empire into the fires of oblivion?

In the astral, the hundreds of pairs of eyes and their silver faces gathered to witness this extraordinary event.

Then Nelan knew what they were.

They belonged to a very special brand of men. He knew some of their names: Oliver, the barrel man; Winterhay, the surgeon; Diego, Drake's *cimarrón* manservant; and Great Nelan Anderson, his old and trusted Danish friend. They were crew members on the *Golden Hind*. Another was Roger Adden's brother, Luke, who, along with all the other seamen aboard the stricken *Marigold*, went to a watery grave off Cape Horn. John Young and the young lad who'd died in Torbay joined all those others who'd lost their lives. These English mariners had laid down their lives in honourable service. Together, they had come in astral witness of this historic maritime event.

Silver eyes.
Silver faces.
Silver seas.

Nelan shook his head in wonder and watched as Drake unfurled a flag in triumph.

"Now that's what I call a Hellburner!" the admiral yelled, to make himself heard above the sheer racket of the fire and the wind.

The fourth and final pair of bells rang, marking the end of the first watch.

It was midnight.

At that precise moment…

The 8th bell rang.
On the 8th day.
Of the 8th month.
Of the 8th year.
In the 8th decade of the year 1500.
Which brought forth the 8th fireship.

All the eights; six of them, like pretty maids all in a row. Regiomontanus had forecast the event to happen in the 88th year of the century. Could anyone have planned for such an extraordinary coincidence? So, how did it happen? Nelan's best explanation was the innate ability of the higher human instinct to read and interpret the signs and seize the moment to ride the crest of the wave of the spirit of the times.

The fire spread across the three masts of the nearest Spanish ship. It leapt from one mast to the next, and then from one vessel to the next, spreading a deathly pall of mayhem and panic in its wake. It licked the top of the mast of each ship in the Armada. The sight of the crowning of the fire was both unerring and ineffable. If this was the astrological crowning mooted by Charles Howard, the man was more than a high admiral; he also had the gift of prophecy.

What happened next defied the laws of nature, because instead of descending downwards and spreading along the decks, the flames crested along the top of the masts. The spirit of fire, relishing this frantic moment of freedom, grew merciful and refused to spiral down the masts of the Spanish vessels. Was this compassion? Could the spirit of fire and its servants, the silver griffin and the salamander, exercise mercy? Perhaps it could, since the element of fire itself was ancient, certainly older than humanity and the planet herself.

Whatever it was, its extraordinary action preserved the lives of thousands of men and animals cowering on the decks of the Armada. It saved them from a death by fire, perhaps the most painful, nerve-shredding way to die. This miracle pierced the hearts of all the crews, both English and Spanish alike, who to a man knelt in the shadows, bowed their heads and prayed to their bountiful God.

The eighth fireship was the last that Drake sent.

Hell had burned enough for one day.

This was the most inexplicable coincidence.

This was the midnight of eights.

31

The Pith of Action and Reaction

Early hours onwards on 8th August 1588

Lit by the stern lights, Drake and Nelan paced the quarterdeck of the *Revenge*. They and all the crew peered to the north-east, where the Armada lay at anchor off the coast of Calais... or did it? What with the night, the billowing clouds of smoke, the bitter brown fumes, the smell of fear, the frantic excitement, and, not least, the raucous anticipation, no one could tell if the eighth fireship had finally broken the stubborn will of their foe.

A Spanish cannon roared into the night... A signal from Medina Sidonia's flagship, but for what? The sounds of creaking masts and flapping sails mingled with shouts from the Spanish mariners. By the soft light of the moon, the English could just make out wherries moving amongst the Spanish vessels. Were they carrying messages from the Duke of Medina Sidonia to his fleet commanders or to the governor of Calais? Was the Armada preparing to flee?

As the bells of the watch tolled and the night advanced, Nelan swore there were fewer stern lights at the Spanish anchorage. Or was it wishful thinking? Had the lions finally prevailed over the eagle? Halfway through the middle watch, around two of the clock in the early morning, Drake received a message from Admiral Howard. Nelan had the honour of reading it out:

Prepare your squadron.
Be ready for the battle of our lives!

When the first slender lance of dawn light pierced the darkness, and the first bell of the morning watch sounded, at half past four of the clock, he could see… what wasn't there. The main body of the Armada had sailed. Finally, the English had broken their enemy's tight eagle-wing formation and shifted them from their moorings. Yes! The Armada had relented!

The burned-out ribs of the English fireships sat forlorn on the Calais jetty. Of the Armada, only the *San Martin*, Medina Sidonia's flagship, and four others remained, all close-hauled and under light canvas. The rudderless *San Lorenzo* crawled along inshore. The other Spanish captains must have interpreted their miraculous escape from the Hellburners as a merciful gesture from the Almighty, and why wouldn't they? Like a bunch of frightened rabbits, they'd not even taken the time to raise anchor. Instead, they'd cut their anchor chains, raised their sails and run before the wind. They headed along the Flemish coast and into the North Sea.

Now, for the chase.

Howard's *Ark Royal* fired a gun, and the buglers trumpeted the signal out across the choppy waters, raising English sails and spirits. Howard headed towards the coast to confront the stricken *San Lorenzo*. With Drake's *Revenge* in the van, the rest of the naval force of nearly a hundred and fifty sails set off to hound the Armada, but they first had to get past the *San Martin* and the other four vessels. The battle edged northwards until Drake spied the rump of the Spanish fleet. They'd hoped to find the Armada spread out like a broken string of beads across the North Sea, but by a feat of disciplined seamanship, the Spanish had once again reformed the eagle-wing formation.

As they headed up the coast, Drake asked for the fleet's position.

"Across the way, m'lord," the pilot replied, "is the small Flemish port of Gravelines."

Gravelines, or was it grave lines or lines of graves? Was this where he'd meet a watery grave? Or the English navy? Or Dee's vision of a British Empire?

Drake sailed the *Revenge* into the thick of the action, closing on the first Spaniard in range. Guns blazing, the English reloaded quickly and fired again. The Spanish were slower to fire and sluggish to respond. In the cut and thrust of battle, the English gleaned that the Spanish gunners were poor in execution, and even worse with their aim.

During earlier engagements along the south coast, the English had steered away from confronting the Spanish for fear of being pummelled by their cannon and boarded by soldiers. But when they fired their cannon at the Spanish, their shot failed to penetrate the thick oak-hulled Spanish galleons.

After the capture of the *del Rosario*, Nelan had noticed that it had transported soldiers and sailors. With each deck packed with supplies and equipment, it inhibited the Spanish powder monkeys from quickly moving gunpowder from store to cannon, meaning it took them longer to reload. Also, the Spanish cannon, unlike the English, did not have wheels, limiting their direction of fire. By now, the Spanish fleet had been at sea for nigh on three weeks and so could not replenish their stocks of gunpowder or fresh water. After engaging in pitched battles since the 29th of July, how much fight and powder did they have left?

With these advantages, and the weather gauge, Drake led the van. This was the moment when the tide in the affairs of Englishmen ran full, and, taken at the flood, led on to fortune. It was time for new tactics; run the gauntlet and close on the enemy once and for all.

Nelan spurred the men on, helped unfurl a sail, then hauled a rope, all the while keeping a lookout for the Spanish. On the gun deck, he ran the duties of a powder monkey, in which his diminutive stature allowed him access to the smallest of places where others dare not tread.

The Battle of Gravelines was a melee of confusion. Ships coming into and out of the line of sight. Cannon thundering here. Clouds of smoke and blackened fumes there. The stench of death. The cry of the victorious. The wail of the vainglorious. The blare of the bugle. The ring of the bell. Climbing the shrouds. The smashing of the mast. Barber surgeons with saw and gag. Broken and severed limbs. The screams and the agony. Hands lifted in solemn prayer. The Commendation for the Dying. The hymn of life and death. Soldiers firing harquebuses from ship to ship. Vessels misidentified. Wrongful messages. Confused gestures. The grit of the valiant. The shadow of the coward. The pith of action and reaction.

The first cannon fire sounded midway through the morning watch, around six of the clock. Fourteen hours later, the English broke off the engagement. It had been a long day, a day of glory, and a day of death, a day of seamanship, and of military valour.

Like two beaten-up fighters, drunk with exhaustion, the two fleets retired for the night to nurse their wounds, count the cost of the battle, gather what intelligence they could about the opposition, and prepare their battered and broken ships for the next day's encounter.

32

A Trinity of Miracles

9th–10th August 1588

During the night, the wind blew hard, filling the sails. The last embers of the full Harvest Moon shone down equally on all men, stirring the blood of both high admirals and lowly deckhands. On land, the workers scythed the crops, gathering the harvest. At sea, the masts creaked, and hundreds of ships spread out across the waves. The harvest was the time of the reaper, yet in the battle to come, who was to be reaped, the English or the Spanish? It had to be one or t'other, because the reaper, once called, could never return empty-handed.

The two fleets resembled a pair of demonic twins playing hide and seek up the northern coast of the Netherlands. Always within sight of the other, they seemed joined by invisible cords of antipathy. Restless and relentless were the English. Then again, so were the Spanish, who persisted in pressing onward, no matter the difficulty or obstacle. When morning broke, the wind moderated and shifted to the north-west. In the English van, Drake and Howard were watchful of the rearguard of the Spanish fleet, manned as ever by the valiant Medina Sidonia.

There was movement in the massed ranks of the Armada. The Spanish changed tack. Nelan and the other hands peered at the waters, every wave and spray, every rise and fall of the swell. The run and the slope of the seas had subtly changed. The water was a muddy brown colour. That spelled danger. That spelled sand.

The Armada drifted inexorably towards the treacherous shoals off the Dutch coast.

"Sands ho! Sands ho!" cried the barrel boy.

"By God, he's right. There," Drake said, with an air of delicious anticipation. "That's the Zeeland sands. If they don't change course by the next sounding of the bell in thirty minutes, their slender hopes of victory will be shipwrecked."

With their accustomed bravery, the enemy preferred to lay to, turn and fight rather than suffer the ignominy of shipwreck on a strange shore. Howard responded by sending the order to stand off and then on, with short tacks.

"The high admiral has tuned his tactics to perfection," Drake murmured. "Even lying to, wind and current drag the Armada to leeward. No anchor in the world can hold a ship fast in shifting sands. Besides, they've cut theirs, so it's no longer an option for them. Aloof we'll stay. Here we'll wait and watch the hand of the Lord destroy our enemy."

"They must be on their knees, praying to their saviour," Nelan said. "After all, He's emblazoned on their flag."

"Let's see if it does them any good," Drake said with a wry chuckle. "Me, I reckon they're bracing themselves for the shame of a stranding."

"In those shallows, there's barely a handful of fathoms for the leadsman to call," Nelan said.

"I'm enjoying watching the finest, largest fleet of ships in the world drift onto the sandbanks. If we had any shot and powder left, we could finish them off. It would be a merciful killing. But we've none, so we'll let the waves and the Almighty do it for us!"

Just as it looked like the Armada was heading into the arms of a shipwreck on a strange shore, the wind backed. Even those nearest the shoals in the van managed to weather the deadly sands and stand away into deeper waters.

Their enemy was so close to annihilation, and at the last moment, the wind had inexplicably changed direction and sent them scudding away from danger. In a few more minutes, the great galleons and galleasses of the Armada would have piled ignominiously into the Zeeland sands, to the humiliation of their king.

Nelan wondered about the cause of this propitious intervention. Had the Spanish occultists, far away in their ivory towers in Toledo and Granada, worked a windborne marvel? Or were they assisted by the hand of God, which both gentlemen and mariners on board the *Revenge* declared? Whatever the cause, a miracle had saved the Armada from a desperate peril.

Drake thumped the gunwale in frustration. "Well," he said, "they evaded our attacks along the south coast. They escaped the fireships by the skin of their teeth. Now, they've avoided the sands. Hate to admit it, but these are a trinity of miracles."

"Yes, m'lord," Nelan agreed.

"It matters not a jot," Drake said. "We've retained the weather gauge. The wind and tide are with us. The Armada can't turn around and sail back to the Netherlands coast. They'll never rendezvous with the Duke of Parma."

"This near-miss sounds the death knell of King Philip's Great Enterprise. You named three miracles for the Spanish, but the greatest one unfolds before our very eyes."

"And that is?"

"England's repulse of the Armada."

"By the Lord, that sounds good to hear."

"This is redemption," Nelan chimed.

All day, the fleet trailed the Armada, keeping them in sight but never veering within range of their big guns, their cannon and their culverin. The Spanish re-formed their well-drilled eagle-winged formation, but its feathers had been ruffled, if not plucked. Many of the ships of the Armada, having severed their anchor chains, placed themselves at the mercy of current and swell, wind and wave.

Limbs ached, and tempers frayed. Every man plumbed the depths of his reserves of courage and stamina. At the embers of the battle, no one wanted to die or suffer a terrible injury.

The next day, the two fleets, ever shadows, headed north and passed the English port of Hull. But the day soon revealed yet another miracle: Howard sent a message confirming the number of casualties the fleet had suffered; one hundred seamen. That was it! There were more ships in the entire English fleet than that. Ever the man to bring the divine into the mundane, Drake conducted an impromptu service during which they gave thanks to the Almighty.

Afterwards, Drake hung over the gunwale, his eyes flitting left and right, always winsome, but watchful. Nelan stood next to the man and breathed in the expanse of the sea. A long silence ensued. They belonged to the sea and to the men of the sea. On land, folks were always in a hurry, rushing to finish work, go to Mass, shop at the market, get to the inn, or argue with their husband or wife. Landsmen filled any void, any moment of quiet, with chatter, chortle or chunter.

At sea, the pace was slower yet faster at the same time. Nelan watched the cats' paws and the spray, sending wisps of white foam into the fresh sea air. The freedom was glorious; the feeling of the wild expanse of water was unlike the confinement of land.

In this moment of quiet reflection, Nelan asked, "How is it possible that our tally of dead mariners numbers just five score?"

"I see the hand of the Almighty," Drake murmured, his eyes moist with emotion.

Nelan reflected for a moment and then said, "We can say with more certainty than ever that we are as far from defeat as the Spanish are from victory."

33

Horses at Sea

11th–12th August 1588

The next day, Drake asked for their position.

"To port lies the coast of Northumberland," the pilot told him.

"We follow our orders," Drake said, "and continue the chase."

That afternoon, the barrel man yelled, "Man overboard!" and pointed off the starboard bow.

Nelan rushed to the gunwale. In the distance, bobbing up and down in the waves, was someone's head.

The bosun asked, "Who's this so far from land?"

"It's certainly strange," Nelan agreed.

As they sailed closer, one mystery was solved, but another arose.

"I don't believe me eyes," the barrel man yelled. "It's a bloody horse!"

"What?" Nelan cried. "A sea horse?"

"Nah!" came the reply. "A black horse with a hairy mane."

"Never seen a horse swimming in the middle of the sea," Nelan said. Nor had any of the crew.

The poor creature panted, and, barely alive, kept dipping its head underwater and then resurfacing.

"More of 'em ahoy!" came the cry from the barrel man.

There were mules and horses. They sailed through a herd of swimming animals, only their heads bobbing incongruously above the waves.

"The poor creatures. Can we stop and haul them aboard?" Nelan asked.

"You knows we can't do that, lad. But it tells a story, that them Dons is desperate," the bosun let rip. "They've thrown 'em overboard, like emptyin' the bilges."

"Yes, but why?"

"Save fresh water. Gotta be. No other reason."

"Yes, you're right, bosun," Nelan said. "The creatures weren't for the sailors, they were for the soldiers. The horses were to serve the invasion. This is the best sight we could ever see. It means the Dons have given up landing on our shores. Quick, get the admiral and let him know the good tidings."

On Fish Friday, they reached the Firth of Forth off the coast of Scotland. The abandonment of the horses and mules convinced Howard that both England and Scotland were delivered from the fires of the Inquisition. The High Admiral of the Fleet raised the flag and despatched wherries to inform the other captains of a simple three-word order: head for home. To celebrate this poignant and joyous moment, Howard joined Drake on the *Revenge*.

While sailing north up England's east coast, Nelan had looked for the clouds of the scarlet pall on the hills of Northumberland, and, to his immense relief, noticed they were thinner and sparser than before. The further north they'd sailed, the more the land appeared free of its suffocating influence. Just as the Spanish had lost the Battle of Gravelines, they'd also been defeated in the occult war.

After snaring each other for a round fortnight, the two fleets resembled a couple of punch-drunk wrestlers. Both staggered around, barely staying upright. With nothing left to give, they had no fight, no munitions, no supplies, and, worst of all, barely any ale. All they had was bravado. The English reminded Nelan of a latter-day David, small in stature and accomplishment on the world stage, pitched against a Goliath whose empire stretched from the Indies to the Americas. David had won, and had almost, but not quite, gained a knock-out. Because Goliath still lived and showed incredible resilience.

Despite their religious differences, the Spanish had earned a deep respect from the English for their seamanship, courage, fortitude and resolute self-discipline. Medina Sidonia had bravely led the line, with his vice-admirals following close behind into the heat of the battle without reserve or hesitation.

The English had surprised not only the Spanish but most of all themselves. They wore the badge of never-say-die belligerence. A tangible threat to their beloved country had elicited this great emotional fervour from each one of them. They had valiantly defended the Island of Angels and her Queen against Spanish imperial might.

Fifteen days ago, they'd sighted the vast array of the Armada ships off the Scillies. For those who witnessed them, those days had been an unforgettable experience. All the English sailors, as well as the many ordinary landsmen and women who had helped victual the fleet and support the endeavour, could march in triumph draped in the garlands of victory. Then the sailors would sit down with their families, wives beaming with pride, and tell their children of their valour and courage, and, like all returning heroes, exaggerate every part of it.

For it had truly been a feat of self-sacrifice and perseverance, as Dee had predicted.

While the crew celebrated the good tidings, Howard and Drake shared a private conversation, which Nelan overheard.

"Vice Admiral, do you think it's all over?" Howard asked.

"No, not at all," Drake said. "After this defeat, the enemy will feel humiliated, but they are brave and strong. At Gravelines, our cannon got close enough to give their ships a pounding. We peppered their hulls and bows with our shot, but look, you can see it up ahead. Most of their fleet is still under sail. During that time, they've kept to their damned eagle-wing formation. I wish I had some of the glue they use. While ours is a story of defiant persistence, theirs is one of great survival against the odds. Incredible. With such endurance, so long as the Armada ploughs through our waters, the nagging possibility remains that they'll sail around the coast of Scotland, tack south through the Celtic Sea, and try for one last time to pierce the iron defences of Devon, Dorset and Cornwall."

"We will be vigilant," Howard said. "I'll return to court and tell the Queen myself."

"Aren't you reluctant to do that?"

"Why? What do you mean?"

"If I may confide in Your Lordship," Drake said. "My inkling of these coming times is that a man may better serve his sovereign from the safety of an ocean-going vessel. I, for one, am wary of the machinations of the court."

"I understand your concerns," Howard said. "But surely we are above such petty considerations."

"That may be, but the rules of the game are changing. England was once an insular isle, her people inward-looking and downtrodden. But we've sailed the world and defeated its most powerful navy. Now, England needs men who are outward-looking, prone to discovery and adventure."

"I think you are right."

"Look at the history of our island," Drake went on. "From the sixth century, we've followed the edicts of the Vatican. Fifty years ago, King Hal broke from Rome and we became a Protestant nation. For a short period under Queen Mary, we reverted to Catholicism. Then Queen Bess brought us back to the Anglican Church. See the recent pattern, a lurch from one religion to the other and back again. This alternation is both mother and father to doubt, uncertainty and suspicion."

"These times are unstable," Howard agreed.

"They are that," Drake said. "But you watch how this all unfolds. After the repulse of the Armada, I fear there'll be more bloodletting, but it'll be on our own doorstep. People's tolerances will harden like iron. Alas, one day, the Queen will leave us. When she does, it's likely she'll leave no heir, so a stranger to the court will ascend the throne. Whoever succeeds will probably cull those now in her favour and introduce their own sycophants."

"We must face these issues with boldness and courage," Howard said.

Drake nodded, and Howard left to return to the flagship.

What a fascinating conversation. Even Drake was wary of the vicissitudes of the court, and to avoid them, preferred to stay at sea. In their different ways, both Drake and Dee shared similar sentiments about court life. With these thoughts in mind, Nelan approached Drake with his bag packed to leave.

"Where are you going?" Drake asked.

"The *Revenge* is set fair for Plymouth. Can I have your permission to rejoin the crew of the *Roebuck*?"

"I'd like you to remain on board the *Revenge*," Drake said. "You conjured that mysterious entity, the silver griffin, striking fear into Spanish hearts. When all seemed lost, it turned the battle and forced them to cut their anchors and run away."

"That was the mysterious midnight of eights."

"It proved to be the change in our fortunes we'd worked so hard to achieve!"

"Then, m'lord, grant me this one favour. I'm a married man now. My wife and I…"

"… And I have a mistress," Drake sighed, gazing longingly out to sea. "I can't be away from her for too long."

"I know. The *Roebuck* is sailing to Deptford, from where I've a short journey home. And I have to report to Sir Francis Walsingham."

"The secretary, there's him to consider. Then, yes, request granted."

"Thank you."

"I trust you'll let bygones be bygones," Drake said. "Please forgive me my failings. I am a man of fervour, impetuous like fire. I love the heat of battle, the thrust and parry of conquest, the sheer elation and joy of discovery. Yet, I am a God's man, a proud Englishman, and a Devon man at that. I've defended the honour of my country with every fibre of my being, and I so desire to return this nation to its path of destiny. As a nation needs a leader, so does the world. England shall be that leader. That is what Dr Dee has foretold.

"It was nearly eight year ago when the *Golden Hind* moored at the Hoe. I'd sailed her around the world with a motley crew, you amongst them, eh? But think on't. That was an immense achievement for us, our Queen, and the Island of Angels. In their lifetimes, few men create a legacy of such enduring richness. Yet here we are, you and I, alongside our brothers in arms in the English fleet. In these fifteen days, we've forged a second legacy."

"So we have," Nelan said. "On that note, I bid you goodbye, Admiral."

"Fare-thee-well, lad."

He took his leave of Vice Admiral Sir Francis Drake with a touch of rue and sadness. As the wherry ferried him to the *Roebuck*, he reflected on Drake's prescient words. The man was right. They may have won the Battle of Gravelines and repulsed the Great Armada, but the war had not reached a decisive conclusion, not least in the astral realms.

While sailing back down south, Nelan again saw clouds of scarlet pall clinging to the flatlands of East Anglia. They'd repulsed the Armada. The influence of the Vatican had receded. So, how was that possible? Further north, the scarlet pall had weakened and diminished, yet it remained in the south. Then he realised; yes, the pall had diminished, but it had revealed another layer of scarlet ambiance beneath it.

This one was not Spanish, nor did it originate in the Vatican. But he had an inkling as to whose it was, and who had caused it to appear. This time, he had the means to remove it permanently, and free the angels of the island for good.

PART 3

THE MEETING OF PURPOSES

34

A Voyage of Remembrances

17th August 1588

As dawn broke, Nelan roused himself from a restless sleep. He'd dreamed of rain slanting onto canvas, sails flapping in the cold and gusting winds. Amongst the fierce storms, he'd glimpsed a fleet of ships buffeted by a northern gale, struggling to stay on course, short on rations, and even shorter on patience. It must have felt contrary to the normal seafaring instincts of those Spanish mariners that the way back led them northwards, away from home.

On a promontory in the distance, he'd seen high granite cliffs, and, across a narrow sea corridor, another segment of land, an island. On waking, he rubbed the sleep from his eyes and realised that he'd been astral travelling. He'd seen the Armada pounded by storms, and spread out like pieces of wreckage on dark, troubled seas. He guessed the headland was John O'Groats, meaning the islands opposite were the Orkneys. The Armada had dragged itself to the most northerly point of the Scottish mainland.

In the rays of the early morning, the *Roebuck* tacked up the Thames. The river narrowed, quickening the flow. Passing Tilbury on the northern shore, he saw thousands of soldiers milling about. Some drilled on parade, while others erected tents and constructed fortifications. There was a hive of activity with man and horse, wagon and mule, and a force of arms, with harquebus and pistol, spear and pike. Scores of small boats were moored at a temporary pier with almost as many on the other, south, side of the river at Gravesend. As they tacked upriver, Nelan hailed the men digging a trench.

"What are all you men doing here?" he asked.

The man with cabbage ears rested on his spade, and announced, "We be buildin' a big depot 'ere. Oh, an' a bridge a' boats from 'ere to Gravesend, over yonder. These be our defences agin' the Don. And I tell ye, master, not one a' them'll pass us by 'ere at Tilbury Fort."

"Glad to hear it. Your name, soldier?"

"I be Bardulf, master."

"Bardulf, eh? We've met before. You're the gravedigger."

"The very same! Fancy seein' your good self 'ere."

"Who's in command here, Bardulf?"

"The mighty Earl a' Leicester, we's his land army." With arms akimbo, he added, "Listen, any day now, 'is troops is gonna be inspected. Yeah. By none other than Her Majesty the Queen 'erself."

"Good Bardulf," Nelan cried. "Then tell the earl we've chased the Spanish as far north as the Firth of Forth."

"The fifth of fourth, you say?" Bardulf replied, cupping his hand to his cabbage ear.

"No, the Firth of Forth."

"Too many fifths and fourths for simple Bardulf."

"Listen, tell him anyway," Nelan yelled, and left him digging his trench. The last time he'd met him was at the cemetery at St Mary the Virgin in Mortlake. Both of them had moved on since then.

The *Roebuck* sailed past the Palace of Greenwich before mooring at Deptford on the south side of the river. The naval dockyard had barely changed since his last visit five years before. They were always building ships there, especially ships of war. Even now, a group of men swarmed over the spine and ribs of a great hull under construction. Surrounding the dock were towers and cranes, wharves and warehouses, and a multitude of craft, from galleons to merchantmen, carracks to caravels.

Ships that had limped back from Gravelines occupied some of the docking bays. One of them was the *Mary and John*, the supply vessel that had taken him from London to Plymouth all those years ago. Although unaware of it then, now he knew how portentous that short passage was for him. It ended one unfortunate part of his life, his imprisonment in Marshalsea, but launched another, far more extraordinary, episode: the voyage across the seven seas and his burgeoning apprenticeship in the astral arts.

Gathering his belongings, he went to find Jacob Whiddon.

"Nelan, you have been a credit to the *Roebuck*. I shall mention you in despatches. Your premonitions were invaluable. Because you insisted we load the bundles of sticks from the *del Rosario*, we successfully repulsed the invincible Armada."

"Thank you, Captain," Nelan said.

"What Simons said about you to the admiral was unforgivable," Whiddon said. "I'm ashamed that he bore false witness against you. It almost cost us the battle."

"Do you know why he did it?"

"He was jealous of your abilities." Whiddon heaved a sigh of regret. "I've clapped him in irons and he'll answer for his actions before a court martial."

"You're right, Captain, I'll be careful," Nelan said. "I warned him that Pedro de Antón had got aboard the *Golden Hind*. I assumed he'd inform Captain Fleming, but did he?"

"No, he did not, Nelan," Whiddon said. "Simons's lies and treachery have brought shame to the good name of the *Roebuck*. Now, let's look to the future. Tell me your plans."

"I love the fire and the flame and working with the furnace, so I'm going to join the Worshipful Company of Blacksmiths and start my own forge."

The bosun interrupted them, saying, "Man on the wharf askin' after the capt'n. Says he's the purser of the *Mary and John*."

Whiddon hobbled over to the gunwale. The man hailed up to them, "We're needing some help, Capt'n."

"What kind of help?" Whiddon shouted.

"Hah. How about all kinds?" the purser scoffed. "Listen, our hull's shot to pieces. We've manned the pumps from Gravelines to Gravesend. There's men sufferin' from their wounds. Mostly powder burns. There's others dyin' a' starvation. On top of all that, we none of us got no pay for our troubles, not a penny farthing. And we's gaspin' for a drop of ale."

"What about the victuals in the warehouses here?"

The purser laughed. "Nah. Only a few barrels a' sweet Spanish sack!"

"We've been at sea for a week and we're low on supplies ourselves,"

Whiddon replied. "But I'm sure we can spare you some flour and a barrel or two of ale."

"That'll ease the men's discomfort," the purser replied. "Thank ye, Capt'n. May God bless your ship and all who sail on her!"

While the crew loaded the supplies onto the *Mary and John*, Nelan bade farewell to Whiddon. "Captain, it's been an honour to serve with you. I hope that, one day, the balm of the sea will heal your broken heart."

"Until that day comes, you'll find me on the quarterdeck following the ebb and flow of the tides," Whiddon said, and they shook hands. As Nelan left the *Roebuck*, he wondered what would become of Jacob Whiddon. Would he grow into another Francis Drake and marry the mysteries of the sea-kind, or would he heal the wound in his heart and marry the mysteries of woman-kind?

For the first time in nine days, Nelan set foot on dry land. As before, when first stepping back on land, his feet wobbled, and he felt unsteady until he adjusted his sense of balance. No more pitch and yaw.

He found a wherry to take him upriver. The wherry master heaved away at the oars, and sallied forth with the tidings from London town.

"Ah, lad," he said, "we 'eard 'bout them fireships in the city some four or five day ago, it was. There was much ale drunk on that day, I can tell ye. But then other pamphlets got writ down, and we 'eard a different story. The town crier, well, he cried that the Armada had avoided the fireships, escaped our fleet, and was come to git us all. That put a stop ta the celebrations, but not for long."

On the north bank, bands of men marched in line bearing harquebuses and pistols, bodkins and cutlasses, rakes and spades. Others erected rudimentary fortifications and dug trenches.

"See that?" the wherry master said, pointing to them. "The militia's ready for them Dons. They ain't gonna pass, oh no. Our yeomen will stop 'em dead!"

The rhetoric boasted admirable defiance, but Nelan feared their army of untrained soldiers armed with pikes, daggers and a variety of agricultural implements would be no match for the Duke of Parma's battle-hardened troops.

They passed carracks and small craft heading downriver. Adorned with rich tapestries, one carried important folk dressed in white ruffs and silk cuffs. Their ladies fluttered fans in the hot breeze and kept the sour smell of the river from their delicate nostrils. To the delight of all, minstrels strummed a gentle tune. When they nearly collided with it, his wherry master was having none of their high-blown manners.

"Oi! Mind where you're goin', will ya."

"I'll have you know, we're to Tilbury, you rude man," said one of the toffs, and took another quaff from his beaker of wine. The boats passed by without further ado.

The wherry rowed past the White Tower of London, and even the gritty old wherry master turned his face away from the ubiquitous row of rotting skulls jammed into the spikes on Traitor's Gate. Further on, London Bridge basked in the shadows of the afternoon sun. On it, hordes of folk moved back and forth 'twixt the City and Southwark. His pleasant dreams were soon banished. Up ahead, several men and a woman weren't dancing the Tyburn jig but dancing the Bridge jig. They must have been there for a goodly while, because the crows had pilfered their eyes, and the corpses stank like the bilges!

"Who are they?" Nelan asked.

"Hah! Spanish vermin!" the wherry master replied, spitting into the waves in disgust. "Them be 'eretics what sowed the seeds of rebellion agin' our noble Queen Bess."

"What evidence did they have to convict them?"

"Evidence, master?" the wherry man snorted. "Don't need no evidence. It was on the say-so of none other than Secretary Walsingham hisself. An' that were good 'nough for the courts at the Bailey. So 'twas good 'nough for me!"

Drifting beneath the arches of London Bridge, they approached Queenhithe Docks. It kindled fond memories of his apprenticeship as a smithy, where he'd learned the ways of the forge and the furnace, the fire and the flame, and where the salamander had first appeared to him. On nearby Bread Street, he'd first met his beloved Eleanor in her parents' bakery. He remembered with fondness those halcyon days, and that special moment when their two spirits joined in harmony, and they promised themselves, one to the other, in the presence of Eleanor's Cross.

Nelan watched the wherries and boats rowing back and forth along the river. Ebb and flow, constant change, yet always the same. *Semper Eadem.* They ferried dignitaries up the river to Hampton Court and Richmond, and down the river to the palaces at Whitehall and Greenwich.

In the late afternoon, as the wherry passed Barn Elms, he saw the golden field of wheat, swaying in the breeze, where he'd enjoyed playing as a boy. Beyond the field was the same wood where, nearly seven years ago, he'd dug up the throck. The discovery of that plough head had altered the course of his life.

Beyond the crest of the Barnes-Chiswick ox-bow, the wherry passed the hamlet of Sneakenhall. Seeing the house of the St John family made him shrink inside. Once a thriving home, it was now deserted, with mud plastered on the windows, birds nesting on the roof gulley, and a door hanging off its hinges.

In his days at Westminster School, Nelan had been a neighbour of St John's stepsons, Guillermo and Pedro. Both had died consumed by vengeance and sacrificed at the altar of the element of fire. Ironic too that both Nelan's parents, Agnes and Laurens, had also lost their lives to fire. Where was St John? he wondered. Still captaining the annual Spanish treasure ship up the Pacific coast of South America, and so as far away from the tragic memories of Sneakenhall as he could get?

They rowed on, passing the Leg O'Mutton, a pond named after its shape, and the empty mansion of his mentor, Dr John Dee. When the wherry master pulled in at the Mortlake jetty, he paid him handsomely.

Nelan was home. The oak tree he used to climb was still there; firm, strong, and full in leaf; a magnificent specimen. Under its canopy was a sprinkle of acorns. Seeds for the future. Summer was going; autumn was coming.

Though he'd been away for less than a month, the joy of return was exquisite. Perhaps because of what had been achieved and what had been sacrificed, this was a moment to savour, and more precious than any other homecoming. Slowly, serenely, dusk fell around him. His heart beating like a drum, he saw his house by the river, swathed in evening shadows. A dog howled. It got louder as he approached. For a moment, he froze. Then he recognised the bark.

"Holdfast!" he cried, as the dog bounded towards him, wagging his tail, and slobbering over his hand.

"Hello, boy," he said, stroking the hound. "Have you been looking after my Eleanor?"

The housemaid opened the front door and said with a broad smile, "Welcome home, Master Michaels."

"Thank you, Margaret."

Eleanor waited for him at the entrance, grinning. When she could restrain herself no longer, she ran to him. They embraced long and hard, holding each other tight as if to let go would mean losing each other again. She smelled as sweet and as wild as a rose in the hedgerow.

He whispered:

I can't ask for more,
Dear Eleanor, Eleanor.
It's you I ad-ore,
Eleanor, Elean-or.

She held him at arm's length and looked him up and down.

"What are you doing?"

She inspected his hands, prodded his chest and belly, and then playfully brushed his codpiece. "What do you think? I'm carrying out an inspection," she said.

"What are you looking for?"

"Leaks, of course."

He chuckled. "Found any?"

"No. My report to the admiral will declare the good ship Nelan fit and ready for action!"

They both laughed, and she said, "I'm just relieved you're home in one piece. Thank you for the letter. Adden delivered it and it warmed the cockles of my heart to read it."

"I'm glad!"

The cook prepared a hearty meal of roast lamb flavoured with a sprig of rosemary from the herb garden. Margaret filled their glasses with a Spanish sack. As he sipped the amber-coloured liquid, Nelan felt a delightful irony, because the wine came from one of the barrels Drake had requisitioned during his sack of Cadiz the previous year.

"A sweet wine, for my sweet lady," he purred.

"A fine toast for my fine hero," she replied.

"Tell me, what have you been doing in my absence?"

"I was called out for a birth," she said, puffing out her chest. "But Matilda is in poor health."

"I'm sorry. So what does that mean for you?" he asked. Giving birth represented far more of a mystery to him than astral travelling, insofar as he had some experience of the latter, and absolutely none of the former.

"I'll get called out more often."

"Why? Oh yes, Bridget. What happened to the poor lass?"

"She's in Newgate awaiting trial."

"You must be careful, my love."

"I will be, as you must be."

Although it had been less than a month, he'd missed her every moment of every day. She was part of him, as he was part of her. Perhaps they formed a single purpose.

They went to bed and enjoyed a long night of passion.

35

Belled and Jessed

21st August 1588

That day, a messenger delivered a request from Walsingham summoning Nelan to the fox's den. As he mounted his steed, the flies, gnats and mosquitoes flitted around, intoxicated by the day's golden hues.

On his way to Barn Elms, Nelan pondered how the fleet had achieved the great repulse of the Armada. Curious it was that the two fleets only fully locked horns in French waters, at Calais and Gravelines. It was as if some invisible force separated them one from the other, which only dissolved once both fleets had departed English waters.

Today, the 21st of August, formed the cusp between the astrological influence of Leo and Virgo, the Queen's birth sign. He kept wondering about the sign of Leo. Then he got it. It was obvious. He walked around it. The ox-bow was the same shape as the symbol for Leo, a sort of upside-down 'U' with curls at either end… The shape that a bird flying high over that part of the river would see.

The English fleet had shadowed the Armada from the 29th of July to the 12th of August. This fifteen-day period fell exactly in the middle of the astrological month of Leo, and so filled the hearts of the English mariners with the courage of the king of the beasts.

What of the midnight of eights? Who could have made up the eighth fireship, on the eighth bell, on the eighth day of the eighth month of the eighth year of the eighth decade of the century – and all of that falling on the full Harvest Moon? England seemed to be more in harmony with a powerful incoming celestial influence. Whatever the reason, at that moment of Octavian change, providence smiled on the Island of Angels and the gate opened for the British Empire.

All the way from Penzance to Dover, the Spanish mariners would have seen the white cliffs and green pastures of southern England, and the scarlet pall resting on its sacred land. They were so achingly near, and yet so far from bringing her to heel.

Arriving at Barn Elms, a voice cried out, "Who goes there?" He recognised the short, squat and rotund form: the secretary's steward.

"Please, Master Adden, put your wrath beneath your feet. It's me, Nelan Michaels!"

"Well, well, well, if it ain't the return of the prodigal son. Last I clapped eyes on ya was in Dover port."

"So it was, Master Adden."

Outside Walsingham's office, Adden said, "Wait here, lad, the secretary's busy. He'll call you when he's good 'n' ready. Got it?"

Nelan nodded, and Adden left him on his own momentarily in the same anteroom as before. This time, Nelan didn't hear the voices of the flames, but he could hear other voices coming from inside Walsingham's office.

"My lord, his skills benefit us, they already have," Walsingham was saying. "They give us intelligence we could never receive otherwise."

A second man replied, "That may be so, but the Devil informs him, the Devil, Master Secretary. Do you understand that?"

"I do, my lord, but—"

"There is no but, Master Secretary," the other man was shouting. "He uses astral arts, which are strictly forbidden in the eyes of the Church. That's why the conjurer of spirits, the summoner of angels, Dr John Dee, has been ejected from our land. Good riddance, too, if you ask me."

"I hear you."

"Let me make myself clear. To me and the other members of the Privy Council, these skills are heretical."

"What are you asking me to do?"

"I won't tell you. You know what you must do, or we'll do it for you!" the man said. Nelan heard a door open and slam shut, so assumed the man had exited by another door.

Who was he? Only a senior member of the Privy Council would dare address Walsingham with such command. The conversation rang alarm bells in Nelan's mind. It was further evidence of the change in the rules of the game about which Drake had spoken to Howard. Nelan nervously fiddled with his jerkin, wondering what to do. It had placed both him and the secretary in a dangerous position. For a moment, he considered leaving. But before he could decide, Adden appeared and ushered Nelan into the office.

Walsingham sat behind his desk, scrawling notes on a scroll. He seemed unaware that Nelan had overheard the conversation with the other person, whoever he was. With a dismissive gesture of his hand, he invited Nelan to take a seat. The man wore the same jerkin, white ruff and black Tudor hat that he wore a month ago. His eyes were as keen as ever, taking in every detail. His face, like a granite crag, looked beset with worries. The miniature portrait of his two dead stepsons still adorned his desk.

"Nelan, the paymaster general reported delays in receiving the casket from you. John Brewer will face the full force of Her Majesty's fury. And I've disciplined Adden for his folly."

A gruff man who saw dangers around corners, Walsingham kept his emotions on a tight leash. Even at this moment of national celebration, his stern countenance barely managed a thin smile. With high jinks in the streets, who else would keep a clear head and manage England's clandestine interests at home and abroad?

"Nelan, these are difficult times. But you have done a good job. I hear you helped prevent the Armada from combining with the Duke of Parma," Walsingham said, although his words sounded insincere.

"Thank you."

"But you have questions to answer," Walsingham growled.

"I do? What are they?" Nelan said, his heart beating like a drum. He thought Walsingham was going to mention his conversation with the other member of the Privy Council. Instead, he brandished a scroll and said, "The governor of Plymouth prison has written to me, implicating you in the fire that destroyed the chapel there. What have you to say for yourself?"

"I was unjustly imprisoned, because there had been no theft. The casket with the Queen's shillings was never stolen. When I realised that, I had to escape to retrieve it, and then to deliver it to the paymaster general. That was the mission you gave Adden and myself, but if you had told us of the decoy casket, we could have avoided this misunderstanding."

"I didn't trust either of you with that information," Walsingham said. "But you started a fire that destroyed Her Majesty's property."

"That was unfortunate, but necessary. But, I was careful there was no loss of life."

"Don't belittle a very serious offence."

"I'm not," Nelan said. This time, he was determined to stand up for himself and justify his actions. "Weigh that against the benefits of my escape. If I had been stuck in prison all that time, I could not have helped the fleet repulse the Armada!"

Walsingham scratched his beard, and after a moment's reflection, said, "That's true, I have heard the same. Her Majesty the Queen has read Captain Whiddon's report, which mentions your occult intervention in the battle."

"That's… wonderful," Nelan said, breathing a sigh of relief. If his name had reached the notice of the Queen, surely she'd protect him from the predators on the Privy Council.

"Is there anything else you wish to report?"

"Yes, m'lord."

"What is it, Nelan?"

"I, err…"

"Be quick," Walsingham said. "I've a wherry on the river waiting to take me to Greenwich Palace for a council meeting. We're planning an Armada Thanksgiving at St Paul's taking place at the end of the month. The Queen will attend, as will all the admirals and officers of the fleet."

Nelan was going to tell him that, when wearing the shoes that never wore out, he'd seen the storms beating against the hulls of the Armada in Scottish waters. And he wanted to speak about Madima's vision and the dirty scarlet pall suffocating the Island of Angels. But in the light of the overheard conversations between Howard and Drake, and now between Walsingham and a senior member of the Queen's Privy Council, Nelan decided this was not the moment to mention the arcane art of astral travelling. Instead, he said, "I would like to join the Worshipful Company of Blacksmiths."

"No, for the moment, you work for me," Walsingham said with a growl. "Come to the Armada Thanksgiving and bring your wife. We'll discuss your future as an intelligencer."

"I look forward to that."

"It may be the last opportunity to see Her Majesty amongst her people."

"Why's that?"

"In the light of the threat of the Armada, the Privy Council strongly advised her to cease all public appearances, but she insists on showing herself to her beloved people. We have doubled the guard on Her Majesty's person. More watchmen patrol the city streets. We've hired more searchers to guard our ports and protect our borders. My spies will infiltrate the courts and castles of every noble in the land, and report the slightest suspicion of recusants, priest holes and Papist insurrections."

"I see."

"But as I've told you before, my intelligencers can't foresee events as you can, Nelan. That's why I need you to tell me if you detect any Catholic plots against Her Majesty in the lead-up to the Thanksgiving."

"Of course, I'll do that," Nelan said.

Walsingham piled his papers into a stack and prepared to leave, saying, "I will root out the conspirators and burn the heretics," before slamming the papers down on the table. He sounded so dogmatic that it was almost papal!

He brushed past him and was out of the door before Nelan could utter a by-your-leave. So much for Secretary Walsingham; a worried man, and a man to worry about.

A few days later, Nelan and Eleanor strolled hand in hand along the riverbank, enjoying the glint of the sun's rays on the waters. The birds sang, and the ducks played on the river until a couple of marauding swans chased the little creatures away. There were bullies even in the animal world.

Heading home, they stopped near Dr John Dee's empty house to admire a flock of geese flying over the river, majestic in their formation. They were heading for winter pastures. Perhaps it was a sign of things to come. Dark clouds gathered on the horizon. A storm brewed. The air chilled. Rain and wind came howling in from the west. They sought shelter beneath the lintel of the front door.

While they waited for it to pass, Nelan said, "I'm worried about Walsingham. I had to justify my actions at the Plymouth jail to him. He's overwrought with the work and now he sees enemies amongst friends."

"He's always like that," Eleanor said. "It's difficult to walk away from a man like him."

The rain slanted into the roof and pummelled the dry earth, which drank it up with thirst aplenty.

"But that's exactly what I want to do. Oh, he's invited us both to attend the Armada Thanksgiving at the end of the month."

"That's wonderful," she purred. "It'll be a magnificent occasion for the country. We might get an audience with the Queen."

"Perhaps, but listen, my love. I've overheard two important conversations recently. In one, Drake claimed that he chooses to stay at sea to avoid the dangers of court life. In the other, a member of the Privy Council told Walsingham to stop using my services."

She puffed out her cheeks and said, "Then you must leave Walsingham's employ as soon as you can. But you're not going to join Drake at sea."

"No, I wasn't saying that."

"Then what are you saying?"

"I tried to tell Walsingham that I want to leave his employ, but he put me off and said he'll talk to me about it at the Thanksgiving."

"Good, I'm glad to hear it. I hope you'll conclude matters with him then."

"I do too."

"I get the feeling you've got more to say. Come on, I'm your wife. Out with it."

"Yes, then I'll tell you a secret about him. You remember the Babington plot? Walsingham had intercepted a letter from Mary to Babington. He called it the bloody letter."

"What of it?"

"Walsingham got his chief forger to add a postscript to it."

"He did! But why?" she asked.

"To make sure he got Mary's head on a platter."

"And he was prepared to fabricate evidence against her! How can a senior member of the Queen's Privy Council justify such an abuse of authority?"

"The phrase he used to justify it still rings in my head. He said it was 'For God, for the Queen and for England'."

"Oh, so that justifies forgery?"

"In his defence, they didn't introduce the bloody letter with the forged postscript at her trial."

"Why not?"

"They'd gathered enough other evidence to convict her."

"That does not excuse such a flagrant abuse of power. Nelan, he's a dangerous man in a dangerous position."

Nelan nodded, and watched the rain stream down in a waterfall in front of them.

After a while, Eleanor said, "I've got a sad tale to tell too."

"Go on, I'm listening."

"While you were at sea, Bridget was found guilty of witchery and now rests in the arms of Our Lord."

"Oh, my God, Eleanor. After you served the barbel at the meal to celebrate the midwife's oath, I had a bad feeling about you and midwifery."

"You already told me that."

"I know, but Bridget has been executed simply for performing her duties. It's dangerous to continue. You have to leave."

She nodded slowly and said, "I'd like to, yes. But I am bound by my oath to continue. I can't just walk away."

"Then, we're both belled and jessed."

"That says it all," she said, and held her hand in his.

The rain slanted into them and they cowered beneath the lintel.

Eleanor had to shout to make herself heard. "Last week, in Mortlake, they put a woman in the stocks simply for enquiring of a sorcerer how long Her Majesty might live. The villagers threw rotten vegetables and stinking abuse at her. A Barnes girl, a mere snip of a lass, got charged with witchery by the local butcher. Everyone knew he'd only accused her because she wouldn't open her legs for him. Now she's locked up in Newgate. The magistrate found a Putney woman guilty of using enchantments on her husband. Tied to a cart, they paraded her around the village. This has happened in the last fortnight since the Armada threatened our shores."

"The repulse of the Armada should have made this country a safer and better place to live in. Instead, it's suffocating our freedoms."

"It looks that way," Eleanor said. "But what about your astral travelling? The closer you get to Walsingham, the more heretical those things will appear. He deals with hard evidence, not clairvoyant visions and subtle prognostications. How long do you think it's going to be before a witchfinder comes knocking on our door?"

Eleanor fell silent, though her words had stoked up a whirlwind in his mind. This was England, and it would never be perfect. Yes, the country suffered the plague and the ague, famine and poverty. There was cruelty and injustice. They'd endured the rampant Papists and the invincible Armada. But Eleanor was describing a witch hunt in the shires and alleys of old England itself. And where would that end?

She hadn't finished. "When will you take notice? When I bring you bread and water in your cell in the Tower? Will you want me to watch you scratch your name and your last testament on the walls of your cell before you believe me?"

She folded her arms and turned her head away in disgust. The storm beat against the house, and the thunder and lightning cracked over their heads. The raindrops bounced back up and slashed their shoes and leggings.

"Well?" she asked. "What are you going to do?"

"I hope Walsingham will free me from his employ at the Armada Thanksgiving. What about your midwifery?"

"Don't worry, I'll find a way to leave the midwifery services. After the Thanksgiving, we'll both be free of our chains."

They waited until the storm passed and the rain slowed to a light drizzle, then stepped into the clearing air and sloshed back home along a muddy path.

36

A Woman in Travail

29th August 1588

He came around after another unsettled sleep. He remembered how, once upon a time, he had been so excited to wear the shoes that never wore out. Now his slumber was so restless that he couldn't even find them. August grew old, and so did he. Along with the recent upheavals, his life mirrored the same doubts and uncertainties that plagued the nation.

Some things never changed, as in *Semper Eadem*. After a shortage of manual labourers due to service in the militia, farmers struggled to gather the harvest. Disturbed by the harvest gatherers, swarms of field mice overran the villages and hamlets, followed by gnats and flies. The wherry masters rowed the courtiers up and down the river, shouting and abusing their passengers. The local clergy carried on their pastoral duties, demonising the Papists as heretics and the Catholic contingent as traitors. The ecclesiastical courts convicted adulterers, fornicators and slanderers. Yeomen practised archery on the common. In the market, the local fishermen sold salmon caught in the river. Vagabonds hung around the stalls, begging for alms before the watchmen moved them on with threats of the stocks. Local constables arrested thieves and poachers who'd then spend an uncomfortable day parading around the village in a cart.

Early in the afternoon, there was a loud knock on the door.

Nelan opened it and asked, "Oh. It's you, Ned. What can I do for the local watchman?"

"Master, I be after Mistress Eleanor," Ned said, the sweat beading on his forehead. "She be needed in Putney – a young lass is a callin' for her."

"What for?"

"For midwifery, master."

"We've an important engagement to attend. Is it really necessary?" Nelan asked.

"I hears Matilda be poorly, so it's only your mistress can 'elp."

Pulling a shawl over her shoulders, Eleanor arrived at the door.

"Ah, Miss Eleanor, come quick. The bairn's due."

"Of course," she said.

"Eleanor. Do you have to go?"

"There's a woman in travail, and there's no one else. I'm sorry, but I have to attend to her."

"How long are you going to be away?"

"Ask that of the Lord."

"What about the Armada Thanksgiving?"

"If the bairn comes in time, I'll find you back here, or if it's later, at St Paul's," she said. "Ned, who's the mother?"

"Alice Taylor, Miss," said Ned, swiping away a fly buzzing around his face.

"Who's Alice?" Nelan asked.

"She moved back in with her mother," Eleanor said, "after her husband was sent to fight with the militia in the Netherlands."

"Who will help you with the delivery?" Nelan asked.

"I'll ask Margaret."

"Let me go with you," he said.

"You know you can't be present at the birth. I'll take the open carriage. Margaret, tell the cartman to fetch it to the front door."

"Yes, ma'am," Margaret said.

"I'll take Holdfast for company," Eleanor said. "Come on, boy," and the dog bound up to her and licked her hand.

"Promise you'll be careful."

"I promise," Eleanor said, and left with Ned, Margaret and Holdfast.

Without her vibrancy, the house seemed empty, so he went outside and watched the wherries pass up and down the river and tried to think about the precarious situation he was in where Walsingham was concerned. Surely, tomorrow, the secretary would confirm that his services were no longer required as an intelligencer. But Nelan feared that Walsingham might have him arrested to bolster his flagging reputation amongst the Privy Council. Even if he extricated himself from Walsingham's grip, would he ever be able to leave the secretary's shadow? While he waited, he explored the astral realms, and found nothing untoward there that would threaten Her Majesty at the Thanksgiving. He gave thanks for small mercies!

Would he continue to receive inklings, visions and premonitions? Was he destined to forge his own path in the astral, wearing the cloak of the salamander, in service to the higher? Or would he fall foul of the changing rules that oppressed anyone at odds with the new shining world order?

As evening fell, he fretted like a worried rabbit. The cries of the birds seeking a roost for the night sounded anxious and wary. Flocks of geese and ducks roamed the banks of the river, unable to settle.

He took a horse and rode over to Alice Taylor's hovel outside Putney, and knocked on the door. Margaret answered.

"Can she come to the door?"

"I'll go ask 'er."

Margaret came back and said, "Master, she can't leave the birth, not for all the silver in the Isles. It's takin' longer than expected."

"Send her my love," he said. "And tell her I hope to see her at St Paul's."

"I will," Margaret replied.

By the time he returned home, it was dark.

37

The Armada Thanksgiving

30th August 1588

He lay awake in the early hours, tossing and turning, anxious about his and Eleanor's predicament, and England's plight. Across the Narrow Seas in the Spanish Netherlands, the Duke of Parma had at his command a disciplined army, poised to invade at a moment's notice. The Armada resembled a wounded animal and was just as dangerous. Its vessels carried troops intended to supplement Parma's soldiers. Nelan needed to know where they were now and get an inkling of their plans.

Could he conjure his special shoes? Softly, he rubbed the three wavy lines beneath his middle finger until he drifted off to sleep. In the deep, still quiet of the night, he occupied his salamander astral form, and searched the astral realms for the Armada. Recently, he'd found it off the Orkney Islands. Now, he hunted for it around the north-west tip of Scotland, its coastline as rugged and unwelcoming as the weather.

In his mind's eye, he saw ships battered by sleet, high winds, and even higher waves. They wore the torn, shredded flag of the Madonna. It was the Armada. From John O'Groats, they'd sailed as far as the west coast of Scotland and north of Ireland. That route was the long, lonely way home, but the only course open to them. Soon, they'd turn south into the coastal waters of the Emerald Isle. From there, would they set sail for home or take the back door through Wales into the Island of Angels?

He drifted back to sleep until a rustling sound outside the front door woke him up. Hoping it was Eleanor, he rushed to the front door, only to find it was the red rays of dawn. He dressed, and told Flint and Alexander that should Eleanor and Margaret return soon, to tell his wife to join him at the St Paul's Thanksgiving.

He set off to catch a wherry to Queenhithe. From there, he'd head to Fleet Street to join the procession. Without his wife, he'd attend the Queen and the nation's Armada celebration. He felt a pang of sorrow, for Eleanor would have felt honoured to curtsy before the reigning monarch. But at least he'd checked to see if she was safe and well in Putney.

He felt the pull and sway of the wherry, and the water rushing through his fingers, as the wherry scudded along the Thames. It stopped near his old school at Westminster to pick up a member of the Anglican clergy waiting by the jetty.

"I'm Pastor Christopher," the man said. His voice was hoarse, probably from delivering too many blistering sermons.

"Nelan Michaels."

"What's your business today, Master Michaels?"

"I'm attending the thanksgiving celebrations at St Paul's."

"Mmm, I'm engaged there too, but on the way there, I have to collect some items for the service at Whitefriars Stairs."

"Can I ask, how long have you been pastor at the school?"

"Ah. Many years, too long for me to remember. Why do you ask?"

"I'm an old pupil."

"Ah. Yes, I remember now," he murmured, shifting uncomfortably. "Weren't you involved in an incident in which a boy died?"

"Yes, that was me. Guillermo died in a gunpowder explosion."

"It was a most awful day." The pastor's eyes glazed over. As if recalling a distant memory, he murmured:

No! I run out of the door. You are a heretic, you die! You burn!
It's Easter. It's the time to cleanse the world of sin!

Hearing those words again, after nearly thirteen years, sent cold tremors of anger through the chambers of his soul. "Wait," Nelan said. "They were the exact words Guillermo yelled at me as he tried to ignite the gunpowder. So… you heard him?"

Pastor Christopher nodded.

"But... the school steward accused me of inciting the incident. If you heard him say those words, you must have witnessed the entire incident. Which means you know that Guillermo started the fire, not me."

"Yes, but..." Christopher said.

"But what? You're a pastor. For God's sake, why didn't you say anything at the time?"

"I-I..." the pastor stammered.

"Damn you! After all these years, you owe me an explanation."

The pastor turned his eyes away from him and drooped his head.

"Yes, I'll confess. I was first ordained as a Catholic priest. When that incident happened, I had just converted to the Anglican faith. I had my first placement at Westminster School. I'd reported to the school steward that very morning, so how could I contradict his version of events?"

"A man of the cloth, you should have told the truth. Instead, you allowed yourself to bear false witness! In doing so, you condemned me to years of pain and distress, caused the death of my father, and the destruction of my father's house!"

Pastor Christopher scrunched up his face. Nelan thought the man was going to weep, but he composed himself and said, "I'm ashamed I didn't speak up. I admit, you did not murder Guillermo. The boy blew himself up. I know you tried to help him."

"I hope you can see that it's not what we do that condemns us, but what we don't do, or what we fail to do!" Nelan growled.

They sat in silence for the rest of the journey, each man haunted by their own memories. The wherry docked at Whitefriars Stairs. Scores of boats of all shapes and sizes descended on the jetties and docking bays along the river. Many were adorned with screens for the ladies to shelter from the sun, while minstrels played tunes louder than their neighbour, creating a cacophony of tabor and trumpet, lute and flute.

Nelan jumped out of the wherry. He had to get away from Pastor Christopher. The man disgusted him. He stumbled to the nearest street corner and vomited. Though the pastor had finally corroborated his story, it was too little, too late. Since the incident, Nelan had grown up and changed. To free himself of its memory, he resolved to no longer be bound by any guilt or shame about it.

Mingling with the crowds, he headed towards Fleet Street. A man wearing a velvet doublet complete with jags and a fine white ruff stood on the corner, calling out, "Buy it here! The Queen's speech. Only a farthing!"

"Who are you and what's this about?" Nelan asked.

"I'm Thomas Deloney and this is a report of the Queen's speech. I heard her deliver it ten days ago to her troops at Tilbury Camp! How her words roused the spirit!"

"I'll take one," Nelan said, and he read:

My loving people, we are persuaded by some who are careful of our safety to take heed how we commit ourselves to armed multitudes, for fear of treachery. But I assure you, I do not desire to distrust my faithful and loving people.

Let tyrants fear, I have always so behaved that, under God, I have placed my chief strength and safeguard in the loyal hearts and goodwill of my subjects.

Therefore I am come amongst you, not for my recreation and disport, but am resolved in the midst and heat of battle to live and die amongst you all.

I know I have the body of a weak and feeble woman but I have the heart and stomach of a king, and of a king of England too, and think foul scorn that Parma or Spain or any prince of Europe should dare invade the borders of my realm.

Rather than any dishonour shall grow by me, I will take up arms, and by your concord in the camp and your valour in the field, we shall shortly have a famous victory over those enemies of God, my Kingdom, and my people.

These stirring words were those of a woman royal in title and finesse. Staunch, resolute and defiant, they epitomised the sentiment of requital in the motto *Honi Soit Qui Mal Y Pense*. Despite, or perhaps because of, the severe threat to her beloved country posed by the Armada, the Queen had grown into a personage regal in both stature and character. His mood lightened, and he looked forward with intense interest to seeing her.

There was a gathering excitement in the air, a kind of rampant anticipation. For the thatcher and the tinker, the haberdasher and the vintner, the cooper and the ostler, it was a rare treat and high privilege to lay eyes on their queen.

The bottleneck to cross Fleet Bridge delayed his progress, which was softened by the sounds of a minstrel strumming his lute and singing:

> *The rose is red, the grass is green,*
> *Serve Queen Bess, our noble queen.*

Nelan tapped his foot to the catchy tune, and soon the crowd sang along with more heart than harmony.

The packed inns hosted much merriment and conviviality amongst men and women alike. On the corner of Old Bailey, a Winchester goose ruffled her feathers at him.

"Come over 'ere, young lad." She beckoned to him while bouncing her considerable assets in the palms of her hands. "Me's curious," she said with a wicked grin. "Is your credentials as great... as you are little? For methinks, out of small things, great things shall arise."

"They do and they are," he said with a wide grin. Standing on tip-toe, he dropped two farthings into the gaping chasm that passed as her cleavage. They disappeared into the blackness, possibly never to be seen again. Ignoring her pleadings and thank-yous, he headed for Lud's Gate. St Paul's loomed up ahead. The streets were jammed like fish in a barrel.

Flags, streamers and bunting of scarlet and purple, red and white adorned the processional route. The aldermen had affixed long evocative tapestries to the walls. One depicted the Queen's accession, while another showed her seated on the coronation throne surrounded by the glory of Westminster Abbey. Sir Francis Drake's fantastic world voyage featured in a third. A fourth depicted the execution of Mary, Queen of Scots, just last year. A fifth illustrated the repulse of the Armada. These represented the high points of the age.

A vagrant called to him. The man was slumped against the wall, begging bowl by his side, his clothes torn and his hair tarred black as pitch.

"By the Lord, it's Little 'imself!" the voice said, drawing on a leather flagon.

"Tom Blacollers! What happened to the bosun of the *Golden Hind*?" Nelan asked.

"The sickness got me," Tom said, coughing into his sleeve. His teeth were black as rot, and his beard was matted and twisted like an old rope.

"I'm sorry."

"'Tis the Lord's will, an' that of our Queen Bess," he added with a sigh of regret. "But I ain't alone. There's mariners aplenty rottin' on Deptford wharf. By the toll of each watch, another good sailor falls asleep in the deep abyss."

"Is that so?"

"These men, me an' others," Tom went on, "we give our last breath for England and for Bess. But for the want of a bandage, a sup of ale, or some simple solace, we're left stinkin' in the bilges."

Tom spat blood and phlegm, and God knows what else, onto the ground.

"Mother Britannia ought to care for her own," Nelan murmured. Delving into his purse, he added a penny to Tom's begging bowl.

Up ahead, two men approached through the crowd. One was exquisitely attired in a padded doublet, white ruff and cuffs, black cloth hat and tight breeches. The other, his assistant, shouted, "Alms for the poor. Alms for the poor."

"Come here." Nelan waved them over to him.

The gentleman said, "I be Master John Piers, the royal almoner."

"It's a bleedin' miracle, it is," Tom grunted, his face creased into a deep frown. "Years servin' in the navy and look, I call 'em, and the master almsman comes with me just rewards."

"Here's alms for your service. I hope this provides you with some comfort," the almoner said, dropping another penny in his begging bowl.

"Most kind of ya." Tom slurred his words before taking another swig.

"Thank the Queen, for I am but her loyal and faithful servant."

Up ahead, a man yelled, "Clear the way!"

The man wore a silver griffin emblazoned on his chest. It was John Tunnall, the town crier. The crowd parted before him like the Red Sea, leaving the centre of the street clear for the procession. A group of aldermen wielding pikes marched stiffly behind him. A buzz of expectancy circled around the crowd.

"Is she there? Can you see our Queen Bess?" one asked.

"Gawd bless 'er," another said.

Dressed in velvet cloaks and chains of gold, the aldermen led a procession of sailors carrying trophies won from the Spanish in the heat of battle. One carried a torn banner, another a charred ensign, a third the famed Madonna emblem of the Armada. As they passed on their way to be hung in the cathedral, the crowd cheered and applauded.

"We stuffed them Dons good 'n' proper," one chimed.

"An' don't these burnt-up flags shows it?" cried another.

Mingling amongst the throng were several burly, thick-set men. Wearing shifty looks, their long black capes made them conspicuous on this warm late August day. Walsingham's intelligencers were keeping a wary eye out for conspirators who would harm the Queen.

A flurry of trumpeters led the main procession of gentlemen, footmen and equerries, while the mayor of the City of London, arrayed in his scarlet attire, brandished the royal sceptre before the Queen's carriage. In deference to their Queen, they carried their hats in their hands. On seeing the white steeds drawing the Queen's chariot, and Elizabeth herself attired in silver armour and a gilded crown, the crowd shouted their acclaim, and waved their coloured flags and gay streamers. Her escort consisted of members of her Privy Council, the Yeomen of the Guard, the Lord Chamberlain, the ladies of the court and the Captain of the Guard. She entered the city through Lud's Gate and soon paraded into the atrium on the west side of the cathedral.

With the pageantry of England in full flow, the blare of the trumpets lifted the spirits of yeomen and noblemen alike, and gently raised the angels of the island from their slumber.

Once the Queen had entered St Paul's, everyone raced to the atrium, blocking the main entrance. Nelan darted up the narrow lanes by the side of the cathedral, before nipping into St Paul's Cross churchyard, where a group of men were hauling logs and kindling from carts to erect a bonfire. He hurried past them towards the east end of the cathedral.

He found a ramp down to the sacristy, at the base of which twelve clergy stood in animated discussion. Pastor Christopher was one, and he said, "Nelan Michaels, how delightful to see you again."

Behind the pastor, a man in a brown cassock pulled a hand-drawn cart, with a rough tarpaulin thrown over its contents.

On seeing Pastor Christopher and the man with the cart, one of the clergy said, "Well, about time, too. We've not long before the service. Have you brought them?"

"I have," Christopher said, tousling his grey locks. "Here they are," and he pulled off the tarpaulin covering the cart, revealing a collection of old church vestments.

"We're to don these robes, eh?" one of the clergy thundered. "Look! This one's got scorch marks. And this one's torn."

"We're specifically asked to wear them," Pastor Christopher replied.

"But these are gold," the man said, squidging up his nose. "Only Roman Catholic priests wear gold vestments. We're Anglican clergy. We don't wear papist cloth!"

The other clergy jerked back a step, as if someone had spoken the secret name of Lucifer himself.

"You had better put them on," Pastor Christopher said.

"Why? On whose say-so?" one of them asked.

"The Queen's," Christopher said. "She wears silver. We wear gold. She's also asked for us twelve pastors to lead out the bishop. Each of us will hold a candle and a bell."

"Bell and candle. If we had a book, it'd be an exorcism," the man suggested, drawing a smirk from the others.

"Whatever you think," Christopher said, "the Queen is the governor of the Church of England, so we obey her commands."

"Aye. You have a point," the clergyman said.

Nelan interrupted. "The golden robes are symbolic, and I have an inkling that we can make a difference with them here today."

"How's that?" Christopher asked.

"I'll show you in due course," Nelan replied. "For now, can I borrow this silver bell? Thank you."

With a visible reluctance, the pastors donned the tattered gold robes.

After the thanksgiving service, the procession moved outside. In the hour before dusk, the twelve pastors led the bishop into St Paul's Cross churchyard. Each held a bell and candles that fluttered in the breeze. With his back bent, the old bishop struggled up the steps of the pulpit. The people swarmed around, while the Queen sat on her throne some distance away to hear his homily. Dressed in scarlet robes and mitre, the bishop lavished praise on the Queen and the Privy Council, paid tribute to the Royal Navy and its commanders for their courageous service, and praised the Almighty for saving the country.

This was the moment. The flood was at the full. Nelan had waited for it all his life. He seized it without hesitation. Heart beating wildly, he marched into the middle of the churchyard. Surrounded by hundreds of people, admirals and captains, aldermen and dignitaries, the Queen looking on, her yeomen about to pounce, he raised his right arm and rang the silver bell.

This simple act silenced the audience. The bishop guffawed. The twelve pastors froze. The hounds ceased their barking. Even the crows stopped squawking. Heads turned to the Queen for a signal. Like the emperor in the Coliseum in judgement of a gladiator, would her thumb point up or down? After an excruciating pause, she smiled and, with stately grace, nodded her head.

With the Queen's endorsement, Nelan recited from a tract he had long ago committed to memory:

> *In the name of God the All-powerful, Father, Son and Holy Ghost, by virtue of the power which has been given of binding and loosening in Heaven and on earth.*
> *Ex Insula Angelorum. The Island of Angels, no less.*
> *For always was it so and always thus to be.*
> *Let the angels of the island be loosened from their binding!*
> *Fiat! Fiat! Fiat!*

The twelve pastors echoed the last line.

Standing in front of Pastor Christopher, Nelan knocked the candle from the man's hand, then snuffed it out, extinguishing the flame. The other pastors chucked their candles to the ground and stamped them into the earth. The light went out.

Nelan grabbed Christopher's gold vestment by the shoulder blades, and, in one bold, swift movement, ripped it from his body. Then he threw it down onto the ground and stamped on it with cold anger. In the thrall of the moment, the other pastors ripped off their robes with an enthusiasm bordering on delight and ground them into the earth.

Nelan yelled into the gloaming:

Bell, Book and Candle shall not drive me back.

A pall of silence descended on the churchyard and all in it. In that moment, Nelan felt a weight lift from his shoulders, the weight of centuries of heavy papal oppression, from the Roman occupation to the Spanish reign of Mary and more, much more.

The warden strode into the churchyard, flaming torch in hand, and kissed the fire against the base of the bonfire. Warming the souls of the faithful, the pitch in the bonfire billowed clouds of black smoke into the evening air, sending the signal to light beacons across the land in a mass celebration of that poignant and mysterious moment. The fire blazed into the heavens with such ferocity that the bells of the cathedral trembled, then shuddered, and then murmured. As the clapper thudded against the bell, it rang, and all the bells rang in sweet harmony.

Fiat! Let it be done. And the miracle was done. Because they rang of their own accord, without human intervention. At first, they pealed slowly, until the bells boomed over the city rooftops and across the shires, summoning a response in kind, until every bell chimed from steeple and tower.

This was the signal for every beacon to be lit along the ancient Celtic leys, along the North and South Downs, along the Michael and Mary line and the other Druid trackways, and along the old church network.

On their own, the flame of the candle and the ringing of the bell were impotent, but with the addition of the missing third component, the 'book', or the service, involving the spoken word, they became a trinity. He'd realised this while on board the *Revenge,* but only now could act on it.

The combination of the Bell, Book and Candle dispersed the historic lingering remnants of anxiety and terror. No more would the dread fear of the burning bundle of sticks stalk the isle. The scarlet tide had been repulsed. After the heat and bluster of battle came an exorcism and joyful thanksgiving. The Queen was radiant in her silver armour.

Amidst the resounding delight of the people, as they raised a cry of high joy, a silver face appeared in the astral above the churchyard, and another and another, until a fine silver rain fell on the heads of the congregation, filling them with the lithe spirit of the living fire.

The exorcism was done. The Gordian knot cut. The scarlet pall dispersed, releasing the angels of the land to inspire the people and send them on quests around the world to discover what they were meant to discover.

Could this be the mystery of the game of bowls, of the kissing of the mistress, of how the curvature of the ball echoed the crescent or eagle shape of the Armada? Was the midnight of eights a mere coincidence, or was it a coalescence of many threads coming together for a purpose, hidden at first, and apparent only later? Was there no such thing as a coincidence, only a current of power running down and along the many chains of connection, joining this thread to that, which the fallible minds of men interpreted as miraculous?

As he pondered these matters, Nelan turned to find Sir Francis Walsingham behind him with two other dignitaries.

"This has been a fine exhibition of your talents," Walsingham said, pointing to the candles and robes lying forlorn on the ground.

"I did it for England," Nelan replied.

"Of course you did," Walsingham said, rather too glibly for Nelan's liking. "In the meantime, may I introduce you to Sir William Cecil, the Lord Burghley."

"Greetings, my lord."

The other dignitary said to him, "Greetings, Nelan."

A shiver went down his spine as Nelan heard the man's deep voice. This was the man who had spoken to Walsingham like he was a cur.

"And this," Walsingham said, "is the sponsor of the *Golden Hind*, Sir Christopher Hatton."

"Greetings, my lord," Nelan said. Now, he'd met the English Triumvirate.

Walsingham said, "If you'd care to join us in the atrium for the culmination of the thanksgiving, there's someone who'd like to ask you about what we've all just witnessed."

38

The Atrium

Early evening on 30th August 1588

His nerves trilled with a heightened sensitivity. He hoped this represented an end and a beginning for him, his adopted country and her angels. Perhaps now they could navigate the gaps and crevices in people's prejudices and superstitions. Perhaps one day, with the help of the angels, Britain would explore the world, become a custodian of great invention and a creator of fine art, and fulfil Dr Dee's vision.

Gliding on that air of success, he strode forth to meet the most prominent lady of the times, Queen Elizabeth, Gloriana herself. As he emerged into the atrium, the central court outside the west entrance, three groups of men were building three more bonfires. He noticed something sinister about them – the men had set stakes in the middle of the bonfires and surrounded them with logs, twigs, planks and kindling. These were for burnings. Nelan gulped. This was not how he had expected the thanksgiving to end. The crowd did, because they were ready for the entertainment, and jostled for the best view. Behind them, an old yew tree cast early evening shadows across the court.

"Nelan, the Queen awaits you," Walsingham said.

His only regret was that Eleanor hadn't made it in time. She would have loved the ceremony and the pageantry, and the privilege of meeting Her Majesty.

The Captain of the Queen's Guard ushered him into her presence.

Dressed as a warrior queen in her silver armour, she sat to one side, giving her a clear view of the atrium. The attendants bustled and chased around to finish the entertainment before sunset.

To the beat of the drum and the blare of the trumpet, the marshall strolled into the middle of the atrium, and announced, "My Queen, my lords, ladies and gentlemen, yeomen and aldermen all, this is the last part of the ceremony, when we give thanks to our Queen, and to our God, whose winds blew away the Armada."

The crowd cheered and threw streamers and flags high in the air to salute the Queen for this, her finest achievement.

The marshall went on: "We end the thanksgiving with a demonstration of how we uphold the law of the land. For without the law, and the Queen, who, with God's grace, gives us the law, we are but primitive savages. These burnings are a cleansing and a final sacrifice to God's law."

As the crowd applauded, three carts trundled over the cobblestones into the centre of the atrium. They each carried a person wearing a long white robe with a hood over their head. Wailers and mourners, beating their chests, followed the first two carts. A mangy hound and an older woman attended the third.

Someone in the crowd yelled, "Let's see 'em burn!"

"Douse 'em in flames!" cried another.

Edging forward like blind folk, the three descended from the carts. From their smaller bodies and demeanour, Nelan saw they were women. The pikemen kept the crowd at bay. The crowd booed and heckled. A few threw rotten fruit and vegetables at the women. The condemned wore hoods, hiding their identities and, for the moment, their crimes. The pikemen fastened them to the stump in the middle of each of the bonfires. From her movements, Nelan thought he recognised the third woman, but before he could look at her more closely, the crowd surged forward, roaring vitriolic abuse.

The dog accompanying her seemed familiar, but as he turned to catch another glimpse of it, Walsingham tapped him on the shoulder and said, "Nelan, I want to speak to you about your future employment. After deliberating with the other members of the Privy Council, I have reluctantly agreed to let you leave."

"I-I'm pleased… to have been of service," Nelan stammered, although he wasn't sure if the secretary was being ironic, or using another of his famous euphemisms. He hoped that the termination of his employ with Walsingham would see an end to any hidden, unresolved malice he or they might have had towards him.

"Oh, and the Queen will see you now," Walsingham added.

Nelan thought he heard Eleanor's voice and glanced over his shoulder to find her, but she was not amongst the crowd. He sighed in disappointment. Turning his back on the bonfires, he faced Her Majesty. Legs shaking, hands moist, Nelan approached Gloriana herself. This was a great privilege, to meet one of the most important personages of the age, the personification of Britannia, who sat on a throne on a podium looking down on her beloved people. Standing in front of her as upright as a maypole, the mayor held the sceptre of state. As the angels of the island danced around her, she sparkled. With her charisma, she inspired greatness from her people and repulsed the evil that would arrest it.

"My Moor," she said, using her nickname for him. "Introduce me. Who have we here?"

"This is Master Nelan Michaels, Your Grace," Walsingham said.

Nelan mumbled, "It's an honour to enter your presence, Your Highness." With a long high sweep of his hand, he bowed to her and to what she represented; a royal human being, and all that was associated with that high attainment. Behind him, he heard sounds of a scuffle. A dog howled. A woman yelled. Etiquette forced him to keep his eyes on her.

Behind him, he heard the marshall announce, "These three wretches are sentenced according to the provisions of the Witchery Act, whereby if someone has perished through the practice of witchcraft, their crime is punishable by death."

Even if he had wanted to turn around, Hatton, Cecil and Walsingham stood in a phalanx behind him, blocking his rear view of the bonfires.

Cecil stepped forward next to him and said, "The witches are ready, Your Highness."

"Thank you," the Queen said, "but first I shall converse with this gallant young man."

She turned her gaze on him, her green eyes assessing his every movement. His heart beat like a drum, and his mouth was as dry as an autumn leaf.

"Master Michaels, you are indeed a canny character. We intended this service to be a thanksgiving to cleanse our land of the poison of the Spanish and Vatican presence. That was why we donned the silver armour, to complement the priests' golden robes. Your improvised version of the Bell, Book and Candle was an effective and fitting way to exorcise the land of its demons!"

"I'm glad you thought so, Your Majesty. Dr Dee taught me well."

"It is so. We've read with interest various reports of your escapades at the Battle of Gravelines where we're reliably informed you conjured an entity, a silver griffin no less, to combat the Spanish threat. Our profound thanks are due to you for that."

"It was my honour and my duty, Your Majesty," he murmured.

"We are minded to reward your valour and service. We can offer you a licence to trade with far-off lands. Or perhaps you'd prefer a pension and an official title."

"You're very kind, ma'am," he replied, his head spinning with excitement.

All ruff and robe, Cecil leaned in towards her and asked, "Shall we proceed, ma'am?"

She deigned not to reply but looked at Nelan, who bowed his head in deference.

"Ma'am, the torches are lit."

"I know you are my 'Spirit', Cecil, but I can see that for myself."

Cecil stood still, despite the rebuke.

"Where were we, Master Nelan?" the Queen asked.

He was about to reply when a hush descended on the atrium. The Queen looked up, her attention drawn by an incident in the atrium.

In that pause, a woman cried out from the crowd, "She's not a witch. She's innocent!"

The woman's voice… the yew tree… and those words… jogged a distant memory.

Wait. I had a premonition of this… in Dover… I know the dog. It's Holdfast. Oh, God! I know who's tied to one of the stakes!

"Ma'am, please," he said. "The bonfires. May I look?"

The Queen gave her assent.

As Nelan turned, Cecil asked, "Ma'am? Shall we?"

"Hold the fire!" she snapped.

Holdfast scrambled over the kindling and climbed to the top of the bonfire. With back bent and paws forward, the hound yelped at the feet of one of the witches. Holdfast clenched the hem of the witch's long white robe in its jaw and tugged at it. It snagged on the hood. To retrieve the hound, a yeoman clambered up the bonfire, but slipped on the logs and tumbled back down to the ground. The crowd erupted with hilarity. With one last tug, Holdfast pulled off the white robe, hood and all.

"Eleanor!" he cried.

His wife lifted her head and searched him out with her eyes. A ball of cloth gagged her mouth.

His legs buckled. His mouth went as dry as fire, and his chest felt like it supported the weight of the world.

"*Save me! Untie me!*" she said. But her voice. He didn't hear it with his ears. He heard it in his soul. Hands clasped in prayer, he plunged to his knees.

Behind him, he felt the Queen's eyes on him.

"*I'm innocent. Don't let me die by fire.*" Again, Eleanor's voice in his soul.

"Ma'am, the witches, the burning?" Cecil asked.

"*I tried to save the mother... I couldn't... I had to choose.*" Eleanor's voice was desperate.

"Ma'am, the crowd grows impatient," Cecil added.

The Queen waved him away, saying, "They can wait, my Spirit. Leave us be, Cecil. We will talk to Master Michaels. Now, what ails thee, sirrah?"

"O-one of the accused..." he stammered.

"Who is she to you?"

"My wife."

"Ma'am, we delay the proceedings," Cecil said.

"Cecil, then delay we shall. This is our land. These are our people. We shall do whatever we can to protect them."

Cecil bowed in deference.

Nelan cleared his throat, lifted himself up to his full height, and looked at Her Majesty. Her eyes resembled a couple of lithe green emeralds, wizened and wary, and yet soft and kindly. "Your Majesty offered me a reward for my valour and service," he said. "I beg you, ma'am, release my wife, who is innocent of these crimes."

Elizabeth thought for a while. The world waited. The crowd waited. So did Nelan, his heart thumping like a tabor. Finally, she turned to Cecil and asked, "This burning is at our discretion, is it not?"

"Madam, yes, provision can be made… I suppose."

"You suppose, Cecil? In our presence, you shall do more than suppose!"

"Yes, ma'am. It is a matter for the governor of the Church."

"Who might that be?" she snarled.

"You, Your Majesty."

"Thank you! Then inform us of this woman's witchery, the wife of Master Michaels here."

"I must defer to Sir Francis, ma'am," Cecil said. "He deals with the case."

"My Moor," the Queen said. "Speak truthfully of this woman's supposed crimes."

"She's a midwife, ma'am," Walsingham said, "who attended a birth where the mother died but the infant lived. She used sorcery and incantations to kill the mother and take the child for herself."

"Alas, an all-too-common crime these days," the Queen murmured, as if to herself. She turned to Nelan and asked, "Is this true? Why would your wife do that? Is she barren that she has no offspring?" Nelan noticed a rueful look on the Queen's face as she asked the last question.

"It is true, ma'am, that the Lord has not blessed our marriage with children," he replied. "But my Eleanor is of warm heart and kindly disposition. She is a goodly woman."

"How do you know of her innocence?"

"She told me so."

"How? Were you present at the birth?"

"No, I was travelling here. But she just spoke to me."

"How is that possible when she is bound and gagged, and over yonder?"

"I know, ma'am. But I heard her voice… in my soul… as clear as sunlight. Dr Dee taught me how to listen to someone at distance."

"We miss the doctor's good counsel, presence and wisdom. Your wife, what did she tell you?"

"She said that there were severe complications during the birth.

Unable to save both mother and child, she had to choose one or t'other, and chose the infant. She's distraught."

"I can understand that she would be, and I am inclined to believe your testimony."

"Do you want us to proceed with the burning?" Cecil again.

"Cecil, never has my Spirit lacked so much spirit! Don't you hear anything I say?"

"Ma'am?"

"We are England. And England has seen enough death. Death is never a solve and never triumphant. Stop the burning. On this day of thanksgiving, we are of a mind to exercise clemency. We hereby declare that the goodly wife of Master Michaels has no crime to answer, and is free to go. Release her."

"And the other two? The burning deters any would-be conjurers and merchants of enchantment."

"Deny us not, sirrah!" she thundered. "Release all three of them. By the will of England, and by our will, they are free to go. *Fiat! Fiat! Fiat!* Marshall, dowse the torches. We have seen enough burnings. Let the land hear no more lamentation."

"Your Highness, you saved the country," Nelan said. "Now, you've saved the life of my wife. I don't know how to thank you."

"Go to her with my blessing. She needs you," the Queen said, and ushered him away with a regal wave of her hand.

The pikemen untied Eleanor. Nelan helped her down from the top of the bonfire. The stark memories of the smell of the burning wood of his mother's pyre and the odours of the fire at his father's house stung his nostrils. The fear slowed his heart. His legs barely held him up as he embraced his beloved. They held each other hard, afraid to let go. Her pain and anguish gushed over him like a bitter wind, chilling him to the bone.

She could just about breathe God's air. Such was her terror, she was as good as dead to the world. He pulled away from her. He touched her cheek, wiping away the hot tears from her face, white with fear and raw with relief. Eleanor didn't appear to know what had happened to her, or where she was. The fire in her eyes had gone. He helped her into the cart, and she cuddled up to Holdfast. Margaret sat next to her and said, "Oh, master, if you weren't there talkin' with Her Majesty, my mistress be gone to Heaven be now."

"True enough," he said, as he took the reins and steered the cart across the cobblestones and out of the atrium into the streets of London.

Margaret sang soft lullabies to ease Eleanor's fractured mind. Beneath her joyful tunes lay a timbre of worry.

"Yesterday evening, when I came to Alice's house, you told me everything was fine with the birth," he said.

"Oh, master, it was," Margaret said. "After you left, it got all dark and dingy, and me an' Alice's ma, we lit them candles. There was awful cryin' and yellin' in pain. The baby's breech, and Eleanor's strugglin' to save 'em both. She delivers the infant, all squirmy like a little frog. We're all praisin' the Almighty when all of a sudden, Alice, the poor dear, she's bleedin' all over the straw. Next thing, she lets out this long sigh, an' she's climbed the stairs to the gates of Heaven. We all cried to the Lord. Even Holdfast is wailing at the ripening moon. Ned goes to fetch the constable an' the priest."

"Then what happened?"

"When he gets back, there's another fella with 'em. Give me the creeps, he did."

"What was his name?"

"Oh master, methinks it were John. An' his hand was all twisted an' deformed."

"That's John Halton, all right."

"He was dishin' out the orders to the constable, he was."

"Then what?"

"Well, this John talks to Alice's ma, all alone they was. Next thing, she's spittin' bile, and accusin' the mistress a castin' a spell on her daughter, all so the mistress can have the newborn for herself. The mistress accused of witchcraft! No! She'd never do summat like that. But the fella John says the mistress is Bridget, the lass executed for witchery. The constable arrests my mistress. Me, I'm beatin' this John with me fists. But the constable, he drags mistress off to Newgate. Me 'n' Ned go there with her. Holdfast too. Can't leave her on her own there, can we?"

Nelan shook his head. "Good, I'm glad you stayed with her. Where's the infant now?"

"With Alice's ma."

What on earth was John Halton doing at the birth? And what

did he say to Alice's ma to make her turn on Eleanor like that? Nelan smelled a rat, because John Halton worked for Walsingham.

He was so worried about Eleanor that he couldn't think about it. Perhaps she'd wake up soon. While he prayed for that moment, he shuddered to think how close he had come to losing her altogether. Eleanor tied to the bonfire post, a man eager to light a fire beneath her feet, and Cecil urging the Queen. Horrific! Exactly like Nelan's mother. Agnes, her name. In agony, she died. The Inquisition had executed her, but it was the English Triumvirate who had plotted to put Eleanor to the torch. She was one of their own, yet that didn't deter them. And during a thanksgiving. The only thanks were due to the Queen for her clemency.

The ghosts from his past still haunted him. Years ago, Guillermo had tried to set fire to him, but instead, had set himself on fire. As the fires took hold, Nelan desperately tried to help the young Spaniard. But the consuming flames had sparked in him a terrible memory of Agnes's brutal murder and he had frozen. Pastor Christopher's tardy confession had eased his conscience and finally freed him of any lurking vestiges of guilt.

From that day thirteen years ago, his life had resembled a runaway horse. He was the unfortunate rider, frantically trying to stay in the saddle, grab the reins and slow its gallop. Whenever he succeeded, some new unjust accusation would pull the reins from his flailing grasp, like the theft of the paymaster general's casket.

During the thanksgiving service, he had successfully repeated his own version of the Anathema – the rite of the excommunication using Bell, Book and Candle. He was as astonished as everyone else at the bells it had caused to ring – *of their own accord!* Since then, the scarlet pall in the valleys of the Isle had dispersed. His rite had worked!

Once again, there was joy in the land and the land was in joy.

39

The Funeral

2nd September 1588

In the three days since the terror of the atrium, Eleanor had slept and rested, and although she had improved, her mental healing was too slow for Nelan's peace of mind. He felt dreadful about her predicament. She was like a ghost without substance, her mind elsewhere, not present. He wanted his wife back, so they could laugh again and be happy together. The same thing had happened to him, that mindless frozen state, unable to respond, so he knew exactly what she endured.

Lingering in the nether regions of life, Eleanor mouthed incoherent words and phrases to herself, her eyes focusing on nothing and everything. Nelan prayed for her recovery. The severe threat of the burning in the atrium had been a shock and a deep wound in her mind. Would she ever revive? Every time he looked at his lovely wife, instead of a feeling of love and warmth, his cup was filled with bitterness and remorse.

Why, oh why, did she insist on helping Alice Taylor? He wanted to forgive Alice's ma, despite her false accusation against his Eleanor. So he attended Alice's funeral, which was held at the little chapel in Putney, close to Barn Elms.

When he saw Alice's ma, he offered out of kindness to pay for the funeral expenses. After all, she'd suffered the tragic loss of her daughter in childbirth. To his astonishment, she refused, insisting that she'd pay for it out of her own pocket. Yet, a lowly widow living in a run-down hovel, how could she afford to do that?

These confused thoughts ran through his mind as he stood by an open grave, the smell of freshly dug earth stinging his nostrils. The pallbearers lowered Alice Taylor's earthly remains into the open grave. Alice's ma, clutching the newborn in swaddling clothes, wept tears of grief. On leaving the cemetery, she turned to him and said, "I'm sorry."

As he headed home in the wherry, he had a nagging feeling that something was drastically wrong, and it wasn't just Eleanor's wounded state of mind. Why did Alice's ma apologise to him? What was John Halton doing meddling at the birth? The man and his deformed hand perhaps had a deformed part to play in her arrest. He was one of Walsingham's intelligencers, which meant the secretary must have known about her arrest for witchcraft. When Nelan first saw Walsingham at the Armada Thanksgiving, why didn't he tell him the news about Eleanor? He could have easily sanctioned her release. But he didn't. Cecil had repeatedly pressed the Queen to start the burnings, which Nelan had barely stopped in time.

Nelan felt vulnerable, as if vultures circled above him, but he'd only see them when they pounced. He watched flocks of geese heading for warmer, safer climes and their winter homes. It was that time of year. A change of seasons. A change of rules. Then he realised; it was time to fly the nest. To protect his family, he couldn't stay in Mortlake any longer. That night, he went to sleep restless and worried.

40

The Awakening

3rd September 1588

The early rays of dawn slunk into the room. During the four days since the Armada Thanksgiving, he'd tried to work out the events that culminated in the atrium at St Paul's. Finally, he drew the pieces of the puzzle together.

There was only one conclusion: Walsingham had planned it all. When the constable was called to attend Alice Taylor's death, like an old fox, Walsingham must have sniffed an opportunity to wreak revenge. Then, on learning that Eleanor was the attending midwife, he'd acted swiftly and ruthlessly, despatching John Halton. But for what purpose?

Walsingham had ordered Eleanor's arrest, an act of vengeance prompted by the secretary's earlier conversation with Sir Christopher Hatton. To save his own skin, Walsingham had to prove to Hatton and Cecil that he could sever ties with Nelan. The secretary had been reluctant to target Nelan before the Armada Thanksgiving because he knew Captain Whiddon had named Nelan in his despatch to the Queen. Instead, Walsingham had targeted his Eleanor. The secretary had probably even arranged for Nelan to be present in St Paul's atrium to witness the lighting of the bonfire. By all that was sacred, Walsingham had contrived the entire scheme.

When Nelan had offered to pay for Alice Taylor's funeral, her mother had insisted that she'd settle it herself. Yet she was a lowly, impoverished woman who could not have afforded to pay for the service on her own. Ah! So, Walsingham, via John Halton, had bribed her to invent the story of Eleanor's witchery. The Taylor woman had traded on the death in childbirth of her own daughter! That was why she'd apologised to him. The guilt had loosened her tongue.

The Triumvirate conspired against him. If they had executed Eleanor, they knew it would have destroyed him and severed his astral connections. But they had not reckoned on the Queen pardoning her.

If they had tried once to snare him, they'd try again. He had to act fast. Careful not to wake Eleanor, he sneaked out of bed to find a particular object. He groped around in the dark until he found it and then tucked it in his purse. Grabbing a candle, he tiptoed downstairs and opened the front door. The two primordial forces of creation were locked in their perpetual dance; the darkness fought to banish the light; the light fought to brighten the dark.

Holdfast settled next to him on the doorstep. From there, he could see Dr Dee's house, a shell of what it once was. If only the good doctor was there, he'd have called upon the angels of the isle to heal Eleanor's illness.

He was about to receive a message. He didn't know what it was, only that it involved the ruby salamander pendant. As he held it, it throbbed with an uncanny presence. With each pulse, he received a different image. First, he saw rows of shelves stacked with letters and cyphers, manuscripts and books. Then he got a picture of the dark wood panelling of the door and the walls, the thick oak floorboards, and the tiny window, giving the room a confined, closed-in feel. Then came an image of a long wooden desk, full of papers and scrolls, quills and inkwells. He recognised the miniature portrait on the desk showing the secretary standing behind a seated woman and two young boys: Walsingham's stepsons.

He was 'seeing' into Walsingham's office. But how? During the months that the ruby salamander pendant had sat in Walsingham's desk, was it possible it had absorbed the subtle vibrations within his office, which now provided Nelan with an astral window into it?

What he witnessed wasn't something in the past. It was happening at this moment. At first, he heard the voices of two men, and then he saw their blurred images. The astral mists cleared, and it was as if distance had shrunk, and he was present in the room, listening to their conversation.

"Is everything prepared?" Walsingham was saying.

"It's the middle of the night, but, yes, the constables and pikemen are ready, m'lord." That was John Halton.

Walsingham then perused a document and read:

This warrant is for the arrest, detention and trial of Nelan Michaels of Mortlake for the wilful destruction of Her Majesty's property."

"What exactly did he do?" John Halton asked.

"He burned down the church at Plymouth prison."

"Despicable!" John Halton said.

"Then serve the warrant now, if you please!"

Nelan didn't need to hear anymore. It would not take the constables long to follow the Old Church Road from Barn Elms to Mortlake.

He woke Eleanor, Flint, Margaret and Alexander. The day after returning from the atrium, he'd packed a few essential belongings, prescient that he'd need them. Flint and Alexander loaded the bags into the wherry. The waxing gibbous moon hung in the night sky, lighting their way into a new life.

As they launched the boat into the river flow, he said to Flint and Alexander, "I've got the tiller. You two, get rowing. We've a journey to make."

Eleanor hummed quietly to herself, and let her hands run through the water as they pushed off from the jetty and drifted into the flow.

Margaret's anxiety boiled over. "Master," she said, "we're leavin' home like we's being chased, but I don't see nobody runnin' after us. And we got all these bags in the wherry. Even Holdfast's here with us. Where we all goin' in the middle of the night?"

He glanced at her innocent eyes, and it drove him to answer her as best he could. How could he tell her that a triumvirate of puritanical men dominated the Queen's Privy Council? And that those same men were jealous because Nelan's astral skills had repulsed the Armada and saved the country? He had grown too powerful, having earned a personal audience with the Queen. What ingratitude! What duplicity! But that's what they'd done.

Despite appearances to the contrary, the Triumvirate also deeply resented his intervention during the Armada Thanksgiving ceremony when Nelan had used the bones of the Catholic rite of excommunication. To their narrow minds, this was heresy, even though it successfully lifted the scarlet pall deposited by the Spanish and the Vatican.

Nelan felt sick as a dog, just like when he discovered Walsingham's flagrant misuse of power in forging the postscript to the bloody letter. Damn right, it was a bloody letter. And now the Triumvirate had blood on its hands, the blood of England's future, but not for long. Because the scarlet pall was no more, meaning that the angels of the island could now release the nation and the people's destiny to bestride the world stage.

Nor could he reveal to her that the Triumvirate was using the cover of darkness to conceal his detention from the Queen, or that a force of constables was at that very moment making their way to arrest him.

All he said was, "Margaret, it's not safe to stay here anymore."

"Oh, master. I never lived in no big house afore. Me, I likes it. Can we come back here soon?"

"This has been my home too and I love it," he admitted. "But I don't know when we might return." Of late, it had been full of happy memories after his homecoming from the repulse of the Armada. But at the atrium, the claws of destiny had ensnared him and, after that, everything had changed. He'd rescued the Island of Angels, but it had cost him his freedom and he'd almost lost his Eleanor. What else could he do but run away?

"Where we goin', master?" Margaret asked.

"First, we're heading for Shooters Hill. Do you know where it is?"

She shook her head, smiling a guilty smile as if she ought to have known.

He guided the tiller around the crest of the ox-bow. Soft mists rose from the reed beds by the banks of the river. Swans, ducks and geese swam across the waters. Keeping their heads low, they slunk past Barn Elms. The black metal weathervane stalked the roof of the mansion – the old fox. Well, a spymaster had to be a wily soul. With the river in flow, and the moonlight dancing on the waves, they made good headway. As dawn broke, they moored the wherry at the jetty at Woolwich.

Shooters Hill straddled the south bank of the river. Holdfast led them across the way before climbing Gibbet Hill. At the summit, a couple of hounds raced towards them, sniffing and licking Holdfast. They trudged towards a circle of wagons. A cluster of shire horses grazed near the Gyptian camp. He spotted a familiar face amidst the long dawn shadows.

"Kazia!" he cried, and the Chovihano greeted him with full Gyptian respect.

"The Fyremaster himself," she said, eyeing him up and down. "You've brought the family, I see."

"This is Eleanor, my wife, and here's Margaret, Flint and Alexander. Holdfast, you know."

"Oh, yes. Finally, I get to meet your beloved. I see you eventually found her, but from her expression, it appears you've lost her again."

"She's endured a terrible experience, staring death in the face. Since then, she's lost her wits, and the light's gone from her eyes. I've brought her here especially to see you, as I'm hoping you can use your magic and bring her back to me."

"I'll do what I can."

"I know you will. Thank you."

"Since we last met, I've lost my brother," she said.

"I'm so sorry about Jasper. He did not deserve to die, and certainly not alongside that traitor Francis Throckmorton."

"Thank you for insisting he had a sup of ale. It lent his ending a much-needed dignity. I admire your courage in making such a kind gesture."

"I could do nothing less for him. Wait… How did you know about that?"

"Oh, I was there."

"I should have known. Jasper asked me to look after you."

"He would," Kazia said with an air of rue. "But I can look after myself. I have many friends in both worlds."

The other Gyptians welcomed Nelan with a jest or a wink and shook his hand with friendly vigour. He broke his fast with them and laughed at their childish antics. Kazia took Eleanor for a long walk. While he waited for their return, he watched Holdfast play with the camp dogs and smiled at the young Gyptian men as they drew blushes from Margaret with their bold but respectful advances.

He felt at home amongst these folk, more so than he'd done at the court with all the aristocrats and aldermen. He shared two things in common with the Gyptians; they were recent immigrants to the Island of Angels, drawn to the land to assist in its growth and nurturing. Also, they were a folklore people who valued the guidance received from the astral.

After the gruelling night journey, he fell asleep and woke up at dusk. Holdfast licked his face. Someone giggled. He knew that laugh. It was one he'd feared he'd never hear again.

"Eleanor!" he cried as he got up, and she smiled that wonderful smile, and he felt as tall as the main mast on the *Golden Hind*. He knew that, like the *Golden Hind*, she'd come back from an incredible journey and that the amazing Kazia had broken the spell that bound his wife in chains.

"How?" he asked, shaking his head in awe, and holding his wife's soft hands.

"Ask Kazia," Eleanor said. "Her gentle warmth melted the frozen part of me."

"It's a miracle," he murmured, close to tears. "Thank you."

"Don't thank me," Kazia said. "I am but a means for something higher to work its way through me and into the world. The same as it does with you."

"Yes, it does."

"The angels of this land thrive in your company. I see you have made their concerns into your concerns."

"That was Madima's vision."

"D'you remember the midnight of eights?"

"Of course. What about it?"

"It was a change of octave. We have entered a new epoch. We are young in it, like children, and so we need to learn its language."

"I thought as much."

They talked and ate and danced and imagined. They sang to the angels of the island, and the angels heard their songs and sang back to them, and their souls rejoiced.

Kazia said, "You remember when the fires spoke to you, saying:

By the warm,
I'll be sworn."

Nelan nodded.

"Well, you know that was the angels of the isle speaking to you."

"Yes, I do now."

"That was their guidance, to which you listened. You believed in them."

During the night, Nelan had a prophetic dream. When he awoke in the morning, the Gyptian camp was packed and ready to leave.

"It's time for us to move on. You're welcome to come with us," Kazia said.

"We've other plans," he said. "But Margaret, Flint and Alexander want to join you, if you'll have them."

"We'd like that," Kazia said.

"When we last met," he said, "you spoke about my future: the ringing of the bells, the words of the prayers of the Almighty and the light of the blazing fire. Your insight into the Bell, Book and Candle enabled me to clear the way for England to fulfil her destiny."

"I'm glad you discovered the inner meaning of my prophecy," Kazia nodded.

"We have to take our leave of you and the Island of Angels," he said.

"Where are you going?"

"Last night, I had a dream about John Dee. He's in a town called Třeboň in Bohemia. He's calling us there. We'll head for Deptford, where we'll catch a carrack across the Narrow Seas to the continent."

"Now, you're leaving for faraway shores; you're a runaway too."

"Yes, I am. Walsingham is after me."

"He'll not find you in distant Bohemia. You're still young. He and his Triumvirate are the old guard. There'll come a time when it'll be safe for you both to return."

"I hope so," he said. "For now, we prepare for this new epoch and its rules."

"What are they?"

"There are three, like the three wavy lines on my palm, the mark of the salamander:

Work it out for yourself.
Find those of kind.
Be surprised at nothing."

"I can feel it coming," Kazia said, her eyes bright with the fire of enlightenment.

Eleanor took Kazia by the hand and said, "You've kindly given me a second chance at life. For that, I will be eternally grateful to you and your people."

"It was the least I could do," Kazia said. "Now I bid you farewell. As long as I draw breath, I shall never forget you. You will both always be in my heart and in my dreams."

"Thank you, Kazia," they said, and bowed to her.

The Gyptian camp set off. Holdfast ran down the slope, barking after their wagons. When he was nearly out of sight, the hound turned and raced back to where they stood.

As Nelan touched the ruby salamander pendant in his purse, he mouthed a silent prayer of thanks. Then he took Eleanor's hand in his, and together they went down the hill to find a boat.

Historical Note about the Dates

Implemented by Julius Caesar, the Julian calendar was employed in Europe until 1582. By then, because of an inaccuracy in calculating the full extent of the year, the calendar had fallen ten days behind the actual date. In October 1582, a new Gregorian calendar was implemented across continental Europe, making up the lost ten days. In England, the Gregorian calendar was not adopted until 1752.

After October 1582, there's a ten-day difference between the Julian and the Gregorian calendars. The days of the week are the same in both calendars, e.g., the 11th of July 1588 in the Julian and the 21st of July 1588 in the Gregorian are both a Thursday.

Because the action in Part One of the novel wholly takes place in England, the dates in that part are derived from the Julian calendar.

In Parts Two and Three of the novel, the action involves countries in mainland Europe such as Spain, France and the Netherlands. So, the dates in those two parts are derived from the Gregorian calendar.

Acknowledgements

The initial idea for this book came to me in September 2020, when I'd intended it to be a single novel, *The Mark of the Salamander*. But books have a way of telling you, the author, what they will be and what they won't be, and this one soon made it clear that it wouldn't fit into a single book, so *The Midnight of Eights* was born.

As always, I owe a deep debt of gratitude to my nearest and dearest, Irene Jones, for her patience and support.

Thanks too to my constant friends, whose ears were regularly bent by my procrastinations: Nick Deputowski, Jackie Carreira, James Harries and Nick Calthrop. Thanks too to Karni Zor and Christine Pearce for helping with the astrology in the story.

Beta readers are a unique breed. I owe a debt of gratitude to Jonathan Posner, Elizabeth St John, John Qjiang, Lynda Newland, Victoria Masters, Dennis Maier and Nancy Hall.

A special thanks to the copy editor and proof reader, whose eye for detail improved the manuscript.

Finally, I want to thank Fiction Feedback, led by the inimitable Dea Parkin.